Sex Drive

Books by Susan Lyons

Sex Drive
She's On Top
Touch Me
Hot in Here
Champagne Rules

Anthologies:

Men On Fire
Unwrap Me
The Firefighter

Published by Kensington Publishing Corp.

Sex Drive

SUSAN LYONS

APHRODISIA

KENSINGTON BOOKS

http://www.kensingtonbooks.com

APHRODISIA BOOKS are published by

Kensington Publishing Corp.
119 West 40th Street
New York, NY 10018

All Kensington Titles, Imprints, and Distributed Lines are available at special quantity discounts for bulk purchases for sales promotions, premiums, fund-raising, and educational or institutional use.

Special book excerpts or customized printings can also be created to fit specific needs. For details, write or phone the office of the Kensington special sales manager: Kensington Publishing Corp., 119 West 40th Street, New York, NY 10018, attn: Special Sales Department, Phone: 1-800-221-2647.

Aphrodisia and the A logo Reg. U.S. Pat. & TM Off.

ISBN-13: 978-0-7582-3825-2
ISBN-10: 0-7582-3825-8

First Kensington Trade Paperback Printing: December 2009

10 9 8 7 6 5 4 3 2 1

Printed in the United States of America

Acknowledgments

Thanks to the usual suspects, my lovely and talented critique group: Nazima Alli, Michelle Hancock, and Elizabeth Allan. And as well, to my agent, Emily Sylvan Kim, my editors, Audrey LaFehr and Hilary Sares, and all the people at Kensington who do such a great job with the Aphrodisia line. Special thanks to Martin Biro for making my life so much easier.

I'll be eternally grateful to Doug for flying me business class when we visited Australia. Not only did it save me from turning into a pretzel, it gave me the idea for this book.

I'm thrilled to be writing another series for Kensington, and have had great fun playing with the "planes" segment of my sexy "planes, trains, automobiles, and a cruise ship" series. I call the series Wild Ride because, for each of the four Fallon sisters, the journey to love truly is a wild ride. The next book—the "trains" one, *Love, Unexpectedly*—is a bit of a wild ride for me, too. It will be released under the pen name Susan Fox in April 2010, and will be in Kensington's Brava line.

Readers are, of course, the reason we authors do what we do. Thanks to all of you for reading romance. I invite you to visit my web site at www.susanlyons.ca, e-mail me at susan@susanlyons.ca, or write c/o PO Box 73523, Downtown Postal Outlet, 1014 Robson Street, Vancouver, BC, Canada V6E 4L9.

1

If someone had asked me a week ago, I'd have said I wouldn't be caught dead buying bridal magazines. However, the resident expert—my newly married secretary at the University of Sydney—told me it was impossible to plan a wedding without them.

Of course *I* had managed my own registry wedding without the assistance of any fancy magazines, but then again, look how well that had worked out. A three-month blip of married life to mar my otherwise pristine thirty-two years of singledom.

Ironic that now it was up to me, Theresa Fallon, with a little help from my sisters, Kat and Jenna, to plan the perfect wedding. On two weeks' notice.

No, not mine. My genius IQ didn't prevent me from making mistakes, but I tried my best to never repeat one, so I'd pretty much sworn off men.

It was my baby sister, Merilee, back in Vancouver, B.C., who'd be bridal-marching down the aisle, a march she'd been dreaming of since, at age five, she'd repeatedly propelled Bride Barbie into the arms of tuxedo-clad Ken.

Merilee was marrying Matt, her soul mate since grade two. You'd have thought fifteen years of love and dreams would have resulted in something more organized than a spur-of-the-moment wedding. However, Merilee'd had a rough time of it health-wise this year, then Matt found a last-minute deal on a Mexican Riviera cruise, and the result was that in thirteen days my kid sister was going to have the wedding she'd always dreamed of.

Except that she, who was frantically catching up the university work she'd missed due to illness, didn't have time to make wedding arrangements.

Merilee needed help, and I loved Merilee. So did our middle sisters, Kat and Jenna, of course, but as always, I was the organizer. The truth was, I liked being in charge. In fact, I preferred doing things myself, so they'd get done right. Snotty? Given my awe-inspiring IQ, my parents' expectations, and the responsibilities that had been foisted upon me at an early age, could I have turned out any other way?

Ergo, I, who *so* didn't relate to the white-lace-and-promises concept, was now on the hunt for a couple of those frilly magazines to supplement the gigantic bible on wedding planning I'd purchased at the uni bookstore. After clearing Sydney airport security late Sunday afternoon, I made for the Newslink store.

A display of hardcover books near the entrance caught my attention. The under-construction pyramid featured *Wild Fire*, the new release from one of Australia's popular novelists, Damien Black. A female sales clerk was plastering "Autographed Copy" stickers on covers that were a touch garish—eerie flames in yellow and red blazing on a black background—but definitely eye-catching.

As a sociologist specializing in the study of Indigenous Australians, I knew Black's name. He was part Aboriginal and wrote paranormal mystery thrillers featuring a police officer who was an Aboriginal Australian.

Though I rarely read fiction, I'd picked up one of the novels. It had been surprisingly entertaining, moderately accurate when it came to the facts, and even, here and there, insightful. But only here and there. Mostly, his work was crassly commercial. The man should devote his writing talents to something serious.

I certainly didn't plan to read another of his books. "Waste of time. Glib and superficial."

"Pardon?" The sales clerk turned to me.

"Sorry." One of the hazards of spending so much time on my own; I had a bad habit of voicing my thoughts. "I didn't mean to say that out loud."

The clerk grinned. "No worries. Lots of readers disagree with you, though. He sure sells well. Me, I can't put the books down. He's kept me up all night, more than once." She winked. "Wish he'd do it in person, though. He was just in signing these books and I gotta say, the man's seriously hot."

"I'm sure 'hot' is an important criterion for making one's reading choices," I said dryly.

A male snort told me someone had overheard.

The clerk glanced over my shoulder. Her eyes widened and color flooded her cheeks. "Oops! Sorry." She ducked her head and concentrated on stickering books.

I turned and saw a man who definitely qualified as hot. His clothes were as simple as you could get—worn jeans, a navy tee—but they showcased a tall, well-muscled frame. His face and arms were tanned dark, and he obviously didn't believe in haircuts. Though I wasn't a fan of long hair, the shiny black waves hanging almost to his shoulders did suit him. He had a strong-featured face with a hint of the exotic, and bright gray eyes that were currently regarding me with a sparkle of humor.

I felt an odd kind of physical awareness. Of him as a man. And me as a woman. Which definitely wasn't the usual way I reacted to a guy. There was something familiar about him, yet I was sure I'd never met him. I'd have remembered that bizarre sense of awareness.

"Not buying a book then?" he asked teasingly, with an Aussie twang.

Embarrassed by my reaction to him, I averted my eyes and muttered, "No."

As I turned to walk away, I heard him say, "Each to his—or her—own."

Why did I feel as if I was running away? I brushed the thought—and the man—out of my mind as I collected a bottle of water, then found the magazine section.

How surreal to be browsing bridal magazines. "Let me count the reasons I hate this stuff." Whoops, I was muttering out loud again. I continued my rant inside my head. *It's a giant industry that manipulates brides into thinking the most expensive wedding is going to make for the happiest marriage. Don't people know that—*

"Excuse me? Are you buying that one?" A female voice broke into my thoughts and I realized a perky young redhead was gazing at me inquiringly.

"What?" I glanced down at the magazine in my hand, featuring the ubiquitous bride clad in frothy white. "I haven't decided."

"It's the last copy. So, if you're not getting it, I'd like to. It's my favorite."

"Then take it." I handed it over. "They're all the same to me."

"Oh, no, they're not!" Her tone suggested I'd said something sacrilegious. "This one's for the *Australian* bride, and that's me."

She pointed to another on the shelf, using her left hand and flashing a small diamond. "That's for the modern bride, the one beside it is more traditional, and oh, that one has the dreamiest things, but they're way too expensive, though some of their ideas can be replicated on a cheaper scale." She grabbed a copy.

As she gushed enthusiastically, I studied the covers, thinking they all looked the same. Merilee had always left bridal magazines scattered around the house, but which had she favored?

The redhead had chosen three. "I'm getting married in April, so we've less than a year to get everything organized. It's so much fun. How about you?"

"Me? Oh, it's not me who's getting married, it's my youngest sister."

"Oh." She glanced at my ringless left hand. "That must be hard. But I'm sure it'll happen for you too, quicker than you'd ever guess."

"God, I hope not." The words burst out, and when her smooth brow creased, I said, "I like being single. Seems to me, we each find the path in life that's right for us. I've found mine."

She was still frowning a little as she raised her left hand and wiggled her fingers, making the diamond dance. "And I've found mine. Maybe you're right, but it's hard to imagine someone choosing to live alone. For the rest of their life."

It did sound rather like a life-in-solitary-confinement sentence, the way she said it. For a moment I remembered the way I'd felt with Jeffrey. Life had been brighter, richer. Happier. At our simple registry ceremony, I'd been euphoric. I might not be a white-lace kind of woman, but the promises I'd made had meant a lot to me. A future, a partnership, a sharing of life, love, work . . .

Sharing? Oh yes, Jeffrey had definitely wanted *me* to share, but he hadn't returned the favor. No, he'd lied to me from the start, then betrayed me. The pitiful truth was, I wasn't the kind of woman who inspired a man's love and loyalty.

"Some of us just do better on our own," I said to the girl. "But I hope you're very happy."

"Your sister, too."

After she'd gone, I chose the modern and traditional magazines she'd showed me. Might as well have both extremes—and see if I noticed the slightest bit of difference.

After paying, I squeezed the magazines into my carry-on. In addition to my laptop and the wedding planning book, it held undergrad exams to grade. Thanks to Merilee's late-breaking news, I was leaving the uni a week before the end of the semester.

When I entered the departure gate, business class was loading. I joined the line, since, as a frequent flyer, I'd had the luck to have been upgraded. On the ten-hour flight to Honolulu— the first leg of my trip to Vancouver—the perks of business class would make a huge difference. Decent food, a couple of glasses of nice wine, space to work, a seat I could actually sleep in.

Now, if only I got a seatmate who put on his or her headphones and left me alone.

The plane had two business-class sections: one on the upper deck, which was more private, and one on the main deck. I was in the main one, assigned to a window seat in one of the side banks of two seats.

The seats in business class were different than the basic ones in economy. Rather than being linked together with shiftable armrests between, these were independent chairs. Kind of like those recline-in-front-of-the-TV loungers, except lodged inside a hard-shelled cocoon frame.

When I arrived at my row, a black-haired man was in the aisle seat, bending to stow a bag under the seat in front, and I couldn't get past him. Behind me, people were making impatient sounds, so I said, "Excuse me? Could I slide by so I don't hold others up?"

"Sorry." He straightened with a quick smile, a disarming one that crinkled gray eyes and flashed white teeth in a dark face framed with too-long hair. The man from the bookstore.

"You!" Definitely not the seatmate I'd have chosen even if he was, as my secretary would have said, eye candy.

His smile quirked into a grin I had trouble reading. "If it isn't the discerning reader." He rose and moved into the aisle to let me go past.

I'm not clumsy by nature, yet I managed to trip over his feet. Big, brown, well-shaped feet in leather sandals.

When I stumbled, his right hand caught my shoulder and held it. "Easy now."

Easy? With the heat of his hand burning through my cardigan? My breath caught and I couldn't move. Something—a kind of energy—came off him. My body felt it like a tingly caress all over, though the only thing he gripped was my shoulder. There was a scent too, reminding me of field trips in the Outback: sunshine on eucalyptus—or gum trees as they're called in Australia. And there was a gleam in his eyes that, if I'd been a more attractive woman, I'd have read as sexual interest. But hot, self-assured guys like him never gave plain, studious women like me a second glance.

I managed to unfreeze my muscles and plunked down in my seat, carry-on and purse on my lap.

"Put your bag up?" he asked, gesturing toward the overhead bin.

"No, thanks, I'll keep it with me."

An elderly woman in the aisle quickly said, "You can put our bag up, if you don't mind."

"I can do it, Delia," the silver-haired man behind her said.

"Course you can, Trev. I just want to make this young man show off his muscles." She gave my seatmate a wink.

He flashed her that dazzling smile and hefted the bag easily. When he hoisted it into the bin, his body stretched in a powerful, graceful motion. Muscles flexed in his arms and, as the left sleeve of his T-shirt rode up, I saw the edge of a tattoo—a dragon?—that appeared to curl around his bicep.

The shirt molded strong shoulders, hard pectorals. It was pulling free from his unbelted jeans. My gaze tracked down the line of his fly to register that the jeans, too, molded something quite appealing.

A shiver of sexual awareness rippled through me, making me squirm. Damn. Rarely did I notice a man in a sexual way. But then, not many men were worth noticing in that way.

He said, "There ya go," to the woman.

Before he could catch me gaping, I busied myself with extracting a couple of student exams from my bag. From the corner of my eye, I noticed the older couple—a fit, attractive pair—taking the seats across the aisle in the middle section.

My seatmate sat down and his physical presence almost overwhelmed me. My uni colleagues were intellectuals like me, and rarely was I with someone like the man beside me. He pretty much exuded sexuality. Thank heavens for the spacious, independent seats. If I'd been crammed next to him in economy, arms and thighs touching each time we shifted position, I'd have ended up a mass of quivering hormones.

Sexual awareness was a rare feeling for me. I'd always, since I was a little kid, been all about intellect, not about the physical aspects of life—and that's exactly the way the opposite sex had viewed me. I was in demand as a tutor, but not as a date. Then I'd met Jeffrey. He'd chosen me from among the other young profs and grad students. He was only my second lover, and with him I'd learned to enjoy my body. To enjoy sex.

I'd thought he was different. That he'd seen me, Theresa the woman, not just my brain. But I'd been wrong.

Easier, and safer, to do without men. The one time I'd decided to experiment again, with an anthropology prof I'd met at a conference in Melbourne, the sex had sucked. Intellectual compatibility hadn't translated into the physical equivalent. Thank heavens I had a low sex drive or I'd sure be frustrated with only my own hand and a vibrator to keep me satisfied.

I wondered what the man beside me was like as a lover. My

guess was, either stunningly skilful or entirely self-centered. Not that I'd ever find out. He definitely wasn't my type, and I'd have bet that went double for him, about me.

Feeling warm, either from the stuffiness of the plane or the effect of my seatmate, I began to wriggle out of my cardigan.

"Help you with your cardie?"

"No, I'm f—" Before I could say "fine," his hand was there again, on my shoulder, easing the navy cashmere down over the sleeveless top I wore beneath it. The top was rust-colored and brought out the auburn in my short brown hair. Plain I might be, but I wasn't entirely without vanity. I strove for a look that was comfortable, practical, and passably attractive. No point trying for a glamour that could never be mine; I'd only have looked pathetic.

He drew the cardigan down slowly, fingers brushing the bare skin of my upper arm, and again I tingled all over. His touch felt like a deliberate caress, but that must have been my imagination.

I slanted a glance sideways and saw the gleam in his eyes that I'd noticed before. His gaze skimmed my shoulder, landed on my chest, and I realized the V neck of my top was pulling down as the cardigan came off. Trapped inside the sleeves, I couldn't reach up to adjust it.

My skin heated and I knew my cheeks as well as my chest were coloring to match the reddish tone of the sleeveless top. My nipples tightened. Finally, my arm came free and I hurriedly pulled up the neckline of my top and turned my back to him so he could work on the other sleeve. And so I could hide my budding nipples. I searched for something casual to say, to mask my discomfort. "Why do Aussies do the 'ie' thing? Cardie for cardigan, barbie for barbecue?"

"Just lazy, I guess. Brissie for Brisbane, bickie for biscuit." I tried to focus on his words rather than on those warm fingers taking far too long getting the damned sweater off my other arm. "But the 'ie' forms are often no shorter. It can't be laziness."

"Huh." He paused. "Footy for football, tinnie for a tin of beer, damned if you're not right. Guess it's our way of making things a little friendlier." With a final seductive stroke, he slid the sweater free. "There you go. Now, let's see what others I can think of. Sunnies for sunglasses."

I turned to face him and took the sweater he handed me. "Thanks."

"Hottie for . . ." He paused, eyes twinkling.

Damn, he was thinking back to the bookstore clerk's comment about him being hot, and my response. Crossing my arms across my chest, trying to salvage my composure, I said, "Hottie? That's one I haven't heard."

The corners of his mouth twitched. "That'd be short for hot water bottle."

I had to chuckle. He'd set me up perfectly. "Not something I've had much need of in Sydney."

"Nah? Got something better to warm your bed?"

"That would be telling." My gosh, was that me? Almost . . . flirting?

"Here you go," a female voice broke in. I looked away from gleaming gray eyes to see a very attractive brunette flight attendant with a wide smile. "Amenity kits from L'Occitane."

She handed us the little bags. "Mr. Black, I see you're all settled. And you're Ms. Fallon. How ya going?" This was the Australian way of asking everything from "How are you?" to "How's it going?" or "How are you doing?"

"Fine, thanks." I was surprised she'd addressed us by name. Obviously in business class the flight attendants had a list of seat assignments.

Her brow furrowed. "You're not traveling together, are you?"

"No," I said quickly.

The man shot me an amused glance.

"Right, then," the woman said, face clearing and another smile flashing. "It's a long flight, but I'll do my best to make it a pleasant one." Now she was looking directly at my seatmate, leaning into his space as still-boarding passengers stepped around her, and I thought she'd put a special emphasis on the word "pleasant."

"That's good of you, Carmen," he said, seeming quite happy that the fabric of her uniform trousers brushed his jean-clad knee. He sent her one of those eye-crinkling smiles.

So he knew her name, too. I could see her being his type. Well, pretty much any man's type. I gathered the two of them had been chatting—flirting?—before I arrived.

Not that I cared, except I'd as soon not be ignored when it came to service. I cleared my throat to remind her I was there. "Thank you." I paused. "Carmen."

She gave me a smile that looked a trifle pitying. Women like her always gave me an irrational urge to spout off the fact that I'd been awarded a PhD—summa cum laude—at the age of twenty-two. Ridiculous, because I knew perfectly well that academic credentials wouldn't impress her. She'd be looking at my average figure, average face, average clothing, and knowing my attributes could never compete with hers.

"May I offer you a glass of champagne?" she asked me.

I swallowed the silly surge of . . . surely not jealousy? "That would be lovely." The treat would be a nice start to a long trip, and maybe distract me from the man beside me.

"Same for me," my seatmate said.

"Of course. Coming up." Was she actually fluttering her eyelashes at him?

When she went to talk to the older couple across the aisle, he turned to me. "All psyched up for ten hours on a plane? Any ideas how to pass the time?" he asked in a suggestive tone.

Great. He was a "love the one you're with" guy who'd flirt with whichever female was closest. Even a woman like me.

The urge to banter had left me. "I have work to do." I slid my tray table out of the arm of my chair and slapped the exam booklets down on it.

"Yeah, happens I do, too." Despite his words, he didn't take out any work, just reclined his seat, adjusted the footrest, and closed his eyes.

Fine. He didn't care whether I chatted with him. I'd got what I'd hoped for: a seatmate who would leave me alone. Not that I wanted the attention of an arrogant flirt like him, but sometimes it truly irked me that men found me so easy to ignore.

I tried to adjust my own footrest, but it didn't cooperate, so I focused on the first exam. I'd barely started when my mobile—no, cell; I had to transition to Canadian terms again—rang.

I pulled it out of my purse and saw from call display that it was my sister Kat. There were four of us, a three-pack plus one, with the one—the unplanned afterthought—being Merilee. I was the oldest at thirty-two, the plain brainiac. Kat was a year younger, Ms. Sociability. She lived in Montreal and handled PR for a gorgeous hotel.

"Hi there," I answered quietly. My seatmate's eyes were still closed. "Can't talk long, the plane's almost loaded." My brain was calculating time. It was five thirty at night here, which made it . . . "Kat, isn't it three thirty in the morning? Are you just coming in or getting up?" Surely even a party animal like Kat wouldn't stay out this late.

"I woke up and couldn't get back to sleep. Did you get the e-mail I sent a few hours ago? I haven't heard back."

"It may be on my laptop. I downloaded e-mail before I left. I'll look at it during the flight. Were you able to swing that leave?"

Carmen was back with the drinks. I nodded my thanks as

she handed me a flute of bubbly champagne. When she placed my neighbor's drink on his tray, his eyes opened quickly enough.

Kat was saying, "Do you know how difficult it is for me to take time off without notice?" She went on about all the people at the hotel who depended on her. My sister. Always the life of the party, be it in her social life or at her workplace.

As she spoke, my seatmate and the flight attendant chatted away, accompanied by considerable eyelash-batting on her part. Didn't she have other passengers to attend to? Or did she plan to spend the entire trip flirting with him, like he was God's gift to womankind?

I broke into Kat's ramblings. "If it's a real problem getting off work, don't worry about it. As I said before, I can handle this."

There was a pause. Then, "Well, of course, I forgot that you've already *handled* one wedding, and so successfully at that."

Ouch. I knew my younger sisters had always resented me: my brains, the responsibility our parents had given me, the way I'd lived up to their hefty expectations. Now I'd pushed one of Kat's buttons, so she'd retaliated by pushing one of mine. My failed marriage.

If I'd been alone, I'd have sniped back about her brilliant ability to always pick the wrong guy. However, the flirtatious Carmen had departed and the man beside me apparently had nothing better to do than sip champagne and listen to my side of the phone conversation. So I said, "Sorry. It would be great if you could get off work and help out." I picked up my own flute and took a calming swallow.

"God, Theresa, you make it sound like it's *your* project. It's *ours*. All of ours. Yours and mine and Jenna's. That's what we agreed. We'll work together to give Merilee the wedding of her dreams."

I dragged a hand through my hair and rubbed my temple, where a dull throbbing signaled the beginning of a headache.

"Right. Of course." There was no question I wanted the best for my baby sister. It was just that I preferred not to work with a team. No one else, especially my sisters, ever met my standards.

"Anyhow," Kat was saying, "if you'd have let me finish, I'd have told you I did arrange the time off. I'll get train tickets and e-mail you the schedule. It's about a four-day trip."

"If you flew, you'd be home in half a day."

"You know I don't do planes." Her voice held a warning edge and I could picture her face, brown eyes narrowed, that vertical frown line bisecting her forehead. She was probably on the verge of a headache, too.

Giving each other headaches was about the only thing we had in common.

I sighed. Kat was the craziest mix of traits. She was fluently bilingual, had done very well in school, held a responsible job, and had dozens of friends and the most active social life imaginable. And yet, she had an irrational fear of flying and appalling taste in men.

Not, of course, that my record with the opposite sex was any better. However, I knew better than to keep trying, whereas she was forever falling for someone new and totally wrong for her.

Knowing no amount of logic would persuade Kat to fly, I asked, "Any word from Jenna? I left her a couple voice mails and e'd her, but no response." Jenna was the next sister, the third of our three-pack, as we'd called ourselves long before Merilee was born. A year younger than Kat, Jenna would be turning thirty soon. She had carved out her niche in the family as the flaky one.

"No. And we did all promise to keep in touch at least on a daily basis."

"You know Jenna. She loathes any sort of rules or accountability."

"True. But this is *important*." Kat gave a frustrated growl. "She's probably off in the wilderness with those birds of hers."

Jenna, who'd never stuck with one job—or man—for more than six months, had followed a surfer boyfriend to Santa Cruz and got involved in a peregrine falcon survey. "I'll try her again from the airplane phone once we're under way. Uh, what's the time in Santa Cruz?"

"Three hours different than me, so it's like, almost one o'clock. Saturday night, Sunday morning. She'll be out having fun, probably have her cell turned off. Or the battery will have run down because she forgot to charge it." We shared a moment of silent understanding. "If you do connect with her," she said, "get her to call me. I'm going to grab a couple more hours sleep, then I'll be in at work getting things organized."

"Tell me about it." My secretary and I had spent a good part of the last twenty-four hours doing the same thing.

"Can't believe we'll all be in the same place at the same time. It's been a while."

"Christmas the year before last."

A loudspeaker voice told the passengers to turn off electronic devices.

"Kat, I have to go. I'll check e-mail and voice mail in Honolulu."

"Right. Safe flight."

As I shut off my cell, I was shaking my head. When my sisters and I had been growing up, there'd been a lot of competitions and petty jealousies. We'd each developed distinct personalities and interests, and those had taken us in different directions. Now, living in four different cities in three countries, we rarely spoke, much less saw each other. Of course we all loved each other, but it was easier for us to love from a distance. It was kind of sad, but that was the way the Fallon girls had turned out.

Now, thanks to Merilee, we were teaming up for the first

time in ages. White lace and promises for her. For the rest of us, a little bit of hell as we tried to make nice—or nice enough—with each other to pull off a wedding in less than two weeks.

"That's not the way to start a long trip," the man beside me said.

"Sorry?" I turned to look at him and saw a twinkle in his gray eyes.

2

Damien Black grinned at the intriguing woman in the seat beside him. The sexy prof who was marking Sydney Uni exam booklets but didn't have an Australian accent. The woman whose conversation on her mobile had given her a stress headache.

The literary snob who thought his novels were superficial crap.

Not that he necessarily disagreed. But, hell, they were fun to write and they were damned lucrative superficial crap. He had the best fucking job in the universe: making up stories, playing with imaginary friends, and getting paid well to do it.

The prof intrigued him, and not only because she was hot in a subtle, classy way. He wondered how she'd react when she found out he was the guy whose books she'd dissed, but he was going to hold off on satisfying his curiosity. They had a long flight ahead of them, and together they could make it a hell of a lot of fun. But he stood a better chance if she got to know him before she learned his identity.

"You've been shaking your head and heaving sigh after sigh," he said. "And not drinking your champers."

She glanced at his empty glass. "Not a problem you've been suffering from, I see."

Had to admit, there was a definite appeal to a woman who wasn't afraid to use her tongue. Banter was a good start. Maybe she'd soften up and think of a friendlier use for that tongue. "Drink up. It'll help your headache."

She frowned. "I don't have—" Then she winced. "Well, maybe the beginning of one."

The flight attendant arrived with the champagne bottle and a big smile. "So sorry, I certainly don't want to neglect you." She filled his glass.

"Ta, Carmen." The flashy brunette had told him her name when he'd first got on the plane and she'd recognized him.

She cocked a brow at the prof. "You don't care for it, Ms. Fallon? Can I get you something else?"

"No, it's fine. I was just on the phone." She held up her closed mobile. "Which is off now, and I'm about to enjoy the champagne."

"Good on you," Carmen said, then gave him a wink before she moved on.

Yeah, Carmen had gushed all over him when he came on board. She'd made it clear she was available for a little action. Her, and about a hundred other girls in the two years since his first book hit the bestseller lists and he'd become a familiar face on TV talk shows. Not to mention, been voted one of the country's ten sexiest bachelors.

The "sexy bachelor" angle had featured prominently in the promo plan his agent and publicist had developed, a fact that at first he'd found humorous but had soon worn thin. This business of women flinging themselves at him had gotten a little old. Truth was, it wasn't all that flattering when females swarmed all over a bloke just because he was famous and supposed to be sexy. Celebrity had its disadvantages.

Truth was, the prof interested him more than Carmen. She

was a turn-on, with an appealing face that wasn't caked in makeup, a slim, shapely bod, and boobs that looked to be all her own. Plus, she intrigued him. The woman presented a challenge. Though she clearly wasn't immune to the physical spark between them, she sure wasn't throwing herself at him.

Could he win her over before she found out who he was?

He held out his glass to her. "Bottoms up, safe trip, don't let the buggers get you down." He'd have said "bastards" but figured it might piss her off.

A chuckle spluttered out of her and her eyes warmed. Those eyes reminded him of the water in a billabong: shades of reddy brown brightened by specks of blue and green, like the reflections of red rocks and trees in blue waters. As with a billabong, a bloke could stare into their depths and lose himself. Especially now, when her amusement made them sparkle as if sunshine dappled the still water.

She clicked her glass to his. "The buggers?"

"Whoever's got you sighing like a high wind through the gum trees."

Her lips twisted, more in rue than amusement. "My sister. Actually, all my sisters." Her eyes widened and he sensed the information had slipped out, laughter creating a chink in her reserve. She glanced away and raised the glass to her lips.

"Ah. Families. Can't live with 'em, can't shoot 'em. Easiest to just avoid them." That was his current strategy with his own family.

"True." She gazed into her glass. "But it's not always possible."

"No?"

She glanced up, eyes narrowing. "I really do need to work."

Why was she so intent on keeping him at a distance? He was about to ask when he felt a hand brush his right forearm.

"Sorry to interrupt," Carmen purred, not sounding sorry at all. "We're readying for takeoff. I need you to fold up your tables. You can hang on to your glasses and I'll be by with more champagne once we're in the air."

He heard a quick swallow on his other side, then the prof extended her glass past him. "I'm finished. You can take this, thanks," she said coolly. He gathered she hadn't exactly warmed to their flight attendant.

"I'll keep mine," he said.

When Carmen had gone, he turned to his seatmate. "You know what they say about all work and no play."

Her lips pressed together, their fullness folded in to make a thin line. When she released them, they were plump and a deep, natural pink. Ripe for kissing.

But her voice was chilly. "Believe me, I do. They make Theresa a dull girl. Which I am. So, you might as well get over yourself and let me get on with my work. I'm sure *Carmen* will be more than happy to let you chat her up."

Interesting. Damien figured he was pretty damned observant for a guy—a writer had to be—and she'd just delivered a whack of information. Not only her name, but the fact that folks thought she was too serious and didn't hold back from telling her. Now, what was that bit about Carmen? Did he detect a hint of jealousy?

This was going to be one interesting flight.

He decided to let Professor Theresa Fallon win this round. When they were in the air, having drinks and appetizers, she'd have to put the exams away.

"Okay," he said easily. "You get on with your work then."

Besides, it wasn't like he didn't have work to do himself. This wasn't a vacation. He'd finished a weeklong book tour in Australia, had a couple days at home in Sydney to get turned around, and was now headed off for a month's tour in the United States and Canada. With him, he had the galleys for *Gale Force*, which had to be back to his publisher in a week. And of course, there was *Scorched Earth*, the book he was currently writing. Or had been, until a plot point had hung him up.

Beside him, Theresa was again studying the exam. Absentmindedly she lifted her hand and rubbed her temple through short, gleaming auburn hair. The gesture made him focus on her slim fingers, which, even with their short, unpolished nails, had a particular feminine grace. Fingers that he'd bet would feel nicer on his skin than Carmen's red-tipped claws.

Usually, the width of the seats in business class was an advantage, but not tonight. In economy, Theresa's arm would've brushed against his on the armrest. Her bare arm against his, the constant whisper of flesh against flesh acting like the friction of two sticks being rubbed together, the way some elderly Aboriginals still made fire. Friction, heat, friction, spark, more friction—then flames.

Of course, if he and Theresa had been touching that way, he'd have had a hard-on. Just being this close to her was enough of a tease to his senses. He was aware of her every movement. Her scent—something earthy yet fresh—made him think of sex in the great outdoors.

Damien shifted, wishing he could adjust his swelling package. Trying to distract himself, he decided to work on his plot knot. He closed his eyes and reviewed what he'd written to date.

The book started with Damien's police detective protagonist being reamed out by his superior. Although Kalti Brown had solved his last case, he refused to reveal exactly how he'd identified the bad guy, and how that criminal had come to die in a freak windstorm. Kalti's secret was that he had a special connection with his totem spirit and the creator spirits from the Dreamtime. When bad people went against the natural laws, the spirits were as determined to punish them as was Kalti, and they worked together in an alliance that was often less than comfortable for him.

As Damien reflected, eyes shut, he was dimly aware of the plane taxiing, then taking off. Of the elderly couple across the aisle telling Carmen they were going to Vancouver to visit family, including a brand-new great-grandchild.

Kalti, now, he was a loner for obvious reasons. But his boss had decided someone should keep an eye on him. Enter Marianna, his new partner. Female, Caucasian. A hard-line, play-by-the-rules cop.

Beside him, Damien heard the prof reach for her carry-on bag and pull out something that rustled. More exam booklets, he guessed, then he returned to his musings.

Marianna was tough and career-focused, and resented being assigned to a cop who had the reputation of being a renegade. She didn't trust Kalti and he, a keeper of secrets, couldn't trust anyone. And yet, partners were supposed to be a team and be able to rely on each other.

The two were assigned to a couple murders that might be the work of a serial killer. There was a ritualized aspect to the killings that made Kalti suspect—

Beside him, Theresa was muttering to herself, breaking his concentration. He heard something like, "For only six thousand dollars, you, too, can look like a strawberry parfait." And then, "Or a mummy." His brain couldn't make sense of what he was hearing. When she said, "Can't weigh more than eighty pounds. If a man hugged her, she'd snap in two," he had to open his eyes and glance over.

What he saw made him laugh. She had a bridal magazine open. "Wedding gowns? What happened to all the work you had to do?"

Her cheeks flushed to match her sleeveless top. "I thought you were asleep."

"Hard to sleep with all that muttering," he teased.

"Oh damn. Sorry. It's a bad habit."

"No worries. But I'm curious. A six-thousand-dollar straw-berry parfait?"

She flipped pages and he stared at a lacy concoction the color of a strawberry milkshake. He let out a hoot. "That's ridiculous." Its droopy lines made him think of melting ice cream, and there was a big pouffy red something-or-other at the waist that was probably a bow but looked like a giant squishy strawberry. "Aren't wedding gowns supposed to be white? I mean, unless you're Asian or something."

"Pink is the latest trend. But yes, most are white or off-white. Look at this."

Another page flip, and he gazed at a pale, sad-looking woman whose thin body was wrapped round and round in what looked like gauze bandaging. A mummy's wrappings. "She looks like a corpse, so I guess it's fitting she'd be wrapped like one."

Theresa giggled. Eyes sparkling, she turned another page. "How about this?"

No tits or ass on this one either. But God, she went beyond skinny to emaciated. "Jeez. A stick-woman." He winced. "Scary. How could anyone find that attractive?"

She shook her head firmly, auburn hair lifting then settling. "I sure don't." Grimly she added, "What a horrible message it sends to young women."

"Yeah. And take it from me, if they look like this, no guy's ever going to marry them." He couldn't imagine any red-blooded man wanting to have sex with a skeleton.

And speaking of sex . . . Damien took the excuse to undo his seat belt, lean over, and let his arm brush hers, feeling a zing of connection.

Then, quickly, he shifted away. Shit, what was he doing? Obviously she was engaged, despite her ringless hands. So much for trying to seduce her.

Didn't mean they couldn't talk, though. He flipped another

page, then another. "Well, this girl's got curves. At least below the waist. Man, look at the arse on her." Then he peered closer. "Or is that the dress, making her look so big?"

"I gather it's called mermaid cut. Yes, it does accentuate the, uh, bottom, curving in like that then flaring out again so she can walk. Or at least hobble."

"Yeah, she sure as hell wouldn't be doing any waltzing in that one."

"Waltzing?" She glanced at him quizzically. "You don't look like the waltzing type."

"Hey, I'm from Oz. 'Waltzing Matilda'?" The truth was, he was one hell of a dancer.

"Yeah, right." Her eyes crinkled with a smile. "Isn't that song about a swagman—i.e., a hobo—dancing with his swag, meaning his skimpy bundle of possessions?"

"Damned academics," he groused. "Take everything so literally."

"How did you know I'm an academic?"

"Grading exams from the uni?"

"Oh, of course."

He glanced back to the magazine. "Hate those dresses with the rigid tops that don't move when the woman does. And why do so many of these models look miserably unhappy?"

"Way to sell a dress, eh? What's the myth they're selling? Isn't it supposed to be, this is the happiest day of your life?"

"Myth? You mean you don't buy into it?"

She shrugged. "I guess it's nice to start out feeling that way. Even if the reality is, you've got more than a fifty percent chance of being miserable."

Whoa. A cynical bride? Of course, she must figure she and her fiancé would beat the odds. "How'd you come up with that depressing statistic?"

"Roughly half of marriages end in divorce. And lots of

spouses are unhappy but don't get divorced. Ergo, there's probably something like a quarter of marriages that are actually happy."

Ergo? What kind of woman said *ergo?* As for her statistics . . . Damien shook his head, bemused. He was thirty-three and had never met a woman who'd made him want to settle down, yet he'd kind of figured on getting married one day. Really married, in the traditional "grow old together" way. As the prof had laid out the facts, it sounded like he'd be crazy.

Absentmindedly he flipped another couple pages. Hmm, here were some dresses that were actually nice, worn by models who looked like real, attractive, smiling women. If he was Theresa, that was the designer he'd be looking at.

When he started to turn the page again, her hand caught his. "Wait."

Her touch felt great, but she didn't even seem aware of the contact. Instead, she stared at the magazine, transfixed. "That one. It's lovely." Her finger brushed the page reverently.

The ivory-colored dress was simple, but prettier than the fancy ones. The strapless top was soft rather than rigid, and decorated with pearls or lustrous beads. A band of lacy, pearly trim ran along the top and below the bustline, then the dress fell to the floor in a slim drift of fabric. A woman could waltz in it and it would bell out gently, romantically, drifting seductively around a guy's legs. And under his hands, her back would be bare, soft, warm . . .

Not that he was into weddings or anything.

But for some reason, he felt a weird twinge at the thought of Theresa in that dress, whirling around the dance floor with another man. Then later, in the honeymoon suite of a fancy hotel, being unzipped. Or did the back have buttons? The dress would slip down her body to pool on the floor, leaving her clad in something white and lacy, very brief, showing off her slim but definite curves.

Double whoa. He shouldn't be thinking this way about another man's bride.

He cleared his throat and tried to sound objective. "It's pretty and you'd look good in it. It'd show off your neck and nice arms. The model's got that long hair all over her shoulders, but the dress'd look better with short hair like yours."

She was staring at him, looking stunned. Shit, was he sounding all gay?

"Me?" she squeaked.

"It's the prettiest wedding dress you've looked at."

"Ooh! Are you getting married, Ms. Fallon?" Carmen was back, resting a hand on Damien's shoulder so she could lean across and peer at the magazine. "Let's see. Oh, those are too plain." She dismissed the page he and Theresa had been studying, and flipped a few pages. "Look! Isn't this one stunning?"

He peered at the picture. "Why's it all caught up in those flouncy things? It looks like mosquito netting."

Carmen's hand squeezed his shoulder. Rolling her eyes, she said to Theresa, "Men. They have no taste when it comes to this kind of thing." Using Damien's shoulder for support—and getting in another squeeze—she straightened. "This calls for champagne. I'll be right back."

"I don't—" Theresa started to say, but Carmen had gone. The prof turned to Damien with a mischievous grin. "I'm with you. That dress does look like mosquito netting."

"Unless your guy's into the whole wilderness safari thing, I'd stick with the other one."

"It's not me who's getting married. It's my baby sister."

"Ohhhh." The one syllable eased out of him slowly, on a breath of . . . Relief? No, it had to be pure sexual pleasure that she wasn't already taken. That she was fair game, to stick with the safari analogy.

"I'm flying to Vancouver, where my parents and Merilee live, to organize the wedding."

"And you're not married yourself?"

"No." Those billabong eyes studied him for a long moment. "Divorced. And not about to give it a second shot."

So, she had personal experience with those divorce statistics. "Sorry it didn't work out."

She shrugged nonchalantly, but shadows clouded her eyes. "It was a learning experience. How about you?"

"Haven't even come close."

"Guess you have more sense than I did."

"Not so sure it's a matter of good sense. I've got nothing against the idea. In principle." He gave her a quick grin. "Or at least I didn't, until you started quoting stats. Just haven't found a woman who doesn't bore me." Even as he said the words, he wished he could call them back. Not that they weren't true, but they made him sound like a—

"Don't think well of yourself, do you?" she taunted.

"Nah." He laughed. "Well, kinda. You have to think well of yourself. I mean, who else is gonna do it?"

She laughed. Man, the woman had a pretty laugh, soft and husky like a breeze rustling through gum leaves. "I'll give you that. But how can you suggest that all women are boring?"

"Not what I said." He paused, setting her up. "Haven't found a bloke I'd want to marry, either."

Another chuckle. "Somehow I don't figure you as gay."

"You think?"

Oh, yeah, he liked her smile, her laugh, the sunlight-on-water sparkle in her eyes. Things were definitely looking up.

He didn't even mind when Carmen arrived with the champagne. At least until she bent toward Theresa to hand her a flute glass, and shoved her left boob in his face.

Not that he had anything against women's breasts. In fact he might've taken Carmen up on her offer if he hadn't been sitting beside Theresa.

But now there *was* Theresa—whose lit-up face had transformed to a disgusted scowl—and he'd rather have her company. She was sexier, prettier, more interesting, and there was that challenge factor. The time limitation, too; he had only ten hours to charm her.

He had to do something about Carmen. Theresa's magazine gave him an idea. Could he persuade her to go along with it?

When Carmen reached for the used glass he'd kept, he said, "Mind getting me a fresh one?"

"Happy to." She pirouetted and headed up the aisle, curvy arse wriggling.

Quickly he turned to Theresa. "Do me a favor. Pretend we're engaged."

"What? What are you talking about?"

"Save me from that woman's clutches."

"That . . . Carmen? But you've been flirting with her."

"Reflex. A stupid one I now regret. Help me out?"

An eyebrow kinked. "You do know, she'd give you pretty much anything you want?"

"She doesn't have anything I want." He glanced up and saw Carmen heading back from the galley. "Please?"

"You're sure?"

Damien grabbed her hand and threaded his fingers through hers. Warm, soft skin; the interlocking of their fingers making him think of their bodies entwining. Oh yeah, his plan already had benefits. "Come on, sugar," he said to Theresa as the flight attendant arrived beside him. "We've let the secret out. You just couldn't resist looking at wedding dresses."

"I, uh . . ." she stammered.

He lifted their clasped hands to his mouth and kissed the back of her hand. Mmm, he could definitely do more of that. But right now he was on a mission, so he lifted his head and turned to Carmen. "I know Theresa and I said we weren't together, but it was a lie. We just got engaged and it's a secret. Don't want the news slipping out before we tell her family."

His explanation might not make a lot of sense to Theresa, but it would to Carmen. She'd know the engagement of one of Oz's ten sexiest bachelors would be big news for the tabloids. The kind of news his agent and publicist would be furious about, come to think of it, because it'd scupper one of the big features of their PR campaign. Shit. Telling Carmen might not have been his brightest idea. Especially given the glare she was sending him.

"But, I thought—"

"Sorry," Theresa broke in. "I asked, uh . . ." Her eyes widened as she no doubt realized she didn't know his name. Quickly she went on, "I asked my fiancé to pretend we weren't together. I hope he didn't go overboard, and make you think, uh . . ."

The flight attendant's eyes narrowed. "No, no, of course not." Briskly she poured their champagne, not offering her congratulations, then shot him a nasty glance as she departed.

"Good on you," he told Theresa, squeezing the hand he still held. Funny how natural it felt in his. "Thanks."

She tugged it free and rolled her eyes. "Don't send inconsistent messages to women. And, by the way, what the heck is your name? I almost blew it when I didn't know my pretend fiancé's name."

A good point, but she'd heard Carmen address him as Mr. Black, and if he said Damien she'd likely recognize his name. He wasn't ready for that. Not when he'd got her to pretend they were engaged, which meant she'd have to act at least semi-friendly. "Day," he said, giving her the nickname some of his friends used.

"Day? That's unusual." She studied his face. "Is it Asian? There's something about your features, your coloring."

He took the opening she'd offered. "My dad's mother was Chinese." He pushed up his left sleeve to reveal the Chinese-style dragon tattoo that wrapped around his bicep. Then he picked up his champagne glass. "Let's drink a toast to—" He was about to finish with, "getting rid of Carmen," when a voice, male this time, spoke from over his shoulder.

"Did I hear you tell the flight attendant you're getting married?"

Startled, Damien almost dropped his glass. He turned to see the older man from across the aisle—who looked too young to be a great-grandpa, with his thick silver hair and bright blue eyes—standing beside him. "Er, yes, that's correct." Correct that he'd said it, at least.

"Many congratulations." The bright eyes went soft, a little misty. "Best day of my life when I married Delia. Every day's been a blessing."

A snort came from behind him. "I'll quote you on that, Trev, next time you're whingeing about the way I cook your eggs."

The man turned and Damien could see his wife, a crochet hook in her hand and a bundle of yellow wool beside the champagne glass on her tray. Her eyes were blue, too, and twinkling above wire-rimmed reading glasses she'd shoved down her nose.

"Better than having to cook my own eggs, isn't it?" the man retorted with a grin, and made his way up the aisle in the direction of the lavatories.

"Want some advice?" the woman—Delia—asked Damien.

"Er . . ."

Theresa leaned past him, arm brushing his, a hint of mischief in her voice when she said, "Yes, please."

"Don't hold a grudge and don't go to bed angry. It festers if you do that. Even if you're furious with the other person, ask yourself, would your life be better without them? If the answer's yes, then climb out of that bed and leave. If the answer's no, give them a big kiss. Talk about what's gone wrong, make up, and get over it and move on."

Damien grinned at her. "Sounds like wise advice."

"It does." Theresa's voice sounded a little sad, and he wondered if she was thinking about her own marriage. Had it been her or her hubby who'd climbed out of that bed? Did she regret it? She'd said she didn't intend to get married again. Was that because she was disillusioned with men, skeptical about marriage, or still in love with her ex?

"How long have you been married?" Theresa asked the older woman. "If you have a great-grandchild, it must be going on fifty years?"

"Ha! Trev and I are almost newlyweds. We married two years ago. The family in Vancouver is mine from my first marriage."

"Well, congratulations," Theresa said. "On the new addition to the family, and on finding happiness a second time around."

"Thanks. And best of luck to the two of you." She pushed her glasses up and went back to crocheting something so tiny it was clearly for the baby.

Damien turned to Theresa and raised his glass again. "To a happy wedding, and a happy marriage," he said loudly. Then he mouthed, "For your sister."

"I'll drink to that." She touched her glass to his.

They both took a swallow, then she said softly, "I want to ask you something."

Had she put two and two together about his name? Warily, he said, "What?"

She glanced past him. "Can anyone overhear us?"

He shook his head. "Not if we speak quietly. The seats are too far apart, and the cocoon effect insulates them. What's your question?"

"What did Carmen do wrong?"

"Huh?"

"You were flirting, encouraging her. Then you decided you weren't interested. What did she do?"

"Her? Nothing. It was you, Theresa." What the hell, why not go with honesty?

"Me? I don't follow. And how did you know my name, anyway?"

"All work makes Theresa a dull girl? You said that, remember? Anyhow, I don't think you're dull. Fact is, I'm more interested in you than in her."

3

Had this very hot man—Day—really said what I thought he had? Flustered and skeptical, I asked, "Interested? In what way?"

He gave me the sexiest smile imaginable. "The usual way."

As in, the usual way a man was interested in a woman. Usual for him—that was a no-brainer—but definitely not for me. My skin heated as if I had a fever, and a pulse fluttered in my throat. Another throbbed between my legs. My dormant sex drive seemed to have woken up.

No man had ever looked at me that way. Jeffrey's interest had been immensely flattering and seductive, but his eyes had never held the heated gleam Day's did. With my ex, I'd of course learned that his interest lay in appropriating my research, and the sex we'd enjoyed was merely a side benefit for him.

And Jeffrey had, let's face it, been a short, prematurely balding prof who on his best day could be called cute. Not stunningly handsome like the man who was gazing at me with such intensity. A man who couldn't possibly be interested in my research.

Day seemed sincere, not that I was any judge of male character. But I still didn't understand. What did he want from me? I swallowed against that fluttery pulse in my throat and forced words out. "The usual way? What does that mean?"

His eyes burned even hotter. "It's a long flight, Theresa Fallon. Bet we can figure out some interesting ways to pass the time."

What ways did he have in mind? A more experienced woman would have known, or at least had a playful way of finding out. All I could manage was bluntness. "Day, if you wanted sex, you could have had it with Carmen."

The corner of his mouth kinked. "True. Not saying I don't want it, but if I did, it'd be with you. When you're in the mood."

"When?" My voice rose. I couldn't believe his audacity. Did he really think I was as easy as Carmen? "Shouldn't you have said *if*?"

A cocky smirk. "Nah. I'd bet on when."

"You're so damned sure of yourself." The words burst out. How dare he! "Doesn't any woman ever say no to you?"

He glanced upward, squinting like he was mulling over my question, then said, "Not in recent memory."

The tone of his voice—amused self-deprecation—somehow defused my annoyance. "Did anyone ever tell you you have a swollen head?"

"You find false modesty appealing?"

"N-no, I suppose not." When it came to my work, I was as confident as he. "If you're good at something, it's silly to pretend you're not." I rubbed my temple, where my tension headache had made a reappearance.

"There you go. I *am* good, I promise."

He meant in bed. Or did he? Maybe my inexperience was making me read him wrong.

He reached over and stroked the hair back from my temple, then rubbed gently, his warm thumb finding the knot of tension.

People didn't touch me, except for handshakes or an occasional brush of bodies passing in a narrow doorway. This touch was presumptuous. Intimate. I should have moved away. But it felt so wonderful. How long had it been since anyone had looked after me?

"Good at what?" I dared ask, not sure how I wanted him to answer.

"Mmm." A small, very wicked grin. "How about curing headaches, for a start?"

"It's not a bad start." Where did he intend to go from here? Did he actually hope to seduce me into . . . whatever limited kind of fooling around we could do on an airplane?

Did I want him to? Right now, the caress that had unwound the knot of pain was winding up a whole different kind of tension. A hum of arousal that flowed through my veins like thick, warm honey.

Day had turned down the certainty of sex with a stacked flight attendant who had wavy black hair, pouty red lips, and no doubt ten times—no, make that fifty times—more sexual experience than I. And yes, knowing the plane as Carmen did, she'd have found a place where she and Day could actually engage in intercourse.

Was the man crazy? Or was it me who was crazy? Leaning closer to absorb the heat coming off that firm brown skin, to inhale that outdoorsy male scent.

I shouldn't encourage him, shouldn't let arousal build between my legs. Because of course I wouldn't let him seduce me. I wasn't that kind of woman.

No, Dr. Theresa Fallon—Ms. All Work—wasn't the kind of woman who attracted a gorgeous man, flirted with him, took him for her lover.

When I put it that way . . . Wouldn't it be nice, for one time in my life, to break out of the mold I'd always been cast in, and to be that kind of woman?

Day seemed to think I was. I'd have figured he was merely picking a convenient target if he hadn't rejected Carmen. For the first time in my life, it seemed a man saw me as a sex object. The feminist in me said I should be insulted, but the truth was, I was hugely flattered.

He stopped rubbing my temple and ran his fingers through my hair in a stroke that was half massage, half caress, pure bliss. It was hard to think rationally. And impossible to resist leaning into his hands the way a cat presses into the hands that stroke it.

"I like your hair," he said.

"I thought men liked long hair."

"The hair should suit the woman. Be shiny, feel nice. Not all glopped up with gunk."

"You think it suits me?" I wasn't fishing for a compliment, just genuinely curious. I'd chosen my hairstyle because it was easy, and I had better things to do than fuss with my appearance.

"Yeah. Shows off your long neck, pretty face." He ran a finger along the outside of my ear, giving me pleasant shivers. "Cute ears."

I'd never thought much about my ears, but guessed they were okay. A pretty face, though? If he wanted to seduce me, he needed more than generic flattery. "My face is average. Not round, not square, but somewhere in between. My features are the same. Not big or small."

He studied me intently. "Huh. Guess that's right. Except, where you say average, I say perfect. Symmetrical."

No generic compliment this, and he delivered it with a sincerity that made me glow.

"Like Goldilocks and the . . . What was it?" he asked, mischief sparking his gray eyes. "Oh yeah. Beds. Who'd want too big or too small, when you can have just right?"

"It was the chairs that were too big and too small," I protested halfheartedly, remembering the story I'd read to Merilee a few times. "The beds were too hard and too soft."

"Ah, well . . ." The spark danced again. "Too soft definitely isn't good. Too hard, though? Hmm, you're the woman. Is there such a thing as too hard, when a gal's in bed?"

Oh my God. My cheeks flamed. This man was so out of my league it wasn't funny.

If I had any sense, I'd tell him not to be crude. Tell him to remove his hand from my neck, where he was caressing my nape in a way that sent more shivers of pleasure coursing through me. I'd pull out the exams and get back to being Dr. Fallon.

Instead, I glanced at his lap. Under the fly of his jeans, an already impressive bulge was expanding. I forgot all about being Dr. Fallon and wondered what he'd look like naked, how he'd feel under my hand as my touch made him grow. Then, how he'd feel between my legs, where my long-neglected female parts had sprung to needy awareness.

Oh God, this sexy, assured, experienced man truly was turned on by me. I'd never had such a sensation of pure female power. It gave me an unprecedented sense of sexual confidence.

Trying to ignore my flaming cheeks, I said, "Too hard? Not in my experience." Day didn't need to know how limited that experience was.

The flare of surprise in his eyes pleased me, and I went on. "Of course, as you pointed out, I'm an academic. Hypotheses need to be tested."

He laughed and his hand clasped my shoulder. "I'll volunteer to assist with that test."

Oh God, what had I got myself into? Did he think I was offering to have sex with him? People did speak of the mile-high club . . .

"Dinnertime." It was Carmen, brisk and professional. "I'm taking orders. We're starting with either Atlantic salmon tartare, pâté de foie gras, or wild mushroom soup. Then your choice of beef tenderloin with peppercorn sauce, coconut curried chicken, or bug salad with mango-ginger dressing."

"Bugs," I said. I loved the crustaceans, with their taste somewhere between crab and lobster. "And the salmon tartare, please."

"The mushroom soup for starters," Day said, "and I'll have bugs as well. And wine. Last time I flew, there was a Lenton Brae Sauvignon Blanc?"

"We have it." Snidely, she added, "You're ordering for your fiancée as well, of course?"

He glanced at me. "Sugar, does that wine sound good to you?"

I didn't know the wine, but played along. "Of course, sweetie." Gathering my courage, pleased to have an excuse to touch Day, I leaned into him and pressed a kiss to his T-shirt-clad shoulder, absorbing an amazing jolt of heat and energy.

Hmm. If kissing his shoulder through cotton was that powerful an experience, what would lips to lips be like? I had a growing—let's face it, irresistible—need to know.

Carmen handed us warm, damp towels and departed.

After I'd wiped my face—a benefit of not wearing makeup—and hands, and placed the towel on my tray table, I said to Day, "What's the wine?"

"It's from the Margaret River region. Dry, crisp, kind of lemony, a hint of spicy oak. Should go well with the bugs and appies."

Hmm. He was getting more interesting by the moment. A

hot-looking guy with a dragon tattoo who was a wine connoisseur. And flew business class. For the first time, I wondered what he did for a living. I was about to ask when his lips quirked up at one corner and he said, "Sweetie? You called me sweetie?"

"You called me sugar."

"It popped into my mind. Because you're so sweet, and all," he teased. "So, d'you call all your guys sweetie?"

"No." I'd called Jeffrey "dear" occasionally, but mostly used his name. I wasn't the endearment type. I gave Day a saccharine smile. "Only you, sweetie."

He laughed. "I like you, you know that?"

"I'd kind of hoped so." I paused a beat. "Since we're engaged and all."

"Speaking of which." He lifted his flute, which had an inch of champagne in the bottom. "Shouldn't we have a toast to our upcoming . . ."

I raised mine, too. "Nuptials?"

Slowly, eyes gleaming, Day shook his head. "Not what I had in mind." He clicked his glass gently against mine, then lifted it and drained the contents in one swallow.

"So I'm supposed to drink a toast to whatever you had in mind?" All the same, hand trembling as I lifted the glass, I did it. It wasn't a promise I'd have sex with him, only a promise to . . . What?

To play his game, which I had to admit I was enjoying even though it made me nervous. Not to mention aroused. He'd banished my headache, made me forget about work, and also, I suddenly realized, made me forget to phone my sister Jenna.

Now I seized on the excuse to distance myself a little, to let some of the sexual tension dissipate. "Oh, gosh, I need to make a call." Jenna should be home by now. Alone? Yesterday she'd said she had broken up with the surfer guy she'd followed to

Santa Cruz. She hadn't sounded heartbroken, but that was no surprise. For Jenna, relationships were about having fun while they lasted, not about the long term.

"Go ahead." Day gestured to the onboard phone, then lay back, eyes closed.

I took a moment to admire the length of his legs, the press of firm thighs against worn denim, the bulge at his groin that had receded since Carmen's arrival but was still impressive. His forearms rested on the arms of his seat, firm and tanned, sprinkled with black hair. My fingers itched to touch his arm. Among other bodily parts.

I dialed my sister's number and waited. After several rings, I was readying myself to leave another voice mail, when I heard her voice, breathless. " 'Lo?"

"Hello, Jenna, it's Theresa." I curled sideways in my seat, away from Day. Not only for the illusion of privacy, but to avoid the distraction offered by his hunky body.

"Hey, sis. Call display didn't show your name."

"I'm on the plane. Did I wake you?"

"Nope. Just got in. There was a beach party. So, you're on your way home?"

"Didn't you get my e-mail? I said I'd get a flight Sunday night."

"Is this Sunday?"

"I think it's Saturday night there." The time differences did get confusing, even for efficient me. As for Jenna, she'd so rarely held a regular job, the days of the week held little significance to her. Nor did keeping track of time. Or keeping track of much of anything. How paradoxical that she'd chosen to participate in a count-the-falcons survey.

"How about you?" I asked. "When are you heading to Vancouver?"

"Still working on it."

"Jenna, you're the one who picks up at a moment's notice

and heads off in a new direction. What's the big issue about leaving Santa Cruz? Did you get back together with what's his name?"

"Surfer-dude Carlos? No, we're history. But wow, the surfing is fabulous right now. I'm getting really good."

"And improving your surfing skills is more important than your sister's wedding?"

Day snickered and I turned to glare at him, but his eyes were still closed.

"That's not what I said."

"Okay, Jenna. Anyhow, if you're tied up, I'll do the wedding on my own. I mean, with Kat's help," I amended quickly.

"Yeah, right. You hate it when we try to help. All you can do is criticize."

"I like things to be done right," I muttered.

"*Your* idea of right, Ms. Perfectionist."

Why could we never act like rational adults? "Let's not argue. We all said we wanted to give Merilee a great wedding, so we need to cooperate. I'll set up a project plan and work out the tasks, then we can figure out who does what."

"Yeah, sure, a project plan," she said disdainfully. "Whatever."

"Of course, you can't actually *do* anything until you get to Vancouver," I added.

She sighed. "I'm trying. Honest, Tree." Jenna was the only one who used nicknames. I was Tree because that's how she'd first pronounced my name. "But it's not easy. I need to raise some money."

"Money?"

"Yeah, like to fly home?"

"You don't have money for the flight?" Hadn't she been working?

"The peregrine falcon survey is volunteer work. I've been waitressing some evenings, but I'm not making a lot."

How could she live like that, especially now she was turning thirty? Normally I wouldn't have bailed her out, but damn it, Merilee was getting married. "When I get to Vancouver tomorrow, I'll book a flight for you and I'll pay."

"Shit, Theresa, I don't need your charity."

Couldn't she just say "thank you"? Annoyed, I sniped back. "Sounds to me like you do. Or, if you won't take it from me, call Mom and Dad. I'm sure they'll pay to fly you home."

"Not going to happen."

Damn her. Ninety-nine percent of the time she was easygoing, but every once in a while—at the most inconvenient moments— she got stubborn. "So, what's your *plan*?" My guess was, she didn't have one. "It'll break Merilee's heart if you're not home for the wedding."

"I'll be there! Honest to God, Theresa, lay off. I'll figure it out."

My headache was returning. "Well, if you have any brilliant ideas about the wedding, give me a call or drop me an e-mail."

"You've got the location booked, right?"

"No, I don't. I haven't even started the project plan. Since Merilee called, I've been kind of busy. Booking a flight, reorganizing my schedule, getting someone else to monitor exams, packing. I'll find a location as soon as I get home."

"A location? You know where it has to be, don't you?"

I'd barely given it a moment's thought. "Where?"

"VanDusen Gardens."

"Why do you . . . Oh. Oh, yeah." Our gran, Mom's mother— who unfortunately now suffered from Alzheimer's—used to take us girls on an outing every Sunday afternoon. Science World, the Aquarium, the beach at Spanish Banks, VanDusen Gardens. Merilee had always loved the rambling, naturally landscaped gardens. I did remember her saying she wanted to get married there. How could I have forgotten?

Could it have something to do with the fact that Merilee, the late addition to our three-pack of sisters, had rarely been the focus of my attention? Or Mom's or Dad's, or Kat's or Jenna's, for that matter. By the time Merilee came along, we were wrapped up in our own lives.

"It's June," I said. "It'll be booked on a Saturday."

"It's a big place. I bet they could squeeze us in."

To put it kindly, Jenna was an eternal optimist. To put it more accurately, she tended to ignore reality. "I'll ask." There might be a last-minute cancellation. Merilee would be so excited if we could hold the wedding at VanDusen. "And if not, maybe one of the other gardens Gran used to take us to."

"Talk to Mom and Dad," Jenna said. "They must know someone who can make it happen. Play the guilt card."

"The guilt card. That's a thought." Our father, who worked at the University of British Columbia, was one of Canada's leaders in researching genetic links to cancer, and was busy with the final draft of a report. Mom was a prominent personal injury lawyer and right now she was preparing to present an appeal in the Supreme Court of Canada next week. Neither had time to help with wedding preparations, yet I knew they wanted Merilee to have a wonderful wedding. They wouldn't mind spending a few minutes pulling strings. Grudgingly I said, "Good idea."

"I'm sure you'd have come up with it eventually." There was a smirk in Jenna's voice when she added, "Once you started typing up that *project plan*."

Jenna wouldn't know a plan if it bit her on the behind, but I decided to take the higher road and not comment. Instead, I mused, "What if it rains? We'd need tents or something."

"It'll be sunny for M&M. Just wait and see."

I rolled my eyes. "Fine, you put in a request with the weather gods, and I'll work out a contingency plan."

Noises from the aisle made me turn, to see Carmen serving people a couple rows ahead of us. "Jenna, I have to go."

"Me, too."

"Call Kat, would you? In a couple hours, when she's up? And e-mail us when you know your travel plans."

There was no response. "Jenna? Oh damn, did you hang up on me?"

Day opened his eyes and grinned as I hung up the phone less than gently. "Man, am I glad I don't have siblings. Is it always like that?"

"Usually. We love each other, but . . ." I shrugged. "My secretary says her sister's her best friend. I haven't a clue what that's like." Of course, I didn't actually have a best friend. Colleagues and grad students I enjoyed talking to, but no buddies.

I'd once thought Jeffrey was my best friend. After, I'd decided I didn't need one.

Day's hand stroked the aching knot in my temple. "You need to learn some relaxation techniques, Theresa."

The tension eased. "Actually, I kind of like this one. Your hands are magic." Yes, I said the words deliberately. When he touched me, I wanted more. Wow, here I was, flirting with a man I knew next to nothing about. Maybe I was wilder than I'd ever imagined.

"You ain't seen nothing yet," he murmured.

I believed him, if he was referring to his hands. They were so nonacademic. Strong, dark, masculine, yet gentle and sensitive. Hands that made a woman melt and burn under their touch. Oh yes, I was coming to believe I could be wild.

Carmen arrived, bearing nicely set trays: appetizers, cloth napkins, fresh glasses. She presented a wine bottle so we could see the Lenton Brae label, then poured for us. "Enjoy," she said flatly.

"She hates us," I told Day. "You realize we're going to have marginal service for the whole trip."

"That's better than a boob in the face."

"Give me a break. You can't tell me you didn't enjoy that."

"Okay, I'm male. What can I say?" He glanced at my chest as if he was wondering what my breast would feel like.

He made me aware of the thin V-necked sweater I wore and the flesh-colored bra designed for comfort, not display. And of the way my nipples had perked up and were doing their best to draw his attention through those two layers of fabric. I imagined his lips sucking a nipple into his mouth and a jolt of desire pulsed through me. Trying to sound composed, I said, "You sure do know how to sweet-talk a woman."

"Yeah, I'm one classy guy." The words were absentminded, his voice husky, his gaze still fixed on my chest.

I unfolded my napkin, picked up a fork. "You do have a certain distinctive charm. Stop staring and eat your soup."

He chuckled. "Distinctive? You sure do know how to sweet-talk a guy, Dr. Fallon." Obediently, he turned his attention to his tray and spooned up some soup. "Or is it Dr.? I noticed Carmen called you Ms."

"It's Dr. But the first time I flew as Dr. Fallon, a woman had a heart attack. They checked the passenger manifest and came to me, thinking I was a medical doctor." I remembered my shock and panic, and gave a shiver. "There I was, all of twenty-two, and I felt so helpless—"

"Twenty-two?"

Damn, there was something about this man that had me revealing things I normally kept private. This was crazy. He was so clearly a player. Yet, in our semi-isolated pair of seats, feeling the buzz from champagne and arousal, I felt a sense of intimacy. Oh, what the heck, I was a strong-minded woman. I could choose what to share and what to hold back, and right now, what was the harm in talking?

I gave a casual shrug. "I was a Doogie Howser kid. Zipped through school. What can I say?" I forked up some salmon tartare and tasted it. It was very nice for airline food.

"Man. Did you do anything else but go to school?"

Besides supervising my sisters while my parents worked? "Not much. My Howser-esque qualities became apparent when I was a baby, so my parents put me on the fast track." No Goldilocks for me; my "fairy tales" had been Greek mythology.

"Why?"

"Uh . . . What do you mean?"

"To what end? So you could have a doctorate when you were twenty-two?"

The question stopped me and I realized I didn't know the answer. "I guess once they knew my potential, they wanted me to realize it." It wasn't like me to be revealing personal information to a stranger, but there was a surprising warmth in those gray eyes. A warmth that eased the ache in my temples, and made my nether regions hum with awareness.

He put down his spoon, soup bowl half empty, and cocked his head. "But why the 'all work, no play' thing? What's so bad about being a kid? Playing with friends, having fun?"

"I don't know," I said softly, lifting my wineglass. "I envied my sisters sometimes, because they had those things. But . . . this is awful; I felt kind of superior, too."

He chuckled. "Yeah, I got that from the phone calls."

I winced. "Did I sound horrible?"

"No. Just like a perfectionist who's impatient when others don't measure up."

I nodded. "That's me in a nutshell."

"Try the wine," he urged, making me realize I'd been hanging on to the glass but hadn't yet taken a sip.

I obeyed, and found it matched his description. He'd summed it up as neatly as he'd just done with me. "It's great."

Day touched my arm, fingers drifting across my skin in a caress, then squeezing gently. "There's a lot more in that nutshell, Theresa. Sense of humor, loyalty, a—"

"Loyalty?" I cut in.

"To your little sister. Taking on her wedding."

My eyes widened. "That's not loyalty, it's just . . . she's my sister. The wedding is really important to her, and I want her to have her perfect day." After all, there had been enough times I, and the rest of the family, hadn't been there for Merilee.

"Course you do." He spooned up some more soup and held out his spoon. "Here."

I leaned forward, feeling inelegant as I slurped it. "Tasty. Want to try the salmon?"

At his nod, I offered him a forkful. He steadied my hand with his, which had the opposite effect of sending quivers from my fingers up my arm.

He took his time about releasing me. "How many siblings are there? Any more phone calls you need to make?"

"No, that's it. I'll check in when I'm in Honolulu airport." I sipped some more wine. "There are four of us, all sisters." I broke off. "You can't possibly be interested in this."

"Hey, until dinner's over and they turn out the lights, what else can we do but talk?"

And what would we do after? I'd intended to work—on the wedding plan, the exams. But that decision could wait. For the moment, with meal trays in front of us, what else could we do but eat, drink, and chat? It was flattering to have a man interested in something other than my latest research project. I'd never see Day after this flight, so what was the harm in opening up a little? In fact, the idea—ships that pass in the night; strangers on a plane—had a strong appeal.

"Okay, here's the Fallon family history. When Mom and Dad got married, he was working on his doctorate—he's a geneticist—and she was going into law school. They didn't plan on having kids for years. She was on the pill, but it's not 100 percent effective. She got pregnant in second-year law. Lucky for me, they decided to have the baby."

"That was you? I'm glad about that decision."

"Mom believed one parent should stay home with the kids

for the first two or three years. Dad's very much the absent-minded professor, so he'd have been useless with a baby. They decided they'd like to have at least two kids, and Mom said, if she was going to interrupt her career path, she was only doing it once. So she whipped us out very efficiently. Me, Kat. Then, trying for a boy, Jenna. They decided the three-pack was enough. When Jenna was two, Mom went back to law school."

Day, who'd been drinking wine as I talked, put his glass down. "Your mom sounds really organized. Guess you take after her?"

"Funny you'd say that. I've always been a daddy's girl, an academic. But you're right, I'm also very organized, like Mom." An outsider's perspective was interesting.

"I bet when you were little they saw you as the best of both of them. They wanted you to superachieve partly for you, but partly because you were a reflection of them."

"Maybe so," I said slowly. It was another perception to tuck away in the back of my mind and mull over later. "You're not just a pretty face, are you, Day?"

4

So she thought he was good looking. Damien grinned smugly. "Hold onto that thought, Prof. It may come in handy later." When she found out his identity.

Theresa frowned, clearly not following his train of thought, thank God. Then she stretched and fiddled with the seat controls.

"Problem?" he asked.

"I want to adjust the back and raise the footrest."

"Here." He bent over and, as he found the control, his hand brushed her thigh. A firm, warm thigh under her cotton pants. "Give me your hand."

Hesitantly, she let him take it and put it on the lever, resting his hand atop to guide it. "Like this," he told her. "You slide it this way, and use your feet to push the footrest."

"Thanks, I've got it."

Reluctantly, he withdrew his hand and let her get settled.

"I'm not used to business class," she said. "My budget doesn't allow for it, but this time I got an upgrade."

"I like it for long flights." *His* budget, thanks to Kalti Brown, could handle the occasional expenditure like this. So far the Kalti books had earned him enough to buy a flat in Sydney and pay the mortgage on a beachfront cottage north of Cairns. He used both for writing. A change of scene often helped reinvigorate his muse.

As for this book tour, his first to North America, a New York publisher had bought U.S. rights to his books and was sponsoring the tour. They covered the basic expenses and Damien was chipping in to give himself a few extras such as flying business class.

At the moment, it was looking like one damned rewarding expenditure. "You quit in the middle of the family saga, prof."

"You're sure you're interested?" She was fidgeting with her wineglass, rotating the stem back and forth.

He reached over to brush the back of her hand. "Positive." A storyteller himself, he liked hearing other people's tales. And Theresa was one of the most intriguing people he'd run into in a long while.

"Stop me when you get bored." She swallowed the last of her wine. "In the family, I was Dad's kid, the academic. Kat was Mom's. Mom's a lawyer—a very successful personal injury litigator—and has always focused on people rather than research. Kat's bright, but no academic. She's outgoing, has a ton of friends. That's the area where she's superior."

"And the third? Jenna, did you say?"

"Yes. For a long time, she was the baby. She acted out a lot, but could be a real charmer. So far, she's spent her life drifting. Never found a focus."

"She didn't carve out an area where she was superior?"

Theresa made a sound that was between a snort and a chuckle. "She excels at being eccentric. She's a nonconformist, a flake. Mom says she's a kook, like Goldie Hawn on a TV show from the late sixties, early seventies, *Rowan & Martin's Laugh-In.*"

Carmen came to take their empty appetizer dishes, replace them with their entrées, and refill their wine glasses. When she'd gone, he and Theresa both tasted the bugs, agreeing they were good but the sauce could have used more ginger.

"The wine does go well with them," she said.

"Glad you like it. So, go on. There's a fourth sister, the one who's getting married?"

"Yes, Merilee. After they had the three-pack, Mom and Dad were focused on their careers. As we girls grew up, I was into school, Kat was being Ms. Sociability, and Jenna was playing at whatever took her fancy. The five of us have pretty distinct, strong personalities."

"Yeah, I bet. If the rest are like you."

She wrinkled her cute turned-up nose at him. "We carved out our own niches, mostly respected each other's boundaries, got our routine down pat. Then, eight years after Jenna, Mom got pregnant again. It wasn't planned."

"Must have been a shock for her. For all of you."

"To put it mildly. Now there was a three-pack plus one, and we all had to adjust. This time Mom went back to work right after a short mat leave. Jenna lost her place as the baby, which made her act out even more. I got stuck with more older-sister responsibilities. But Merilee was an easy child. Not such a strong personality as the rest of us."

Must have been tough for the baby, following in the shoes of three strong and much older sisters. Theresa called them the three-pack plus one, not something like "the Fallon four." "Sounds like the rest of you carved out your niches and didn't leave anything special for Merilee."

"Well, sort of." Her eyes began to dance with that sunlight-on-water sparkle. "She'd disagree, though."

"Yeah?" He put down his fork, gave her his full attention. "So, what's your little sister superior at?"

"According to her, it's love. She's the one sister who has a talent for it."

Love? "Oh yeah?"

She nodded. "I'm divorced and determined never to make the same mistake. Kat wants to marry and have kids, but she always falls for losers. And Jenna, according to Mom, is a hippie who was born in the wrong decade."

"How so?"

"She loves guys, loves sex, believes in the whole free-love, no-commitment thing. She says fidelity's stupid because people aren't hard-wired to be monogamous, so she flits from guy to guy and never intends to settle down. She has a short attention span. She's excited about whatever new idea or man comes along, but not in a deep, real way." Theresa raised her wineglass and slanted him a teasing glance. "Sounds like your ideal woman, right, Day?"

"Hmm." He tilted his head back and reflected. "Yeah, there's a certain appeal to a woman like that. Fun with no strings." He thought about the girls who'd come on to him in the last couple years. The succession of affairs. The sex, sometimes great and sometimes mediocre.

The fact was, the names and faces had grown interchangeable. And he'd started to feel scummy. Like the woman didn't really see him, just the successful, sexy author. And he didn't see them as individuals either, just a series of hot babes.

"But a guy grows up," he said slowly. "Maybe he wants more. Someone he can really get to know. Bit by bit, layer by layer. Connecting, growing closer."

He found himself thinking of his friend Bry, which was a jolt because the last thing either of them was was gay. But in a way, his train of thought made sense. "You know how it is with a good friend?"

Theresa was watching him intently, fork poised in the air as if she'd forgotten about it. "How do you mean?"

"Like, how you first meet someone through a friend or through work." He'd met Bry, a cop, when he was researching his first Kalti Brown book. He'd needed information about the structure of the police department, how crimes were investigated, and so on. "You hit it off, go for a beer, talk about something other than work. Find common interests. Discover you think the same way about things, have the same values."

Her eyes were narrowed in concentration. "Go on."

"The relationship grows. Pals turn into good buds who are there for each other, no matter what."

Now there was a sheen in her eyes. Was she thinking of a close friend? Or maybe wishing that's how it was with her sisters?

"So," Damien said, "what if you had that kind of thing with someone of the opposite sex? A solid friendship plus great sex. Maybe that'd be worth building on, rather than moving on to the next lover."

"Yes, I . . ." She swallowed. "I think it sounds wonderful." Her voice was choked up, like she was on the verge of tears.

Suddenly he realized that he must have made her think of her ex-husband. "Crap. Sorry, Theresa. I didn't mean to remind you of your marriage. I'm an idiot."

"No. But, surprisingly," a tiny smile flashed, "you're a bit of a romantic." The smile disappeared. "And, while that kind of relationship does sound great, how do you know it's real? That you can trust in it?"

"That it'll beat the statistical odds? I dunno. Gut instinct? Leap of faith?" He wondered whether she'd fallen out of love with her husband, or vice versa.

Knowing that the enforced companionship of a long flight could breed its own kind of trust and openness, he tested the waters. "I'm sorry your marriage didn't work out."

"I made a big mistake, falling for Jeffrey. I learned I couldn't trust him."

"Damn. He cheated on you?" The guy must've been a right bastard and a fool.

A corner of her mouth turned up ruefully. "Not in the way you're thinking. Not with another woman. And in fact, he didn't exactly cheat *on* me, he cheated me out of recognition."

"I'm intrigued."

She made a face, picked up her wineglass, and drained it. "For this, I need more wine."

He leaned into the aisle, caught Carmen's eye, and held up his own empty glass. She gave him a nod, then turned toward the galley.

She returned with the wine bottle, filled their glasses, and gathered up their entrée plates and silverware. "For dessert, we have a cheese and fruit platter, lemon cheesecake with pomegranate glaze, and chocolate Cointreau mousse."

"The mousse, please," Theresa said.

"Cheese and fruit," Damien said.

"I'll be right back. Coffee, tea?"

Theresa ordered decaf coffee and Damien asked for the same. Then, when the two of them were alone again, he said, "Go on. Tell me what happened with your ex."

She took a drink of wine, another, then put the glass down decisively. "When we met, he was a tenured sociology professor at the University of Saskatchewan. With my brand-new PhD, specializing in indigenous studies, I'd just won an appointment in their native studies program. I had an idea for a research project, and went to him to get his opinion."

She grimaced. "He was enthusiastic. About not only the project, but me as well. We started dating and he helped me put together a grant application. We had a whirlwind courtship—in a way that would probably strike you as hopelessly dull and academic, but all the same it seemed romantic to me—and got married two months after we'd met."

"He swept you off your feet. I wouldn't have taken you for the type." Damien felt a twinge of jealousy, and also annoyance at the jerk who'd hurt Theresa and made her so cynical. He wanted to touch her, offer comfort, but her arms were wrapped protectively around her body and he sensed she wouldn't welcome it.

"I was young. Naïve. Dazzled by his interest," she said grimly. "Stupid."

He tried to imagine Theresa as a girl who'd had the brains and drive to get her doctorate, yet been naïve enough to be swept up in a romance with a man who'd ended up hurting her. Now she was what? Thirtyish? And still bitter about her ex, and cynical about relationships. "So, what happened next?"

"I'd almost finalized the grant application and was waiting for Jeffrey's feedback. Then he proposed, wanted to get married right away, and everything else got shoved aside. Or so I thought. We had a civil ceremony and a brief honeymoon. When we got back to work, I pulled out the grant application and asked when he'd be able to review it. He said he'd forgotten to tell me, but he'd already revised and submitted it. We just needed to wait to hear back."

"And?"

"When the grants were announced, my project had got funding. But Jeffrey had applied in his own name, listing me as a research assistant but not as coauthor."

"Wanker!"

"When I asked what was going on, he said I must have misunderstood. It had always made sense for him to apply, because I was too much of an unknown to get the grant."

"But it was your idea and you did the work," Damien said indignantly. "You deserved the credit."

"Wouldn't you think? And instead, all I'd be was a researcher again, just like when I was a student at Harvard and the New School for Social Research in New York."

"Harvard?" The woman had a habit of dropping these amazing tidbits. "You went to Harvard?"

"Yes. So did my dad. In medicine. And no," she scowled at him, "I didn't get in because I was a legacy, I had the marks."

She'd lost him. "What's a legacy?"

"At the Ivy League schools in the States, typically ten to fifteen percent of new admissions are the children of alumni."

Did the woman memorize statistics on everything?

"Especially of distinguished alumni," she went on. "The kind who make donations to their alma mater. The entrance qualifications for their children are often, shall we say, a trifle lighter. The kids are referred to as legacies."

"Well, that's crap. Whatever happened to equal opportunity?"

"Exactly. Anyhow, you wouldn't believe the number of people—profs and students—who assumed I was a legacy."

"Until they saw your work." He barely knew Theresa, but was sure she'd excel on her own merits.

Her face lightened with pleased surprise. "Thank you."

He shrugged. "Welcome. And like I said, your ex is a wanker. If you didn't yet have the reputation to get a grant, couldn't he have sponsored you? Or at least listed you as coauthor?"

"Of course. But he wanted the credit. And had no qualms about using me to get it. The whole thing—the seduction and marriage—were all about him. Him and his career."

"Ah, come on." Not that he wanted to excuse the bastard, but how could the guy not have been attracted to Theresa? "He probably fell for you, then got greedy when he saw the chance for career glory."

"I doubt that very much." She put down her now-empty glass. "Anyhow, after that betrayal, I couldn't believe anything he said. I couldn't work with him, got mad every time I saw him. I told him he could find another research assistant, and another wife. After I finished teaching that semester, I left Saskatchewan."

"That's rough." He squeezed her hand where it rested on her tray table.

She freed her hand from under his and firmed her jaw. "I don't need pity. I'm a loner. That's how it's always been, and it's how I work best."

"It's not pity, for God's sake." Didn't she recognize sympathy? "I know what you mean about the loner thing, though." Damien spent days on end writing, only breaking for a run or walk. It wasn't that he didn't like to socialize, just that he got so absorbed in the work. If Bry didn't drag him out for a few beers or a backyard barbie, he could go weeks without talking to a soul other than a grocery store clerk.

Theresa snorted. "You, a loner? Give me a break. You flirt with every female in sight."

He winked. "Didn't say I don't like women. But I do spend a lot of time alone."

"What do you do?"

Crap, he'd walked into that one. If he told her, it'd break the growing connection between them. Fortunately, he could avoid the question because he saw Carmen coming with their desserts. "That looks good," he told her as she handed him a platter with strawberries, grapes, and slices of kiwi fruit and papaya, plus crackers and small wedges of four different cheeses.

"Enjoy," she said, voice flat, obviously still ticked at him. When she'd finished with the meals, he'd have to have a word with her, try to make things right. Ensure she wouldn't tell anyone about his "engagement."

Theresa took a spoonful of her chocolate Cointreau mousse and her expression told him she'd forgotten her question about his occupation. Her full attention was on taste sensations that appeared to be almost orgasmic.

He'd have liked to be responsible for putting that glow of sensual pleasure on her face.

She spooned up another bite, then sucked it slowly off the spoon, eyes closed, and his cock jerked as he imagined those lips wrapped around it.

To further torture himself, he selected a ripe, medium-sized strawberry and reached over to dip it in her mousse. Her eyes opened, narrowed in annoyance, then he held the strawberry to her mouth. She smiled and reached up her hand to steady his, the way he'd done when he'd eaten salmon tartare off her fork. Her mouth opened, then she closed her lips around the chocolate-coated tip of the strawberry.

Oh yeah, he was definitely erect now.

The warmth of her soft fingers against his hand, the glaze of sensual enjoyment in her eyes, the way her lips wrapped around the red fruit. The damned berry was even shaped a bit like the head of his cock.

As Theresa took her time nibbling the fruit from his fingers, he was glad for the napkin across his lap. Especially when Carmen came along to pour coffee.

"Enjoying your dessert, I see." This time her tone bordered on snarky. Unprofessional, yeah, but it had been shitty of him to come on to one woman, then ditch her for another. Sure, all he'd done was flirt, but he and Carmen both knew where they'd been heading.

When she'd gone, he watched Theresa add milk to her coffee and stir. Her bare arm moved in circles, graceful and feminine. A smart, strong woman, yet vulnerable and wary. She must have had other lovers since her divorce, but her ex had done such a number on her, she still mistrusted men. How could a guy be cruel to Theresa? "About your husband," he said abruptly.

The spoon clicked the side of the cup as her hand jerked. "What? Oh, enough said. It's in the past."

"Yeah, but all the same, I'd like to meet up with the bugger in a dark alley. I'd punch his lights out."

His words, the grimness of his tone, clearly weren't what she'd expected. Her eyes widened. "Day! That's . . . you wouldn't. That's so . . . uncivilized."

"You're saying civilized meanness, like white-collar cheating, is okay, but being physical isn't?"

"Well . . ." Her tongue came out and ran across her top lip as she considered. Color rose in her cheeks. "Violence isn't a solution." Her lips tipped up at the corners, then the smile took over, widening on her mouth, making her eyes light. "All the same, I'd like to see it. Jeffrey would . . ." She gave a snort of laughter. "God, he'd be no match for you."

Damien loved seeing her laugh. Man, she was beautiful. "Theresa? The guy was a fool. A woman like you shouldn't be taken advantage of, you should be appreciated. Slowly and thoroughly. By a man who wants to make you feel like the beautiful, sexy woman you truly are."

The laughter had faded from her face as he spoke, to be replaced by wonder. "Day? That's a really nice thing to say."

He shrugged. "It's the truth. Any man in his right mind would feel that way."

"Not so as I've noticed." The humor was back, this time wry.

"Then you haven't been looking in the right places." He picked up a strawberry. "Want another?"

"I think it's your turn." She took the berry from his fingers, dipped it in mousse, and held it out to him.

He nibbled the treat and with the last morsel sucked the tip of her index finger into his mouth.

She gave a startled, "Ooh." A flush colored her cheeks and the exposed V of her chest. Under the thin sweater, her nipples tightened.

It was those nipples he imagined as he sucked on her finger. When he freed her, he teased, "Do you blush when you're teaching at the uni?"

Her hands went up, covering her cheeks. "No."

"Why not?"

"I guess because I know what I'm doing. I'm confident."

"But not with me?" He put a slice of cheese on a cracker and offered it to her.

"No thanks, I'll stick to fruit and chocolate."

He ate the bite himself and fixed another. "You didn't answer my question."

"It's not you, Day, it's men. I'm not confident with men. As colleagues and students, yes, but not, uh, socially."

That was nuts. She had so much going for her. How could she have let one man destroy her confidence? "Jeffrey has a lot to answer for." He broke a grape off the small bunch on his plate, dipped it into her mousse, then held it out so she could take it from his fingers, her soft lips a tantalizing whisper against his skin.

"It wasn't only him. I was always years younger than the boys in my classes. Like, graduating high school at fourteen? You can bet no one asked me to the prom."

"I see what you mean. But once you reach a certain age, when everyone's grown up, the differences don't matter so much." He fed her a slice of overripe papaya and a bead of juice trickled over her bottom lip and down her chin.

He wanted to lick it, but she caught it with her finger. "Yes, but by then I had my doctorate." She stuck her finger between her lips and sucked it, which made his cock jerk inside the confinement of his jeans.

"I'd missed out on all the girlie stuff," she said. She slanted him a glance, wet her lips. "And on Sex."

Sex. The word, coming out of her full lips, sent a surge of

lust straight to his already aroused groin, and he could barely suppress a moan.

"Sure," she went on, "I knew the textbook facts about male/female relationships, but that's not the same thing as being a normal teenager. Trying to decide if a boy really likes you, having your first kiss, wondering how far to go. Knowing when you're in love versus in lust. Knowing when a guy's in love versus just using you." She'd gone from sounding wistful to bitter. Thinking of her ex again.

"Okay. But hell, Theresa, you're grown up now. A beautiful, intelligent, interesting woman. You must've gained a bunch of experience since Jeffrey."

She shrugged. "I wasn't interested in trying again." Quickly she added, "Look, I'm not completely pitiful and naïve. Jeffrey wasn't my first and he wasn't my last."

"I didn't mean that." Only that she was vulnerable. Perhaps he ought to back off. He didn't want to hurt her.

Theresa jabbed a finger in the middle of his chest. Hard. "No!"

He jerked and almost knocked his food tray off balance.

"I see that look in your eyes." She jabbed him once more. "I hate that 'poor little smart girl' look. Don't you go making decisions for me. If I let you . . ." she went even pinker, "uh, feed me dessert, it's because I want to."

Feed her dessert? The woman had to be aware that the dessert was foreplay.

"Not," she went on, "because I'm some loser who's desperate for the attention of a handsome guy. And I want you doing it because you want to, not because you feel sorry for me."

He gave a surprised laugh. His throbbing cock sure wasn't sorry for her. She was damned fine to look at, sexy, and he enjoyed talking to her. He was having the most fun he'd had with a woman in a very long time, even though they were both fully clothed. "No fear of that. But I don't want you getting hurt again."

"God! You and your massive ego." Interesting to note that billabong eyes could spit fire. "Day, I won't give anyone the power to hurt me. If we do—whatever—it's going to be fully consensual. If we're using each other, it's for our mutual pleasure, and that's all."

Using each other? Nah, that's what he and Carmen would've been doing. Her wanting to fuck a celebrity, him just wanting to get his rocks off. He reached over to spoon up some mousse, then held the spoon to Theresa's lips. "Consensual is good. But, Prof . . ."

Slowly she licked chocolate from the spoon, her gaze holding his.

"Prof, if we . . . share dessert, or anything else, it's not about using each other. Mutual pleasure, yes. Using, no. Got it?"

"Y-yes. I do." Her eyes were luminous.

Gently he used his thumb to clean a smudge of mousse from her upper lip. Then he licked the chocolate from his thumb. Her eyes widened. Glittered with sexual heat. "Mutual," he said. "Pleasure."

She nodded as if hypnotized.

Damn, but he was impatient for the cabin lights to dim and give them some privacy.

Fortunately, Carmen and the flight attendant who handled the other side of the business-class cabin were clearing away dinner trays and offering final refills of coffee and tea. Passengers rose, stretched, headed for the lavatories.

Across the aisle, the great-grandparents were yawning and unwrapping blankets. She'd put her crocheting away. Damien would bet his next advance that they'd be dozing off, not staying up to watch a movie.

Theresa slipped the strap of her purse over her shoulder and rose. "Excuse me, Day." She headed up the aisle to join a small queue.

While she was gone, Carmen refilled their coffee cups and offered chocolates. "Or has your fiancée had enough chocolate?" she asked sarcastically.

"Can any woman ever have too much chocolate?" He took one and put it on Theresa's tray, beside her coffee. "Ta, Carmen."

"Right," she said coolly.

Now was his chance for a private conversation. "Look," he said softly, "I acted like a jerk, flirting with you. It was stupid. I'm sorry."

Her face softened a touch. "That's it? An apology, with no attempt to excuse yourself?"

He shook his head. "I was wrong. Period. Again, I'm sorry." He tried out a low-powered version of the smile he knew many women found irresistible. "It's a knee-jerk reflex, flirting with a pretty lady. And this being engaged thing is so new, I'm not used to it. We really want to keep it a secret for now, so please don't spread the news."

"Well, I have to say, you're gonna break some hearts when women find out you're off the eligible list, Damien Black." Her expression was a degree or two warmer when she moved away to serve the people behind him.

He wondered what she'd think when his engagement was never announced.

When Theresa returned, she said, "They give us chocolates, too?"

"It's their version of the chocolate on your pillow." He winked. "Speaking of which—pillows and all—you weren't planning on watching a movie, were you?"

"I really should work." Her voice lacked conviction.

So should he, but hell, this opportunity—this woman—was

too good to pass up. "Don't want to disillusion Carmen. She'll figure our marriage is doomed to failure."

"Oh gosh, I'm *so* worried about Carmen's opinion."

He chuckled. "Besides, remember the 'all work' thing? Isn't the prof allowed some time off to play?"

"Well . . ." Her cheeks were pink again. "Dare I ask what you had in mind?"

"I think you just did." He gave her his full-wattage smile. "Whatever we feel like. A little more talk. Maybe . . ." With his index finger he smoothed hair away from her temple. "A kiss, right about here." Then he touched her nose. "Another, here." And, finally, her lips. "And definitely one here."

"You're—" Her voice came out croaky. She cleared her throat. "You're giving me warning you intend to kiss me?"

"Let's say hope rather than intend." He studied her face, which reflected a mix of embarrassment, uncertainty, and arousal. The physical signals—flushed cheeks, gleaming eyes, beaded nipples—said she was turned on. But would she get over her hangups and acknowledge her desires? "Figure that might be more fun than grading exams?"

Humor sparkled. "Undoubtedly. But . . ." She ducked her head. "Maybe you shouldn't have asked. Maybe you should have just gone ahead."

"No. I want you to opt in."

Slowly she raised her head and gazed into his eyes. "To what, exactly, Day?"

"Three kisses. Temple, nose, lips. And then we'll see."

Those enticing lips curved. "That doesn't sound too awful."

"If it is, we stop there."

The curve deepened. "And if it turns out to be enjoyable?"

"Then it's your turn. You pick the next three things. Kisses or anything else you want."

She sucked in a breath, and he wondered what she was imagining. Something that made her cheeks flame again, and that could only be good as far as he was concerned.

Before he could ask, Carmen stopped beside them. "More chocolate?" She'd lost some of her attitude, he was glad to see.

When he and Theresa both turned down the offer, with thanks, Carmen went on. "We'll be settling in for the night. Do you have everything you need? Pillows, blankets, water? You know how the video screen works? There's a movie guide in the side seat pocket."

Theresa said, "Could I get a bottle of water, please?"

"Make it two," Damien said.

"Of course."

When Carmen had gone, Theresa said, "I don't believe it. She's acting more civil."

"Yeah, well, I apologized."

"Apologized?" She studied him with some surprise. "Hmm. That's kind of sweet."

Sweet. He rolled his eyes. Then he made a trip to the loo, taking the toiletries kit so he could shave and brush his teeth.

When he came back, he noticed that the older gent across the aisle seemed to be dozing, sleep mask covering his eyes. Beside him, his wife was taking out her own sleep mask and earplugs. "Have a good night," she said softly. Was that a twinkle in her eye?

"You, too."

Throughout the business-class cabin, there were a couple people with computers out, another couple reading, and a few who were focused on their video screens. But, for the most part, people were settling down to sleep. Rustlings and hushed voices died away.

Damien got pillows and blankets out of the overhead bin as a female voice came over the loudspeaker, advising them the cabin lights would now be dimmed and instructing them where to find the individual seat lights. "We wish you a pleasant night, and to minimize disturbance we'll avoid walking through the cabin unless we need to. If there's something you'd like, please press the call button or come up to the galley and we'll be pleased to help you."

A moment later, the main lights went off. Now the cabin was illuminated only by faint lights on the floor marking the aisles, a glow where the galley and lavatories were located, and the occasional seep-over around a cocoon chair where a passenger had turned on the seat light.

He leaned toward Theresa. "I can hardly see you," he murmured. "How'm I going to find that temple, for the first kiss?"

5

I could—probably should—have avoided Day. I should have curled into the cocoon of my seat, turned on a light, got started on that wedding project plan.

It'd be silly to let myself be seduced by a charmer, and I wasn't known for doing silly things. But, oh God, he'd got me so turned on with that dessert sharing. Not to mention what he'd said about a woman like me deserving to be appreciated slowly and thoroughly, and made to feel beautiful and sexy.

No man had ever made me feel that way. No wonder I'd never had much of a sex drive when no guy had ever revved me up this way.

Of course it was only a line. But the reality was, I wasn't the kind of woman guys normally tossed their lines at. When was the last time a man had flirted with me even a little? When was the last time I'd had fun talking to a man, not about sociological studies but simply engaging in male/female teasing banter?

Banter? Wait a minute, I didn't *do* banter. The banter gene had been omitted from my makeup. Except, with this man I kind of, sort of, had been bantering. Not entirely clumsily. I'd made him laugh more than once.

Not only that, I'd aroused him. The way he'd aroused me.

"When a person can't see," Day said softly, "he has to rely on touch." Fingers grazed my chin, then soft lips brushed my temple.

So much for moving away. Instead, I held still, my skin tingling where his mouth brushed along my hairline, pressing soft kisses. Then he was moving across my cheek toward my nose.

He'd broken his promise. He'd said—or had he merely implied?—he'd kiss me three times only. Temple, nose, mouth. Instead, he was weaving a daisy chain of kisses, working his way ever so slowly across my skin. A puff of breath, soft lips, a hint of warm dampness. Each sent a tremor racing through me, straight to my sex, which was pulsing with need.

The kisses were closed-mouthed, almost innocent. How could they be such a turn-on? But then, my reaction to this man hadn't made sense from the very beginning.

As an academic, I believed in objectivity. I didn't hedge or rationalize. And, to be totally objective about it, Day turned me on in a major way. No doubt he had that effect on many women but, for me, the experience was fresh.

Oh, my. He was kissing my nose, letting me feel the moist underside of his lips, teasing my flesh with the tip of his tongue. The nose was *not* an erogenous zone, I reminded myself. But my body wasn't listening to me, it was responding to Day. My nipples were hard, yearning for his mouth to give them the same treatment he was bestowing on my nose. And my sex was swollen, damp, achy.

Why was this happening? With Jeffrey, arousal hadn't been there in the beginning. It had grown as he wooed me for a few weeks with intellectual discourse, red wine, and kisses.

And speaking of kisses . . . Day's lips had reached mine.

He gave me one quick peck, then moved away. I waited to

see where he'd kiss next, *how* he'd kiss next. But nothing happened.

"Day?" I whispered.

"That's my three. Now it's your turn."

I knew what I wanted. Why shouldn't I take it? "I don't
think that last one qualified as a kiss. Finish what you started."

"And then?"

"Then I get my three."

My eyes were adjusting to the dim light, and I saw the flash
of his smile as he moved toward me. "Thank God."

He made me feel desirable. As a woman. Period. Not as a
kid genius, not as a top-rated teacher and grad student advisor,
not as a brilliant researcher and colleague. As an attractive, sexy
woman. I could kiss him for that. And I did.

We started slowly, learning the shape of each other's lips. He
nibbled my lower lip the way he'd done my nose, sucking it in,
teasing it with his tongue, sending darts of pleasure rippling
through me.

I did the same thing back, and he sighed with pleasure.

I'd thought I knew how to kiss, but I soon realized I'd
barely passed my GED. Now Day was taking me to university
and I'd be willing to bet, before he was done, I'd have my PhD.

In the past I'd thought kisses were pleasant, but nothing
special. Kind of a practical means to an end. A "hi, it's you, this
is nice, okay now let's get on to something a little more arousing" kind of thing. Not a treat to be savored slowly, deliciously,
like a chocolate mousse-covered ripe strawberry.

We were still nibbling and licking around the edges, like we
were tasting the chocolate. We hadn't even got to the fruit and
my head was spinning, my chest flushed, my thighs clenched.

I'd enjoyed making love with Jeffrey, but now I suspected
my experience with him was another GED-type thing. If Day
was as good at sex as he was at kissing . . .

He had one hand on the armrest of my semireclined seat,

bracing himself. The other stroked through my hair, caressed the planes and curves of my face.

I ran my own hands through his hair, finding it thick and soft, a little springy as if it had a mind of its own. It curled down his neck and I stroked under it, along his hairline, into the soft, hidden skin of his nape.

As we kissed, his breath drifted across my face, scented of minty toothpaste and chocolate. I wanted to taste the inside of his mouth, and by now it was most definitely my turn to choose what we did. I gripped his head between my hands to hold him steady, then thrust my tongue between his lips. He parted for me, I dipped inside, and yes, he tasted as good as he smelled. My after-dinner chocolate mint to suck on and relish.

He angled his head, giving me better access, and danced the tip of his tongue around mine. Then he took his turn at invading my mouth, making a leisurely sensual exploration.

My lips felt flushed and tingling, soft and damp, as his tongue thrust between them. Mirroring the act of intercourse.

And speaking of lips, that other set was swollen and damp, and could really have used some stimulation other than the tight press of cotton between my thighs.

His hand didn't go there, though. Instead, he inched down one shoulder of my sweater and bent to press kisses on the bare skin he'd revealed, working down the V-neckline to the cleavage that now showed. His tongue followed that cleft, then he kissed along the top line of my bra.

I caught my breath, nipples hard and aching.

"There's a better way," he murmured.

Of course there was, but it required privacy and a bed. "What do you have in mind?"

"Take off your bra."

"But . . ." I wanted this man's hands, his lips, on my breasts, but what if someone saw us? I peered past him, seeing virtually nothing but an occasional glow of light many seats away. And, if anyone did happen to walk down the aisle, Day's body would block their view of me.

Wriggling in the seat, I straightened so I could reach up under the back of my sweater and undo my bra clasp. Then I pulled one shoulder strap out the armhole of my top and down over my arm and hand, then used the other shoulder strap to pull the whole bra out the other armhole.

I probably looked no different than I had before, but I felt different. Wanton and sensual, my nipples rubbing against the woven fabric of my top. This was the closest I'd ever come to being braless in public.

"Put that somewhere you won't lose it," Day suggested.

I tucked the bra into my purse, then took one of the blankets he'd stuffed between our seats. When he shook it out and draped it over me, I felt bolder and leaned back in my seat, shamelessly thrusting my chest toward him.

He didn't waste time accepting my offer. He slid his hands under the bottom hem of my top, brushing the bare skin above the waistband of my pants and making me tremble. Then he cupped my breasts. And didn't move. Just held them, letting them settle into his big hands as if they were designed to fit there.

I could see him fairly well now. His eyes were closed and he smiled, not that sexy grin but a slower, closed-mouth smile that looked to me like perfect satisfaction. "Oh, now, that's good," he murmured.

It was, and I could hardly complain about him seeming so thrilled to merely hold my breasts, but I really wanted him to touch my nipples. "It's good, but it could be better."

His eyes opened, squinting at the corners with humor. "I thought it was you gals who were supposed to want the slow foreplay?"

"If you go any slower, I'm going to die of frustration."

"Can't have that. So, Theresa, what would you like?" He

cupped my breasts more tightly, making them even rounder and more sensitive. Then he ran his thumbs around my puckered areolae, circling in a light caress.

His actions made the sweater brush back and forth across my nipples. Stimulation, but not what they craved. It had been so long since a man had touched my body intimately. Yes, I knew I could live without sex, but now that I was seminaked in the darkness with a hot guy, I wanted everything he could give me. A whimper escaped my lips.

Day's mouth immediately covered mine, and I realized what I'd done. If we were going to fool around and escape detection, we had to keep quiet.

"Sorry," I murmured against his lips.

He sucked on my lower lip. Then, finally, his hands were focusing on my nipples, squeezing them gently, rolling them, his fingers doing to them very much what his lips were doing to mine.

And oh my, did it feel wonderful.

He broke the kiss and let go one breast, fiddled with the controls for my chair, and now I was tilting back farther. He eased the blanket aside and peeled my sweater up to reveal my breasts, then his dark head dipped down and he licked around my nipple, using quick brushes of his damp tongue.

And then he sucked it and I barely managed to stifle a gasp of pleasure. I pressed a hand against my lips, a reminder to stay quiet, and buried my other hand in his hair. As his talented lips and tongue worked my nipple, my hips thrust up, craving the erotic press of his lower body.

It couldn't happen, though. The lack of privacy, the design of the seats, didn't allow for it. Damn.

I'd never been a woman who climaxed easily and reliably, but now sexual tension was coiled so tight inside me, I was pretty sure I'd come if only . . .

His fingers might do it.

Would he? Did I have the guts to ask?

He was sucking my other nipple now, his touch so provocative that I pressed my lips against my hand to stop myself from moaning.

Day lifted his head from my breast and trailed damp kisses down the center of my body. When he reached the waist of my pants, he undid the button, then paused. Maybe he was waiting to see if I'd protest. "You're such a turn-on," he murmured huskily. "Lovely bod." He lifted his head. "Theresa?"

"Don't stop," I whispered.

Under the blanket, he undid the zipper and slid a hand inside, brushing my bare tummy above the boy-brief panties I wore.

I shivered, body tightening with anticipation.

He cupped my mound through the thin cotton. As he'd done with my breast, he just held me for a few moments.

I let the sense of his firm heat sink through the fabric, through the nest of curls. Felt the way his middle finger curved between my legs over the damp crotch of my panties, resting over my clit, my labia. My sex quivered, hungered, and I wanted to press up against his hand, yet there was something very sexy about this, about not moving. As I concentrated, I became more and more aware. Each sensation was intensifying, anticipation building.

Now my entire body was trembling with need.

"Pull your pants down," he said.

I gripped the waistband on both sides and lifted up, working the fabric over my hips.

He took over then, sliding my pants over my hips and thighs until they were bunched below my knees.

I lay back under the blanket, nervous but almost unbearably excited, like the hormonal teenager I'd never had the chance to be.

His finger rubbed the crotch of my panties, brushing my clit.

I almost came off the seat. Then reality crashed in on me. Was this really me, Professor—Dr.—Fallon? Half-naked under a flimsy airline blanket, in a cabin with maybe fifty other passengers, opening my legs to a total stranger?

It couldn't be. I was far too practical. Inhibited. Unsexy.

"How about these?" he whispered, tugging on the cotton of my panties.

Oh, how I wanted the touch of his skin against mine. But, "No, I don't have the nerve." God, what was I thinking? Did I have the nerve for any of this?

"S'okay. I'll manage."

He'd manage. I had no doubt a man like Day could manage pretty much anything he wanted to when it came to sex. The amazing thing was, he wanted to "manage" with me.

He might call me "Prof" from time to time, but he saw me as a woman. Not only that, he wasn't focused on his own satisfaction, but on giving me pleasure.

And, damn it, I wanted that enjoyment. Jeffrey had touched me this way, sometimes gone down on me, but it had always been a means to an end, and the end was him inside me, finding his climax. That couldn't happen here with Day, not in this airplane cabin, and it was so erotic and satisfying to have a man concentrate on pleasuring me.

As his fingers again stroked me through the saturated crotch of my panties, I gripped the edges of the seat and let my thighs fall open, giving him better access. I felt nerve endings spring to the alert; my whole being was focused on the tantalizing slide of his fingers and the sensations he aroused.

"Such a sweet pussy," he murmured.

Pussy. Of course I knew the word, but I'd never spoken it. Nor had a man said it to me before. A sexy word. A word for a woman who wasn't inhibited, but sensual and purely female.

A tight, tingly, achy feeling radiated out from where he

touched me, and inside, the tension of arousal coiled tighter. "Oh, God," I whispered.

Looking down, all I could see was the navy blanket and his arm, disappearing underneath. So strange, not to be able to see, yet feeling such intense sensations.

He pulled aside the crotch of my panties, and now he stroked bare flesh, the pads of his fingertips caressing my damp folds of skin. Gliding, pressing, circling, each touch sensitizing me even more. One finger slid between my labia, probing gently, then he was slipping inside me and again I had to stifle a gasp at how good it felt.

Still bracing himself with one hand on my chair armrest, he leaned over to breathe in my ear, "God you're hot, Theresa. Is this good?"

"Oh, yes." The words came out on a sighing gasp of breath. "More."

Another finger joined the first. He pumped gently, circled inside me. Made me imagine his penis, so much thicker and longer, doing the same things. Living up to the promise of that mouth-watering bulge in his jeans.

My internal muscles gripped him, then released, automatically taking up a rhythm that matched his thrusting and circling.

"So sweet," he said. "Wish I could taste you."

The thought of his mouth on me made my hips lift, pressing my sex against the palm of his hand.

His mouth came down on mine, tongue parting my lips.

I started to kiss him back, but his thumb got busy on my clit, pressing and circling, and my entire focus flew south where all the arousal—every moment of it since I'd first seen him— was centering and building.

If I didn't come soon, I was going to die of frustration.

Using his thumb and forefinger, he gently pinched my clit

and squeezed. And inside me his fingers stroked a stupendously sensitive spot. Delicious sensations crescendoed, peaked, broke in waves. My orgasm would have been noisy, but his mouth caught my cry.

After, I tore my mouth from his and gasped in air.

A few minutes later, when I'd begun to catch my breath, I whispered, "Wow. That was . . . wow."

"You're so responsive. So sexy."

I was?

Now that I could breathe again, I let myself sink down in the seat and freed a hand to reach up, catch him by the back of the head, pull him down so our mouths met again. Slowly, loose and satiated, maybe a little sloppy, I kissed him.

One part of my need was satisfied, but something was missing. He'd given me a stunning orgasm, but I had yet to touch his penis. And I really, really wanted to. Besides, what kind of lover would I be, how complete would the act feel, if he didn't climax, too?

I broke gently from his mouth. "Seems to me it's your turn."

He made a choked sound. "I'm so hard, I could explode."

What could we do, given the privacy issue? His seat was on the aisle, and way too exposed. "Let's change seats," I suggested. "Just give me a minute to, uh . . ." I eased my pants back up, under the concealment of the blanket, then we swapped seats.

The cabin of the plane was quiet. The only people who could possibly see our aisle seat were the great-grandpa across the aisle, who was curled facing away from us under his blanket, and the woman seated behind him. She was lying back, face mask on, mouth open, snoring softly. All the same, what we were doing seemed awfully risky.

Perhaps Day sensed my nervousness. "Hey," he murmured, touching my shoulder. "You don't have to."

"No, I . . ." I did want to feel him in my hands, bring him release. Oh, to hell with being sensible. I draped the blanket over him, then, hand trembling, cupped the fly of his jeans.

He shuddered and drew in a long, shaky breath.

Under the worn denim, his erection was a hot iron shaft. Or it would be, if iron could pulse under my touch. My fingers itched to free him. I fumbled with the button at his waist and he helped me, then together we undid his zipper.

Now I could grip his shaft through his underwear. But that still wasn't good enough. I tugged at his waistband and he took the hint, pulling his clothing over his hips.

My hand closed greedily around his naked length, his throbbing heat. I stroked down, felt the wiry tangle of his pubic hair, the firmness of his balls. I stroked up, circled my fingers under the head of his penis, then gently caressed the crown, catching a couple of drops of pre-cum and spreading the warm liquid.

His hips jerked.

I wished I could pull aside the blanket and see him. His penis felt perfect. Everything a woman could wish for, and way more than I'd ever experienced before. My sex, so recently satisfied, gave a twinge of hunger, craving the feel of him deep inside. I repeated my stroke, down his shaft, then up, finishing with a swirl over his crown, and again, faster. His hips thrust and I could hear him breathing hard, trying to be quiet.

I was turned awkwardly in the seat, a position that didn't let me do a tenth of the things I wanted to with his body, but I could pump him, feel his response, and feel my own body yearning for more.

His hand caught mine where it circled his shaft, and at first I thought he was trying to stop me, then realized he was giving me tissues. He'd obviously been thinking ahead when he'd gone to the lavatory.

If I'd dared, I'd have kneeled on the floor and wrapped my mouth around him. But if anyone had walked down the aisle, it would have been obvious what we were doing.

His thrusts had stopped being rhythmic. Now they were erratic and his breathing was getting louder. We had to finish before we got caught.

I let go of his seat, trying to balance, and with one hand I reached down to squeeze his balls while with the other I stroked up his shaft. When I felt his balls tighten and his climax begin, I wrapped the tissues around his crown as he spasmed and jetted.

My body trembled and my sex clutched as I imagined him letting loose this way inside me. God, I wanted that.

When he'd finished, I slid back into the aisle seat, quivering with excitement.

Gradually, Day's breathing slowed. He hauled up his underwear and jeans and tossed the blanket aside. "What was that fancy word of yours, Prof?" he teased softly. "Wow?"

"That was it."

"It's the right one."

He eased out of his seat—my seat—touched his lips to mine, then took the used tissues from me, headed up the aisle, and disappeared into the lavatory.

I shifted over into my own seat, which was still reclined, and lay back, feeling a goofy, euphoric grin curve my lips. Wow, indeed. What an amazing, almost surreal, experience. Did this mean I'd joined the mile-high club? Or did that require actual intercourse?

Oh, how I wanted to have real sex with this man. If fooling around like teenagers felt so good, I could only imagine what he'd be like in bed.

When Day returned and took his seat, I was still grinning. The old Theresa would have been embarrassed, but this one felt sexy, desirable, exciting. I leaned over and murmured, "You're really something."

His lips brushed mine. "Nah. That'd be you." His smile

flashed white teeth, even in the dim light. Then he yawned. "Man, am I wiped. I was up most of the night, packing."

Was that true, or just an excuse for his sleepiness? "You know, there's actually a scientific reason why men tend to fall asleep after sex. Not that this was . . . I mean, we didn't exactly have sex."

"Orgasms count." He yawned again and adjusted his seat so it was reclined like mine. "So, you being a scientist, Prof, you'll excuse me if I doze off?"

"I will." In fact, I felt kind of tender as I watched his eyelids drift shut.

I should have been tired, too, after being up most of the previous night preparing for this spur-of-the-moment trip, but I was too keyed up to sleep.

Trying to be quiet, I eased out my laptop computer, plugged it into the power outlet on my seat, and booted it up.

First I scanned the e-mail Kat had sent a few hours ago. It said what she'd told me over the phone, ending with a note that she'd send me the train schedule once she'd booked her ticket.

I thought of my life-of-the-party sister taking the train. It would be in character for her to find a lover during the journey—as out of character as it had been for me to hook up with Day. Of course, Kat would pick a loser, fall for him, get her heart broken in the end. Whereas I knew exactly what I was doing, and knew there was no deep emotion involved for either Day or me.

What it came down to, though, was a fundamental similarity between me and my sister. Neither of us was the kind of woman who attracted true, lasting love. A pang of regret struck me, but I brushed it away. Kat might long for that kind of relationship, but I was happy without it. I had a highly rewarding career, and I'd even proven—thanks to Day—that I might occasionally have a sexy fling.

I skimmed back to the previous round of e-mails, started by Merilee after the conference call when she'd told us about the wedding.

> Hey, big sisters, this is so cool! I can't believe I'll see all of you in 2 weeks.
>
> I'm so excited about the wedding!! You know how I've been waiting for this moment all my life. It feels like finally I'm fulfilling my destiny.
>
> And no, guys, that doesn't mean I'm going to dump the whole school/career thing and devote my life to a man. You and Mom have trained me better than that <g>. It just means, Matt's my other half and I can't wait to be officially united.

I'd felt rather the same when I'd met Jeffrey, fallen in love, and got engaged. I'd believed he was my soul mate.

My soul obviously had rotten taste in men.

Merilee's was much smarter. She'd found Matt when she was seven, and hung on to him. He truly was a sweet guy. Cute, smart, caring. On the career track to be a teacher, the same as my little sis. The most important thing was, he'd always treated her with affection and respect. This wasn't a man who'd ever cheat, in any sense of the word.

I refocused on her e-mail.

> It's so cool of you guys to offer to help with the wedding but, honest, don't sweat it, okay? Yeah, I know I always said I wanted all the stuff, from the calligraphied invitations to the fancy dress to the cute little couple on top of the wedding cake, but if we waited to do all that then we'd lose out on the cruise. And I need that honeymoon cruise with my guy <g>. This year, being sick, it's helped me put stuff in perspective. Love and health are what matter.

Merilee had always been a self-sufficient girl. Not a complainer. It had been a shock to all of us when she said she'd been diagnosed with endometriosis and was scheduled for a laparoscopy. We'd known she'd had a hard time with her periods, but then lots of girls do, and that's what I, and my mom and my sisters, had told her. Who could have guessed she had an actual medical condition?

Well, Matt had. He'd kept telling her to go to the doctor, but she'd listened to us rather than to him. Until this spring, when she was in even more pain than usual.

When she'd e-mailed about the diagnosis, I'd felt so guilty. I'm sure Kat and Jenna did, too, and Mom especially. The guilt had made me even more determined to give Merilee as special a wedding as could be arranged on such short notice.

While I'm being serious, one of the things about endometriosis is that it lowers my chance of getting pregnant. Matt and I figure we better get started sooner rather than later. And we want to be married when we start a family.

This was a good time to be going home. Somewhere amid Merilee's schoolwork and the wedding preparations, I'd find an opportunity to talk to her about her health.

So, anyhow, there was something I forgot to tell you on the phone. I guess it kind of goes without saying, but if any of you want to bring a guy along as your date, that would be great. Jenna, knowing you, you'll have replaced surfer guy by then, but if you do bring someone, try not to shock the 'rents too much, okay? Theresa, I guess you're not seeing anyone? And Kat, are you dating anyone, or between losers? LOL.

Hugs, Merilee

Yes, even our sweet little sister could get snarky at times. She did like to lord it over us that she was the only one who was lucky in love.

Jenna had answered with, Never know who I may pick up on the way home, and I do live to shock <g>.

Kat had responded to Jenna's e-mail with, God, Jenna, be careful, for Christ's sake!

To which Jenna wrote, Like you can talk, Kitty-Kat. You're the one who has shitty judgment when it comes to men.

Kat wrote, Fine, then I'll just come alone. It's not like I'd ever find a man who met with the family's approval. Theresa and I will be each other's dates, right sis?

Before I'd had a chance to answer, Jenna had popped back with, Tree, you gotta get back in the game, big sis. Your hoo-ha's gonna shrivel up and die if it doesn't get some male attention soon.

That was when I'd checked e-mail and got into the conversation. My message read, At least my hoo-ha is selective.

As I read my post of less than twenty-four hours ago, I fought to hold back a giggle. Right now my hoo-ha, as Jenna so quaintly put it, was quite happy. Maybe Day wasn't exactly what I'd had in mind when I'd typed the word "selective," but he did have talented fingers.

For a moment I closed my eyes and played with the fantasy of taking Day to my sister's wedding. He'd blow the family's collective socks off.

Not that it was going to happen. Our little fling was purely in-flight entertainment.

And speaking of entertainment, it was time to stop slacking off and get on with one of my tasks. Since the computer was open, I'd focus on wedding planning rather than exam grading.

Knowing it was almost impossible to get either of my parents by phone, I typed up an e-mail asking them to look into VanDusen Gardens, and saved it in my Drafts folder. When I was between flights in Honolulu airport, I'd find an Internet connection and do e-mail.

Then I opened my project-planning program and started a file titled, Merilee's Wedding. I typed headings for Item, Target Date, Ideas/Notes, Progress, and Completed.

Then I entered, as the first item, Identify Venue, with the target date ASAP, then VanDusen? and Can parents swing it?

All right, what next? Time to consult the wedding bible. I put the computer on the floor, pulled out the fat book I'd bought, and skimmed the first chapter. Realizing I was squinting—my vision got worse when I was tired—I put on my reading glasses.

Then I retrieved the computer to make more notes. Under Item, I typed Legalities. For target date I put a ?. Then I typed the notes, No blood tests are required because both are of age and Canadian citizens. Need marriage license. Where/when/who can get it? Do online search? Does Merilee already know?

I consulted the book again, then went back to my project plan and typed, Officiant. ASAP. If wedding outside, who can officiate? Religious or civil? M probably doesn't care, so long as it's romantic. "White lace, pretty flowers, romantic promises. That's what she wants."

"Your sister?" Day's groggy voice almost made me toss my computer in the air.

6

Damien grinned at the shocked expression on Theresa'a face.

"Don't do that to me," she said, staring at him above her reading glasses, one hand planted over her heart. "I thought you were asleep."

"I was." He reached over and touched her arm, because it was hard to look at her and not touch her. Her mumbling had woken him, but she was so damned cute, he couldn't be annoyed. The woman was definitely intriguing. Smart, sassy, sexy, sensual—but then she had those less sophisticated traits, like blushing and muttering to herself, that made her even more appealing.

And she was so much fun to tease. "Yeah, but it was hard to sleep through all that stuff about licenses and officiants and white lace. What the hell's an officiant anyway?"

Her face scrunched up in embarrassment and she pulled off the glasses. "Was I talking to myself? Sorry. An officiant is the person who officiates at a wedding."

"You academics know all the big words," he teased.

She reached down and hefted a book that must have weighed

five pounds. "Believe me, I know only about a hundredth of what's in this book. I could have happily lived the rest of my life without learning the rest."

He glanced at the title, which read *Planning for Perfection: The Wedding Planner's Bible.* "Your sister's getting married this month and you have to do all the stuff in that book? What are you, some kind of miracle-worker?"

"Of course I can't do *all* of it. But I don't want to miss anything important, and I want to have as many of the frilly touches as possible. Merilee's that kind of girl." She wrinkled her nose ruefully. "She's pretty much my opposite."

Yes, Theresa was feminine and sexy, but not the frilly type. She had the kind of look that went with the bridal gown they'd both admired.

He'd like to see Theresa in a dress. Not a wedding dress, of course. A sundress would be good. Pity she was connecting on to Vancouver—as he'd gathered from her conversations with her sisters—rather than stopping over in Honolulu like he was. He could find some mighty fine ways of killing a day and a night in Hawaii with this woman.

Could he persuade her to change her plans? Though she was conscientious about the wedding, she'd been as into their under-the-blanket play as he had.

He imagined the two of them sharing the oceanside hotel room he'd booked. Of him stretching Theresa out on the bed with the balcony doors open and a soft ocean breeze drifting in. Removing her clothes slowly, one by one, watching her chest flush, her nipples perk up . . .

He drifted back to sleep, and horny dreams.

When Damien woke again, it wasn't to muttering. Theresa had put her computer and book away and was stretched back in her seat, sleep mask across her eyes, blanket draping her. Sleeping as neatly and efficiently as he imagined she did pretty much everything.

Except sex. That was one place where she seemed less in control, more spontaneous. Thank God.

He'd love to know what she could really be like, with privacy, time, a comfortable bed. Oh yeah, he had to persuade her to overnight in Honolulu. That is, if she didn't freak out entirely when she realized who he was.

Damien was awake now, so decided he might as well do some work. He cranked his seat up from its reclined position, turned on a reading light, then glanced at Theresa. She didn't move.

Soon he was engrossed in proofing the galleys for *Gale Force*. The galleys were his last chance to catch mistakes, so he always concentrated hard on them. He might write superficial crap, but damned if he was going to let any inconsistencies or typos slide by if he could help it.

He was in the middle of Chapter 2 when Theresa exclaimed, "Oh my God, you're Damien Black!"

Startled, he jerked, then turned to her, a finger to his lips. "Sshh. People are asleep." Well damn, he'd thought she'd be out for another couple hours. Now, here she was awake, and she'd figured out his identity.

She had shoved the sleep mask to the top of her forehead and was glaring at him. Her face, illuminated by his seat light, was a study in embarrassment and horror.

"Writer of superficial crap." He held up his hand like a kid at roll call. "Yeah, that'd be me."

"I . . . I . . ."

"Don't know what to say?" he teased.

"I'm so embarrassed." Her voice was low now. "I had no idea, in the bookstore. But that's why you looked familiar; I'd seen your photo before." Then she scowled. "You knew I didn't know, and you let me keep on thinking—Oooh! And that's why Carmen was so—Oh, you really are slimy." Her voice had risen again as her annoyance built.

"Sshh," he repeated, getting ticked off himself. "So, what was I supposed to say? Hello, I'm the guy who writes those books you think are so glib and superficial?"

"You let me . . . I thought . . ."

"Okay, maybe it was a little scummy not to tell you who I was before we, uh, fooled around. But I wanted you to give me a chance. I figured, if you knew I was the writer you hated, that'd prejudice you against me."

Her eyes were still narrowed. "I didn't say I hated your books. I read one and it wasn't bad. Just . . ."

"Yeah, I heard you the first time."

"What you did wasn't fair. It wasn't right."

"What? Letting you get to know me before you judged me?" He struggled to keep his voice low, but damn it, this was one of his hot buttons. "Let me tell you, I'm damn tired of people making assumptions about me just because I'm 'that writer.' "

As he spoke, her gaze had gone from angry to troubled. Her eyes softened with comprehension and maybe sympathy. "I always hated it when everyone saw me as 'the brainiac' and didn't get to know me."

"Besides, you did know my name. Carmen addressed me as Mr. Black and I told you my name was Day."

"You told me it was Chinese," she protested.

"Nope. You told me it was Chinese. I didn't correct you."

"You're not the most principled person in the world, are you?" But the rancor had mostly died from her voice. Then she frowned. "Wait a minute, I thought you were part Aboriginal Australian. Isn't that the hype? That you write about an Aboriginal police officer?"

"That's another quarter of my ancestry, through my mom's mother." He twisted around in his seat and shoved up the sleeve of his T-shirt to display the tatt on his other arm. It was his own totem, done in the x-ray style of Aboriginal art, showing the skeleton and internal organs.

She stared at his arm, then reached out to trace the design. "An eagle?"

"Sea eagle." Her soft touch sent whispers of arousal through him, reminding him of the intimacies they'd shared, and he shivered.

She jerked back her hand and focused on his face. "A Chinese dragon on one arm. A Chinese grandmother. You're born in the year of the dragon, yes?"

He nodded, feeling a smile begin. No one would ever call Theresa stupid.

"And a sea eagle. Your totem animal? Your mother saw a sea eagle when she first felt you move in her womb?"

Another nod. "Yeah. I got the tatts when I was fifteen, getting in touch with my roots."

"Hmm. You were young to be making a decision like that. Bet you didn't ask your parents." Absentmindedly, she pulled the sleep mask off her head and ran her fingers through her hair.

"No. They yelled a lot. Told me I was an idiot and I'd live to regret it."

"Did you?"

Damien shook his head firmly. He wasn't a guy who communed with the spirits the way his protagonist Kalti did, but all the same those tatts had become a part of him, as much as his hands and his creativity.

The prof's gaze had softened, so he dared ask, "Can you accept the fact that, even if you think my writing stinks, I'm not such a bad guy?"

Her lips twitched. "I never said 'stinks.' You're exaggerating."

"Theresa?" Now he dared to reach over, tug the blanket free of her forearm, and run his fingers gently over her soft skin. "We made a connection. Don't blow it over something, uh—" He broke off before he could say "silly."

"I don't like being deceived."

He thought about her ex and winced. "I know. I'm sorry for that. It won't happen again."

"Well . . ." She shrugged. "I guess I can see your point. About not wanting me to prejudge you."

"Friends again?" he wheedled, running his hand down to press the back of hers.

Her hand twitched, then slowly she turned it over and interlocked her fingers with his. "I guess. Though maybe we should keep away from the subject of your writing."

"Sounds wise." Except, had the writer been born who could resist reading bad reviews? Or asking the reviewer what the hell was wrong with her taste?

Theresa's hand was so warm and soft in his. This was the perfect opportunity to turn off his seat light, cuddle up, and initiate some more sex play. "So, is it just *my* novels or do you think all fiction is superficial?"

Her hand tensed and she huffed out a breath. "Day. Damien? I don't want to fight."

He raised his free hand in a protest, a vow. "No fighting. Just satisfy my curiosity."

After a long pause, she said, "I don't read much fiction. I don't see the point to it."

"Yeah? What do you do for entertainment? TV or movies? Music?"

"Uh, I listen to some music, but only as background when I'm reading journals or working. I watch the occasional documentary or news program. And I travel, doing research and attending conferences."

"Listen to yourself. I ask you about entertainment and you tell me about work."

She pulled her hand free and her chin lifted. "I told you. All work, no play."

The woman must have a genius IQ to have hopped through

all that schooling like a kangaroo on amphetamines, so how had she managed to miss the fact that her parents had done a real number on her? He grabbed her hand back and squeezed it, even though she didn't respond. At the moment he was more interested in her life than her views on his books. "Let's try this from another angle. What gives you the most pleasure in life?"

"Uh . . . I guess . . . teaching. Seeing students get fired up." Now she turned toward him. "It's amazing how many Australians—like people in other countries that were colonized—don't understand their own history, especially as it relates to indigenous people. And they don't realize that government funding and policies are doing so little to help. Even after taking a class or two, most still don't really grasp it, but each year there are a few. I know they're going to be more responsible citizens, maybe even work to improve things."

"That's great." He'd been raised in a "white" middle-class household, but those drops of Aboriginal blood had sensitized him to the fact that Australia's indigenous people had got, and were still getting, a raw deal.

"Your books . . ." Her voice was low. She'd looked away from him, biting her bottom lip.

Right, that's how this had started out. "Yes?"

"I only read one and it was more than a year ago, so maybe I'm not being fair, but you don't seem to take on the issues."

"What do you mean?"

"Your police officer is a full-blooded Aboriginal Australian. He's got some kind of mystical, spiritual connection with mythical beings. Right?"

"Yes. With his totem and with ancestor spirits from the Dreamtime. Although some would argue they aren't mythical."

She nodded. "True. Anyhow, I gather your protagonist always solves the crime, and it's a struggle for him to hide the involvement of the spirits."

"Right." It sounded formulaic, but what the hell, most successful mystery series depended on some kind of tried-and-true blueprint.

"And he has trouble with the other police officers and his superiors because he's secretive."

"Yes."

"Not because he's Aboriginal per se."

"How'd'ya mean?"

"Discrimination, Damien. Indigenous Australians frequently face discrimination—in terms of education, health care, housing, and in the workplace."

"I *know* that." And Kalti Brown did deal with some, but it was never a big part of the story. "When people read fiction they're looking for escape, not nasty realities."

She did that chuckle-snort thing again. "Serial killers and annihilation of bad guys by ancestor spirits are fine to read about, but prejudice against Indigenous Australians is too nasty?"

He hated it when people got on his case about what he chose to write. Thank God for his agent and editor. They said every writer attracted criticism, and the more successful he got, the more there'd be. They told him to never fall into the trap of thinking he had to justify his writing to anyone. His only job was to produce the next fantastic book.

Now, here he was, justifying. His own damn fault. The prof had suggested they not discuss his writing. "One's entertainment. The other is social criticism. Preaching to the reader."

"What's wrong with a little preaching? People need to hear the facts. Lots of Australians act like ostriches, thinking the government has everything under control. Avoiding the truth."

He didn't avoid it in his books, just didn't belabor it. "Then teachers like you can educate them." Each person chose their career and he'd found a great one. He didn't appreciate being hassled about it.

"You're one-quarter Aboriginal Australian. You have a totem on your arm. You should care about this."

"I do. But . . . Look, it's not like I grew up Aboriginal. My grandfather died in an accident when I was a baby, and my Aboriginal grandmother went back to her family. They lived in the country and we never visited them. The Chinese side, by the way, lives in New Zealand. My parents were both pale enough they could pass as white and that's what they did. They raised me as a white kid."

"And yet you got that tattoo. And your mother told you about your totem animal."

He sighed. "My mother said they were at the beach, and this sea eagle swooped down just as she felt me move for the first time. She didn't say anything about totems. Then, when I was fifteen, I ran away from home. I felt like I didn't really know who I was, with this whole hidden side to the family. I found my Aboriginal grandmother and her people, and went to visit them. They taught me some things, like about totems and the Dreamtime."

"You identified enough with them to get the tattoo, and you've never had it removed. And author hype emphasizes your Aboriginal roots. That's how I heard about your books."

"Yeah, well, that was my publisher's and agent's idea. A hook when the first book came out. Aboriginal writer with Aboriginal hero." He grimaced. "I wasn't so keen on it myself. And it pissed my entire family off."

"Really? I guess if your parents had raised you as white . . ."

"Yeah, they didn't want the Aboriginal association. And my Aboriginal granny and other relatives were mad because they thought I was exploiting them and what they taught me."

She was silent.

"Well?" he demanded. "Is that what you think?"

She nibbled on her bottom lip again, then her hand squeezed

his. "My guess is, no. I think you just wanted to write a good story."

"Too right." Damn, if this almost-stranger who didn't even like his writing could understand that, why couldn't his grandmother and her kin? "Thanks."

She studied his face and he saw shadows shifting in her multicolored eyes. Seemed to him like there was something else she wanted to say. Instead she just squeezed his hand again. "Maybe this is a good time to change the subject. What should I call you, Day or Damien?"

"Whichever you like."

"Damien, I think." Her lips curved. "That is, when I'm not calling you sweetie."

That grin reminded him of something. "You still haven't told me what you do for fun."

Her eyes widened. She was quiet for a few seconds, then she gave a small smile, showing that appealing touch of vulnerability. "To be honest, this is the most fun I've had in a long time."

Touched, he curved his palm along the side of her face. "It's the most fun I've had, too."

She went from vulnerable to skeptical in an instant. "Give me a break. You can't expect me to believe that. I'm sure you've had better—" Her voice had been rising and she broke off, then continued in a whisper. "Better *sex*—real sex—with a dozen women in the last year."

Yeah, he'd had plenty of real sex. But, there'd been something particularly erotic about fooling around with Theresa in the darkened plane. Besides . . . "It's not only about the sex. It's everything. The silly wedding dresses, the way you talk to yourself, those billabong eyes—"

"Those what?" she interrupted. "Did you say billabong eyes?"

"Yeah. They make me think of a pool of blue water reflecting the red cliffs overhanging it, the green leaves of gum trees rustling in a warm breeze." He broke off, disconcerted at the words that had come out of his mouth. It was one thing to write this kind of shit in his books—and the truth was, it didn't come easy for him—but it was something else to say it to a woman. "It's a compliment, honest."

Her lips curved. "And a poetic one. Hey, you could be a writer."

He smiled back. "Anyhow, on the subject of fun. You're interesting, different, challenging. Being with you is fun."

"Yes." She ducked her head, flushed. "That's what I meant, too. Not just the uh, almost-sex, but being with you. Even when we disagree." She darted a look through her lashes, eyes twinkling. "Looking at you's no hardship either, sweetie."

"Back at you, sugar."

She raised her head. "You make me feel female."

"News flash." He touched her unconfined breast through her top, felt the nipple harden. "You are."

"I don't normally feel that way. I'm the professor. You know, gender neutral."

"You may be a prof, but you're most definitely not gender neutral." His cock wouldn't respond this way to anyone who was less than 100 percent woman.

"Short hair, no makeup, tailored clothes, always wear pants. Always working."

He shook his head, then ran his fingers through her hair, separating the silky auburn strands. "Sexy hair that shows off your long neck and pretty ears." He rimmed an ear with his index finger and felt her tremble. "Perfect features, billabong eyes, rosy lips." His fingers traced down her face to rest on her very kissable lips. "Why the hell would you need makeup?"

Her mouth curved under his touch.

"Tailored clothes? Yeah, have to say, I'd like to see you in a skirt." He dropped his hand to her shoulder, caressed it, then drifted his fingers down her arm. "This top is good, though.

Shows off those nice shoulders and arms, and the V-neck is classy. Low enough to give a guy ideas, but not so low that it's tacky."

"I—"

"Hold on, I'm not finished." Threading his fingers through hers again, he continued. "As for always working, well . . . Sometimes you're critiquing wedding dresses—or novels. Sometimes you're squabbling with your sisters, and sometimes you're doing your little sister a very big favor."

He clicked off his seat light and, in the sudden darkness, tugged her hand toward him. "And sometimes you're turning me on something fierce." He pressed their joined hands over his erection, which jumped eagerly.

"I do like doing that." Her voice caught, then she gave a husky giggle. "Touching you turns *me* on."

"Hate to think it was one-sided."

She stroked him through his jeans. "Want to get under the blanket again?"

"You know what I really want? I want to get into you."

There was a pause. Damn, had he been too crude?

"I'd like that, too."

Tentatively, he said, "There's always the loo. It's not romantic, but it's private."

"Could we sneak in there without anyone seeing?"

"Everyone's asleep. Course we can."

"Really?" Her hand clutched him tight through his jeans.

Oh yeah, Theresa was turned on, too. She only *thought* she was a stuffy professor.

"I'll go first, make sure no one's watching. If the coast is clear, I'll leave the door open a crack and you'll see the light." He removed her hand, adjusted his swollen package inside his jeans, and headed up the aisle.

No one else was stirring in the business class cabin.

He eased open the door of the loo and glanced inside. Yeah,

it was an airplane john, but it was clean and neat. Hoping Theresa wouldn't lose her nerve, he stepped inside and slid the door partway shut. Then he took a paper towel and wiped drops of water from the sink and counter.

A few seconds later, the door moved and she was there, squeezing in. Damn, there wasn't much space. Neither of them was huge—him at six foot and her at maybe five six—but they weren't tiny, either.

He shifted one way to close the door behind her just as she moved in the same direction, and she stomped on his foot. Hurriedly she stepped back, only to lose her balance and crack her elbow against the sink. "Ouch." She rubbed it. "Funny bone." Even in this ugly artificial light, her eyes sparkled with laughter.

"This isn't supposed to be funny," he grumbled in a teasing tone, finally managing to close and lock the door. "It's supposed to be sexy."

"Sexy would be, mmm, a brass bed, candles, romantic music."

Trust a female. That sounded more like *romantic* to him. "Sexy would be you naked."

"Both of us naked. But I don't think we could ever get our clothes off in here." Doubtfully, she gazed up at him. "This probably isn't going to work."

"Course it will."

"Oh, you know that, do you?" She raised her eyebrows. "You've done this before?"

"Uh . . ."

"You have!"

"Well, yeah. Is that so bad? I mean, you know I've had sex with other women."

"Of course. I just didn't realize you'd done it on a plane before." She cocked her head. "How many times?"

"Uh, twice. Once with a flight attendant, once with another passenger." Discomfited, he shrugged. "Long flights and all."

"Oh, yes." Her eyes narrowed dangerously. "Passing the time on a long flight. I'm quite aware of the phenomenon."

Too late, he realized that had been one of his come-on lines to her. Damn, he didn't want her to think she was an interchangeable female. "I chose you over Carmen."

Her eyebrows rose.

Okay, maybe that hadn't been the most brilliant thing to say, either.

Then she shook her head vigorously, as if to banish troublesome thoughts. "Right." Her voice was brisk. "You did. And the truth is, we're in this for mutual pleasure, right? So, since you've done this before, you must have worked out the logistics."

True. Before, he'd yanked his pants down and sat on the john. One girl had hiked up her skirt, the other had pulled down her own pants, and they'd sat on his lap. Quick, efficient. Meaningless. Superficial.

He damned well didn't want his and Theresa's mile-high club experience to be superficial. And right now, all this talk was ruining the sexy mood. "Oh, damn." He caught Theresa's head in both hands and bent down to kiss her.

She didn't move for a moment, perhaps deciding whether she really wanted to go ahead with this. Then, in a rush, she stretched up so the fronts of their bodies pressed together tightly, wrapping her arms around his back. At first her lips were shy, her body tense, but he seduced her mouth and soon she loosened up and threw herself into the kiss.

Kissing her standing up was a revelation. Their bodies fit together perfectly. He'd been wrong about her height. She must be five seven, five eight. Tall enough that, when she rose up on her toes, her soft breasts pressed against his chest, her pelvis cradled his hard-on.

Earlier, they'd talked about dancing, and now he could imagine it. Her out of her tailored clothes, wearing a swirly skirt and heels, him leading with a hand on her back, a little hip action. And speaking of hip action, what the hell was he doing, thinking about dancing?

He reached down, finding the hem of her sleeveless top, easing away from her so he could pull it up her body and over her head. He tossed it toward the sink.

Naked breasts. Oh, man. They looked as good as they'd felt when he'd groped them under that blanket. Her skin was creamy, her nipples the soft pink of a rosebud. Totally, utterly, beautifully feminine. Reverently he caressed a nipple, circling her waist with his other arm.

Her skin puckered, the areola tightening as he watched, the nipple beading. A flush tinged her pale skin. Even the ugly light didn't detract from the magic of watching her body become aroused by his touch. She sucked in a breath and her breasts lifted, thrust forward. Then, when she breathed out, they sank back. Had he ever seen anything as fascinating as Theresa's breasts rising and falling as she breathed?

"I want yours off, too," she murmured, trying to pull his T-shirt up his back.

He yanked it over his head. Then he grabbed her in his arms so their bare chests pressed and rubbed against each other, her breasts soft and cushiony and unmistakably natural.

There was nothing in the world to compare with the texture, the soft weight, of a genuine breast. "God, woman, I wish we had the space and time for me to do justice to your breasts."

"Do justice?" she asked huskily.

"Oh, yeah. And to the rest of you as well. This mile-high thing is going to be about as frustrating as it'll be satisfying." That hadn't been the case when he'd done this before. He and the women in question had been more concerned with getting their rocks off than spending time on caresses and kisses.

"I'd like that, too. But I'm nervous about someone catching us."

She was right, but damn, he wanted time with her. "Honolulu," he said, stroking the smooth skin of her back. Her soft hands moved from his shoulders down to his lower back where they lingered in a particularly erogenous spot. "I'm overnighting in Honolulu. Stay with me, Theresa."

"I can't. I have to get to Vancouver, start work on the wedding."

He cupped her buttocks and pulled her closer against him, pressing his erection against her belly. "I've got a hotel room on the beach. A big bed. We'd have lots of time." He dropped a kiss on her full lips. "Lots of privacy."

She nibbled her bottom lip. "I have responsibilities."

"All work? Come on, Prof. Give Theresa a day off to play. The woman deserves it."

A quick grin. "She does. But her sister deserves a great wedding."

He sighed. "How about if we compromise?" As he spoke, he punctuated his words with little kisses and nibbles, starting with her lips. "Stay over and we'll both do some work, as well as have time to play." He bent to kiss the hollow at the base of her throat. Her collarbone. "You haven't speed-read that whole big bible yet, have you?" The upper swell of her left breast.

Her nipple. He laved it, then sucked it into his mouth like a whole strawberry, swirling his tongue around it, squeezing it between his lips.

She moaned and tangled her fingers in his hair.

He released her breast and she said, "No, don't stop."

"Say you'll stay over with me."

"My luggage is checked through."

"Honolulu has stores. We'll buy you a sarong."

She giggled. "I'm not the sarong type."

"Could've fooled me." He licked her right breast, sucked on her nipple, then pulled away. "Oops. You haven't said yes yet."

"You're going to deny me sex unless I say yes?" Her voice held humor and arousal.

"That's pretty much the plan."

"That would be blackmail."

"Add that to the list of my sins. Glib, superficial writer, deceiver of women, and now blackmailer. Yup, I'm your basic scumbag." He circled her areola with one finger and watched the skin tighten. God, the woman had to give in soon because he was dying to make love to her.

"A sexy scumbag, though." Her eyes gleamed and she ran her hands over his chest, pressing into his pecs, threading through dark curls of hair, teasing his own nipples. "I guess you're not leaving me any alternative."

"Really? You'll stay over? Share Honolulu with me?" Was that really him, sounding so pathetically excited and grateful?

"Yes." She still sounded doubtful. Then she repeated, firmly, "Yes. As long as I can get a flight to Vancouver tomorrow."

"Awesome!" He leaned over to suckle her right breast.

Again she gripped him by the hair, but this time she hauled his head up. "Damien, if we're going to have lots of time and privacy in Honolulu, I really think we should, uh . . ."

"Get on with it before we get caught?"

She nodded.

"Yeah, you're right," he admitted reluctantly. "I just want to make it good for you."

"It'll be good." She gave a soft laugh. "As good as airplane lavatory sex can be."

She deserved more. "It'll be great in Honolulu," he promised, capturing her hand, bringing it to his mouth and kissing it.

"I believe you. But right now, let's enjoy the moment."

Her hands reached for the waistband of his jeans.

7

I struggled with the button of Damien's jeans. It wasn't like me to be crazy with curiosity over what a man's genitalia might look like. But he had me so aroused, and all the sight and touch indicators had suggested his equipment was quite spectacular.

His erection was so big it pulled the fabric taut, and it was a fight to force the metal button through the rough denim, then another struggle to work the zipper. But I persevered, and the tab slid down, the teeth parted.

The swollen head of his penis thrust out of the top of black cotton briefs, glossed with pre-cum. An image of pure masculine vigor and sensuality that made my body hum with need.

Vaguely, I was aware of him jerking the jeans down his legs, of the fact that the briefs were actually boxer briefs that hugged his balls and the tops of his muscular thighs, but then they were disappearing, too, and I sucked in a breath when my gaze took in his full, rigid length.

I'd been right about spectacular. In comparison, Jeffrey and my other two lovers were . . . "unimpressive" was the most polite word I could come up with.

Fascinated, I curled my fingers around him, feeling a pulsing, tensile strength that made my sex throb in response. Throb, clench, and gush in response. I'd never felt so purely physical. All I wanted was to envelop him, sheathe him, absorb him all the way into my core. Then feel him plunge back and forth, pressing against all the sensitized spots that were crying out for attention.

I stroked up and down his shaft, his soft skin and throbbing heat inside the curve of my hand, the backs of my fingers brushing the dark curls of hair on his lean belly.

His muscles tensed and he groaned.

My mouth watered, craving the taste of him, but not even Damien's luscious penis was going to make me kneel on the floor of that lavatory.

He pulled away from me, sheathed himself with a condom he must have taken from his jeans pocket, and sat down on the closed toilet seat. Now it was his turn to unfasten my pants, to unzip them and work them over my hips, taking my panties with them.

If I hadn't been so turned on, so focused on his hard-on and my aching need, I'd have felt self-conscious as, one foot at a time, I took off a loafer, slid the pant leg over my foot, then stepped back into the shoe. Then I tossed my pants and underwear on top of our shirts and turned to him, utterly naked except for a pair of navy loafers.

Damien's gaze caressed my breasts, drifted across my belly, lingered at my groin. His eyes glittered. "Oh, yeah, you're one hot woman. Now come here. Sit on my lap, Theresa."

When I took a step toward him, trying to figure out how to straddle him, he shook his head. "Can't do it that way. There's not enough room for your legs."

"Then how—"

Firm hands grasped my hips and he turned me.

"Oh." My voice squeaked out. "Oh, right." I'd never had sex this way, sitting so my back was to a man's front. I regretted that I wouldn't be able to see him, but mostly I just wanted him inside me. Whatever it took.

I sat gingerly, straddling his thighs, his erection sandwiched between his body and the curves of my bottom. What was I supposed to do next?

"That's a girl," he murmured, pressing a hot, moist kiss into the nape of my neck. One hand came around to stroke my breast and the other slid between my legs, finding my creamy, needy center. He gave a grunt of satisfaction and caressed me, stoking sensation.

Good as it felt, I was nervous about taking too much time. "We should do this now."

"I'm sure as hell ready if you are. Lift up a little."

His thighs were warm and strong under me. All I could really see of him was his knees, and I braced my hands on them as I raised my body. He struggled to tilt his rigid penis and bring it forward, then the crown probed between my legs, making me gasp. With one hand, Damien parted my slick, swollen folds, then he was easing in and, oh my, it felt so good.

And then it hurt a little, and I tensed. It had been so long since I'd had a man inside me, and never one who was built like Damien.

"Easy, Theresa," he murmured, breath warm on my ear. "We'll take it nice and slow."

His words helped me relax, then his thumb was on my clit and the last thing I could do was relax. His penis pressed inside me an inch or two farther, a sexy hint of everything he had to offer. His thumb circled and stroked, and all the arousal that had been building centered and magnified. I trembled with desire—and anxiety—at the thought of him filling me.

I could feel myself get wetter as with each subtle motion he slid in farther. Oh God, I wanted, needed, to climax.

He took my clit between his thumb and index finger and squeezed gently. The pressure was so good, so intense, I came apart under his hand, barely managing to remember that I couldn't cry out.

As I rode the waves of orgasm, Damien eased farther inside me and my body loosened around him, took him in, clung to him with pleasure. When he was all the way in, he murmured, "All right?"

"God, yes."

"Do what feels good. Control the action."

Cautiously I levered myself up, then down, feeling the slide and friction of his flesh inside mine. His hands held my hips, helping me keep my balance, and I moved faster, riding him so it felt like he was pumping in and out of me. A soft moan of pleasure escaped my lips.

"You're so sexy," he said. "Your long, slim neck and back." The words came out between pants. "Curvy arse. The cleft between your cheeks."

"I feel sexy. You make me feel sexy." I'd never controlled the lovemaking this way.

In some ways it seemed impersonal because I couldn't see his face. I was staring at the back of a silver metal door and around me was the cold starkness of a generic airplane washroom. Better to look down. And, oh my. Each time I raised up, I could see his inner thighs where the skin was pale, almost tender looking. The furry roundness of his balls. The base of his penis and the way his shaft disappeared inside me.

Oh yes, this view was sexy, and so was the way he filled me, deep and hard. Both were a real turn-on, but the disadvantage to this position was that his penis didn't brush my clitoris, and I usually needed that stimulation in order to come.

Damien's hips were lifting, his penis jerking. He was close to orgasm.

"Touch yourself." He gasped out the words.

Somehow, he knew this was what I needed. His hands were

occupied, holding my waist, but he didn't want to come and leave me behind.

Of course I masturbated occasionally, but I'd never touched myself when I was with a lover. I was too inhibited. And yet, here I was having sex in an airplane lav with the hottest guy I'd ever met. And my body was heavy, achy, on the edge. I really, really wanted that second climax.

"Come on, Theresa," he gasped, for the first time sounding impatient.

To hell with my inhibitions. I lifted a hand from his thigh, feeling him grip my waist tighter so his heavy thrusts wouldn't unbalance me. Then I touched myself the way he'd done, stroking my nub, pressing, squeezing it a little. Remembering the feel of his much larger, rougher-textured hand.

Damien's hand. Damien's penis pumping into my slick channel, filling me deeply.

The orgasm caught me by surprise, and it was all I could do to choke back a moan.

He plunged again, hard, then again, and buried his face in my shoulder as spasms rocked through him and into me as he, too, climaxed.

After, I collapsed heavily on his lap, my whole body weak, trembly, and totally satisfied. His arms circled me and I rested mine atop his. "Wow. If that's what it's like in an airplane lavatory, I can't wait to try a bed."

"Insatiable female," he grumbled against my shoulder.

"You're the one who—" I jerked upright. Someone was rattling the door.

"It's okay," he murmured. "I locked it. They'll use the other one."

So much for basking in the physical afterglow of great sex. My body was taut with anxiety. "We have to get back to our seats. Oh God, what if someone sees us come out?"

"They'll be envious. C'mon it's not a crime, like smoking in the lav."

"Well . . ." He had a point, but on the other hand, our behavior was awfully undignified. I was a Harvard graduate, a university professor. And he was a—

Oh. My. God. I, the esteemed professor, was screwing in the loo with a celebrity.

I smothered a giggle, then levered myself off his lap. When he bent to pull up his jeans, I shifted as far away as I could in the cramped compartment, to give him room. How on earth was I going to get dressed? Both standing up, we took all the available space.

Damien reached around my naked body to grab his shirt from the sink. "You sit on the toilet lid while I finish dressing, then I'll pop out and go back to my seat. Lock the door behind me, then you'll have some room and privacy."

"Okay." I spread tissues on the lid and obeyed, arms wrapped around myself.

After he'd pulled the shirt over his head, he bent to drop a kiss on my nose. "Whoever told you that you're all work?" Then he was reaching to open the door and I scrambled upright so I could slam it shut behind him and secure the lock.

When I was alone, I stared at my reflection. Pink cheeks, pink chest and breasts. I'd never seen myself this way. Sexy, tousled, embarrassed yet thoroughly satisfied. If sex with Damien was this great in such an unappealing, cramped environment, what would it be like in a real bed?

Oh my gosh, I'd agreed to stay in Hawaii with him. And I couldn't wait.

Rattling and clanking sounds outside the lavatory door brought me to my senses. I splashed cold water on my face and soaked paper towels to wash myself. Then I dressed, glad I'd thought to bring my purse and bra. After I combed my hair, I looked more or less normal. I took a deep breath and put my hand on the door lock. Was anyone outside?

Squaring my shoulders, I thrust open the door and stepped out.

Luck was with me. No one was there. As I moved past the tiny galley, the flight attendant who served the other side of the cabin was pouring juice. She grinned. "I hear you're engaged to Damien Black. Good on you, you lucky girl."

"Carmen told you? I hope she also told you it was a secret. And yes," I couldn't hold back a grin, "I'm very lucky."

It struck me that, if Damien ever did get engaged, his fiancée would indeed be a lucky girl. Not that he was my type, of course. I wanted a man who was far more serious, and had a social conscience. But the guy did have a lot going for him.

As I made my way back to my seat, I saw a few people were stirring, chatting quietly, watching their video screens. A glance at my watch told me we had about an hour and a half before we'd be landing.

Damien greeted me with a knowing grin and squeezed my bottom when I slid past him to take my seat. His long, wavy hair was a mess—from me dragging my fingers through it. Gently I reached up to finger-comb it, sliding my fingers through the rich silk, thinking that a mix of Aboriginal, Chinese, and Caucasian blood made for great hair, as well as those slightly exotic, handsome features.

"I like the way you touch me, Tezzie," he said softly.

"Tezzie?"

"Theresa's pretty, but I want something more personal. I'm an Aussie, after all. Tezzie seems just about right."

Wonderingly, I said, "The only person who's ever given me a nickname before is my sister Jenna. She calls me Tree, which dates back to her being a baby and not being able to pronounce my name."

"Nah. Tezzie's softer, more fun. Suits you better."

"I like it." It was a good name for this new me, the woman who was having a fling with Damien Black. I also liked the fact that he'd made up a special name for me.

The cabin lights blinked on, startling both of us, and a female voice announced that juice and champagne would be served shortly, followed by breakfast.

Damien's hand gripped mine. "We cut it tight on our timing. If we'd have stayed in there another five minutes, there'd have been a queue at the door."

In fact, drowsy people were shuffling up the aisle, and the lineup had already started.

"I'd have died of embarrassment." Though the experience would have been worth it. I gazed at him, filled with a sense of unreality. I'd never done anything so outrageous in my life. "You're a bad influence."

He gave me a wicked grin. "Or a good one. It's all a matter of perspective."

I couldn't help but grin back. "So it is."

When Carmen came by with a reserved smile, heated towels, and a tray of drinks, we both accepted glasses of orange juice. Damien persuaded me to have a glass of champagne, too.

After Carmen had moved on, he held up his flute in a toast. "To you and me in Honolulu. With a bed."

Oh God, yes. "I'll drink to that." We clicked glasses, drank, then I said, "I'll have to e-mail or call my family. My parents and Merilee are expecting me at the house tonight." I raised a hand and scrubbed my palm over my forehead. "What am I going to say?"

"The truth won't cut it?" A humorous light made his gray eyes dance.

For a moment, I indulged in imagining my family's reaction. Shock? Envy? Worry? No, probably not. "They'd never believe me," I said wryly. "It's so out of character."

Having drunk his toast, I now blended my remaining champagne with the orange juice to make a breakfast mimosa. "Damien, why are you staying over in Honolulu?"

"Got to do a reading at a store." He followed my example with the beverages and took a sip. "I've just done a tour in Australia, and now I'm starting a month-long one through America, with a couple stops in Canada, too."

"Wow. You've really hit the big time."

He shrugged. "I'm better known in Australia, where I was first published." There, his books topped the bestseller lists. "But an American publisher bought foreign rights and has published my old books, plus released an American edition of *Wild Fire* to parallel the Aussie edition. They're putting some money into promotion, hoping to create the same kind of popularity in North America."

"I can see that working."

"Yeah?"

"I think your stories will have the same kind of appeal as they do in Australia, and maybe even more because of the novelty factor of the foreign setting and the Dreamtime spirits."

"That's what my agent says, but it's good to have another perspective. Especially from someone who thinks I'm a crappy writer."

"I never said that. You have a talent for storytelling."

He pretended to reel with shock. "My God, an actual compliment. I don't believe it. So why are you so down on my writing?"

This was surreal. I'd just had sex with this man, we'd clicked champagne flutes to toast more sex in Hawaii, and now we were back to literary criticism. I didn't want to be rude but I didn't want to be dishonest, either. I considered his question as I sipped my mimosa. "It's just that you have talent *and* celebrity, and you could do so much more with them."

He snorted. "Should've known it was too good to believe. Look, I do the best I can."

"I'm just saying, you're part Aboriginal, you have an Aboriginal Australian hero, you know the indigenous people have a raw deal. You've developed a huge audience in Australia. You could be using your writing skill to bring broader awareness to the problems."

"Just because someone's born into a group that's disadvantaged, that doesn't mean they're obligated to devote their life to fighting for that group's rights."

"No, but—"

"Talk about the pot calling the kettle black." He leaned toward me, brows raised. "Women are disadvantaged in society, but you haven't chosen women's rights as your field."

"No. But I've never really experienced problems due to being female. Any discrimination against me occurred because I was so young."

"Well, I'm only one-quarter Aboriginal and I never experienced any discrimination."

He'd drawn a pretty effective parallel. "I see your point."

Carmen interrupted our conversation by bringing us breakfast trays. Fresh fruit, omelets, croissants, and jam. She poured coffee for both of us.

I tore off the end of a croissant and nibbled it. "All right, I concede," I told Damien. "You're no more obligated to be an activist for indigenous rights than I am for women's rights."

"Too right." He nodded, then concentrated on eating his omelet.

I tasted my own, but I'd never been one for big breakfasts. A croissant and fruit was much more my style.

After a few minutes, he said, "Why *did* you end up studying indigenous people? I bet your dad wanted you to go into his field."

Remembering a fourteen-year-old kid standing up to her father, the eminent geneticist, I gave a rueful chuckle. "Yes, but I'm not big on microscopes. And Mom, who's a litigator, wanted me to follow in her footsteps." My strategy had been to deflect the two of them away from me and into arguing with each other.

"They're both strong personalities," I told him. "I wanted to find something special of my own, not just follow one of them. What I did get from them was a desire to help others. To make a difference in the world." I gave him a pointed look, which he ignored.

"But why indigenous studies when you're Caucasian?"

"There was a girl in grade six. A First Nations girl, Becky. I was younger than the other kids and Becky was older than them. She started school late, got bounced between home and foster care. Top that off with some learning problems . . ." I shrugged. "You can imagine."

"Poor girl."

"But she was the only one who treated me like a real kid, not a brainiac geek. Perhaps because we were both outcasts. Or because she was more open-minded. People called her dumb, but that wasn't true. The system had failed her."

"What happened to Becky?"

"We became friends, studied together. I figured out she was dyslexic. She'd never been in one class long enough for anyone to realize it. Once our teacher knew, Becky got the assistance she needed and did fine. She graduated high school, got into college, became a social worker." I gave him a meaningful look. "She's helping her people now."

"Yeah, yeah. She's a better person than I am." He rolled his eyes. "So, Becky was your experience with discrimination."

"Yes, and I learned that one person can make a difference. Me, then the teacher. And now Becky is making a difference in a bunch of people's lives."

He nodded. Then he eyed my half-finished omelet. "You gonna eat that?"

I handed my plate over. "Go ahead. I'm not a big breakfast eater." The fruit looked good, though, so I spooned some up.

"Despite Becky, you left Canada. You specialize in Indigenous Australians, not First Nations Canadians."

"I started out in Canada, but my experience with Jeffrey spoiled it for me. I didn't want to work in the same field as him. I needed a big change. I liked Australia because it's a long way from Canada, yet has a similar history and similar issues when it comes to indigenous studies."

"Okay, so how are you making a difference for Indigenous Australians?"

Hadn't he been listening last night? "Researching and publishing. Teaching."

"Finding the few students each year who listen and learn, and maybe become better citizens."

All right, he had listened. So, why the question? "That's right."

"And how about those publications? Who reads them?"

"They're in professional journals. And I present papers at conferences."

"Hmm." He picked up his coffee cup, studied the contents for a few seconds, then took a swallow.

"Hmm what?"

The cup went down slowly, and he turned to me with a level, almost steely gaze. "You're bright, a Harvard graduate. I assume you're talented in your field. Seems to me, maybe you could be doing something more with that talent."

Oooh! He'd turned my words back on me. Indignantly I glared at him. "I'm a tenured professor, multipublished. I advise graduate students as well as teaching undergrad courses, and I present at international symposiums. What more, in your *esteemed* opinion, should I be doing?"

"Talking to the real world." He spoke quietly, but with more than a hint of challenge.

"The real world? I haven't a clue what you mean. Do, please, enlighten me."

"Look, I'm not criticizing." His gaze softened a touch. "Just saying your messages conflict. You think I should use my writing skill to preach to the world at large about discrimination. So why shouldn't you do the same?"

"I'm an academic. I write scholarly papers."

"I'm a novelist. I write fiction."

I gave an exasperated sigh. "What I'm saying is, my audience is academia. Professional colleagues, students."

"A narrow audience. Why not broaden it?"

"And do what?"

"Dunno. Come down from the ivory tower and write pieces for magazines, newspapers? Popular versions of those scholarly papers?"

I wrinkled my nose. "Academics tend not to have a lot of respect for other academics who popularize—commercialize—their work."

"And it's about academic respect? I thought it was about having a social conscience."

He didn't get it. He was so clearly not an academic. I picked up my coffee cup, only to find it was empty, and put it down again none too gently. "Fine, you've made your point. Neither one of us understands what the other is doing, and we have no right to criticize."

He nodded slowly, then held out his hand. "Truce? No more career counseling from people who don't know what they're talking about?"

I considered a moment. "Fair enough." I took his hand and we shook, then he held on to my hand and I let him. Though I was still steamed up, why let our differing viewpoints get in the way of the rapport we'd established? We were casual sex partners, that was all.

"Want more coffee?" he asked.

"Please. If you see Carmen."

He held up his right hand, and in a couple minutes Carmen arrived with the silver pot and filled our cups. She took Damien's empty tray, then glanced at mine, where half the fruit and croissant remained. "Still working on that?"

"No, I'm done. Unless you want it? Sweetie?" I added the "sweetie" to let Damien know I wasn't holding a grudge.

A gleam of humor lit his eyes. "I'm full. Thanks anyhow, sugar."

When Carmen had taken our trays, I said to him, "I do hope your book tour's a big success."

A grin flashed. "Thanks."

"It must be fun, traveling around, meeting fans." It was a kind of celebrity I'd never sought, but I did know the satisfaction that came from being respected in your field.

"There's good and bad. I like seeing new places. Some of the folks at stores and local TV and radio stations are great. And I never get tired of hearing someone say they love my books."

"I can imagine." Of course his work was as important and personal to him as mine was to me, and I was sorry I'd been so critical. "What's the bad part?"

"Bizarre travel schedules. Administrative crap that goes wrong. Stores that forgot you were coming and didn't order your books. Signings that weren't advertised, so no one shows up." He chuckled. "Signings that *were* advertised, and the only person who speaks to me is a little old lady who wants to know where the loo is."

"You've had signings where no one came?" Wouldn't that be kind of like having no students enroll for your lectures?

"Oh, yeah. Especially in the beginning. It'll happen again on this tour, because I'm not well known in America. But tours are as much about getting to know the booksellers, so they'll hand-sell your books, put up a display, order the next one. And about media exposure."

"Do you plan the tours yourself?"

"God, no. I'm a writer, not a planner. I have a part-time admin assistant who works with the people at the publishing houses. I go where I'm told, and contact her if there's a screw-up like a flight being changed." He sipped coffee. "What gets old really fast is the nights alone in a hotel room. Yeah, I always have writing to do, but those rooms are impersonal and depressing."

"I doubt you ever have to be alone," I joked.

"Nah, maybe not." His mouth kinked up at one corner. "But picking up girls on the road gets to be pretty impersonal and depressing, too."

Ouch. I stuck my chin out. "What about me?"

"You?" He shot me a puzzled look. "What do you mean?"

"I'm a girl you picked up on the road. Or flight, in this case."

"You're different."

"How? You can hardly say we're kindred spirits. We've spent most of our time arguing."

A quick laugh. "Yeah, right. But all the same, it's different. I dunno how, I'm not that analytical. It just is."

I liked the sentiment, even if he couldn't put it into words. "Thanks for clarifying that for me," I teased. "You do have a way with words."

He laughed, squeezed my hand, and pulled our clasped hands over to rest on his thigh. "Maybe it's attraction of opposites. You gotta admit the attraction exists, Tezzie." He inched our clasped hands higher, until they rested against the bottom of his fly.

Underneath the denim, he was beginning to grow. Feeling him, remembering how he looked naked, how he'd felt inside me, brought an instant rush of arousal.

"Yes, it exists." Attraction of opposites. It wasn't a thing I'd experienced before, because I'd always stuck to my own kind.

With Jeffrey, I'd marveled at how alike we were. How compatible.

And look how well that had worked out.

"Let's talk about Honolulu," he said. "We'll stroll the beach, drink mai tais, I'll buy you a sarong and a thong bikini—"

"No way!" I narrowed my eyes.

"I'll take you to bed and we'll find out how fantastic we can be together. Sound good?"

Maybe he was right about that opposites thing. Perhaps that's why we had such amazing chemistry. For twenty-four hours, why not stop being analytical, practical, and responsible, and let loose and have fun?

I nudged our clasped hands an inch up his fly. "A thong bikini, eh? Tell you what, I'll wear one if you do."

8

Damien let out a surprised laugh. "No bloody way I'm wearing one of those things."

"My sentiment exactly," Theresa shot back at him, a twinkle in her eye.

A guy had to like a woman who didn't let a squabble get blown out of proportion.

"Oh gosh," she said, "What about my luggage? It's checked through to Vancouver."

"We can ask Carmen about getting it offloaded." He frowned. "But if we're engaged . . ."

"Our luggage would be together." She finished his thought.

"Is there anything you really need?"

"Let me think. My work's in my carry-on, along with a change of undies. I can buy shorts and a light shirt. As for toiletries, the airline amenities kit and hotel miniatures should do." She shook her head. "No, I'm okay. Let's not bother."

Wow, a low-maintenance woman. What a treat.

When the flight attendants came through to do the final

check before landing, Carmen said, "Congratulations again. When's the big day? And where are you getting married?"

"We haven't set the details yet," Damien said. "We need to tell our families first."

"I'm sure they'll be thrilled. Unlike the single female population of Australia."

When she'd gone, Theresa cocked her head in his direction. "You're *that* well known?"

"Er, I was voted one of the ten sexiest bachelors in Oz this year," he admitted.

"Jesus." She raised her brows. "How did I miss that news flash?"

He ran his fingers up her bare arm slowly, just skimming the surface. "You wouldn't have voted for me, Tezzie?"

She shivered. "You're so damned full of yourself, Damien Black."

All the same, she hadn't said no, which made him grin smugly. "Guess I'll have to prove I belong on that list." He secured her hand in his as the plane descended for its landing.

Once they were down, he stowed his gear in his carry-on while she turned on her mobile and checked messages. "Friday," she muttered.

"Should I ask, or are you talking to yourself again?"

"Sorry. That was Kat, the next oldest sister. She's in Montreal, the head of PR for a luxury hotel."

He heard a note of pride in her voice. Even though she and her sisters had their issues, there were bonds of affection, too.

"Anyhow," she went on, "she's booked train tickets."

"She's the one who doesn't fly." He'd overheard Theresa's side of the conversation.

"She'll be home Friday, and that'll be another pair of hands to help with everything." The prof didn't sound thrilled to pieces.

"Let me guess. You'd rather do things yourself than share work or delegate."

Her mouth squeezed into a rueful expression. "What can I say? I'm efficient. When we were kids, Mom would put me in charge of getting the chores done. I'd try to organize the others, but Kat always had something going on with her friends, and Jenna'd forget the moment after I told her what to do, so it was easier to do things myself."

"You had schoolwork, though. Those accelerated courses must have taken a lot of time."

"Sure, but . . . When the others did pitch in, it was slapdash. They didn't do as good a job."

Damien grinned. He could imagine the bossy older sister ordering the others around, not being satisfied with the results, and letting them know. If he'd been Theresa's sibling, he'd probably have said, "Fine, next time do it yourself." Family dynamics. He'd learned it was easier to avoid his family than deal with all the crap.

He and Theresa gathered up their belongings as the plane taxied to the gate. When the arrival bell dinged, Damien opened the overhead bin and took down the older couple's bag. "Nice meeting you," he said.

"You, too," the man said. "By the way, we're Trev and Delia Monaghan. And I've enjoyed your books, young man. Just read the latest before leaving home."

"You know who I am?"

"Overheard the flight attendant. And don't worry, we won't be telling anyone about your secret engagement."

"Appreciate that."

"But you get that date set, son," Trev said, "and marry the girl before someone else scoops her up."

"Yes, sir." Damien faked a salute.

Theresa leaned past him to say, "Have a wonderful visit with your family."

"Thanks, dear," Delia answered. "And don't forget that advice I gave you."

"We won't."

Damien stepped back to let them go down the aisle first, then he and Theresa took their place in the queue.

Once they were into the airport, they both lengthened their stride and passed the people who were walking more slowly. "Feels good to stretch," she said.

"Sure does." He glanced around. "Nice airport. It's my first time in Honolulu."

"I often stay over. It breaks the trip." She sniffed the air, an appreciative expression on her uplifted face. "Mmm, I love the feel and scent of the air here."

Now that she'd mentioned it, he realized how balmy the air was. And scented with tropical flowers. Kind of like at his place in Queensland. This wasn't the unpleasant climate control so typical of airports. In fact, the airport was only partially roofed and a couple of small birds darted around. "Whoever designed this place got it right."

"There's even a garden. You can go for a walk or sit on a bench. But right now, I need to see about getting my ticket changed."

Since she knew the airport, he let her take charge. For a macho dude, he sure had a pack of women bossing him around. Editors, agent, publicists, admin assistant, and now the prof.

Damn, he was glad she'd agreed to stay overnight. In fact, he was so glad, it was disconcerting. Likely he'd have had no problem finding a woman to share his bed, but he didn't want just any woman. He wanted Theresa. A control freak with a streak of vulnerability. Frustrating, challenging, intriguing. Sexy. Fun.

With brisk efficiency, they retrieved his baggage, then Theresa found the ticket desk and made her inquiry of a stunning young Hawaiian woman.

"Want the good news first, or the bad?" the woman asked with a smile. Then, without giving them a chance to answer, she went on. "Yes, Ms. Fallon, I can get you on the same flight as Mr. Black, but business class is full, so I can't give you an upgrade."

"D'you have two seats together in economy?" he asked.

"Yes, if you don't mind being downgraded."

"Hmm," he mused. "A business-class seat and service versus..." He studied Theresa, faking a cool, appraising gaze, but badly enough she'd know he was kidding.

She stuck her nose in the air. "Separate seats are better anyhow. By the time I've spent a day with you, I'm sure I'll be getting bored." The corners of her mouth twitched.

The ticket agent glanced from one to the other. "So, uh, you do want separate seats?"

Damien reached over to wrap an arm around Theresa. "No bloody way."

At first her body was tense, as if she wasn't used to this kind of physicality, then she softened and melded against him, putting her arm around him too.

White-tipped fake nails tapped quickly on a keyboard, then a printer hummed, and the agent handed him an envelope. "Here are your tickets. Mr. Black, you'll need to check in tomorrow with your luggage. Now, Ms. Fallon, I can see if we can get your baggage off the plane."

"No, that's all right, thanks. But can you make sure it's held in Vancouver?"

"Of course. I'll notify our people at YVR." The Hawaiian grinned. "Good excuse to shop in Honolulu, isn't it? As if a girl ever actually needs an excuse."

They thanked her and moved away from the counter, Damien shoving the ticket folder in the back pocket of his jeans. "Let's get a taxi."

She groped his butt—no, she was pulling out the folder. "You should take better care of this. Let me put it in my bag."

The joys of being with a control freak. He'd never lost tickets in his life. Well, except for that one time in Melbourne . . . If she wanted to be in charge, let her. His ego could handle it.

She zipped the tickets into an inside compartment of her purse. "Taxis are this way."

He followed her, backpack slung over one shoulder, tugging his wheeled bag.

When they climbed into the next cab in line, the middle-aged Hawaiian driver said, "Where to?"

"Waikiki Beach." He pulled out the hotel confirmation e-mail. "The Queen Lili . . ." Damn, Aboriginal Australian names weren't so unpronounceable.

"Queen Liliuokalani?" Theresa asked, the syllables gliding melodically off her tongue, though she sounded skeptical.

"Yeah, that'd be it." He showed her the e-mail printout.

"Gotcha," the driver said, pulling away from the curb.

"That's quite the hotel," Theresa said. "Right on the beach."

"You've stayed there?"

She snorted. "Hello? I'm the one who flies economy."

"Mostly I'm in budget hotels. But I decided to splurge since it's my first time in Hawaii." He'd imagined working out the airplane kinks with a long run on the beach, then having a burger and a couple drinks in a beachside bar, followed by some sightseeing. Now all he could think about was Theresa naked in a big bed.

She was way over on the other side of the seat, so he slid over, reaching for her hand. Instead of meeting his grip, she gestured to her seat belt. "Do yours up."

"Is there a rule you don't follow?" he grumbled.

"Not if the rule's there for a good reason." She watched as he did up his belt, then, eyes twinkling, added, "Like that one about not, uh, what is it? Smoking in the lavatory on a plane?"

"Gosh, no," he teased back. "I sure wouldn't want to, uh, *smoke* in the loo."

Now she did let him take her hand, but it sure as hell was

frustrating, not being able to even rub thighs. Oh well, he could entertain himself with thoughts of how they were going to heat up that bed.

Apparently, the prof's thoughts were taking a whole different tack, because she said, "She was the last monarch of the Hawaiian islands."

"Huh?"

"Liliuokalani. She was quite a woman. She didn't want to lose Hawaii to the foreigners. She did her best to preserve the monarchy and keep the islands for the native people."

"Fighting a losing battle." He didn't know a lot of history, but he did know that the native people always got screwed.

"Yes. The American immigrants—especially the wealthy, powerful ones—wanted Westernization and of course control of the economy. They overthrew the monarchy, deposed Queen Liliuokalani, and set up a provisional government, which became the Republic of Hawaii."

"Who took over from the queen? Let me guess, some white guy."

"Good guess. Sanford Dole."

"You actually remember his name?"

"Dole pineapple? It was his cousin who founded the pineapple empire." She ran a hand through her hair, lifting wisps of bang off her forehead.

The cab was stuffy, so he lowered the window, though now that balmy Hawaiian air was scented with exhaust rather than flowers. "And then Hawaii became an American state?"

"No. The American president was Grover Cleveland, and he actually favored the monarchy. He believed it had the support of the Hawaiian people, which was no doubt true. Anyhow, there was lots of politicking and an attempted uprising. Liliuokalani did eventually swear allegiance to the Republic of Hawaii."

"That must've burned her off something fierce."

"I imagine so. Not only for herself, but for her people. The loss of independence."

"As always happens when the white man 'discovers' a new country." Bitterly he thought how true it was in Australia, with the Aborigines and Torres Strait Islanders. In fact, a court had even held that the lands were vacant when the colonizers arrived. Basically, saying the Indigenous Australians weren't human beings. It pissed him off whenever he thought about it.

Theresa was going on. "Yes, precisely. So then, in, mmm, I think it was 1898—the U.S. president was McKinley by then—Hawaii was annexed to the States. It didn't actually become a state until something like the late 1950s."

How about that? He'd assumed the American states had all been states for a century or more. The prof sure made him feel ignorant. "How do you know all this stuff?"

"I've studied all the indigenous societies in the world."

"Here you go, folks," the taxi driver's voice broke in. "The Queen's hotel."

With a start Damien realized he'd missed the entire trip from the airport. Maybe there'd been scenery, but he'd been caught up in Theresa's story and the intent expression on her face.

He started to get out and almost strangled himself on his seat belt. By the time he got around to the trunk, the driver was extracting his bag and their carry-ons and handing them to a hotel porter, who made a small stack on a luggage trolley.

Damien pulled out his wallet, handed the driver some American bills, and said, "Thanks, mate. Keep the change. And I'll need a receipt."

"Thanks." The driver glanced up at the hotel. In a neutral tone he said, "Things sure would've been different if Liliuokalani'd got her way."

As he drove away, Damien studied the hotel. Two cream-painted towers, their balconies dripping with purple bougainvillea, were connected by a much lower building with a palm-thatch roof. The porter, a tanned young man with streaky-blond hair who Damien would bet was a surfer, gestured toward the glass doors. "Good morning. Welcome to the Queen Liliuokalani."

The greeting reminded him it was only nine in the morning here. And, because of crossing the international date line, it was nine o'clock *yesterday* morning. His mind boggled at the concept. It was almost as if there was a parallel universe, one in which he had yet to even leave for this trip.

A universe in which he hadn't met Dr. Theresa Fallon. Tezzie. No, he didn't like that universe at all.

Together they stepped into the lobby and he gazed around, appreciating the design. Under the high thatched roof, airy rattan and glass furniture was scattered, and vivid purple orchid plants decorated every surface. A soft breeze wafted through, carrying the scent of ocean, tropical flowers, and a hint of sunscreen.

The other side of the lobby had no wall. It was open to a landscaped area with a pool, lounge chairs, and tables with umbrellas, and beyond that the beach. The wings of the hotel extended in a ragged V-shape away from the lobby, framing the pool and garden, a formation that would give every room an ocean view.

It had been something like fourteen hours since he'd left his flat in Sydney, and his sandaled feet itched longingly at the thought of walking on damp sand. But when he glanced at Theresa, another part of him had an even bigger itch.

Another lovely Hawaiian woman—did Hawaii make any plain ones?—greeted them at the reception desk. He had no desire to flirt with any of these women. Looking at them was like admiring a lovely picture. The only woman he wanted to get intimate with was Theresa. The sooner the better.

He'd arranged for an early check-in, and soon the clerk was handing him an envelope with two key cards. "You're on the tenth floor in the Plumeria Tower, Mr. Black." She gestured. "Over there, the northern tower. Chase will take you to your room."

"Just follow me," the porter said, his smile a white flash against deeply tanned skin.

In the elevator, Damien brushed his shoulder against Theresa's. She gazed up at him and he saw uncertainty in her eyes. Second thoughts?

When the doors opened, he let the porter precede them down the hall and hung back to ask, "Are you okay?"

"A little nervous. Staying with a stranger . . ."

"I'm not a stranger. I'm that crappy writer who's one of the ten sexiest bachelors in Oz." He leaned close to whisper in her ear. "And who's the best lover in the entire country."

As he'd intended, she giggled. "Oh, right. How could I have forgotten?"

They had caught up to the porter, who had opened their room door. Damien stood back to let Theresa enter first, then found more American bills and tipped the porter. Then he put out the "Do Not Disturb" sign and followed Theresa into the room.

It was attractively decorated in the same light and airy style as the lobby, with watercolor paintings of Hawaiian scenes and a couple of orchid plants gracing tabletops. Morning sun slanted through the tilted louvers of a pair of wooden doors.

Theresa opened them, revealing the balcony, which he recalled from the hotel's Web site was called a lanai. She stepped outside. "Oh my."

He moved to stand beside her in the sunshine, near a railing decorated by bright purple bougainvillea. "So this is Waikiki." He glanced right and left, absorbing the view. It reminded him of Surfers Paradise on the Gold Coast. A lovely long stretch of beach rimmed by high-rises and shopping. Even the bougainvillea and the plants in the garden below—coconut palm, hibiscus, red ginger, and frangipani—were familiar.

"Not many people on the beach," she said. Despite the giggle a few minutes ago, her voice sounded strained. "I guess tourists are sleeping in or having breakfast. Are you hungry?"

He put an arm around her, feeling tension in her shoulders. "Yes."

She turned to face him. "Then we could go down and—"

"For you. We have unfinished business."

"I s-suppose we do." Her voice faltered.

That touch of vulnerability made him feel protective. Damien brushed his lips against hers. He wasn't going to rush things, but hell, he was on a lanai on Waikiki Beach with one very sexy woman. Not kissing her wasn't an option.

Her arms came around him, but loosely, tentatively. "Damien, I feel grubby from all the travel and, uh . . ." And mile-high sex, she meant.

The woman would have sex in the loo with him, but she was too shy to talk about it afterward. It was kind of cute.

"Me, too. A shower would sure feel good." He dropped another kiss, this time letting his lips linger against hers. Slanting his mouth, licking the delicate outline of her top lip, nibbling the fullness of her bottom lip. Then he eased away. "Want to shower alone or together?"

"Oh! I, uh . . ." A frown crinkled her brow. "Would you be offended if I said alone?"

He shook his head, disappointed. "After all these hours with me, I can see how you'd like a few minutes of privacy." Perhaps she had girl stuff to do, like shaving her legs, that she'd just as soon he didn't see.

She smiled up at him. "Thanks for understanding."

Okay, that made him feel better. He cupped her face. "Just don't change your mind." Then he kissed her gently, lingered on her lips until she responded, then took the kiss deeper, tongue flirting with hers.

Her arms came around him, her body pressed against his, so there was no doubt she could feel the way his cock had come to attention. She wriggled her hips, moving her belly back and forth across the bulge in his jeans, which of course grew. Then she pulled away and said breathlessly, "I won't change my mind."

Great. Alone with a hard-on. When she went inside, he remained on the lanai for a few minutes, though the tropical air wasn't designed to cool a guy down.

He pulled himself together and went inside to open his luggage. The shower was running behind a closed door, and he could imagine Theresa standing under the spray.

He put a handful of condoms on the bedside table, laid out a pair of shorts and a casual shirt for later, then unpacked his computer and plugged it in. Still the shower ran.

Wet skin, a froth of soap bubbles gliding down her sleek body. Damn, a guy could only take so much of this.

Damien went out on the lanai with his mobile to check messages. The store where he'd be doing the reading tonight wanted him to call and confirm he was in town, which he did. A message from his agent said his new release had, for the first time, hit the *New York Times* extended list for bestselling hardcover fiction, at number twenty-five. The U.S. publisher's promo efforts had clearly made an impact.

A *NYT* bestselling author. How about that? This was definitely his lucky day.

Damien sauntered back inside, leaving the lanai doors open so the breeze drifted in and a swath of sunshine cut across the tiled floor. The shower was off now. Was Theresa combing her hair? Rubbing lotion into her skin?

He pulled off his shirt and tossed it into the old pillowcase he used as a traveling laundry bag, then called, "There's a guy out here who's in serious need of a shower."

"Out in a minute." The words were garbled. Ah, she was brushing her teeth.

When the door opened, he stared eagerly, hoping she'd be naked or maybe in a skimpy towel. But no, this hotel had to provide bathrobes. The big, bundly white terrycloth ones. All the same, Theresa looked cute and sexy, her cheeks pink, short damp hair fluffed up around her face, long legs and bare feet sticking out the bottom of the shapeless robe.

Her eyes widened at the sight of him. "Oh, you're . . . um . . ." Her gaze tracked his naked torso.

"Getting ready for my shower." Just to mess with her, he reached for the button at the waist of his jeans.

Her gaze followed and lingered. Then she jerked her head up. "You go ahead. I'll, uh, wait for you."

So, the prof had gone shy on him again. "It's okay if you want to get started without me," he said suggestively.

"No! I mean, uh, I'd rather wait."

"Okay. I won't be long."

The bathroom was steamy and smelled of something herbal and pleasant, reminders that just a few minutes ago a naked Theresa had been in here. Quickly he stripped off his jeans and boxer briefs, easing them over his erection, and rushed through his routine. The hotel soap and shampoo were labeled "Green Tea and Rosemary," so that must be what smelled so good.

It would've felt great to linger under the pounding spray, but something way more fun awaited him, so he rinsed off and dried himself sketchily. Normally, he'd just have pulled on a clean pair of briefs, but he didn't want to come on too strong, so he wrapped himself in the other robe. Without underwear.

When he walked out, Theresa was at the desk, sun gilding her auburn hair, plugging in her own computer next to his.

Flushed, she said, in a rush, "I really should call Vancouver. And get e-mail going. Let everyone know about my change of plans."

"The flight hasn't even left Honolulu yet. You have lots of time." He walked over and rested a hand on the collar of the robe, then eased the fabric down so the sun could touch her skin and he could caress her nape. "We have a date, remember?"

She ducked her head, giving him better access. "I'm not very experienced at this."

How did she manage to make him feel tender and horny, all at the same time? He slid his hand along her neck to her jaw, then cupped her cheek and tilted her face toward him. "That doesn't matter. What matters is, do you want this, Tezzie? You and me, doing all the things we couldn't do on the plane?"

Her lashes lowered, then she blinked and gazed straight at him, those billabong eyes dancing with green and blue sparkles in the morning sunlight. "Yes, I want it. Sorry to be so... waffly." Her jaw firmed. "I wouldn't be here if I didn't want this. If I didn't want you, Damien."

Those were words that heated him even more than the sun that burned through his robe. The sun's touch warmed him from the outside, but Theresa's desire kindled a spark that made his blood fizz and his cock surge with need.

He caressed her cheek, stroked damp hair back from her face. "Then let everything else go for an hour or two. Right now, all that exists is the two of us." He bent to kiss her and her lips met his, warm, giving, seductive.

When he straightened again, her gaze drifted down to the neckline of his robe, the V where one side wrapped over the other. Where his tanned skin and curls of dark hair were a stark contrast to the white terry. "You want me to take this off?" He touched the robe's belt, which he'd looped at his waist.

Slowly, her gaze following his hand rather than returning to his face, she shook her head and edged the desk chair around so she sat facing him squarely. "No. *I* want to take it off you."

"Be my guest."

Hand trembling slightly, she took hold of one end of the belt. The way he'd looped it, one pull would undo it.

She tugged. When the belt fell, the bulky robe loosened, but not enough to reveal his body. He stood in front of her and waited.

She raised both hands to grip the sides of the robe at mid-chest. And paused. Her shoulders rose and fell as she took a deep breath. Then she spread the sides wide.

Her breath sucked in with a gasp as she saw he was naked and aroused.

As if mesmerized, she rose slowly to her feet and eased the robe off his shoulders. It fell to the floor. The sun caressed his back and her eyes blazed a heat trail across his front.

"You really are beautifully made," she murmured.

"Glad you approve. See anything you'd like to touch?"

A quick grin, a glance upward under eyelashes. "All of it."

"Then it's all yours."

Hesitantly she touched his shoulders, running her hands over them and down his upper arms, then squeezing, feeling the muscle and bone below. "How did you get to be in such good shape? And so tanned? Writing's a sedentary, indoors job."

"I run, swim, work out. I need to, because yeah, it is sedentary, and I've always been a physical person."

She began to explore his pecs and when her fingers circled his nipples, he caught his breath. Then managed to finish his thought. "Exercise helps me work out story problems, too."

"Really?" She glanced up, then went back to teasing his nipples. "I do the same thing. When I've been working so long my thoughts are muddy, I change into shorts and go for a run."

How about that? The idea of Theresa in shorts was almost as

arousing as the touch of those soft, persistent fingers, whose every tweak made his cock throb and twitch.

Her hands traced his ribs and down over his abs, which tensed under her touch. A quick circle of his navel, and then one hand gripped his shaft. Lightly, tentatively.

He let out a moan of pleasure.

Still holding him, she sat in the desk chair again, then subjected his cock to a brush-of-fingers exploration that covered every inch of skin. From the base, where his hard-on jutted out of a nest of dark curls. Up the raised, throbbing vein that was so responsive to each stroke. Lightly ringing the top of his shaft, just under the crown. Then, finally, brushing and circling the head, finding a drop or two of pre-cum and smoothing it into his achingly sensitive skin.

He pulsed under her hand, trying not to thrust, but arousal was hot and thick in him. Burying his hands in her hair, he said, "Hey, Prof, you're killing me. Have you almost finished your research?"

"I believe in being thorough." Her voice was throaty and, when she raised her face to his, he saw how flushed she was.

Thank God he wasn't the only one who was so turned on. "Could you be thorough wearing fewer clothes?"

9

Staring up at Damien, I had a sense of unreality. This couldn't be me, in a luxury hotel on Waikiki Beach, with a man who'd been ranked one of the ten sexiest bachelors in Australia.

A man who deserved that ranking. His body was amazing, hard and masculine, gilded by the sunlight. On him, the dragon and sea eagle tattoos didn't look overdone or tacky; they gave him an intriguing edge.

His coloring was beautiful, his features strong. An illustration of how mixed-race heritage could produce gorgeous offspring. Oh yes, he was a treat to behold. But the most incredible thing was the ardent blaze in his gray eyes, the huge engorged penis filling my hands. The indisputable evidence of how aroused he was. By me. An academic, not a sex goddess.

And yet, the heat that pulsed through me—that tightened my nipples, turned my skin pink, made me tingle and ache between my legs—was all about sex. And the size of his erection, the desire in his eyes, did make me feel like a goddess.

But . . . he'd been with so many women. Women who were

prettier, sexier, far more experienced than I. How could I possibly measure up?

Not that he'd complained so far. Which meant, I must be doing all right.

I was intelligent. I could take my cues from him. Learn as we went along. The way my fingers had learned how his penis liked to be caressed.

My instinct—my craving—right now was to lean forward and take him between my lips. But he'd said he wanted my clothes off, so instead I let go of him and rose. My legs were shaky and my fingers trembled as I reached for the belt of my robe. On the plane, he'd sort of seen my body, but only in the cramped, poorly lit lavatory.

"Uh-uh." His hands stopped me. "I'll do that."

I stood, breath fast and shallow, quivering from head to toe as he undid the knot I'd tied. Then he shoved the robe off my shoulders. I fought the instinct to grab it, and instead held my arms away from my sides so the terry fabric slid down freely. My gaze followed the robe and saw it fall in haphazard white folds on the sun-kissed terra-cotta tile.

Leaving me utterly naked, exposed in bright sunlight to Damien's scrutiny.

"You are so beautiful."

His words, spoken in a tone that sounded reverent, made me raise my eyes to his face. He didn't notice, because he was staring at me with a smug "oh man, look what I've got" smile tugging at his lips and lighting his eyes.

I knew my body was okay. Not fat, not skinny. Breasts either a B or a C cup, depending on the bra. An average body, functional and healthy but nothing to write home about. Then I remembered what Damien had said about Goldilocks, and how average really meant perfect.

All these years, I'd thought the only special thing about me was my intellect. And no one had told me anything different.

But Damien's expression was giving me a whole new, flattering and exciting, message. It gave me the courage to raise my hands and cup them under my breasts, plumping them up and offering them to him. "See something *you* like?" I echoed the words he'd spoken earlier.

"Everything."

A thrill that was arousal, but more than that—a brand-new female power—rippled through me. "Just going to stand there and look?"

"Trying to figure out where to start."

No longer nervous, I drifted my right hand down from my breast, across my abdomen, out to the flare of my hip, then back in across the top of my thigh. Ending with my thumb a couple inches away from the V between my slightly spread legs. "There are no bad places."

I'd meant no bad places to start, but he interpreted differently. "God no. All your places are very definitely hot."

My guess was he'd go straight for my breasts, but he surprised me. He lifted both hands and ran his fingers through my hair, which was almost dry. He stroked back from my temples then forward, fingers gently caressing my ears, my cheeks, down to my lips, my chin. My neck, out to my shoulders, down my arms. As if he was learning, memorizing, the outline of my body.

His touch was more sensual than overtly sexual, but it brought every cell to alertness.

When he reached my fingers, he squeezed lightly, then released them and started again, this time at my breasts. But rather than tease them the way he'd done on the plane, he used that same drifting caress. Over them, down my rib cage, abdomen. Thumbs skimming my pubic hair, making my sex tense in pleasant anticipation.

But no, now he was stroking outward, to the curve of my hips, moving down the outside, following the same path my own hand had taken a few minutes ago. Coming to rest with his thumbs almost touching my sex. I held my breath, wanting him to travel those couple more inches, to brush against the damp, swollen flesh that hungered for his caress.

Instead, he took his hands away and stood, arms at his sides, not touching me. Except with his gaze, which traveled back up, retracing every inch of the path his hands had taken. He finished by looking into my eyes, smiling almost bemusedly. "I'm one hell of a lucky bugger."

Then he stepped closer, put his arms around me, pulled me against him so every sensitized cell in the front of my body came into contact with his heated flesh. His hardness against my softness. My breasts flattening against his firm pectorals. His erection pressing insistently against my stomach.

Arousal made me tremble and I wasn't sure my legs would support me. I wrapped my arms around him and lifted my face for his kiss.

Now he stopped being gentle. He slanted his mouth across mine, opened my lips with his tongue, and thrust inside. On the airplane, I'd thought how a kiss mirrored sex. Then, the kiss had been a leisurely, sensual exploration. Now, his kiss was urgent, demanding. Between us, his penis was rigid. Moisture dampened the inside of my thighs as my body wept in need.

He broke the kiss, stepped out of the embrace, and I moaned in protest. But then he lifted me, carried me, dropped me on the bed with more haste than finesse. He kissed me again, hard, then left my lips and dropped a frenzy of hot, moist kisses over my face, my chest, then my breasts.

I grabbed his head and held him there, pressing myself against him as he teased a taut, aching nipple into his mouth. The suction of his lips, the flick of his tongue, soothed my flesh and at the same time tormented it. Everything inside me focused, clenched, craved more of this delicious torture—yet craved release, too. "Oh God, Damien. What are you doing to me?"

"Is it good?"

"Oh, yes!"

He switched his attention to my other breast, and my pelvis writhed, thighs squeezing together. I was on the verge of climax. A stroke between my legs and I'd come. I'd never imagined my breasts could be so sensitive. So sexy. My whole body was like an amazing discovery. The way it looked, the way it felt, the way it responded.

I wanted Damien to keep doing what he was doing, but I also wanted the orgasm that was so close.

Finally—*finally!*—he made his way from my breasts, kissing a leisurely—far too leisurely—trail south. "Such soft skin," he crooned.

"I have softer," I muttered in desperation.

"Sorry?" He raised his head.

"Damien, please?"

A wicked grin crossed his lips. "Oh, am I being too *thorough*?"

I loved the way he was appreciating my body, wringing every ounce of awareness and arousal from it, but I couldn't take much more. I'd never before experienced this feeling of being so sexually on edge, so ready to burst. "It would be good if you got to the point soon."

"Your wish is my command." He moved lower, breath grazing my pubic hair, and I spread my legs in welcome, too needy to feel inhibited. Then he blew a stream of warm air across my sex and I gasped at the featherlight caress. My hips lifted, begging for more, and then his mouth came down on me. A quick, hard swipe of his tongue along my slit. Everything inside me leaped to attention, centered, clenched. My whole body tensed. Waiting.

Then he sucked my clitoris into his mouth and the sweet scrape of his tongue brought the orgasm rocketing through me. I cried out. No, to be honest, I screeched. With relief, satisfaction, astonishment that my body was capable of such ecstasy.

He held me as I shuddered, then gradually drifted into a sort of melty, blissful daze. My eyes were closed, and I was only vaguely aware of the bed rocking as he moved. I heard a rip, opened my eyes, saw he'd torn open a condom package.

My body promptly woke up again. As it did, I noticed the jerkiness of Damien's motions, the frenzied glitter in his eyes. And just how engorged his penis was as he struggled to roll the condom down its length. It dawned on me that he was as turned on, as needy, as close to climax as I'd been a few minutes ago. He was hot for me. Seriously hot for me.

The thought was as exciting as his beautifully masculine, aroused body. I ached for him all over again. "I need you, Damien." I opened my arms, drew him down on top of me.

We kissed, open-mouthed, a little sloppy with passion, as our bodies adjusted to each other. I felt as if he was branding me with his heat, his strength, his vitality. But I wanted him to do it from the inside, too. I widened my legs, raised my knees.

He reached between us, stroked my sex, spreading the moisture, testing my opening with his finger. Then the head of his penis probed me, slid in a little, and I gasped, slightly sore from the last time. He rested, waited, and my body relaxed, then he thrust in a little more.

I could feel the tension in him, every muscle taut with the effort to restrain himself. If he felt anything like I'd done when he'd been teasing my body, he must long to plunge forward and drive straight to climax, but he was holding back. Waiting for me to loosen up so he wouldn't hurt me.

Knowing that, trusting him, I stopped tensing and he slid in farther. Then he eased out, slipped back in. Out and in again, each time wetter, deeper. And each time, I took him. I surrounded him, gripped him, melted around him. Felt the delicious pressure of his hard flesh against my slick channel.

"Feels so good," I panted as excitement built again. "Give me more."

"God, yeah." He thrust harder and I raised my hips, my legs, higher, changing the angle to take him more deeply.

The base of his penis brushed my clit, which was already sensitized after my first climax, and I whimpered with pleasure. Grasping his firm butt in both hands, I felt his muscles tighten as he plunged into me. Now there was no discomfort, just a long, luxuriant slide of flesh against flesh inside me, a shifting pressure against the swollen bud at my entrance. And that sense inside me of everything becoming alert, gathering, building.

Damien held my head in his hands and now he scraped a breathless kiss against my lips. "Can't hold on, Tezzie. You got me so hot."

His hips pumped harder, faster, and I heard my own voice gasping, "Oh, oh," with each stroke, as my body got closer, closer, and then Damien jerked convulsively and everything inside me came apart again as he groaned with pleasure.

After, we collapsed together, and I was barely aware of anything except his warm weight and the sound of us both panting for breath.

A few minutes later, he raised himself on his forearms, smiled, and gave me a gentle kiss. "Wow again."

He rolled off me and went to deal with the condom. When he returned, he brought a bottle of chilled water from the minibar. No glasses. He *was* a guy, after all. But he did open the bottle and hand it to me first, not to mention support me with an arm as I sat up.

Refreshed, I handed him back the bottle and lay down again while he drank deeply.

I felt as if he'd turned me into a whole different person. A real sex goddess. "This feels so decadent," I told him. "Sunshine slanting in, tropical air, great sex. And it's only mid-morning."

He yawned, raising his hand to cover his mouth, and the yawn was a jaw-cracker. "It may only be mid-morning," he said, "but I'm beat."

"So am I." A sense of lassitude and well-being had sunk in, bone-deep. Could I ever remember being so content? I yawned, too, then curled on my side to watch as he put the bottle down and stretched out beside me.

"Come here." He extended his arm and urged me closer until my head rested on his chest.

"I should phone Vancouver." But another yawn rippled through my body.

"Later," he said sleepily.

Well, maybe I'd just cuddle here for a couple more minutes. This was something I'd missed almost as much as sex. Not that Jeffrey had been much for cuddling. A few minutes each night, then he'd kiss me on the forehead and roll over, saying, "We need our sleep."

He'd assumed, right from the beginning, that we couldn't sleep in each other's arms. My ex was self-contained. Tidy and efficient—in his appearance, his work, his personal life. He had clearly defined boundaries. Except when it came to appropriating my research project.

Usually, when I thought about his betrayal, I felt residual hurt and anger. But right now, with my body relaxed and satiated, Damien's arm around me and his warm chest rising and falling beneath my cheek, the scent of frangipani and sea air and sex in my nostrils, it was hard to summon even an iota of a negative emotion.

Damien—my lover!—shifted position and kissed my hair. I expected him to roll away, but instead he squeezed my arm. "Phone later. Work later," he murmured, the words coming lazily, his breath stirring my hair. "Buy clothes later. Lunch, mai tai."

"Piña colada." I could imagine the pineapple-coconut-rum taste in my mouth.

His chest rippled as he chuckled. "Whatever you want, Tezzie. Now, let's nap."

"Mmm. Twist my arm."

"Don't have the energy." But he did stroke it, a gentle up-and-down caress. That slowed. Stopped. His breathing had slowed, too; his chest barely rose and fell under my cheek.

"Damien?" I whispered.

No response. He was asleep. With me cuddled in the curve of his arm.

I dropped a kiss on his chest and murmured, "Thank you for today." Then I gave in to the urge to let go and drift into sleep.

When I woke, I felt almost drugged, my eyelids too heavy to open, my mind coming back to awareness slowly. Normally, I was either up half the night, my brain so busy with ideas that I might as well work, or dead asleep to be jerked awake by the alarm. This feeling was different. Oh, right, I'd been traveling. Was tired from a long flight, jetlag . . .

I lay curled on my side, the way I normally slept, but something definitely wasn't normal. There was a body curved around me, spooning me. A male body. An aroused male body.

Damien. In a flash, everything came back to me.

What on earth had I done, taking up with a complete stranger? Was this the stupidest thing I'd ever done, or perhaps the smartest? Did it matter? Because the reality was, I'd done it. I was in Honolulu with a very sexy man and there was an impressive erection nudging my backside.

My body was definitely awake now. Between my legs I felt a

warm, pleasant ache, partly from having had great sex and partly from anticipating more. I wriggled backward, pressing against Damien.

"Oh, you're awake, are you, Tezzie?" He kissed the nape of my neck.

"Mmm. Something woke me." I wriggled some more.

He licked my nape, blew warm air across the damp skin. His arm was around me and, as he'd done before, he stroked my arm, up and down in a soft, tantalizing caress. He shifted position so his penis nudged between my thighs.

I opened my thighs, let him slide between them, then closed my legs so his shaft was trapped there, nestled against my labia and my clit. He pumped his hips gently, sliding back and forth in tiny, rocking movements as the stimulation made me wet. I squeezed my thighs tighter, concentrating on the subtle but sexy sensations. If we kept doing this, I might come. Especially if I reached down to fondle the crown of his penis and press it harder against my clit.

Or if I tilted my hips and he slipped inside me.

But this time, before I came, I wanted to taste him. I slid away and turned toward him. "Lie on your back."

With a curious smile, he obeyed. His erection rose against his stomach, thick and firm. A needy craving between my legs urged me to just straddle the man and get on with it, and I was pretty sure he wouldn't object. But I'd never seen such a tempting penis—oh damn, what was wrong with calling it a cock?— and I wanted to make a closer inspection.

I scooted down the bed and took him in my hand, lifting his erection away from his body, studying the taut skin, engorged vein, satiny crown. With a featherlight touch I caressed him all over, then circled him with my other hand and pumped up and down a few strokes. Imagining him inside me, my whole body tightened with need, nipples hard, sex throbbing and wet.

"You can go harder," he muttered. "It won't break."

"That's a relief," I teased. I tightened my grip for a few strokes, then bent down and began to lick him. With my tongue, I followed the same path my fingers had taken. Exploring every inch of skin, flicking against the vein, licking under the head of his cock and then over the crown. Catching salty pre-cum.

His breathing was audible, fast and a little raspy.

Then I took him between my lips and sucked him in.

"Oh, yeah, Tezzie. Feels so good."

I took as much of his length as I could, and circled the base of his shaft with my fingers. Then I tightened the suction with my mouth, firmed my tongue-strokes around his shaft, squeezed harder with my fingers and pumped.

He jerked, shuddered. "Jesus! Oh, man, yes."

With my other hand I caressed his balls, felt them tighten as his hips rose. Then he grabbed me by the hair, not gently, and pulled my head away from him. "Stop. Enough. I want to be inside you when I come."

"The sooner, the better."

"Really? Thank God." The comment was heartfelt, and he further telegraphed his urgency by grabbing a condom package from the bedside table. He ripped it open and handed me the condom. When I fumbled with it—I'd never in my life put one on a man, and his cock looked much too big to accommodate it—he grabbed it back and sheathed himself. "Lady's choice. What do you want?"

I answered by straddling his pelvis, one knee on either side, his cock rising between my spread legs.

"Good choice. You sure look hot up there." He smoothed his hands up my thighs and gripped my waist. "And you get to do all the work. I can just lay back and watch."

"You mean you don't intend to move at all?" I teased, gripping his shaft, raising up on my knees, bringing his tip to rest against my opening.

"Mmm." His gaze was intent, watching what I was doing. "Don't think I could be in bed with you and not move. You're too f—too damned sexy."

I'd never been fond of gratuitous cursing. I figured it was lazy, a communication habit of people who couldn't be bothered finding the correct word. But right now, I thought maybe the word he'd been going to say was the exact right one. With the head of his cock brushing the damp folds of my pussy, I told him, "Say it. Say what you were going to say."

Now his gaze slanted up to meet mine. Staring into my eyes, he said, "You're too fucking sexy, Tezzie."

A thrill rippled through me. I was. With him. He made me passionate, erotic, a little wild.

Using my free hand, I opened myself, then I took him in. Only perhaps an inch. "Yes, I am. I am fucking sexy." Another inch. "And so are you, Damien Black." Then I sat down on him, encompassing his full length in one long, hot glide that made both of us gasp.

Locked together, neither of us moved for several seconds.

Then he said, "Lean forward." His hands tugged on my waist, pulling me toward him.

I tilted down, bracing my hands on his shoulders. "Oh, yes." At this angle, the base of his shaft rubbed my clit, which was swollen and eager. He could reach my breasts, too, a fact he demonstrated promptly by cupping them in both hands.

"Now." He squeezed my nipples gently between thumbs and index fingers, making my insides quiver. "Now move."

I obeyed, starting with slow, small motions, but we were both too aroused to settle for that. Soon, I was lifting almost to the top of his cock, then slamming down to grind and twist against him. Sexy sensations flooded through me, from where he filled and stroked me inside, where my crotch rubbed against his curly hairs, his shaft pressed my clit, his fingers tweaked my nipples. It was a sensual overload and I was rapidly reaching the point of explosion.

Damien, too. His hips rose to meet me, plunging his cock deeper, and deeper still. Rubbing my clit faster, harder with each stroke. Then he groaned and his rhythm became frenzied as he began to climax, and those final strokes deep in my core arched my back and brought me tumbling along with him.

After, when I'd started to breathe again, I slid down to lie on top of him, with him still inside me. "That was wonderful."

"Oh, yeah." He stroked my back from shoulder to waist, shoulder to waist, over and over. Hypnotically.

I could have fallen asleep again. But there were things I needed to do. For a few minutes, I indulged myself in cuddling, then pulled away. "I really have to contact my family."

He gave a good-natured laugh. "Yeah, yeah. I know. And we both have work to do. But in an hour or so, we'll go buy you some clothes, have lunch, and plan out the rest of the day."

"Sounds fair. I'm going to take a quick shower. Alone," I added. Then I grimaced. "Wish I had those clothes now. I hate to get back into the same ones. And the bathrobe is too warm." Thank heavens at least I always traveled with fresh undies in my carry-on.

"Don't have to wear a stitch, as far as I'm concerned," he said cheerfully.

"Dream on."

When I finished my shower and pulled back the shower curtain, I saw a white cotton sports shirt hanging on the hook on the bathroom door. I dried off, then slipped into it. It covered me to mid-thigh and the loose-weave fabric was cool and light. I studied my reflection in the mirror as I brushed my teeth. In my humble opinion, I looked kind of cute and sexy.

A girl wearing her guy's shirt after they'd made love. Even though I wasn't much of a movie-watcher, I did know enough about popular culture to be aware the image was often used, and now I could see its appeal.

When I stepped out of the bathroom, Damien was lying on the bed, naked. Another image with definite appeal.

"Thanks for the shirt," I said.

"My pleasure. It looks much better on you. Great legs, Professor Fallon." He swung off the bed, reached under the shirt to give my panty-clad bottom a squeeze, then headed into the bathroom.

I decided to check e-mail, to see if there was anything I should know about before I phoned Vancouver. A message from Kat confirmed what she'd said in voice mail.

> Hey, sis. I've booked the train tickets and am forwarding the e-ticket so you'll see the schedule. Maybe someone can pick me up at the station?
>
> My boss gave me flack about taking a holiday with no notice, but what the hell, I have an assistant. He did just fine when I went to Cape Cod last year.

Cape Cod. Yes, Kat had gone with the man she'd been head over heels in love with at the time. I tried to remember his name, what he'd done for a living. Had he been the international financier from New York, or maybe the Olympic gold-medal skier? Kat had gone through so many love affairs, the details merged. And each time, she was convinced the man was "the one."

Would she ever learn? Ever develop good judgment when it came to men? Or was she, like me, destined for a solitary life?

I could deal with it—maybe with the addition of an occasional hot fling—but I wasn't sure Kat, despite her successful career, would be happy on her own. My poor sister. It must be tough on her, seeing Merilee get married.

In the bathroom, the shower shut off. I imagined Damien—

the man who'd taught me I was fling-worthy—naked, fresh and clean, dripping water. Beginning to towel off. I toyed with the notion of knocking on the door and asking if he wanted to come out and play.

No, I had to have *some* discipline. Besides, my body was so satiated, the last thing I should be thinking about right now was more sex. I turned back to my sister's e-mail.

After all, how often does a Fallon girl get married? So far, only once, and you didn't even invite us. (Bad girl!) And that obviously jinxed your marriage, so we can't let that happen to Merilee. Not that anything could jinx her and Matt, right? I mean, they've only been each other's "one and onlys" for how long? 15 yrs!

Do have to wonder why the kid has all the luck . . . You thought you'd found your guy and he turned out to be a loser. And me, yeah, I can hear exactly what you're saying. I keep repeating the same mistake, and you at least learned from yours.

But Theresa, I don't WANT to be cynical like you. I want to believe there's a great guy out there for me. That I deserve love, and that I'll find it.

I sighed. I'd believed the same thing myself when I met Jeffrey, but his betrayal had convinced me I was wrong. Of course Kat deserved love—we all *deserved* it—but if she was going to *find* it, she needed to learn a different strategy.

Feeling a little sad for the both of us, I read on.

So, anyhow, guess what? I'm bringing a date to the wedding!!!! Yes, it's a guy, and he's good-looking and successful. And very, very nice. His name is Nav. Honestly, Theresa, this man is NOT another of my bad choices. You and the 'rents and the sisters will all approve of him. HON-

> EST!! <G> He'll probably fly out a day or 2 before the wed-
> ding.

I groaned. "Honestly? Oh, give me a break." It was no big
surprise that Kat would have found a new man. She never went
long without one. But there was something different this time.
She wasn't gushing that she was madly in love with this one.
Maybe she *was* learning a new strategy. Perhaps for once she
was taking it slow, getting to know the guy before flinging her
heart at him. Who knows, maybe this Nav would give her the
love she deserved and was so hungry to find. Of course, odds
were she'd chosen another loser, but at least this time she might
find out before she'd fallen head over heels.

> BTW, re the wedding. We'll need invitations, right?
> M&M need to come up with a guest list ASAP. I know Mer-
> ilee always wanted hand-calligraphied invitations with RSVP
> cards enclosed, but there won't be time. Phone calls would
> be a hassle, having to provide all the info and get people to
> write it down. So I was thinking, why don't we do e-vites?
> I'm really good with graphics, I could design something in
> the next couple days, if you get the list from M&M. Oh, and
> we could use the list to plan the bridal shower and make
> sure one of Matt's friends is arranging a bachelor party. Let
> me know what you think.
> Hugs, Kat.

Invitations were already on my project plan, and Kat's suggestion was a good one. I made a mental note to update the
plan.

There were no other family e-mails, just a couple from the
uni that I'd deal with later.

I had just picked up my cell to call Vancouver when the
bathroom door opened and Damien came out. Naked. No

robe, not even a towel. Just six feet of naked male perfection, looking completely at ease in his body.

"Hey," he said, "how ya going? Talked to your folks?" He wandered over to the dresser where he'd laid out a small stack of clothes, picked up a pair of white boxer briefs, and began to put them on.

White underwear could be boring, but his great body and dark skin turned them into a sexy image that would have made a great advertisement for underwear. Or sex.

This casual intimacy was totally foreign to me, but that didn't stop me from staring appreciatively. "Uh, no, I was just going to call. I've been checking e-mail."

He pulled on a pair of tan shorts. "I've got galleys to proof. I'll go out on the lanai, give you some privacy. An hour, right?" Shirtless, he squeezed my shoulder and dropped a kiss in my hair, then gathered up his work and went out to settle in a lounge chair.

There was something appealing about the idea of Damien and I being compatible enough that we'd give each other the space to get on with what each of us needed to do.

Speaking of which . . . I dialed the number of our family home in Vancouver, the one that was now occupied by only Mom, Dad, and Merilee.

Merilee answered, sounding unfocused.

"Hi sis, it's Theresa. Were you asleep?"

"Oh, hey! Good to hear from you. No, I wasn't asleep. I'm working on a paper. Can't believe how much I missed, being off sick."

"You could have skipped the whole semester and started fresh in the fall."

"Then I wouldn't graduate next year with Matt. No, I'm really lucky they gave me an extension, and I can do this. Besides, in two weeks this'll all be behind me and I'll be on a Mexican Riviera cruise with my husband." Her voice rang with joy.

"Speaking of weddings, can you and Matt find time to do an invitation list? Kat says she'll design something nice for an e-vite."

"Cool! Great idea."

"So I guess we'll need names, e-mail addresses, and who they are—like, whether they're a friend of yours, friend of Matt's, family of Matt's, or whatever."

"Sure. D'you need it for when you get home or can it wait until tomorrow?"

"Uh, well . . . I'm not actually going to be home until tomorrow."

"What? But I thought your flight—"

"Change of plans. Long story, and nothing bad." No, Damien was definitely a good thing. "I'm staying in Honolulu overnight, same as I usually do."

"Okay, sure. I'll let the folks know. Oh, and we planned a welcome-home barbecue for tomorrow. But I guess you won't be home in time for dinner?"

I winced. Usually, I could be counted on to appear on time. "No. Sorry to screw up everyone's plans."

Merilee gave her tinkly laugh, which always made me think of wind chimes in the breeze. "Don't worry, it was me who did that. Or, rather, Matt, finding that deal on the cruise. Like, could the timing have been any worse? Mom preparing for her Supreme Court of Canada case, Dad finishing the report on his latest research grant, me with the semester to make up? You and Kat and Jenna all busy with your own lives. And Matt's swamped, too, because he's back at his usual summer job at his uncle's firm and he has to train someone to take over for him while he's away honeymooning."

"Merilee, are you two sure you want to get married now? It's such a rush, and we'll never be able to put together the kind of wedding you dreamed of. Why not wait until next summer? You could still go on the cruise this year."

"No. Matt and I want to start our life together. Try to get pregnant. The wedding . . . Okay, I won't lie." She gave a quick laugh. "Like I could lie to any of you about the kind of wedding I wanted. I never made any secret of it, the way I mooned around with those wedding mags. But Theresa, things happen that make you think. Make you grow up and realize what's really important."

The certainty in her voice made me smile, albeit a little mistily. Merilee's life *had* changed this past year, and she clearly knew what she wanted. My baby sister had grown up. Though . . . "You always did seem pretty mature to me," I acknowledged. "For your age. Self-contained, self-sufficient."

She didn't answer, and I wondered if we'd lost the connection. "Merilee? Are you still there?"

"Self-sufficient? Well, I had Matt, didn't I?" There was an edge to her voice. Bitterness? It was unusual, because typically Merilee was sunny and sweet, the nicest kid of all of us, the one who had slipped through life smoothly. Until this past year, and the endometriosis.

"Yes, of course you had Matt." And yes, I felt a twinge of guilt for not having been a better big sister. "Anyhow, if you two are sure about the wedding, then we'll do our best to give you a great one. Now, what else? Oh, I'm on the same flight as planned, just a day later, so I get in around midnight. I'll catch a cab and come home and go to bed, then see you all in the morning. Kat's booked train tickets and will get home on Friday. And Jenna—"

"Let me guess." Her tone was lighter again. "She doesn't know her plans yet."

"She needs to work out her finances."

"When doesn't she?" Merilee, eight years Jenna's junior, had always managed money—and everything else—efficiently. "I bet Mom and Dad would pay for her flight," she said.

"I told her that, and I offered, too. She says she doesn't want charity."

"Then she should get a real job."

"I know."

We were both quiet for a few seconds. Then I said, "Well, neither of us is going to change Jenna." Though I worried about what life would be like for our footloose and fancy-free sister as she grew older. Of course, maybe she'd have one of those priority-changing experiences Merilee had spoken about, and finally grow up. I just hoped it wasn't a bad one.

"True. Listen, Theresa, I really need to get back to this paper. But Matt and I'll do the e-vite list. Promise."

"Great. See you soon. Sorry to inconvenience everyone with the change of plan."

"No problem. Take care. Enjoy Honolulu." Then she gave her wind-chime laugh again. "Wait, what am I saying? This is you, Theresa. You'll be in a hotel room working. So I guess I should say, I hope you get lots done."

If she only knew. Not that I'd ever tell my family about Damien. Or would I? I gazed out to the lanai, where he was sprawled in a lounge chair, manuscript pages in one hand and a pen in the other. My lover. My very hot lover. The one who'd turned me into a sex goddess.

My family thought they knew me so damned well. Maybe I'd drop a hint, to tantalize them and keep them off balance. For now, I contented myself with saying, "Thanks. You, too."

After hanging up, I went back to e-mail.

First, I sent my new flight information to Merilee, with cc's to Mom and Dad, and a reminder about the e-vite list. Then I sent the e-mail I'd saved in my Draft folder, asking my parents to see if they could pull strings and get us into VanDusen Gardens for the wedding.

And then I replied to Kat's message.

Hi Kat. Glad you got the tickets. I should be able to borrow someone's car and meet you at the station.

Yes, you're right about invitations. I think e-vites are a good idea. I talked to Merilee and she agrees. She and Matt are going to put together a guest list. So, when you have time, go ahead and do something up. I'm sure it'll be great.

She definitely had the skill, but she worked for a very up-scale hotel and was used to doing international PR. To be safe, I added,

Just remember, this is M&M, not some ritzy hotel you're promoting!
Oh, BTW, I won't be in Vancouver until tomorrow night. I'm in Honolulu overnight. There's e-mail (obviously!) and you can reach me by cell.
Heard anything from Jenna? I told her to call you. She's trying to work out her travel plans.
Talk soon. Theresa

And then I called Jenna. No answer, so I left a message, repeating my offer to pay for her flight home. "How about we make it your thirtieth-birthday present?" I suggested.

After hanging up, I opened my wedding project plan, but my mind was still on Jenna.

Hard to believe she'd soon be thirty. When I'd reached that age, I was a tenured professor at the University of Sydney. I'd presented papers to the United Nations Permanent Forum on Indigenous Issues and been published in every journal of any significance.

I'd celebrated my birthday by taking my secretary out for a very nice dinner, telling her it was a thank-you for extra work she'd put in. She'd had no idea it was my birthday. I didn't want any fuss, just a good meal, a bottle of wine, and pleasant company.

Kat, who'd turned thirty last year, had spent her birthday in Cape Cod, with the guy whose name I didn't recall. Jenna would probably spend her landmark birthday by picking up some new hottie and screwing his brains out.

Not that there wasn't something to be said for that particular course of action. I glanced out to the lanai, where male eye candy was stretched out, brown skin gleaming in the sunlight, reading intently.

10

Damien finished a chapter and smiled with satisfaction. The people at his publishing house had done a great job—so far, he'd picked up only a few small errors—and he liked the book. He always felt nervous when he read his own work in galley format, knowing that was how the book would be printed unless he made changes. What if, at that stage, he suddenly found an error in logic or a major inconsistency? Or worse, what if he decided the whole story sucked?

It hadn't happened yet. Didn't mean he'd stopped worrying, though. But so far, with *Gale Force*, he was happy.

Realizing he was hungry, he checked his watch and saw he'd been working for more than an hour. A glance inside showed Theresa curled up in the desk chair, long legs bare and shapely under the tails of his shirt. She had the wedding planning book spread open and was typing and muttering. When he rose and moved to the open lanai door, he could hear her.

"Wedding cake. Big, fancy, tiered cake with romantic topper. Separate slices to take home? Groom's cake?"

He stepped through the door and she glanced up.

"Groom's cake?" she repeated, eyes dazed.

Not sure if it was a question, or just her mind stuck on the last thought, he answered anyhow. "Chocolate. Well, unless the guy doesn't like chocolate. But what man doesn't?"

Her gaze sharpened, focused. "Or woman. But do you think we need one?"

"Jeez, I'm no wedding expert." Still, he'd been to a few. "People usually have them. They're not fancy white things with icing swirls and roses like the wedding cake, they're a big, flat cake."

"Sheet cake. Yes, I remember from my secretary's wedding. It had some picture drawn in icing on the top."

"Yeah, like a surfboard or footie ball. Something the groom likes doing." He winked at her. "Some hobby he'll likely have to give up once he's tied down with a wife."

She grinned. "Don't look at me, I'm not pro-marriage."

Any bachelor in his right mind would be thrilled to hear his lover speak those words. But Damien couldn't help but think what a pity it was her ex had been such a scuzzy bastard. A woman like Theresa shouldn't shut herself up in an ivory tower. She had so much going for her, a guy would be damned lucky to find a woman with her beauty, sexuality, and intellect.

Of course, she could be a real pain in the arse when she got argumentative.

But now she was smiling, eyes bright and sparkling, not a criticism or argument in sight.

He touched her soft cheek. "Done enough work, Prof? Time to hit the shops and buy you something sexy, then find some lunch?"

She pressed into his hand, then moved away, getting up and stretching. His shirt lifted higher up her thighs, giving him naughty ideas. "Sure," she said. "I'm hungry." She stuck a bookmark in the wedding book and heaved it closed, then came over to him, rose on her toes, and planted a kiss on his lips.

"I'm being irresponsible, Damien, but I won't regret it. I deserve some fun."

"Damn right." He kissed her back, harder and deeper, then shoved her away before he gave in to temptation. "Get dressed and let's go out." Part of him would be entirely happy to spend the whole day in this room, but the fact of being in Honolulu for the first time, with a special woman on a sunny day, made him want to go out and explore.

Theresa gathered up her clothes and went into the loo. He pulled on the shirt he'd laid out earlier, stuck his sunnies in the shirt pocket and his wallet in his shorts pocket, and wondered how long it would take her to get ready.

The door opened and she emerged.

Most women spent half an hour on their hair and makeup, and didn't end up looking near as fine as Theresa. Of course, with such natural good looks—dark brows and lashes, rosy mouth, great bone structure, soft, clear skin—she didn't need much fancying up. Yeah, her natural beauty was a real turn-on.

"What are you staring at?" she asked nervously. "I know these clothes aren't right, but they're all I have with me."

"It's not that. You look great. That's all." She didn't even look too out of place in her cotton pants and sleeveless top, but he guessed she'd be hot once she got outside.

She raised her eyebrows, but didn't ask him to expand.

When he was writing, it was this kind of stuff that gave him trouble. He could write ten pages of action and dialogue in an hour, yet it often took him at least that long to draft one line of Kalti's emotional response to a woman.

"Oh crap, that's what's wrong!" he said.

"Wrong?" She glanced down her body. "What's wrong?"

"Not you. My book. The one I'm working on." He took her hand and tugged her toward the door. "Something didn't feel right but I couldn't figure out what it was." As they headed for the elevator, he went on. "My cop protagonist Kalti has been assigned a new partner. And I know what a lot of their issues and conflicts are. Like, she's scientific, logical, skeptical, and he's the guy who . . ." He paused as they stepped into the elevator.

"Who believes in Dreamtime spirits, and they come alive for him," she said. "A fact that he hides from his colleagues."

"Too right. But if he and Marianna are partners, they need to be able to trust each other."

"A man who's keeping secrets is hard to trust," she said with a touch of bitterness.

"True. But Kalti can't tell her—can't trust *her*—because she's an outsider to his world. She'd never let herself believe in the spirits."

The elevator doors opened and they both stepped out. "So," he said, "all that stuff sets up great conflict. But something was missing."

"And you've realized what it is?"

"Uh-huh." They'd crossed the lobby, and now stepped outside into the sunshine. "Sunscreen for you." Her skin was a light golden brown. "And sunnies and a hat." He slipped on his own sunglasses.

"I hate hats. But yes to the rest. And to shorts, definitely."

"A sarong," he teased. "With a bikini top."

She ignored the comment. "Let's head over to Kalakaua Avenue. Now, go on, what did you figure out about Kalti and his new partner?"

"He's had casual relationships with women, but this is the first time he's had a female partner. He has to see her as a woman, not just a partner."

"Isn't that sexist?"

"It's human nature. Trust me, a man notices if a person's male or female. So, does he think less of her, discriminate against her, or does he defend her when other guys make sexist remarks? Does he overprotect her in a dangerous situation? Does he lust after her?"

She nodded. "I see what you mean. And, on that note, she'll not only notice he's a man, but that he's Aboriginal Australian. What does she think about that?"

"Like, does she think of him as a boong?" Deliberately, he used one of the derogatory terms that, along with coon and abo, were used by racist people. "Or, if she isn't prejudiced, does she defend him against racial slurs, which might piss him off because he can take care of himself?"

"Well? What *do* they think of each other?"

"Good question. One I haven't answered. I got caught up in the action of the story and forgot about the more subtle, personal stuff." The stuff that, while being tougher to write, added essential texture and depth.

Her fingers wove through his and she hugged his arm against her. "The issues you're talking about—like discrimination, whether it's blatant or subtle—are important."

She was right. And maybe in this book they'd come to the fore more than they had in the past. Some instinct had made him give Kalti a female partner, but if he hadn't met Theresa, he might not have figured out the deeper implications and possibilities. Dealing with perceptions and prejudices could give this book additional depth and conflict and, who knew, those issues might even feed into the story line. Once he got started writing, he never knew exactly what words were going to flow through his fingers.

They'd been weaving through other tourists, most in shorts and many sporting vivid Hawaiian shirts and tees. The streets were pleasant, with coconut palms offering some shade, overflowing flower baskets hanging from Victorian street lamps, surfboards displaying historic information, and ginger and frangipani perfuming the air.

He and Theresa stopped at a red light and she tilted her head up to him. "The subtle, personal stuff, like you were talking about, is really interesting. Small things can reveal a lot." She touched the sea eagle tattoo that was hidden under his shirt sleeve. "Like your tattoos."

"Symbols of teen rebellion."

"Symbols of two different heritages, ones that your parents avoided acknowledging. A statement of independence. You wanted to be your own person, and you recognized that your Chinese and Aboriginal heritage was part of that."

"I guess." Yeah, this was the kind of thing women did so much better than men. Not only analyze subjects like this, but have the words to express them. Man, it was going to be a challenge weaving this kind of stuff into his book.

The light turned green and they began to cross the street.

"Do you have any contact with the Chinese side of the family?" she asked.

"My grandmother died when I was young, but I'm in touch by e-mail with a grandaunt who lives in New Zealand."

"I guess you know what it means to be born in the year of the dragon."

He did. When his Chinese grandaunt had first told him, he'd been thrilled to learn he was a dragon. But to spout off about it to Theresa would sound egotistical, so he shrugged.

Her eyes gleamed in the sunlight. "The dragon is one of the most lucky, powerful of the Chinese Zodiac signs. A person who's born in the year of the dragon knows what he wants and is determined to get it. He has a natural charm and charisma, and easily influences others. People enjoy his company, turn to him for advice. He's often the center of attention."

Damien gaped at her. "Jeez, prof, you're a walking encyclopedia."

"No, I'm a good researcher."

"You researched me? My tattoos?"

"I was overdosing on wedding stuff and needed a break."

Well, how about that. Was it intellectual curiosity or was she really interested in him?

"This store," she said, steering him through an open door.

They'd passed a dozen shops and he had no clue how she'd chosen this one. Efficiently she went about selecting white shorts, a sleeveless top with a subtle pattern of seashells in sand and white, another in pale blue, flip-flops, sunglasses, and sunscreen.

"Bikini and sarong," he reminded her, guiding her to a different section of the store.

"I don't . . . I've never been much of a beach person."

"Why am I not surprised, Prof? But lighten up, you're at Waikiki. We have to at least walk down the sand, dip our toes in the ocean." He pulled a sarong off the rack, one that wasn't too flashy, patterned in muted shades of green and blue. "Here, this goes with your eyes."

Those eyes flashed. "Did you want to pick the bathing suit, too?"

Without hesitation he reached for a bikini with a string-tied top and a thong bottom. The briefest one he could find. In plastic-flamingo pink.

His choice was so outrageous, it made her laugh.

He chuckled, too. "No? Okay then, your turn to pick."

She glanced at the one-pieces, which were what he thought of as grandma suits. Way too much fabric. And most were in garish patterns that hurt your eyes. Her hand hovered beside a bikini, then she grabbed the hanger. And another couple besides. "I'll try these on."

"Feel free to model them for me."

But she didn't, just came out holding a simple one that was the subtle green of gum leaves. She paid for the purchases—eyes glinting dangerously when he offered to buy them for her—then disappeared into the changing room again. When she came out, he whistled. The shorts and tank top showed off her soft curves and long limbs, and suited her coloring. She looked more relaxed, definitely not like she belonged in a uni office.

"Want me to sunscreen you?" he offered.

"Already done. Now I just need to, uh, get some underwear, then let's find lunch. I'm starving. Breakfast was a long time ago."

And, in her case, had consisted of some fruit and half a croissant.

Though she hadn't let him pay, she had no qualms about handing him the string-handled carrier bag bulging with her travel clothes and new beachwear.

When they found a lingerie shop, she said, "You stay outside. I don't need advice."

He'd have liked to goad her into buying sexy undies, but gave in. "Okay. I'll check out this shop." He headed toward a store that featured Hawaiian shirts and board shorts. Inside, he bought a Waikiki Beach T-shirt to commemorate the occasion.

Then he hung out on the sidewalk for a few minutes, until Theresa joined him carrying a promisingly tiny bag. "All set?"

"Yes, and I need food," she said.

"Let's head over to the beach. Find a place where we can eat by the water."

"Sounds nice."

Hand in hand—and how great it felt to be holding hands with this auburn-haired babe in her casual summer clothes—they strolled to an attractive open-air hotel restaurant where they were lucky enough to get a table on the ocean side. Sheltered from direct sunlight, they both took off their sunglasses and smiled at each other.

A waitress with long, wavy blond hair and a Hawaiian-print dress came to ask what they'd like to drink. He glanced at Theresa. "Piña colada?" When she nodded, he said, "And I'll have a mai tai."

While they waited for their drinks, they studied the menu.

"Normally I'd go for shrimp salad," she said, "but I'm so hungry, I'm going to have grilled mahimahi. How about you?"

"Coconut shrimp with french fries and a salad."

Their waitress returned with their drinks, big glasses with colorful paper umbrellas sticking out of them, a purple orchid decorating his and a white frangipani on Theresa's.

After they ordered, Damien held his glass out. "Here's to being seated beside the right person on a long flight."

She clicked her glass to his. "I couldn't have said it better myself." After sucking some of the creamy liquid through her straw, she gave a satisfied sigh and sat back in the padded seat of the rattan chair.

They both extracted the flowers and umbrellas from their drinks. He picked up the frangipani. With its golden centre, ivory petals, and pink tips, the blossom was delicate yet resilient, kind of like Theresa. "Go tropical, Tezzie. Put the frangipani behind your ear."

She took the flower and admired it. "They call it plumeria here."

"Whatever you say, Prof."

Hesitantly she tucked it into her hair and Damien nodded approval.

Thinking that this was quite the life, he sat back, sipping his mai tai. At home, he mostly drank beer or one of Australia's excellent wines. But his first time in Hawaii called for something different, and the potent rum drink was perfect.

A few yards away, past a stretch of grass and the hedge of bougainvillea and palms that marked the edge of the hotel property, bathing-suit-clad people strolled along the beach or lay in the sun. Some were tanned so dark they must do this every day. Others were blindingly white and lathered with sunscreen, and several were so red they'd be hurting tonight. Tourists who hadn't learned that the sun's kiss should be treated with respect.

"This is such a luxury," Theresa said.

"You know, they do have beachside restaurants and tropical drinks in Oz," he teased.

"I know. I do go out occasionally. But I don't think I've ever had such a sense of being relaxed and pampered." Her eyes danced. "Maybe the great sex has something to do with it."

He curled his fingers and polished them against his chest, in a taking-credit gesture. "Too right it does."

That might explain why he, too, was feeling on top of the world. He couldn't imagine a single place he'd rather be, or a person he'd rather be with. Now, if only the waitress would bring their food before his stomach began to growl.

Theresa took another sip of her drink. "These go down much too easily." She smiled across the table. "I never finished what I was saying about the dragon."

"There's more?" Not only was she into research, apparently she had a perfect memory.

"He likes to be the leader, and he's a good one. He likes power, too, and has lessons to learn about flexibility and compassion."

"You mean he's a control freak like you?" he joked. His personal opinion was, he'd learned a whole lot about flexibility since he'd started working with a team of women.

She made a face, then went on. "Then there's the other tattoo. The sea eagle. The eagle flies high and symbolizes power, courage, and freedom. Spirituality and transcendence, too."

"I'm not such a spiritual guy."

"Your alter ego, Kalti, is."

"He's not my alter ego," he said automatically. People were always asking if Kalti was really him, and the answer was no.

"If a writer chooses to write about one character over and over, rather than write different books about different kinds of people, I figure that character must resonate with him." She raised her brows in a challenge. "He identifies with his protagonist, and the protagonist probably manifests a lot of his creator's qualities. Or ones the author wishes he had."

A novelist *wrote*. Or at least Damien did. "You're sure you're a sociologist, not a literary critic?"

"Fine. Back to the eagle. He's *supposed* to have excellent vision and insight, as in 'eagle-eyed.' I guess some eagles are better at that than others, or maybe having only one-quarter eagle blood has dimmed the power."

He snorted, and finished off his mai tai.

She chuckled and went on. "The eagle faces challenges, is brave, versatile and patient, and he survives. Maybe your eagle blood gives you some of the flexibility your dragon lacks."

"You don't believe this stuff, do you, Prof? You being an academic and all."

Her brows drew together. "I don't know. My dad's a strong advocate of hard science. He'd say, nothing exists unless there's objective evidence of it. But talking to Canadian and American First Nations people and the Indigenous Australians . . . Things happen that don't have an easy scientific explanation."

He leaned forward, nodding. "I saw that when I visited my Aboriginal relatives. For example, a man broke his arm so badly it was all twisted around, with the bone sticking through the skin. I figured he needed to get to a doctor or he might lose the whole arm. But they wrapped it up and the *karadji*—healer—performed a ritual and communed with the spirits, and within two or three days the man was lifting his little boy with that arm. Seemed to me, it healed like magic. Way faster than Western medicine could have done it. I still don't know what to make of it."

She nodded. "Of course there's the explanation that if people believe in something, reality can be affected. That may be what happens with a healing ritual or a spiritual experience. On the other hand, as much as there's no concrete proof that spirit ancestors and totem animals do exist, there's no concrete proof they don't."

"Well, Prof, you've surprised me. I'd have expected you to be more hard line."

The waitress arrived with their lunches. Sizable helpings, and the food looked great. "Thanks," Damien said. "And I'll have another mai tai. Theresa, want another drink?"

"Why not?"

After what she'd said about being so hungry, he'd figured she would dive immediately into her meal, but instead she gazed at him thoughtfully.

"Damien, you said your Aboriginal relatives think your books exploit your heritage and their beliefs. But you put the spirits in your stories not to make the books sell, but to honor the possibility that the spirits exist. Right?"

"Er . . . Honestly, for me writing isn't such a deliberate, conscious process. The first thing I had was Kalti, and I knew—don't know how—he was Aboriginal. So of course he had a totem, and I guess it was the sea eagle because that's the one I know best."

The waitress returned with fresh drinks and he nodded his thanks before going on. "I didn't know if I'd ever sell the book. I'd written two before, and got a pile of rejections. But when I started out with Kalti, he really came to life, and I just typed what I saw, and what he told me. The ancestor spirits were *there*. It's not something I planned."

"Interesting. You're intuitive, spontaneous." She wrinkled her nose. "The opposite of me. I'm analytical. Can't do anything without developing a project plan or at least making a list."

He held out his glass to her. "And we've both done pretty damned well for ourselves."

"That's true." She clicked her glass to his. "Now, let's eat. Did I mention, *hours* ago, that I'm starving?"

He watched her dig into her fish, which was topped with toasted almonds and served with rice and sea asparagus, then picked up one of his popcorn shrimp and bit into it. It was great, the shrimp fresh and succulent, the batter crisp and tasting of coconut. Next he tried a french fry, which was also delicious, just the right combination of soft potato, oil-crisped skin, and salt.

"Want a shrimp?" He speared one with his fork and extended it across the table.

Theresa took a nibble off the end. "Good, but I like mine better. I'll steal one of your fries, though, if that's okay."

"I don't think it's stealing if you ask. Help yourself."

She offered him a bite of her fish, then they both agreed they preferred their own dishes and ate hungrily. Every once in a while, her hand darted across to poach one of his fries.

As they ate, they talked about what they'd do after lunch, and she agreed they had to walk Waikiki Beach. He checked his watch. "It's after two, and I have to be at the bookstore around six thirty. I should be finished by eight, eight thirty. What say we have dinner after that, since we're having such a late lunch?"

"Sounds good. Maybe I should buy something a bit more dressy for dinner."

"I'm sure shorts are okay, but suit yourself." He paused, slightly nervous. "Sorry that I've got some business to do."

She glanced down, fiddled with the paper umbrella from her drink. "I could, uh, grade exams while you're gone." Avoiding his eyes. Not wanting to come right out and say she didn't want to come to his bookstore thing? And why would she, since she disapproved of his writing?

He told himself he wasn't disappointed. Besides, it might prove to be one of those events where not a soul showed up.

All the same, it would be rude not to invite her. "Or you could come along with me."

She lifted her head and studied his face, expression neutral. "Are you asking to be polite, or because you want me there? Either's okay. I mean, I can understand, after the way I insulted your books . . ."

"It's not that. Remember what I said, about sometimes the only one who talks to you is a person asking for directions to the loo?"

"Hmm." Her lips curved. "Then I guess I should come, so you'll at least have one person to talk to. Oh, I could pretend I don't know you, and gush about how you're my favorite author."

He chuckled. "Nah, you don't have to lie for me." Then he reached over to touch her hand. "But it'd be great if you came."

"Then I will," she said matter-of-factly, freeing her hand and pinching another fry. "But I'm definitely buying a dress."

"You could wear the sarong and bikini top," he joked.

"You never give up, do you?"

"Not on a good idea."

When they finished their meals, the waitress asked if they wanted dessert. "The mud pie is the best," she said. "Kona coffee ice cream, a chocolate wafer crust, and chocolate sauce with a hint of espresso in it. Who can resist?"

Theresa groaned. "That sounds lovely, but I'm too full."

"Nothing, thanks," he told the waitress, then when she'd gone he said to Theresa, "Later, when we've walked and digested, I bet we can find ice cream cones."

The bill arrived and, with minimal argument, Theresa let him pay it. Then she said, "I know you want to get out on the beach, but would you mind if I stopped to get a dress? I promise, I'll pick the first one that's halfway decent, and not try on a dozen."

"Oh please, not *decent*."

He let her drag him through one shop where she didn't see a single thing she liked, then into another that met with her approval. She made him plunk his arse in a chair near the door, saying, "Wait here. I don't need editorial comment."

It wasn't much more than five minutes before she returned, carting another bag.

"Hey, you're not going to show me?"

Her grin was mischievous. "You'll have to wait. Besides, isn't it beach time?"

Oh yeah, he wanted to stick his toes in the ocean.

However, when they were back in their hotel room and she emerged from the loo, his body rapidly came up with a different priority. "Oh man, look at you."

She still had the plumeria blossom in her hair and she wore the green bikini top, which was classy, sexy, and set off her terrific body and pretty coloring. The green matched one of the shades in the knee-length sarong she'd wrapped around herself. Damien liked sarongs. They were feminine and enticing, highlighting a woman's curvy hips and slim waist, showcasing her legs. Making a guy imagine what lay beneath.

The bottom of that green bikini.

His cock stirred inside his board shorts, which were the only clothing he wore, and he reached for the sarong fabric she'd tied at her waist. "You're just asking to be unwrapped."

She darted away. "The beach?"

He groaned, released her, and willed his cock to subside. "Yeah, yeah."

"I've slathered on sunscreen and I have my sunglasses. Do I need anything else?"

How refreshing to be with a woman who didn't feel the need to tote a bag full of junk wherever she went. He patted the pocket of his shorts. "I've got the room key and some money. That should do it."

They made their way down to the courtyard, an oasis of interestingly shaped pools surrounded by ceramic tile, lush green vegetation, and bright tropical flowers. Most of the lounge chairs by the pools and the seats at umbrella-shaded tables were occupied, the guests sipping fancy drinks or reading paperback novels.

Damien could never stop himself from scanning the covers of people's books. There'd been a couple times when he'd been in a coffee shop or airport and seen someone reading a Kalti Brown novel. Of course he knew his sales stats—or as accurate a picture as royalty statements could give—but seeing real live human beings engrossed in his books was a high.

And so was stepping out the gate that guarded the pool area, and onto the pale sand of Waikiki. He caught Theresa's hand and hustled her, laughing, through a half dozen tourists who were strolling along the beach, and down to the edge of the ocean. There, past the burning heat of the dry sand, he kicked off his sandals and she did the same. He gathered up both pairs and hooked the fingers of his free hand through the straps.

Then he stepped into the water, pulling her along with him. It was warm, the gentle waves rippling over their feet and onto the sand. Around them, toddlers played in the shallows, older kids squealed as they jumped around and dove through waves, and farther out, adults swam. He wanted to be out there, knifing through the water. "Are you a swimmer?" he asked Theresa hopefully.

She shook her head. "Not much of a one. It was never a priority."

He knew that if he asked, she'd sit on the beach and wait while he went for a swim, but he got lots of chances to swim back in Australia. Right now, he'd rather be with her. "Let's walk." He turned in the direction of Diamond Head and they started out, him walking in the water, kicking it up from time to time just for the heck of it, her on the firmly packed damp sand above the waterline.

"This is nice," she said. "I've never done this before, even though I've stayed in Honolulu several times."

He wondered if, the next time she overnighted here, she'd come down and walk the beach and think of him. Or maybe, the next time she'd be with some other guy. Or she'd come alone and some guy would hit on her—like the ones who watched with hungry eyes as she strolled, seemingly unaware of their admiring gazes.

Feeling possessive, he let go her hand and instead wrapped his arm around her, pulling her close to his side. She smiled up at him and reciprocated, her slim arm circling his waist, thumb hooking into the pocket of his shorts.

As they strolled, he felt the shift and play of her muscles under her silky skin, and had to fight against his body's response. Sweet torture. But he wouldn't trade a moment of it.

They paused to watch surfers trying to catch some wimpy waves, and tourists in an outrigger canoe, then again to admire the sand castle a little boy and girl were building. The boy trotted back and forth, digging up pailfuls of wet sand and plunking them down where the girl pointed, then the girl did the fine work of smoothing everything into place, following a design that existed in her mind.

"Nice teamwork," Theresa said. "Brains and brawn."

"Just like you and me."

She tipped her sunglasses down her nose and slanted him a glance over the top. "Oh, I think you might have a brain or two in that pretty head of yours."

They chatted easily as they strolled, mostly commenting on what was going on around them. Damien could've walked for miles, enjoying the interplay of the sun's heat and the freshness of the ocean breeze. The soft abrasion of sand on the soles of his feet, the tiny waves tickling his toes. The scent of sunscreen and ocean. Mostly, the woman whose body moved beside his, her sarong brushing his legs.

"How about taking off the sarong?" he asked when they neared the end of the beach, where there were fewer people.

She hesitated, then untied the knot at her waist and unwrapped the fabric.

The bikini bottom was brief, tied with strings at the sides. "Oh yeah, that's nice." He drank in the sight. Theresa was perfect with her golden skin, toned body, soft curves, sparkling eyes.

They turned back to retrace their steps. He admired her slim waist and the feminine flare of her hips, undulating seductively as she strolled along the water-packed sand. "You're making me horny, beach girl."

"You're not the only one. You don't look half bad in those shorts, surfer boy."

"Wanna fool around?" He pinched her arse.

She swatted his hand. "Damien! Not on a public beach."

"Just kidding." But he filed the idea away. Maybe after dinner they could find a deserted strip of sand. "But there's a hotel room waiting for us."

"Something to look forward to."

It was true. Though he wanted to make love to Theresa again, he was in no big hurry. This was so damned perfect. Sun, sand, breeze, ocean, all shared with a vibrant woman who totally turned him on. A woman who was sexy, responsive, fun in bed. Thank God for the number of orgasms he'd already had with her, or his cock would be tenting his shorts right now.

"It's a pretty beach," she said. "I'm trying to imagine what it looked like before the hotels and stores and tourists."

"You been up to Queensland, seen some of the beaches there?" he asked.

"I haven't been to the beaches. Are they nice?"

"Most beautiful ones in the world," he boasted.

"Mmm, and of course you've seen all the others so you can compare."

"Nah. But nothing could beat them. And some are quite undeveloped." He thought of his cottage at Palm Cove, with the beach stretched out in front in both directions. Miles of clean near-white sand with only a few people. Usually he went for a run in the morning to wake up, and again in the evening to clear his head and unwind before bed. When he needed to work out a story idea, he'd walk for miles, go for a long swim, or just flake out in the sun.

He imagined strolling that beach with Theresa. Going back to his place and making love while the wooden ceiling fan stirred the air that drifted in the open windows. Then lighting the barbie and grilling fresh bugs, washing them down with a bottle of Lenton Brae Sauv Blanc. The cottage was a place where he could work productively and also relax. Maybe she could, too.

Since he'd met Theresa, he'd been living in the moment. Doing his best to charm his pretty seatmate, realizing how much fun she was, inviting her to stay over in Honolulu. He hadn't thought past tomorrow morning. Until now.

They both lived in Sydney. She'd be heading back after her sister's wedding and he'd be returning when his book tour wrapped up. They could hook up again, hang out, date. Be lovers. Have fun together. If she wanted to.

The prof seemed devoted to her work. It didn't sound like she took much time off. But maybe that was because she hadn't met a guy who made her want to.

Was he just a temporary diversion, or might he hold a bigger place in her life? He was coming to hope for the latter.

"Do you always read the same passage?" Her voice broke into his thoughts.

It took him a moment to figure out what she meant. "At signings? Usually. People's eyes can glaze over quickly, so I choose something that's less than five minutes. From near the beginning of the book."

"The goal being to hook them into buying the book?"

"There you go. But also, to avoid spoilers. And give them a taste of my writing. If it's not to their taste—" He squeezed her waist. "Like, if it's too *glib* for them, or too violent, or whatever, then they shouldn't buy the book. I don't want that kind of sale, where the reader's dissatisfied. And maybe tells other people my writing sucks."

"That makes sense."

As they walked on, he wondered if he should sound her out about seeing each other back in Australia. Nah, he didn't want to rush her. "Hey, Tezzie, feel like something sweet?"

"Would that be you?"

"Ice cream as an appetizer and me for dessert."

11

Preceding Damien into our room, I thought that the day so far had been one treat after another. The last being my passionfruit gelato and his chocolate macadamia nut ice cream cones, which had melted faster than we could lick them. Hands and mouth sticky with gelato, body glossed with sunscreen and sweat, the promise of sex ripe in the air, I said, "I need a shower."

"That's what? The third today? I think we should be good greenies and conserve water this time."

A shared shower. Something I'd never done. Privacy had always been a big thing for me. But today, knowing I was with a man who liked my body, I felt confident enough to say, "By all means, let's go green."

When we'd reached the hotel grounds, I had tied the sarong around my waist again. Now, in the hotel bathroom, Damien untied it. It dropped to the floor and my gaze followed it. Staring at that pile of flowered fabric, I turned and offered him my back. He untied the strings of my bikini top and it too fell away.

"Now that's pretty," he said.

I lifted my gaze and realized what he was seeing. My almost-naked back and then, reflected in the mirror, my front view. Skin flushed from the sun and breeze, breasts pale in comparison except for the pinky-brown areolae and rosy budded nipples. My cheeks were pink too, my hair tousled. I pulled the plumeria blossom from my hair and set it on the counter.

Then I looked past my own image to Damien's reflection, and the heat in his eyes. He hooked his hand into the waistband of the board shorts that hung low on his hips, and shoved them down, leaving him naked. With a cock that was, without either of us touching it, growing and lifting its head.

He reached out to pull the string tie at one side of my bikini bottom. It thwarted him.

"I knotted the bow," I confessed. For me, it took guts to walk down a beach in a bikini. I sure hadn't been willing to risk a bow coming loose and the bottom falling off.

He chuckled and tried again, untying first the knot and then the bow. One side was all it took. Still tied together on the other side, the two scraps of fabric fell loose. I parted my legs and the suit tumbled to the floor.

Damien's eyes gleamed. "You have one fine arse for a desk-bound professor."

"You give such sweet compliments." All the same, his words and expression made my breath hitch, as did the sight of his now-erect cock. My sex throbbed in recognition, and hunger and moisture gathered between my legs.

He stepped forward to press his front against my back, trapping his erection between us so it rose between the cheeks of my behind. He reached around to cup my breasts, then rested his chin on the top of my head and stared into the mirror.

I stared too. His larger body framed mine, his skin so dark in comparison. He was so much *more* than I—his hair midnight black, his arms big and strong and dark as they crossed my honey-gold skin—and yet we complemented each other. I looked slim, almost delicate. Subtle in line and coloring. And he looked bold. This was what male and female were supposed to look like together.

The reflection, as much as the feel of his rigid cock, the tease of his thumbs stroking my nipples, was a total turn-on. My inner thighs were damp, my sex hungry for his touch.

He let go of one of my breasts and I watched his hand drift down, stroke over my abdomen, drift through the auburn curls of pubic hair, and I tensed in pleasant anticipation. Then, with his palm cradling my mound, he slid his fingers between my legs.

I sighed with relief and need, pressing against him, my body asking for more. Watching my pale hands move across his dark skin, I caressed his arms, feeling the soft hairs, the firmness of muscle under his skin. My hands were sticky from melted gelato, my skin was sticky with sunscreen and perspiration, my crotch was sticky with sex juices. I should have wanted to climb into the shower, but I didn't.

I wanted Damien to climb into me. With one hand I reached back, between our bodies, and gripped the pulsing heat of his shaft.

His fingers stroked my labia, then between, and now a couple slid inside my channel and began to pump slowly in and out.

"Oh, yes." My thighs tightened and internal muscles gripped him, heightening the delicious sensation.

"So tight and wet, Tezzie," he murmured, breath tickling my ear.

Following the same pumping rhythm as his fingers, I stroked up and down his cock.

"Oh, yeah, that's good." He began to lick my ear, circling around, nibbling the rim, and I arched back to give him better access.

Then—"No!" I pulled my head away. "Sunscreen."

"I forgot. They should make edible sunscreen."

"I wish they did."

"What do you want?" he asked, fingers still working inside me, making it hard for me to concentrate on anything but his touch. "Sex in the shower? Or here? Now, like this?"

"Like . . . ?" My hand stilled on his shaft. What did he have in mind?

"Lean forward. Brace yourself against the counter."

At the thought, arousal gushed around his fingers, dripping onto my inner thighs. I let go of his cock and he eased his fingers out of me as I leaned toward the counter, gripping the edges with both hands, bowing my body so my bottom thrust toward him. I bent my head, closing my eyes, now feeling too exposed and self-conscious to look in the mirror.

I heard a tearing sound, a condom wrapper. He nudged my legs farther apart. Again his hand settled between them, opening me, then the head of his cock probed my entrance, where it felt like every sensitized cell was reaching out to him crying "yes." I tilted my backside a bit more, finding a better angle, and he slipped into me. Just a little way.

Then his hands were on my hips, bracing him the way I was braced against the counter, and he began to thrust gently. Sliding in another inch, then back out, then in again, and each slide brought new and wonderful sensations. His balls slapped softly against me each time he thrust.

Slip, slide, I was getting wetter. I became aware of the noises our bodies made together: a damp, sucking sound, accompanied by pants and whimpers. We smelled ripe and raw, of sweat and arousal, an earthy odor. The sounds, the scents, were animal. Primitive.

"Look," Damien urged, and slowly I raised my head.

His gaze met mine in the mirror. Staring over my right shoulder, his face was rigid with concentration, his cheeks flushed and eyes burning with silvery fire.

I glanced at my own face—noting eyes wide with surprise, embarrassment—then quickly looked away. Instead, I watched the way we moved together. My body rising and falling as I matched his strokes, thrusting back against him each time he plunged into me. My arms were taut but my breasts bounced softly. Between my legs, just before the bottom of the mirror cut off my view, I could see his cock as it entered me.

I bent lower, taking all my weight on one forearm, and stretched the other arm between my legs. Reached back to caress the slippery base of his shaft where it emerged from my body, coated with my juices. To stroke him each time he slid out, then let go when he surged back in.

I watched our bodies where they joined, as they joined. Seeing what we were doing at the same time I felt it. It was messy, elemental. His pulsing, driving heat filling me, withdrawing, filling me again. My hands gripping him, letting go, brushing his balls, bumping against my clit. Grasping and fumbling and stroking and rubbing. It was hard to separate the sensations, to know which he was creating and which came from my own hand, but it didn't matter, everything felt so amazing.

And now I felt that preclimax sensation, that sense of something inside me coiling tight, building to the bursting point, a sweet ache that climbed higher until I didn't know how I could stand it any more.

He changed angle slightly and now he was hitting that incredibly sensitive, magical spot inside me, the same one his fingers had found on the plane. "Damien, oh yes!" The coil of tension shattered and unwound in pulsing waves that made me cry out.

He groaned, "God, Tezzie," and surged hard, fast, then exploded inside me so forcefully that I climaxed again before the ripples of the first orgasm had faded away.

Our bodies rocked together, then slowly we disengaged from each other, still breathing hard. Damien peeled off the condom, flushed it away, then studied me, shaking his head. "Man, that was something."

"It was." I realized he must have found my G-spot. Territory no other man, or even my own seeking fingers, had managed to locate before.

"Here I had plans for a slow, sensual shower," he said, "soaping you all over."

Mmm, that sounded good. "We still need to shower."

"Then let's get going. Can't be late for the signing."

He turned on the tap, adjusted the temperature, and stepped in. "Come on in, the water's great."

I joined him and ducked under the spray, letting it hit the top of my head and run down both sides of my sun-kissed body, enjoying the freshness against my sticky skin.

When I stepped back from under the spray, he squeezed a dollop of shampoo onto one hand and rubbed his palms together to spread it evenly, releasing the scent of rosemary into the moist air. Facing me, he ran his hands over my hair to spread the shampoo, then began to rub with his fingertips. His touch was lighter than when he'd worked the tension knots out on the plane, somewhere between a caress and a massage. After he'd lathered my hair, his fingers continued down my neck, easing out any remaining kinks.

"Feels so good," I murmured.

He guided me back into the spray and rinsed my hair, taking care no shampoo ran down my face. Then he lathered fancy soap onto a washcloth and rubbed the cloth over my skin in gentle circles, starting at my shoulders and working down my back.

Feeling almost drunk from the combination of sunshine, fresh air, and sex, I stood, swaying a little, luxuriating in his attention.

He finished my back, began on my front. My nipples hardened under the gentle abrasion and it seemed he paid particular attention to them. "So pretty and pink," he said, and I looked down to see how rosy and pert they looked, poking out from a froth of soap bubbles.

When he slid the washcloth lower, then between my legs where it felt abrasive, I moaned.

He stopped immediately. "Are you sore?"

"A little. I'm not used to, uh, this much sex in a day." Or any sex, for that matter, unless it came from my own hand.

"Sorry if I hurt you."

"I didn't feel it when we were—" I stopped, not knowing whether to call it having sex or making love. "But now I'm a bit sensitive."

He replaced the washcloth with his own soapy hand, gliding over my skin with the lightest touch. "Better?"

"Yes." In fact, if he kept it up, it would be arousing.

But he quickly moved away from the sensitive areas and picked up the washcloth again, stroking it down my thighs.

When he'd finished washing me, I stood under the spray to rinse off, then took the cloth. "It's my turn."

"Much as I'd like that, we'd better not. It'd be too much of a turn-on and you're in no shape to . . ." He winked suggestively.

"Hands work, too," I said, feeling bold. "If you'll recall from last night on the plane."

"Oh yeah, I definitely remember. But we're running out of time. Let's take a rain check."

I did want to primp a bit before going along to the signing as his . . . whatever. Date? In fact, when I'd done my private shopping earlier in the afternoon, I'd not only bought a dress, shoes, and a shawl, but also mascara, eye shadow, and lip gloss.

So I left Damien in the shower and dried off as he whistled "Waltzing Matilda" off-key. This reminded me of being married, sharing the bathroom with someone.

Although, come to think of it, when Jeffrey and I had been married, I'd been quick to scurry into a dressing gown. Yes, he'd told me I was beautiful, but I'd still felt self-conscious, thought of myself as plain. He'd never made me *feel* attractive.

And Damien, who could have his pick of pretty much every single woman in Australia, not to mention a number of married ones, did make me feel that way. I found myself humming "Waltzing Matilda" along with him, no more in tune than he, as I rubbed lotion into my skin.

He came out of the shower and toweled off, then, occupying mirror space side by side, he shaved while I applied light makeup. Then I kicked him out of the bathroom while I got dressed.

First, the new underwear. Though I normally wore boy-brief panties and plain cotton bras, this time I'd indulged in some fun, feminine items. Now I put on a peach underwire bra and thong made of satiny soft cotton with an eyelet pattern. And then the dress I'd chosen. It was a formfitting sundress with a scooped neck and buttons all the way down the front, the skirt ending several inches above my knees. I'd studied various tropical patterns, then decided to go with classic black, which made the outfit seem a bit dressy without being too formal.

Stepping into medium-heeled black sandals, I studied my reflection. When had I last bared so much skin? I bit my lip. Why hadn't I thought to ask Damien what he'd be wearing, and what he considered appropriate for a book signing? Cautiously I emerged from the bathroom.

He was out on the lanai, but stepped inside when he heard my heels clack on the tile floor. In a black short-sleeved cotton shirt tucked into khakis, his longish black hair damp and gleaming, he looked casually elegant.

His eyes widened in appreciation. "Wow. That may even be sexier than the sarong."

"You look great, too. We even match. I'm glad I went for black rather than tropical."

He strode toward me and clasped my shoulders. "You know those buttons are gonna drive me crazy."

I gave a self-satisfied grin. Yes, I'd hoped he would imagine undoing them. "You never did see what I bought at the lingerie shop."

He groaned. "You're wicked, Tezzie."

Not only had no one ever called me wicked before, I'd never even imagined such a thing. But damn, it felt good.

He turned me away from him and gave me a light slap on the bottom. "Let's go before I succumb to the lure of those buttons."

Chuckling, I picked up my purse and the inexpensive but pretty shawl—gauzy black shot through with gold and silver threads—I'd purchased. "I'm ready. How far is the bookstore?"

"Only a few blocks. Should we call a cab?"

I rarely wore heels, but these shoes were comfortable. "Let's walk."

As we left the room, I noticed he'd slung his carry-on bag over his shoulder. "What are you bringing?"

"Bookmarks and pens to hand out. A sign-up book for the e-newsletter my assistant sends out each month. And my laptop computer. It has trailers for this book and my next one."

"Trailers?"

"Short videos. Like for a movie or TV show."

"People do trailers for novels?" I asked as we stepped into the elevator.

He shook his head tolerantly. "Sure can tell you're not into fiction. Yeah, trailers have been around for years now. They're on MySpace, YouTube, author Web sites, publisher sites, review sites. Some bookstores will play them."

"You don't make them yourself, do you?"

"I work with a designer. We discuss content, visuals, sound, and he makes it happen. We have a good time. He's Aboriginal Australian and has fun with special effects for the spirits."

"I'm learning a lot. It's more complicated than with academic texts. We don't do book tours, make trailers, and so on."

We strolled through the lobby and I thought how noisy—how "look at me"—my high-heeled shoes were, clicking on the tile. But for once, I didn't mind being looked at. I slipped my hand through the crook of Damien's arm, straightened my back, held my head up proudly. Tonight, I was with one very sexy man, and looked as if I belonged here.

Outside the hotel, late afternoon was fading into evening. The sun was still out, but lower in the sky. The streets were busy, clogged with traffic and tourists, some people heading back to hotels and others starting out for drinks and dinner.

I saw several people noticing us. We stood out in our simple clothing, a bit more elegant than the typical summer garb. Perhaps people thought we were going to some fancy club. Maybe they even thought we were celebrities. And in fact Damien was, at least in Australia.

When we arrived at the store, he stared into the window and gave a rueful laugh. "Well, they did get books. Just an awful lot of them."

The center of the big display window was filled with an elaborate construction of several dozen copies of *Wild Fire*, with a poster advertising tonight's event. "That's good, right?" I asked. "They must think the book's going to sell well."

"Mmm. Or the publicist sold them a bill of goods, and they're going to be pissed when no one shows up." He put his hand over mine and gripped tight. "Here goes."

Was he actually nervous? This hot, sexy, amazing man was nervous? How very . . . sweet. I squeezed his hand in return. "If people don't show up, it's their loss." And I meant it. I might wish he wrote more serious books, but I knew both he and his writing were compelling.

"Thanks, Tezzie."

Our eyes met for a long, silent moment, then hand in hand we walked into the store.

A middle-aged Caucasian woman with deeply tanned skin and obviously dyed blond hair rushed up. "You're Damien Black. I've been watching for you. I'm Marietta Harper, the events organizer. This is such a thrill."

Damien shook her hand. "Marietta, it's me who's thrilled. This is my first event in Hawaii. My first time here, in fact. What a terrific place, and thanks so much for that super display in the window."

I swallowed a smile. Whatever happened tonight, Damien would handle it brilliantly.

Despite her tan, the woman managed to blush. "My pleasure. We've had posters up for the last week, we've run ads in the papers, and it's been in the events handout that goes in every customer's shopping bag."

"Couldn't ask for more. Except, of course, that a few people pay attention and show up."

The two of them exchanged a knowing glance. "Wish I could guarantee it," she said. "You certainly deserve it, but the truth is, it's unpredictable. We're competing with the beach, not to mention mai tais and pupus."

"Pupus?"

"Appetizers. Anyhow, you know how it is in the publishing business these days. So many people are into electronic media rather than good old-fashioned books. And prices are high, especially for hardcover."

"There's more value in a hardcover book that you can read over and over," I said, "than in a few fancy drinks."

"Dear, you don't have to convince me," she said fervently, then gazed at me curiously.

"Sorry," Damien said. "Marietta, this is my friend, Theresa Fallon."

Friend. That was a nice word. And I did feel as if we'd become friends. Maybe that was crazy. Our relationship had started out as a fling, but now, to me, it felt like more.

I didn't have time to pursue that train of thought because she was pumping my hand warmly. Then she said to Damien, "Congratulations on your placement on the *New York Times* bestseller list."

"Thanks. Yeah, I'm pleased."

So he'd hit a U.S. bestseller list as well. He hadn't mentioned that to me. When I'd first met him, I'd thought he had a swollen head, but I'd since learned otherwise.

Marietta went on. "Let me show you the setup. I hope I've thought of everything, but be sure and let me know if there's anything else you need."

We followed her as she said, "For fiction events, we put the speaker's table and the chairs right at the entrance to the fiction section so people can't miss it."

There was a table with a chair behind it and a couple dozen chairs in front. I listened with interest as Marietta and Damien discussed the setup and format for the event. Then she said, "When you're nearing the end, staff will put a table over there—" she pointed—"and pull some of the books from the window. People can bring them over to you to sign."

The muscles in Damien's throat worked. "Right."

Was he wondering if anyone would be buying? At least Marietta's plan would allow the staff to determine how many books to bring, depending on the size of the audience. I could imagine how embarrassing it would be if there were five dozen books stacked there, and only three people in the audience. I'd never have the guts to do this sort of thing.

Damien reached into his bag. "Is it okay to hand out bookmarks?"

"That's great. I'll have one of the staff do it as people come in."

"Thanks." He handed her a bundle, then pulled out his computer. "I have book trailers for all my books. Maybe your staff could set the computer up and run them for folks?"

"Good idea. Want to boot it up and show me how to access them?"

"Sure." The two of them bent over the computer, then Marietta took it away and I saw her conferring with two young salespeople.

I glanced at my watch. Ten minutes to the seven o'clock start time. A few people were wandering around, looking interested but uncommitted.

Marietta bustled over to them. "Here to see Mr. Black? You're in for a treat. I just finished *Wild Fire* myself, and let me tell you, I haven't read anything so exciting in ages. Come in and get comfy." The woman was upbeat without being pushy, and the chairs began to fill.

"I don't think they're all looking for the bathroom," I murmured to Damien.

"Marietta's done a great job."

"Mmm. I'm sure that's it. Your books couldn't possibly have anything to do with it."

He chuckled. "Seems there's a few folks who like that glib, superficial shit."

I poked him in the ribs with my elbow. Then I gazed at him, feeling nervous, excited, proud. In a day, I'd come to care for this man. It would be a troubling thought, if I wanted to dwell on it. Which I didn't. "I'm going to find a seat before they're all taken. Good luck."

"Thanks." He brushed my cheek lightly, almost as if he was stroking a good-luck charm. "I'm glad you're here, Tezzie."

I chose a chair near the back, wanting Damien's fans to get the best seats and also curious to observe the audience. I'd picked up a handful of bookmarks and now studied one, seeing that the design was simple, eye-catching, and effective. One side featured *Wild Fire*; the other had covers and blurbs for his previous Kalti Brown books and the next one in the series.

When about two-thirds of the chairs were filled, Marietta stepped to the front and cleared her throat. "Welcome, everyone. We have a real treat in store for us. Damien Black is one of Australia's hottest authors—and, as you can see, ladies, I do mean *hot*."

Several women chuckled and Damien, who'd taken the seat behind the table, gave his sexy grin. He truly did look hot, with his long, shiny black hair, his strong and slightly exotic features, the black shirt setting off his dark skin and hair, the white flash of his smile.

"He's been voted one of Australia's ten sexiest bachelors, but on top of that he's a very accomplished writer. His first two books, *Thunder Struck* and *Killer Wave*—" she took them off the table and held them up—"have hit the bestseller lists in Australia, and now his new release, *Wild Fire*, has done the same, not to mention hitting the *New York Times* list."

She held up the new book. "He'll be reading tonight from *Wild Fire*—and let me tell you, it's a page-turner—and he'll also talk to us about his writing, and answer questions. Then, of course, he'll sign the books that I know you're going to want to buy. So, because you didn't come here to listen to me, I'll turn things over to Damien Black." She stepped to the side.

There was a polite ripple of applause as Damien stood and came from behind the table. "Thanks, Marietta." He hiked one butt cheek up on the table, looking casual, relaxed, and friendly. "And thanks to all of you for forgoing sunset on that amazing beach, not to mention a round of mai tais and pupus, to come and visit with me. I hope I'll make it worth your while." Again he grinned, and again a few people laughed.

The man was a quick study, picking up what Marietta had

said, even the word pupus that he hadn't known before, and incorporating it.

"First, I'd like to tell you a bit about what I write. In Oz they say my books are genre-benders. Stores aren't sure whether to shelve them as mystery, paranormal, or thrillers. You've probably all noticed this trend in the publishing world. Used to be, there were clear boundaries in commercial fiction. A book was a mystery, sci fi, a romance, a thriller. It was shelved in a particular section and the cover art told you if the book was going to be a cozy mystery or a hard-boiled one, a historical romance or a sweet contemporary or a sexy one. When you picked up a book, you knew what you were getting. Right?"

Heads had begun to nod even before he got to the question at the end.

"These days it can be confusing because there's more selection. We still have classic genre books, but we have genre-benders as well. Paranormal cozies, erotic historical romances. Erotic paranormal historical interracial romantic suspense—and whew, that's a mouthful!"

More chuckles. Clearly, Damien knew what he was talking about, and his audience was relating. Not only to his words, also to him as a person. As a teacher myself, I gave him full points for presentation. He was more effective than many of my colleagues, speaking without notes, his voice full of energy and loud enough to carry without booming, his face animated as he made eye contact with first one person, then another. Of course, it didn't hurt one bit that he looked gorgeous and had a charismatic personality.

"And it's a more interesting world for readers, right? You sure aren't going to get bored." He caught my eye and winked. "It's more fun for writers, too, because we're not stuck having to conform to rigid guidelines about what's appropriate in a mystery, a romance, sci fi, and so on. We get to write what interests and challenges us.

"Now for me as a reader, I've mostly been into mysteries and thrillers." He grinned. "Typical guy, right? Someone needs to get killed, something needs to get blown up."

Oh, he'd definitely hooked his audience. And as he spoke, people who'd been walking by on their way to the fiction section had stopped to listen, then found seats.

"So, my protagonist, Kalti Brown, is a cop. He's challenged to solve some pretty nasty crimes. Now, I'm not a guy who does real well with rules, and it would've been hard for me to write a straight-arrow cop. No surprise that Kalti turned out to be a guy who has some problems with authority."

I grinned to myself. Earlier, Damien had denied that Kalti was his alter ego. Maybe he didn't even realize it himself.

"Somehow I knew he'd be Aboriginal Australian, but I didn't know until I started to write that he has a special connection with the Dreamtime creation spirits and his totem animal. With a spirit world that—" He broke off. "Well, does it exist or doesn't it?"

The audience stared raptly at him. By now, every chair was filled and a few people were standing at the back and along the sides.

"Does any god or spirit exist?" he went on. "Yes, in the minds of the people who believe. But in actual, scientific, measurable reality?" He glanced my way, the hint of a grin tugging at his mouth.

"Paranormal fiction has exploded since the beginning of the twenty-first century. Do vampires, shape-shifters, superheroes with supernatural powers, ghosts, and so on really exist? I doubt anyone cares. They're just having a hell of a good time reading and writing about them."

Damien leaned forward, *Thunder Struck* in his hands. "The heart of a book is the hero. He's got to be strong, larger than life in some ways, but he's got to ring true. Gotta be human.

Have a touch of vulnerability. Readers like to root for the under-dog, right?"

Several people in the audience had leaned forward, too, and heads nodded.

"So here's Kalti. A bright guy, a competent cop, but a bit of a renegade. An Aboriginal Australian, which means he's not au-tomatically one of the gang. It's kind of like being a female cop. You have to work twice as hard to win respect."

I was glad he'd mentioned that point rather than ignoring the discrimination issue. It seemed as if the audience could re-late, too. A number of women were nodding. A few native Hawaiian men as well, and a couple of black men.

"Add to that the fact that Kalti's helpers are supernatural be-ings and he has to keep their existence a secret—and, well, the poor guy's typical workday isn't a walk in the park."

More chuckles.

Damien picked up *Wild Fire*. "Let me give you a taste of Kalti's world."

The audience settled back in their seats, relaxed but atten-tive.

He opened the book close to the beginning and began to read.

"We got another media release." The words, spoken over the phone by Zachary Tennant at the Sydney Morning Herald, *hit Kalti like a roundhouse punch to the gut. He sucked in air, felt a rush of nausea.*

Hell, no, not another. That meant the fire at Dawson Fertilizer hadn't been a one-off, a vendetta, or insurance fraud or accident. Six people had died in that blaze, including the accountant's baby girl.

"You sure it's the same guy," he asked, hoping against hope.

"Looks the same to me. Same format—a press release, printed, generic—reporting the fire. No location, just a blank with 'de-

tails to be provided later.' " Tennant paused. "It gives a time, Detective Brown." His tone told Kalti it was going to be bad.

"Tell me."

"One o'clock tomorrow morning."

He cursed. It was ten at night now. Sheer luck Tennant had found him at work. Except, most of the team had been working overtime on the Dawson case. The fact of that little girl dying— a dad losing both his wife and his only child—hadn't let them sleep.

"Fax it over," he said. "I'll send someone to pick up the original."

"I'm saving space for it in tomorrow's paper." Tennant's voice was soft, full of regret. "Give me a different story to run, would you? A story about how the fire was prevented, the arsonist in jail."

"We'll do our best." But as he hung up, Kalti knew the odds were against them.

"Listen up!" he yelled, letting his anger out. "The Herald got another media release about a fire."

Curses spat into the hot, dry room, a room that stank of overwork and frustration. So far, every lead they'd pursued on the Dawson case had resulted in a dead end.

"John, grab the fax that's coming in," Kalti said, "and everyone gather round." He was the senior of the officers in the room, so he took charge.

When the team had gathered around his desk, he studied the fax. "Looks like the same deal as Dawson. Media release says the fire's timed for one o'clock, so we've only got three hours. You guys, get to work on your computers, figure out where he might target. Pass on leads to the officers on patrol, get them to do drive-bys." Kalti planned on hitting the street himself, to see if his totem sea eagle would appear and guide him.

"Figure the same MO as Dawson?" Al Chan asked.

"That's all we can do," Kalti said. "Which means we're look-

ing for someplace big—lots of property to destroy, a spectacular blaze, maybe chemicals or fuel to ignite. A place that's mostly shut down at night. But not entirely," he added grimly. "It wasn't an accident there were people at the Dawson plant that night. He knew there'd be staff working late, because they always did at the end of the month. This bastard wants to take lives."

12

Damien glanced up and saw his audience had grown. Everyone, including Theresa, looked focused, absorbed.

The power of the written word. *His* written words. Savoring the moment, he bent his head to the book and read on, letting the audience feel Kalti's frustration when his superior officer barged in, took charge, and refused to let Kalti leave the building.

The tension in the room was as much a presence as the hum of the air conditioner, the bitter odor of stale coffee. Along with the others, Kalti tried to work, but his gaze kept going to the clock on the wall. Watching the hands tick toward one o'clock. Powerless.

Shit. Enough. Chained to a computer here, his efforts were futile. On the street, his totem might come to him.

He surged to his feet and headed for the door. "I've got the flu. Gotta go home."

"Damn it, Brown, you get back here!"

He slammed the door to block out his chief's command.

There'd be hell to pay tomorrow, but tonight a sick bastard was targeting innocent people and Kalti had to try to stop him.

No time to wait for the slow old elevator, he pounded down two flights of stairs and threw open the door. For a moment he froze, scenting the air, waiting for guidance.

Yes! A sea eagle swooped down with a fierce, scolding cry, its extended claws barely missing the top of his head.

Kalti raced for his unmarked police car while the eagle swooped again, impatiently. "I'm coming," he yelled as he flung himself into the vehicle.

But in the pit of his stomach he had a sour, sick feeling that told him he was too late.

Damien stopped reading, closed the book, and reached behind himself to put it on the table. The audience—about three dozen people now, including Theresa—watched him intently.

A middle-aged woman in the first row leaned forward and demanded, "Well, what happens? Does he get there in time?"

He grinned. "Ah, that'd be telling. You'll have to read the book if you want to find out. For now, do you have any questions you want to ask?

"Are you Kalti?" an earnest young woman in Goth makeup and clothing, with tattoos up both arms, asked. "Like, do you have Dreamtime spirits helping you?"

He got this question with some regularity. From people who believed, or wanted to believe, that the spirit world really existed. "If I did, it wouldn't have taken me so long to get published."

Laughter greeted his words. Then he went on. "No, I don't have Dreamtime spirits helping me, or not that I'm aware of. As to whether Kalti is me, no, he's a fictional creation."

Three or four hands were waving in the air, and he pointed to a man who asked him about police procedure, and how accurate his books were.

"I have a good friend who's a cop and he tells me what really happens. I bend the truth occasionally, to make for a better story."

"Don't readers get upset," the man asked, "if you're not completely accurate?"

"Sometimes." Damien grinned. "And I remind them this is fiction. You know what, Kalti Brown doesn't actually exist, so why should it be so surprising if I make up some other details?"

He got some more laughter. Then he pointed to a middle-aged woman with curly brown hair.

"I've read your first two books," she said, "and Kalti's dated some women, but things never get serious. When's he going to have a real romance?"

"Same time as all of us." He paused, seeing her frown in puzzlement. "When he meets the right woman." Which just might be in the book he'd started, when he went back and re-worked it. Kalti's new partner was his opposite in many ways, and the two of them struck sparks, but that could make for challenge, fun, great sex. He glanced toward Theresa, saw her smiling as if she was enjoying herself.

He was one lucky bugger that so many people had shown up and seemed interested in his work. Maybe it was juvenile to want to impress his girl, but hell, that's how he felt.

He noted that Marietta, who'd been sitting in the back row, had risen and was helping her staff stack copies of his books on a table.

For the next question, he chose an attractive young Hawaiian woman. He'd seen her walk past when he'd started to speak, then she'd stopped and taken a seat.

"I just got my B.A. and I'll be going to graduate school in sociology," she said in a soft voice. "I've been thinking about a thesis topic, and I was interested when I heard you say about your hero being Aboriginal Australian, and about discrimination and having to work extra hard to prove himself."

"Yes?" Where was she heading with this?

"It would be interesting to compare the experience of Aboriginal Australians with that of Native Hawaiians."

He remembered what the prof had said about the queen with the mellifluous name, and how her people had lost their independence. "Yeah, I think that would be a great topic."

"Do you have any suggestions of where I might start? Like, a few similarities?"

"Uh, I'm afraid I'm not up on Hawaiian history." So much for impressing his girl. He glanced toward Theresa, who was leaning forward, eyes gleaming, mouth open as if words were longing to escape. "But I know someone who could give you a better answer." He beckoned to Theresa. "Come on up, Prof."

Her eyes widened. "I, uh . . ."

"Help me out?"

She rose, looking both eager and uncertain. He watched proudly as she walked toward him, his sexy lover in that tantalizing black dress. When she reached the front, he caught her hand, tugged her closer, then let go. "Folks, this is Dr. Theresa Fallon from the University of Sydney. She specializes in indigenous studies."

A few people clapped and Theresa flushed. He thought it was cute that this woman, who lectured at a university and made presentations at conferences, felt nervous about speaking to his small audience. "Go on," he urged. "Can you give this young woman some ideas?"

"First, yes, I think it's an excellent thesis topic. As for similarities—well, in general terms, colonization of new lands has tended to have similar results in most instances." She stood stiffly, hands clasped in front of her. "Appropriation of resources and especially land, introduction of diseases to which the native population has no resistance, violence, depredation and segregation of indigenous people in a system of reserves. All of course based upon and precipitated by the colonial presumption of innate superiority."

She'd loosened up, her posture more relaxed, her voice confident. Hitting her stride. Unfortunately, interesting as this information was, she was presenting it the wrong way for this forum. People were shifting restlessly.

He touched her arm, stopping her, then whispered in her ear, "It's not a university class. Could you make it a little more folksy?"

Her shoulders rose, tightened again, then she took a deep breath and let it out. "Sorry, I've been lecturing. You can take the professor out of the lecture hall, but it's hard to take the lecture hall out of the professor."

People were smiling; she was winning them back.

"Let me give this another try," she said. "In Australia and in Hawaii, the mentality of the colonizers was that they had discovered new lands. Lands inhabited by creatures that in some ways resembled humans, but were subhuman. Being subhuman, they had no rights. No rights to land or to physical safety."

And now she'd captured her audience.

She stared out at them, expression fierce. "Imagine that tomorrow, some race from outer space invades our world and decides we're all subhuman. Tomorrow, you have no rights. Your houses, your land, will be taken from you. You might be killed. If you're a woman, you might only be raped. Multiple times. Your children will be taken away, to be brainwashed into no longer believing anything you taught them. And quite possibly to be abused."

Damien had stepped back, giving her the stage. Damn, she was something. Pretty and classy and sexy, but smart, impassioned, and effective as well.

"But I'm talking generically. These things have happened to almost every native population of every land that's been colonized. You asked specifically about Hawaii and Australia. To give one example, let's use apologies. In Australia, the Stolen Generations is a term used to refer to the children who were forcibly removed from their families starting in 1869 and continuing for more than a century. After great debate, the government issued an apology, but it took them until 2008—yes, 2008—to do so."

Damien winced, embarrassed at his country's poor record.

"Now to Hawaii," Theresa went on. "It took the U.S. government one hundred years to apologize for overthrowing the Kingdom of Hawaii, and to acknowledge that the Native Hawaiians never legally relinquished their sovereignty over their lands. In Australia, the doctrine of *terra nullius* held that the lands of Australia were vacant when the colonizers arrived. Vacant!"

The young Hawaiian who'd asked the question was nodding, lips parted, looking excited, and the rest of the audience seemed to be engaged, too. Damien could have listened to Theresa for another hour himself, but all the same, he tried to never spend too long on any one question, so others would have their chance.

He touched Theresa's arm again. "Fascinating as this is, some others had their hands up."

"Of course." She gave the girl a warm smile. "If you want, come see me after and I'll give you my e-mail. I can tell you some places to start."

"Cool! Thanks so much."

Damien wanted to put his arm around Theresa, whose face glowed with satisfaction, but instead he just smiled and said, "Thanks, Dr. Fallon."

"My pleasure."

As she returned to her seat, Damien pointed to a man who was waving his hand.

"Where do you get the ideas for your books? Do you worry you'll ever run out of ideas?"

He'd heard this one many times before, gave his usual answer, and moved on to the next question. Marietta held up two fingers to signal it was almost time to wind up. "We have time for one last question."

"When's the next book coming out?"

"*Gale Force* will be out in six months. You can always check my Web site to see what's going on. Or sign up for my electronic newsletter."

Marietta stepped up to the front. "This store has an electronic newsletter, too. Register for it, and we'll be sure to let you know when Damien's next book hits the shelves. Maybe we can even persuade him to come back and talk to us again." She dimpled up at him as the audience clapped enthusiastically. A salesperson clicked a small digital camera.

Then Marietta went on. "We've set up a table over there with *Wild Fire* and Damien's previous titles. He also has trailers for his books, and my staff tell me there are some dazzling special effects. So, let me close off by thanking Damien Black for being here."

After another round of applause, people got up and headed away. Most of them, fortunately, toward the book table. The Hawaiian student made a beeline for Theresa.

Damien put some Kalti Brown pens on the table as giveaways, along with his newsletter sign-up book. Then he took a long drink of water and a couple deep breaths. Thanks to Marietta, the tour had started out on a high.

He hoped Theresa hadn't been bored. Whenever he'd glanced at her, which was often, she'd seemed attentive. Now, though, she'd disappeared. Perhaps she and the student had gone for coffee.

A line was forming in front of him, headed by the woman who'd asked about Kalti's love life. "Want it autographed to you?"

She nodded. "Jean."

He wrote, *To Jean, who believes even a loner like Kalti deserves romance,* and signed his name.

She read the inscription and chuckled. "Thanks."

When she stepped aside to write in the sign-up book, a young woman took her place. "It's for my boyfriend Will's birthday. He's a big fan." She giggled. "So'm I, but this way I get credit for giving him a present, and I also get to read the book."

"Hope you both enjoy it." He handed her the signed book and a couple pens.

The line moved along, and by the time the last person had left, he figured he must have autographed at least thirty copies of *Wild Fire*—some people even buying multiples—and a dozen each of his earlier books. This was much better than he'd hoped for.

When he put down his pen, Marietta bustled up. "Would you mind signing stock before you leave?"

"Love to." Books with "autographed copy" stickers tended to sell better. "Have you seen Theresa?" He hoped she hadn't got fed up and gone back to the hotel.

"She said she was going to wander around the store, then you could find her in the coffee shop. I'm glad you brought her. She was great. So informative and passionate."

"Yeah, she sure was."

The young staffers dumped another two or three dozen books on the table, and he began to sign again. After, he stretched his hand, put away his pen, and stood up.

From his bag he took a box of Kalti Brown pens and a bag of chocolate-covered macadamia nuts, and handed them to Marietta. "A small thanks to you and your staff. I know the nuts are kind of like bringing coals to Newcastle, but they're one of Australia's specialties."

"What a treat. We'll enjoy them. Oh, and I'll e-mail a couple of images to your admin assistant to put up on your Web site."

"Ta." He shook her hand, asked for some restaurant recommendations, then headed off to visit the men's room and hunt down Theresa.

Sure enough, she was in the coffee shop, a half-full glass of something that looked like iced tea on the table beside her, head buried in a book. He wondered if she'd bought a book on Hawaiian history or sociology, or another wedding planning book. Whatever it was, it had sure captured her attention.

She didn't look up as he approached. "Hey, Theresa, ready for some dinner?" He rested his hand on her shoulder, feeling the warm, bare flesh on either side of the strap of her sundress.

She jumped. "Oh! I didn't realize you were there."

"What are you . . . ?" He glanced down at the book. "Well, I'll be damned." It was *Thunder Struck*, his first Kalti book. "You didn't have to do that."

She wrinkled her nose and gave him a rueful grin. "I'd read this book before, a year or so ago, and wanted to give it another go. I admit, when you read that passage, you hooked me. I guess there's nothing wrong with a little pure entertainment from time to time."

"Why'd you get this one, not *Wild Fire*?"

"I wanted to start at the beginning." She reached under the table, pulled up a bookstore bag, and held it open.

Damned if she hadn't bought all of his books. "Okay, that's earned you a dinner out."

Laughing, she came to her feet. "Now, what's this about the *New York Times* bestseller list?"

"Only the extended list, but it's a first for me."

She stretched to give him a quick kiss. "Damien, that's wonderful. And auspicious timing, with you starting your book tour."

He hugged her tight, an armful of warm curves, then reluctantly let go. "You look so damn sexy and that row of buttons is so provocative, I'm tempted to say we should go back to the room and call room service." He dropped a kiss in her hair, smelling rosemary from the shampoo and thinking of a summer garden. "But we've got all night to fool around, so let's have a nice meal by the water, maybe take a moonlight walk on the beach."

"That sounds lovely."

"I asked Marietta for the names of some good restaurants and she said our hotel is one of the best. Want to try it?"

"Sure." She glanced up at him through her eyelashes. "Damien, I was impressed. You did a great job tonight."

He took her hand, squeezed it. "Thanks. The feeling's mutual. We make a good team."

As they walked out of the coffee shop, he discovered the light breeze had completely died down and there was a sultry, sensual quality to the flower-scented air. Weaving his fingers through Theresa's, he said, "I could've been here alone. What a waste."

They strolled hand in hand, not saying much, and he wondered if this was the time to talk to her about the future, back in Sydney. Normally he was confident with women, but he'd never been with one like Theresa before. Not only beautiful, sensual, and fun, but smart and career-minded. She intimidated him a little. And so, he kept quiet.

When they reached the hotel, they went directly to the candle-lit restaurant, where the formally clad maître d' said, "You're in luck. An oceanside table just cleared."

Following him, they crossed the restaurant. Tanned, well-dressed people chatted and laughed, light gleamed off wine-glasses and silverware, and the scents of seafood, garlic, and coconut made his stomach rumble.

A few people looked up as they passed, and several male gazes stayed on Theresa.

"You're turning heads," he told her.

"What? No, that would be you."

"Male heads? Huh-uh. That's you."

With a startled, pleased expression, she glanced around, then flushed. "I think you're right."

"Just remember which guy you came in with."

Her eyes softened. "I don't think that will be a problem."

They reached their table and the maître d' held her chair. Their table was beside a huge window, open to the night air and an ocean sky with a nearly full moon. It was laid with white linen and a green and purple corsage orchid floated in a brandy snifter. Ritzy. Damien was glad he hadn't worn jeans.

He settled into his seat, feeling smug. Here he was, an author with a book on the *New York Times* extended list, the first signing of the American tour behind him—and more successful than he'd dared imagine. With the Honolulu evening on one side, the elegant restaurant on the other, and, best of all, the lovely Theresa across the table in that tantalizing buttoned sundress. Oh yeah, he was riding a high. "We need champagne. That okay with you?"

She nodded. "Yes, we do. It's the right drink for tonight."

She was so amazing. Sometimes their minds were on the same track and sometimes opposite tracks, but always she fascinated him.

He opened the wine list and decided on Roederer Cristal. What the hell, it cost more than he'd make off the royalties from tonight's sales, but this occasion was special. When he gave the order, their waitress's smile widened. "Tonight's a celebration?"

"It is."

When she'd gone, Theresa said, "Cristal? Wow. I mean, I knew the *New York Times* list was important and the signing was a success, but I didn't understand how big all of this was."

"Yeah, it's all great . . ." Hell, what could he say? He wasn't some mushy, romantic kind of guy. But the champagne wasn't only about the bestseller list or the signing, it was about her. "Life's been pretty good since I met you."

"For me, too."

The champagne arrived and the waitress opened and poured it with ceremony, a stream of pale golden bubbles into first Theresa's glass, then his. "I'll leave you for a few minutes, then be back to take your order."

Theresa lifted her glass. "To a wonderful book tour."

Weird schedules, cruddy beds, lonely nights in hotel rooms. Walking into stores always wondering if they'd have his books, if anyone would show up. Slowly he raised his glass.

"May they all be like tonight," she said.

Tonight. Theresa's hand in his as they went into the store. Her attentive face in the audience. Her assistance when the questions got tough. And now, finishing off the evening with her. Looking forward to undoing that row of buttons, one by one, and revealing the lovely, sexy body beneath. No other signing could measure up.

A little bummed, he tried to hide his feelings when he clicked his glass to hers. "Thanks for being here." He lifted the glass to his nose, inhaling a complex mix of fruit, flowers, and nuts. Then he tasted, and the aroma translated into rich, creamy flavors on his tongue.

As that commercial said, there were some things money could buy. A wine like this.

There were other things it couldn't. A great book signing. The company of a woman like Theresa. Ah well, tonight he had both. Mostly, he was a guy who enjoyed the moment and didn't worry about tomorrow, so that was what he'd do. "Let's take a look at the menus."

They read, commented, then he said, "I'm going to go with the grilled steak." It was marinated in soy, ginger, and a hint of lime, and served with garlic mashed potatoes and stir-fried vegetables. "If you don't mind me eating garlic?"

"Not if you don't mind me eating Maui onions. I think I'm going to have two appetizers instead of an entrée. The onion soup and the baked blue crab and rock shrimp. Served at the same time."

After they'd ordered, Damien sat back and reflected on the signing, thinking what he could do better next time. And he realized something that hadn't occurred to him before. Nor to his publisher, agent, or admin assistant. He leaned forward. "Can I ask a favor?"

"I'd guess it was something sexual, but you look unusually serious. What is it?"

"I'm going to get more questions like the one that student asked. Some people in Canada and America are going to be interested in how the situation with Australia's indigenous peoples compares to theirs."

"I'd think so." She tapped her champagne flute thoughtfully, using the pad of her finger, not her nail. "This just occurred to you?"

He shrugged. "Like I said on the plane, I write fiction. I think of the stories, the characters. Not the, uh, sociological issues."

"And historical, economic, political, legal, health, educational, and . . . well, I could go on, but I'm sure you see my point."

Unsettled, he stared at her. "I was going to ask if you could give me a crash course, but you're making it sound like I'd need years of university."

Slowly she shook her head. "No. But Damien, maybe you don't need a crash course. You have another option."

Their waitress brought sliced bread, warm and fragrant, and he offered the basket to Theresa. "Go on. What's the other option?"

She took a slice, buttered it, nibbled a corner. Was she stalling?

He took a slice himself. "It's not like you to hold back, Prof. Come on, sock it to me."

That won him a small grin. "All right. You could simply say what you just told me, that your writing is about stories and characters, not about issues. Say you're at the signing to read them a story and to tell them a bit about your writing process, but not to discuss political issues." She frowned. "Well, maybe that's too heavy-handed. But you're clever, charming, you can find a way to redirect a question and avoid answering it."

Was that a compliment? He took a slug of the fine champagne, wishing it was a shot of rum. "No, that doesn't feel right." Before he met Theresa, before he heard her respond to the Hawaiian student's question and saw the audience's interest, it might have. But now it seemed like a cop-out. "How do I learn what I need to know?"

"We can figure out the most likely questions and work out answers. You already have a fair idea of what's happened—and is happening—with the Indigenous Australians. Yes?"

"Yeah, I read the papers, hear the news." And, because he was a quarter Aboriginal, he noticed items that affected the indigenous population. He was almost reluctant to admit it, because his typical response was to feel lucky he'd been raised white. The problems weren't his. Problems like poverty, alcohol and drugs, inadequate health care, unequal access to jobs . . . Talk about a cop-out.

"Now you need to learn a bit about the situation in Canada and the United States," she said briskly. "You're starting in Vancouver, so you should know that a B.C. case, *Delgamu'ukw*, formed part of the foundation for the Australian High Court's reasoning in *Mabo*."

"Which overturned the doctrine of *terra nullius* and affirmed native title, which led Parliament to enact the Native Title Act."

She nodded, eyes flashing with excitement. "There's a parallel in the Stolen Generations issue, too. In Canada, First Nations kids were removed from their families and stuck in residential schools where they were supposed to, in essence, lose everything that made them Indian and become white. And many of them were abused, physically and sexually. There have been lawsuits against the church and the government. It's a huge issue. And there was an apology too, in 2008, by the prime minister."

"Apologies," he reflected. "They're recognition. Acknowledgment. But they don't fix what's wrong. Like in Australia, the government's had this program and that program, but in the end not much changes. There's talk, but little action."

"Exactly."

Her eyes were fiery in the candlelight, all red earth tones now, the colors of the Outback. Challenging him. He said what he knew she was thinking. "Things don't change because too many people, like me, sit back and don't fight to change them."

Something flashed in her eyes. Surprise that he'd admitted it? Then she ducked her head, tapped her champagne glass thoughtfully.

His breath caught in his throat. Was this where she said that a woman like her, who studied the issues, cared about them, and tried to educate people didn't belong with a superficial arsehole like him?

Theresa's shoulders rose and fell as she took a deep breath, then she folded her hands in her lap and looked across at him. "No one has the right to tell someone else they're not doing enough. That's between a person and his or her conscience. And I think my conscience is telling me I've been hiding behind the, uh, academic façade, as you suggested on the plane. Yes, I make a few students think. Maybe my writing reaches other scholars and impacts their work. But the vast majority of Australia's voters haven't the slightest idea what I'm doing because I don't make the effort to tell them."

Her confession—apology?—touched him. "You could," he said earnestly. "Like tonight when you took off your academic hat and talked to that girl and the rest of the audience. You were damned effective, Theresa. If you did that on TV, people would listen."

Her head started to duck again, but she pulled it upright. "I'm shy when I get outside my comfort zone. But that's not an excuse."

He reached across the table. "Give me your hand."

She lifted one hand from her lap and let him link their fingers.

"Theresa, you're amazing. And you're right. I'm going to stop being one of those people who sits back. I want to learn more, and have more of an impact."

Her whole face lit up, and he grinned back at her. Then he lifted his champagne flute. "This deserves another toast. To both of us being better people."

She raised her glass. "To putting our beliefs into action."

They clicked glasses, then both drank.

Damien felt as if the proverbial weight had lifted from his shoulders. Funny how he hadn't even realized the weight was there until it was gone. "Prof, what do you say we start the crash course tomorrow? For the rest of the evening, let's just relax and enjoy being together here in Hawaii."

"Sounds like an excellent plan."

"Okay, then I'm changing the subject. I have a very important question for you."

"Go ahead."

"Just how many damned buttons are there on your dress, Tezzie?"

13

I toyed with the top button. "I'll let you count them later."

"Tease."

Me? Dr. Fallon? I was trying to figure out how to respond when our dinners arrived.

We tasted, shared, then began to eat hungrily. After I'd taken the edge off my appetite, I said, "Have you always written, or were you in some other line of work?"

"Yes to both. Always liked to write, so I got a journalism degree. I worked at newspapers but didn't enjoy it. Being forced to cover stories I had no interest in, take the political slant of the paper or, at best, stick to the boring facts. So I started writing fiction. It's way more fun."

Oh yes, despite our growing intimacy, he and I were different. My life was all about gathering and measuring information, because I'd thought it was only statistics that made an impression. And yet, Damien's readers probably numbered more than a hundred thousand and, I had to acknowledge, my own work reached only a few hundred people.

His eyes crinkled. "I said something at the event tonight

about having problems with authority? So, yeah, I knew I wanted to be my own boss. I wrote a book, submitted, got rejected. Again and again, which pissed me off. I knew I could write, but no one else seemed to see it."

"That must have been frustrating."

"Yeah, but it made me determined to prove them wrong. When I wrote my first Kalti book, I sensed I had something different. It seemed like this was my true voice as a writer. Anyhow, I found an agent who either agreed or took pity on me and took me on." He gave a self-deprecating smile. "Alex suggested a few revisions, I made them, then she shopped *Thunder Struck* and, believe it or not, got a small bidding war happening."

I paused, a spoonful of onion soup raised to my lips. "A bidding war? You mean, with more than one publisher trying to outbid each other to buy the book?"

"Cool, huh? Especially after getting a hundred rejection letters. Anyhow, we sold, got a two-book contract, and the publisher put some marketing dollars behind *Thunder Struck*. It was an author's dream come true, and it doesn't happen often. I was one hell of a lucky bugger."

"What part doesn't normally happen?"

"All of it. Bidding war rather than rejections. Two-book contract rather than selling one and worrying whether you'll ever sell again. A marketing push from the publisher rather than being left to sink or swim on your own. Helped that all of us saw the Kalti books as a series. It gave my publisher something more than a single book to promote."

"And your books are bestsellers." I could understand why. If a reader wanted pure entertainment—and obviously there were lots who did—Damien delivered.

"Yeah. Which wouldn't have happened without the publisher's support. They bought co-op space in stores, sent out review copies, placed ads, arranged tours and interviews."

"Co-op space?"

He took a quick bite of steak. "You know when you walk into a bookstore and there are those tables at the front promoting certain books, and there are end caps, book dumps—"

"Book dumps?" His business, like mine, had its own jargon.

"Those cardboard display boxes? Well, all that promo stuff is paid for by the publisher. And they gave me the full-meal deal."

"That's great. So, you gave up your journalism job?" I savored another bite of baked crab and shrimp.

"It was a gamble. But my publisher wanted the second book quickly. I figured, if they were going to promote me, I was damned well gonna produce for them. The advance was decent, so I quit the day job, downsized my lifestyle, locked myself away, and wrote like crazy."

"That was gutsy. And disciplined." Discipline, I well understood and respected.

"Some days were hard. But my gamble paid off."

"You paid your dues to get where you are." And I respected him for it. In the candlelight, he was incredibly handsome and sexy. But the man was proving to be so much more. It was scary, being attracted to him in so many ways. Starting to care for a man who was only a fling.

He nodded. "I did, but so do most writers. In relative terms, success came easily to me. And I never take it for granted. That's one thing you learn in this business. You may be the flavor of the month now, but next month the publishers and readers may want something completely different." A grin broke through. "Guess that's a good thing. Keeps me on my toes."

I spooned up the last of my soup as he finished his steak. When the waitress asked if we'd like dessert, I said, "I'm full."

"What've you got?" Damien asked her.

She reeled off a list of yummy-sounding treats, finishing with, "My favorite is the coconut cream pie. It's light, tangy, a thoroughly modern, Hawaiian version of the old classic."

"I'll have the pie," he told her. "Bring two forks, in case I manage to tempt the lady."

Manage to tempt me? Those words summarized our history together.

When the waitress had gone, he reached across the table and took my hand, his warm gaze holding mine. "Hey, you with the buttons. Fantastic evening, isn't it?"

Cristal champagne, a moonlit sky, the scent of tropical flowers, the gleam of candlelight. And, most of all, the man across from me. I felt intoxicated by him and this magical night. And it wasn't only the buzz of sexual attraction, but a true sense of intimacy as we got to know each other better and better. The sex between us was wonderful, and so was the conversation—and so was doing nothing at all except staring at his striking gray eyes and the strong planes of his face, framed by wings of glossy black hair.

He seemed equally content to stare back. I thought about my average face, which he'd termed perfect. Was it possible he found my face as attractive, as fascinating, as I found his?

When coffee arrived, it was hard to look away from Damien and thank the busboy. Then our waitress brought a plate holding a fluffy dessert, which she put in the middle of the table.

I pushed it over to Damien. "Yours, I believe."

He took one of the two forks, ate a bite, and a wicked smile crossed his lips. "You're so lucky I'm a generous bloke." This time, when he forked a bite, he offered it to me.

I leaned forward to take it, and an explosion of flavor hit my taste buds. Creamy coconut, toasted coconut, a hint of lime, more than a hint of rum—it was utterly delicious. My expression must have told him so, because he shoved the plate back to the middle of the table. "Help yourself."

He was the one who'd ordered it, which meant I should have been polite and protested. Instead, I reached for a fork. "Thanks, Damien. This is sinful."

"Tastes as good as sex, doesn't it?"

I chuckled, then felt a hum of arousal as I thought about how he tasted. A little salty, a touch musky, definitely a darker, richer taste. "Uh-uh. This is too sweet and light. You taste more like, hmmm, dark chocolate with . . ." I tried to think what food might compare, but gave up. Damien's taste was unique. Delicious.

"Ah," he said softly, "but it's *you* that *I* taste, and you're sweet all right, Tezzie. Sweet, a little tangy, and definitely addictive."

Heat flushed my body. Cheeks, chest, pussy. I imagined him licking me all over. I was almost ready to abandon the coconut pie and suggest we retire to our room. Maybe just one more bite . . . Oh God, it was good.

His eyes met mine, sparkling with humor and sexual promise. Then he picked up his fork and broke off some pie.

I studied him as he munched, and thought back to what we'd been talking about. "You were saying that market trends keep you on your toes. But you're writing a series. Or are you saying, you'd quit the Kalti books and do something else?"

"If sales really dropped. But for now, I'll tweak what I'm doing with Kalti. I have to stay true to his character and meet reader expectations—like, there will always be the Dreamtime spirits and the sea eagle—but I can take him in new directions."

"You have some ideas?"

"Two." He gave me a quick grin, eyes bright. "I mentioned that I gave him a female partner in the new book? Well, I'm thinking there's going to be a romantic attraction. Maybe that woman at the signing was right, and the poor old bugger's due for the joys and torments of a love affair."

"Torments?" I knew that, whether or not he realized it, Damien identified with Kalti. And Damien had just embarked on a . . . well, not a love affair, because it was only a one-time thing. But all the same, what did he mean about torments? He and I had shared some joys, and maybe I annoyed him from time to time, but torment was a strong word.

"I could give her a dress with buttons all the way down the front." His eyes twinkled. "But seriously, a writer has to torture his protagonist. If life's too easy, there's no story."

Hmm. That made some sense.

He leaned forward, elbows on the table, ignoring the dessert. "And there's got to be a certain amount of growth. A character can't stand still or readers get bored with him."

"And for growth, there has to be challenge," I mused. "As in real life." Damien and I had challenged each other, and as a result we'd both resolved to take our careers in a fresh direction. He had also, even though he might not be aware of it, challenged me to see myself as an attractive, sexy woman. A woman who, as he'd pointed out when we entered this restaurant, could turn men's heads.

"Exactly. Growth—character arc—is especially important to female readers. In general, male readers focus on plot, females care more about character."

"Hmm." I paused, fork raised to my mouth. The coconut pie was incredible, but his words interested me more. I was beginning to understand how fiction could reflect and even inspire real life. "So, most books are aimed at both male and female readers?"

"Nope. Techno-thrillers are aimed mostly at men and romance is targeted mostly to women. With mystery and suspense, some go more one way and some are in the middle, like mine. Of the genres, by far the most sales are in romance."

"Really?" Damien was teaching me a lot. "So, most people—women readers?—are romantics at heart?" Like my sisters Kat and Merilee. They'd always had a stack of romance novels in their rooms.

"They like happy endings—so do mystery readers—but romance readers care more about character than plot. Mystery and suspense is about solving the crime, the puzzle, and stopping the bad guy. Romance is usually about emotion—stuff I'm not so great at writing—and character development, two people beating the odds and winning love."

Winning love. With Jeffrey, I'd felt as if love had miraculously landed on my doorstep. Then, when the going got tough, I had assumed he'd never loved me at all. Neither of us had grown one bit from the moment we met until the day we divorced.

I'd grown more, in all sorts of ways, in one day with the fascinating man who sat across from me. And, to my amazement, I'd had an impact on him, too. "Tell me how all of this relates to your Kalti books."

"Like I said at the reading, I'm a typical guy. There's got to be murder and mayhem to keep me happy." In the wide grin he gave me, I saw a glimpse of what he must have looked like as a kid. A bit of a daredevil. And that daredevil lived on, in Kalti. Damien could be a grown-up with a successful career and let his boyish macho side come out to play in his writing.

"So my books are heavy on plot," he went on, "but there's also character development. Kalti's a complex, intriguing guy. A bit of a lost soul, an underdog, a bad boy. Women are fascinated by that kind of man."

"They are?" I smiled a yes at a busgirl who was offering coffee refills. "I don't see the appeal. Maybe it's sexy in high school, but after that it's just immature. And I can't imagine that's the type of man women want to marry." In a husband, a woman wanted, first and foremost, a man she could trust. A man like Merilee's Matt, not like my ex.

"After he's matured and gentled down some. With the help of a good woman and all."

"Seriously?"

"And vice versa. Two people meet, fall for each other, and that's the catalyst for each of them wanting to grow into a better person. That's typically what happens in a romance novel."

"It sure didn't work that way for Jeffrey and me." I made a face. "Which I guess should have told me something, if those romance writers are to be believed." I shrugged off the memory of Jeffrey. And the intriguing thought that Damien's words were a fair description of what had happened between the two of us. Except, of course, our relationship was a short story, not a novel. "Let's get back to Kalti. He's a bad boy because he's a renegade cop, he's an underdog because he's Aboriginal Australian, and he's sexy, yes?"

"Men readers relate to the take-no-prisoners cop. Women like a strong hero and they're intrigued by the other facets of his personality. But I've just realized that they may get tired of him being such a loner when it comes to romance."

I nodded. "Even your male readers would probably appreciate a hot female character, and some sizzling sex."

"Oh crap, you're saying I have to write sex?" He looked dismayed.

"I'd say you're eminently qualified." I shot him a mischievous grin and fingered the button at the neckline of my dress.

He chuckled. "Doing it's not the same as writing it."

As I sipped coffee, I thought back on our conversation. A thread was still hanging loose. "You said you had two ideas for taking the Kalti books in a new direction?"

"Yeah. I want to incorporate some of the issues about Aboriginal Australians, like we were talking about. And the stuff about perceptions and prejudices."

He'd meant it when he said he wanted to make a difference. "I'm glad, Damien."

"It still has to be a good story. Not preachy."

Thoughtfully, I nodded. "I've seen in my classes how students perk up and listen when I tell an anecdote about real live Indigenous Australians."

"Makes sense, doesn't it? We've evolved from people who hunkered around the fire at night, spellbound by the story-teller."

I'd studied enough anthropology to know he was right. In primitive society, storytellers had immense power. The same was true today. And Damien was one of them. I reflected on what he was planning to do. "You have an interesting task ahead of you."

"Oh yeah, I'm gonna have to start back at the beginning with *Scorched Earth*, the manuscript I've been working on." His eyes sparkled in the candlelight, and I could see he relished the challenge. "That'll occupy me nicely, all those lonely nights in hotel rooms."

After taking one final, lingering bite of the delicious pie, I shoved the plate over to him. "You finish this. I've been eating while you've been talking." Then, hesitantly, I said, "I'm not a writer—I mean, my writing is academic—but if there's any way I can help, let me know."

Belatedly I realized what I was suggesting. Keeping in touch.

Damn. I'd intended this to be only an out-of-character fling with a man who "flung" all the time. And now I'd come to care for him, to want more. That was crazy. I was the woman who'd sworn off men, so a "relationship" wasn't in the cards for me—and Damien was a player, who no doubt didn't *do* relation-ships. All the same, the notion of staying in touch was awfully appealing.

He was chewing the final bite of coconut cream pie, looking blissful.

Before he could swallow and answer me, I rushed to say, "I don't mean to sound presumptuous. I mean, I'm sure you'll do a great job of . . . whatever you decide to do." Besides, I was the one who'd criticized his books. Why would he want my assistance?

"I'd love your help."

"Really?" A heady rush of pleasure filled me. Tomorrow wouldn't be good-bye. My heart was racing and I told myself that's what I got for drinking coffee at this hour of the night. Trying to sound businesslike, I said, "We should do some administrative things, like exchange e-mail addresses and phone numbers."

His eyes twinkled as he shoved the empty dessert plate into the center of the table. "You know what, Prof? The *administrative* stuff can wait for tomorrow. Right now there's a moonlit beach out there, calling our names."

Oh yes, that sounded much more appealing.

"And since you ate most of the dessert," he said in a husky, seductive tone, "you're going to have to give me something else to satisfy my sweet tooth."

I remembered how he'd said I tasted sweet. My mouth, had he meant, or other places as well? My sex gave a throb and I bit back a moan of need. "Would a kiss do it?"

"Let's try it and see."

For once I was going to live in the moment, and at this particular moment I couldn't think of a single thing I'd rather do than kiss Damien Black in the moonlight on Waikiki Beach. "We should drop our bags in our room. And change into shorts."

"You are *not* changing out of that dress. Lose the shoes, go barefoot, but the dress stays. Don't you know what I've been thinking about for the last four hours?"

Several dozen things, but I hoped somewhere in the back of his mind, he'd always been aware of ... "The buttons? Undoing the buttons?"

"Oh yeah." He nodded, expression intent, focused on my

neckline. "And since we sat down here, with the moon just outside, I've imagined undoing them on the beach. Seeing the moonlight on your beautiful breasts."

I made a noise that sounded suspiciously like a girly squeak. "You can't. It's a public beach."

He threw back his head and laughed. A sexy pirate laugh that made the other diners turn and look at us. "This, from the woman who had sex on an airplane."

"Sshh." My cheeks, overdosed on sun, breeze, and embarrassment, burned.

We'd had a lazy, lingering dinner, but now things moved quickly. Damien insisted on paying the bill, saying it was his signing, his celebration, and I'd already spent more than enough buying his books. I let him, guessing he made considerably more than I did. While I loved the academic life, the salaries weren't one of the selling points.

Back in our room, Damien exchanged his pants for shorts but wore the same black shirt, now loose and unbuttoned, revealing tantalizing stretches of his tanned, well-muscled torso. We both kicked off our shoes. As I wrapped the filmy shawl around my shoulders, he picked up a colorful beach towel.

"Those aren't supposed to be taken off hotel property," I said, having diligently read the miscellaneous information in our room.

"You going to report me, Prof?"

"Maybe not. If you're really nice to me."

Downstairs again, I realized it was eleven o'clock—God knows what hour back in Sydney—and I was tired from jet lag and too little sleep. But a champagne-like fizz of exhilaration in my blood told me this adventure was too alluring to pass up.

We stepped from the hotel's landscaped pool area down to the sand. It was pleasantly gritty under my feet, like a gentle scrub with a loofah sponge. We walked toward the ocean's edge, where moonlight spilled a silvery-gold path across the velvety water, its swath broken by ripply undulations as gentle waves breathed their way to shore.

"Peaceful," I sighed.

We walked at the edge of the water, me on the higher side where the waves tickled my feet, him a little deeper. Our clasped hands swung gently and from time to time we bumped hips or I brushed my cheek against his shoulder. Everything felt so relaxed and natural, even the tingles of sexual awareness. How could this be? Before, the only thing that had come naturally to me was excelling at school, both as student and professor.

The beach, which had been packed with sunbathers earlier, was now almost empty. "It's quieter than I expected," I commented in a hushed voice. "Maybe because it's Sunday?"

"Sunday." He laughed softly. "I keep forgetting it's still Sunday. Crossing the international date line is so weird. Our flight left Sydney around six in the afternoon on Sunday. It's like Sunday's a never-ending day."

A magic day, created just for us. A day out of time. But I wasn't about to say something so foolish and romantic. "You know, Sunday really is going to end. It's close to midnight." I hoped the spell wouldn't shatter when the day was done.

We had moved past the hotels and now the beach was even darker and more deserted. I might have worried about safety, but Damien's presence banished any qualms. Unlike my academic colleagues, he gave off an aura of strong male capability.

When we'd walked for five or ten minutes without seeing another soul, he tugged me a few feet up the beach. There, he dropped the towel onto the sand and tossed his shirt on top of it. Staring admiringly at him in shorts in the moonlight, I saw the reverse image of a surfer-dude picture. Dark hair rather than blond; midnight sky and water rather than blue; silvery moon rather than golden sun. Edgier. Sexier. My body trembled with hunger for him.

Eyes glittering, he plucked off my shawl, then reached for the neckline of my dress.

"Damien, no." I grabbed his hands to stop him, glancing around nervously and trying to ignore the way my nipples had tightened. "What if someone comes?"

"Then they get a beautiful eyeful. Come on, Tezzie. If Sunday's finally going to end, let's see it out in style." He caught both my hands in one of his, gripping them lightly but firmly. Then, working with only one hand, he undid the next button. And the next.

If I'd said no and meant it, I knew he'd have stopped. Instead, mesmerized, I watched his deft fingers and the sides of my black dress parting an inch or two all the way to my waist. My body quivered at the cool brush of a gentle sea breeze and the heated caress of his gaze. A shock of need zipped through me, turning me hot, liquid, swollen.

He let go of my hands, probably realizing that if I hadn't protested by now, I wasn't going to. I reached for him, but he dropped to his knees and all I got was his thick, silky hair. I wound my fingers through it, anchoring myself as he kissed the front of my body, following the centerline down to where the dress was still buttoned. His tongue licked into my navel, swirled.

He undid the next button and pressed a moist kiss against the newly revealed flesh. And then he carried on. One button, one kiss. Tummy, mound, inner thigh. Each kiss soft, knowing, seductive, and with each one my body trembled with growing need. Finally, he reached the hem. Kissed the tender skin on the inside of my leg. Still kneeling on the sand, he gazed up and tugged on both sides of the dress.

I gave a shrug, let it fall. Stood in my peach eyelet bra and thong, a fine quivering rippling through me, trying to tell myself it was no worse than wearing a bikini.

"That's damn pretty underwear." He rose, shoved his shorts down, and kicked them off. Naked, the moonlight silvering him, the tattoos circling both of his upper arms, he was primitive and stunning. And supremely masculine, with his engorged cock thrusting up his belly.

Despite the hunger inside me, I whispered, "Damien, we can't have sex on the beach. We could get arrested."

"We're not having sex, we're going for a swim."

"Wh-what?"

"You telling me you've never been skinny-dipping?" He reached for the front clasp of my bra and flicked it open.

Of course I hadn't. I knew how to swim, but poorly. I'd never spent time at the beach, never hung out with someone who'd dare me to take off my clothes and run into the ocean.

Shouldn't every teenager have an experience like that?

Better late than never. I flung the bra aside, skimmed the thong down my hips, and sprinted for the water. "Race you."

His delighted laugh followed me as my feet hit the water and I ran in, finding it got colder the farther I went.

Then he was plunging past me, creating waves that surged around me. Suddenly he dove, leaving me alone waist high in the ocean, breasts exposed in the moonlight. Hurriedly I followed his example, shivering with the shock of cold on my face, shoulders, chest.

I came up where it was deeper and my breasts were covered by water. Shaking my head and flinging drops, I looked for Damien.

He surfaced beside me, laughing, sleek as a seal, sexy as only Damien could be. "The water feels great," he said.

"It's cold."

"You'll get used to it. 'Sides, I'll warm you up." He pulled me into an embrace, and sure enough the front of his body scalded mine. How could he be so hot—and still erect—when the water was this cool?

Worriedly I cast a glance toward shore. "Someone might steal our things."

"We can always get another room key," he said nonchalantly.

"Our clothes! I'm not walking into the hotel naked."

"Guess I'd have to do it then."

Somehow, I knew he would and it wouldn't particularly bother him. "Damien Black, you're incorrigible."

"We could steal palm leaves from the hotel garden," he said. "Play Adam and Eve."

"That was fig leaves." I tried to sound professorial as I struggled to hold back a laugh.

"Palm leaves are bigger. I definitely need a big one."

Now I did laugh.

He tugged me closer. "Come on, Tezzie, don't chicken out on me now."

He was right. The time to object had passed. I was the one who'd run into the ocean stark naked, and here I was in the arms of a hot—in all senses of the word—man whose erection ignored the temperature of the ocean.

Damien let go of me and dove again. I stared around, wondering where he'd surface.

My feet were tugged out from under me. I barely had time to suck in a breath before I went under. He released me and I kicked against the bottom, propelling myself upward. I came up, spluttering, and he rose beside me.

"What were you thinking?" I cried. "What if I couldn't swim?"

"You're in four feet of water. And I'd have saved you."

I knew he was right. With no warning, I launched myself at

him, my full weight knocking him in the chest and sending first him, then me, below the surface.

We grappled together, arms and legs flailing, then came up, laughing breathlessly.

Damien smoothed his hands over my head, squeezing water out of my hair, then cradling my face, gazing down into it. "See? This isn't so bad. And no one can see us."

"I'm glad you convinced me." All the same, I eased us into slightly deeper water, making sure my breasts were below the surface.

"Didn't take a lot." His teeth flashed white in the moonlight. "Ah, Tezzie, you're beautiful, sexy, and fun. What a great combo."

"Smart," I whispered under my breath. He hadn't said smart, and it was the first—often the only—adjective people applied to me. No, to Dr. Theresa Fallon. Right now, I was Tezzie, a woman Damien had created and christened. "You're beautiful, sexy, and fun too."

He gave me a comical leer. "So what're two sexy people gonna do, out here in the ocean where no one can see them? We have to keep warm and fight off hypothermia."

"Hypothermia?" I snorted. "Yes, it's cool, but we're in Hawaii."

"Not buying that one? Well then, how about this?" He bent his head and touched his lips to mine, then smoothed his hands down my shoulders and around my back and pulled me close.

I stepped into the embrace, parting my lips and returning his kiss, feeling as if the water must be sizzling wherever our bodies touched. Such a provocative contrast, the cool caress of silky water compared to the heated, tensile press of his chest, thighs. Cock.

When we'd first entered the water, I'd felt daring but nervous. And then I'd been caught up in the sense of play, like a kid. But now I was all woman, with a partner who was definitely all man, and arousal rushed through me in a surge so powerful it melted my insides. My knees turned to jelly, my pussy throbbed with liquid heat. I held tight to him and deepened the kiss, my need urgent, almost as if I'd never had sex before and was desperate for that first erotic taste.

Fiercely he responded, tongue teasing mine as water dripped down our faces. He'd shaved before we went to the bookstore but now was lightly stubbled, and the mild abrasion was another sensual treat. His hips moved, grinding his cock against my belly, and his legs flexed, balancing the two of us amid the gentle back-and-forth suck of the ocean.

"God, Tezzie," he groaned against my mouth, "I can't get enough of you."

I scattered wet, hungry kisses all over his face, his neck, tasting ocean salt warmed by his skin, and he tilted his head back to give me access. "Look up," he said. "The moon's watching."

He was right. The sky was inky and, this far from the lights of the hotels and shops, the moon and stars were bright. The ocean was a velvety blanket, breathing softly around us. I was still gazing up when Damien let go of me and disappeared again, ducking below the surface.

My breath caught as his mouth closed on my nipple, sucking it in. Sensation zinged through me, all the way to my sex, and my clit throbbed. He was less gentle than he'd been before—perhaps because he had trouble keeping steady in the moving water. Firm suction, the rough brush of his tongue, then—oh, my—a quick nip that resonated directly in my clit.

I was so close to the edge, if he'd done it again I might have come. But instead he let go and a moment later surfaced, gasping for air. "God, you taste good underwater."

His words brought an image to mind instantly. Of his body naked under the inky surface of the ocean. His erect cock, bold yet vulnerable.

Without a word, I sucked in air and shut my eyes, then

ducked, hands tracing the sides of his body as I sank to kneel on the sand bottom. One hand on the outside of his thigh to steady myself, I found his erection with my other hand. Curling my fingers around it, I guided it to my mouth and took him in. His flesh seemed cool at first, then almost instantaneously became hot.

Eyes closed, holding my breath, water surrounding my face, the sensations were disconcerting, but I didn't panic because Damien anchored me. His pulsing heat filled my mouth. I swirled my tongue around the head of his cock and he thrust in response. My pussy clenched in a spasm of pure need, of longing for him to plunge into it.

Air running out, I let go and quickly surfaced, water streaming down my face and into my mouth as I opened it, gasping. "I need—"

"This," he interrupted. And again he disappeared below the surface.

He found my sex, hands clumsy for a second as he got his bearings. I spread my legs wider. Two fingers thrust inside me, his mouth closed on my clit, and all the urgency and need came together and I rocketed into orgasm.

When he came up for air, I clutched him, body still shaking, legs like jelly, and somehow managed to say, "Yes, that was exactly what I needed."

He laughed softly. "Thank God you're quick."

I curled my hand around his cock. "I don't think I can hold my breath long enough to . . ." For the life of me, I couldn't say, "give you a blow job." Pumping my fingers up and down his shaft, I went on. "But we could do it this way. Though I really wish . . ." This, I could say. "I'd really like to feel you inside me."

"I have a condom in my shorts pocket. There isn't a soul on the beach."

"Oh God." Sex on the beach. Waikiki Beach. Perhaps the most popular tourist beach in the world. The idea terrified me. And excited me beyond all reason. "We'd have to be quick."

His cock jerked in my hand. "Sure as hell won't be a problem for me."

I stood on tiptoe, steadying myself with one hand on his shoulder, and under the water guided the tip of his cock to my sex, brushing flesh that was swollen and tingling from climax. Feeling my body respond with an "oh yes, I remember this penis; it makes me feel very, very good, and I want more" reaction. "Don't think it'll be a problem for me either."

"Then let's go before I explode right here."

I released him and he caught my hand in his, pulling me toward shore.

My breasts emerged from the water, skin goosebumping. Anxiously I scanned the beach, not seeing a soul. Nor could I see our clothes. The water got more and more shallow, clearing my stomach, my groin. How strangely exhilarating to come out of the water naked, on a moonlit beach. The experience had a primitive, highly erotic quality.

Not that I wanted to walk into the hotel like this. Fortunately, I wouldn't have to. Damien had better night vision than I. He led us unerringly to the towel and pile of clothes.

He grabbed up his shorts, extracted a condom package, and spread the towel. I stood there, shivering from nerves as well as the brush of night air on my wet skin. Then he caught me up in a tight embrace. His firm, hot body was a good remedy for nerves, as persuasive an argument as any he might make verbally.

When he kissed me hungrily, I whimpered, "Hurry, Damien. I want you now."

In a matter of seconds, we were on the towel, his body covering mine, his sheathed erection prodding urgently as I raised my legs to invite him in. He didn't ease into me this time, but plunged deep in one quick surge that filled me and made me gasp with shocked pleasure.

Our bodies were wet, slippery, as we moved together to a fierce primal rhythm. Not kissing, not speaking, just pounding and slapping together, driven by the need to join—to merge and break apart together all at the same time.

Over his shoulder, the moon and stars gazed down on us, so serene and distant compared to our frenzy. Damien's face was shadowed, which could have made him seem like a stranger, but the fire between us was anything but anonymous. No other man could have called forth this response from me. This crescendo of sensation, arousal, primitive need.

He felt it, too, I knew from his labored breathing, the frenzied jerk of his hips.

"Damien," I gasped, as the spiral peaked, then shattered into a climax so forceful I couldn't stifle my cry. A climax that was mirrored by his own pounding release.

After, our bodies still surged together in a rocking motion that gradually slowed, and I became aware of the soft rushing sound of waves lapping the beach. His face was buried in the curve of my neck and shoulder, his chest warmed mine. Everything felt right, natural. Perfect.

Then I came to my senses. "We should get dressed before someone comes."

Lazily he pulled himself off me. "If you insist." He stood, unself-conscious in his nakedness, and stretched. The sight of him in the moonlight took my breath away all over again, and I would have liked to simply lie there and stare. Instead I groped around for my underwear and struggled into it, then rose and slipped my arms through the armholes of my dress. I started on that long row of buttons as Damien pulled on his shorts.

The air felt cool now, on skin that had only minutes before

been burning. I shivered and wrapped the filmy shawl tight around me.

"Cold? You can have my shirt."

"Thanks, but I'm fine." I told the truth, though a girly part of me loved the idea of snuggling into the shirt he'd been wearing all evening.

He slung the shirt on, not bothering to button it, and gave me a quick hug. "What a perfect way to finish off a fantastic day."

"Yes."

As we began to walk back to the hotel, arms around each other, I felt a sense of letdown. The day—our special day—was over. Tomorrow we'd fly to Vancouver and then...Who knew? Maybe nothing. Maybe something, if he did ask for help with his next book. Might we turn into friends? Friends *with* benefits, or without? Now that he'd awakened my long-dormant sex drive, how would I ever be satisfied with a vibrator?

"Australia has terrific beaches, too," Damien said.

"Mmm." From now on, beaches would remind me of him and Waikiki. Which wasn't a bad thing. He'd given me more fun, better sex, a higher opinion of my own femininity and sexuality, than anyone else had ever done. I'd even noticed men watching me, and a rather cute one had tried to pick me up in the bookstore coffee shop. This new confidence was something I'd take away with me, and thank Damien for. In fact, if I wanted sex, I was sure I'd find a man who would provide it.

But he wouldn't be Damien.

Damn it, it was silly to feel sad at the idea of saying goodbye. Silly to let myself care for a man who was so different from me. And yet, Damien was special. He wasn't like Jeffrey—not a man who used me, but one who gave so much to me.

His arm tensed slightly around my shoulders and there was

a hint of hesitation in his voice when he said, "Maybe one night we'll go check out Bondi Beach."

"Check out . . ." Bondi Beach was a long strip of sandy beach close to Sydney. Was he saying . . . ? "You and me? Go to the beach together?"

"Uh, yeah." Again, the hesitation. As if he wasn't sure he really wanted to? Maybe he was just being polite. But then he went on. "I mean, if you want to. I know you're busy with work. And I guess you're used to associating with people who are a little more, uh, intellectual than me, but . . . we've had fun, right?"

Oh, my gosh. He wanted a relationship. And he actually sounded insecure. This man who was, in so many ways, out of my league wasn't sure if I'd want to hang out with him. Whereas I couldn't think of a thing I'd enjoy more. Trying not to act too much like a schoolgirl crushing on the football hero, I tilted my head up to smile at him. "A lot of fun. You're great company, Damien."

He squeezed my shoulders, looking relieved. "So that's a yes?"

"Well, I'm not sure about sex on Bondi Beach," I teased, "but definitely yes to getting together when we're back in Sydney."

A big grin split his face. "I was gonna ask you at dinner, when you offered to help me with my books. Then you went all *administrative* on me, and I figured some moonlight might get you in the right mood."

I grinned back. *My God, I might actually have found myself a boyfriend. And not just any boyfriend, the one all the girls wanted!* "Mmm, I guess it was the moonlight that did the trick," I said, doing my best to sound like a rational adult, not a giddy teenager. "Couldn't possibly have had anything to do with *you.*"

He pulled me close as we finished the walk to our hotel.

By the time we got to our room, we were stumbling from an accumulation of jet lag, exhaustion, and great sex. We must have looked like a pair of drunks. We managed a sketchy shower, then collapsed into bed, sleepy bodies tangled together, and tumbled into sleep.

I was wrapped in Damien's arms when my eyes fluttered open to wince at the brightness of the sun. We'd forgotten to pull the blinds. Nor had we opened the lanai door, and the room was stuffy. I lay quietly for a few minutes, watching him sleep. Thick, dark lashes fanned out above strong cheek-bones—the same combination of gentleness and strength that characterized Damien himself.

I was wide awake and needed to pee, so I slid out of bed. After freshening up in the bathroom, I grabbed his black shirt to cover my nakedness and threw open the lanai door. The flower-scented air drew me outside and I stood, breathing it in. What a perfect morning. Maybe we could go for a jog on the beach.

When I stepped back into the room, I saw he'd rolled away from the light. I doubted he'd object if I woke him by stripping and crawling between the sheets, but on the other hand, this was a good opportunity to check e-mail.

First I dealt with a few messages from work, glad to find that my secretary was handling my sudden departure with her usual competence. Then I opened a message from my mom.

Theresa, VanDusen was an excellent idea. And yes, I did find a string to pull. One of our neighbors is on the Board. She checked with the event booking person and of course the main venues were booked long ago, but there's another area they use only occasionally. It's generally re-served for Board members, staff, and volunteers, but Jane said she'd work things out. It's not huge, but M&M only plan to invite fifty or so people.

It's not by the restaurant or the main lake area, but over in a corner by a stream. Jane says it's pretty. Lawn, lots of flowers, water. Private access can be arranged for wedding guests, so they can park near that corner of the Gardens rather than walking from the main entrance.

You'll need to think about chair and tent rentals.

Yes, tents were on my contingency plan. "Where on earth do you rent tents?"

We can have the wedding at VanDusen, but not the reception. I was thinking, why not use the house? We can talk about that when you're home. See you soon. Love you, darling.

I sent a quick e-mail back saying, Thank you, thank you, thank you!

Next I skimmed a message from Merilee, which she'd cc'd to Kat, saying she and Matt had done their first draft of a guest list. And then there was a message from Kat to Merilee, with cc's to me and Jenna. The subject line read:

Wedding e-vites
Been doing some thinking, and there's a couple of ways we could go. Merilee, those mags you scattered around the house were all hearts/flowers/lace, so maybe you want to go with the whole soft, romantic, traditional kind of thing. But then I was thinking how you and Matt have been M&M forever, and how you always include a bag of M&Ms whenever you give each other a birthday or Christmas present, and I though it might be fun to use the candy as a theme.

Let me know what you think. I can do either. Whatever you guys want.

Hugs and smooches, bride to be!

Merilee had responded with:

Squeee!!!!!! Oh yeah, M&Ms! What a cool idea. It's so "us." You're the best, Kat.

I felt a twinge of jealousy. I was the one who'd taken on organizing the whole project. "Shouldn't I be the best?" I muttered. Then, "God, how shallow."

I talked to Matt and I guess what we'd really like is some combo of traditional and . . . how can I describe it? Fun, distinctive, original. Like, I want a real dress, white and lacy and utterly gorgeous. But some of the other stuff can be less traditional because, you know what, we're young! And the M&M e-vites are just perfect.

They really were. Cute and young and very Merilee-and-Matt.

Mom told me we got VanDusen for the ceremony. Squee!!!! again. You know that's where I've always wanted to get married. !!!!!! (That's me jumping up and down!)

I clicked REPLY ALL.

Love the candy idea, Kat. Brilliant. And Merilee, I think what you're saying makes perfect sense—and it'll allow us lots of flexibility. And of course you're going to have the best wedding dress in the entire world, and be the most beautiful bride EVER. And at VanDusen Gardens!

Here's a thought. What about bags of M&Ms as gifts for guests? Maybe along with a slice of wedding cake? So you'd have tradition plus that distinctive M&M touch?

See you tonight, Merilee. See you, Kat, in a few days. Have a fun train trip home.

Love, Theresa

No message from Jenna. "Big surprise."

"Morning, Tezzie," a lazy male voice, tinged with humor, said.

14

Damien had to laugh.

Theresa'd jumped a mile when she heard his voice. She stared accusingly at him, where he lay in bed. "You startled me."

Well, she had woken him with all her mumbling. But damn, she'd looked cute sitting there in his shirt, muttering at the computer screen between bursts of typing. He'd been propped up on pillows watching for at least ten minutes, with only his hard-on to keep him company. "If it counts for anything, I think you're the best."

"The best what?" She frowned in puzzlement.

"And I don't think it's shallow to want to be the best at whatever you do."

Comprehension must have dawned because she raised both hands to cover her face and peeped out between the spread fingers. "I said that out loud?"

"Unless I read your mind."

"Sorry. I woke you, didn't I?"

"You, the sunshine, the fresh air. Be a shame to stay asleep and miss all that." He patted the bed beside him. "Want to come over and say good morning properly?"

"I . . ." A quick glance out the lanai door. "Yes, but I'd also like to go for a run on the beach before it gets too hot." She glanced back at him, and the way the sheet tented over his hard-on. "And if I sit down on that bed . . ."

"We both know what's gonna happen." And she was right, a run was a good idea. He'd enjoyed walking the beach with her yesterday, but his body was used to aerobic exercise every day, and it would be particularly welcome today. They were facing another relatively long plane flight, arriving around midnight.

In his ideal world, they'd have sex, then a run, then more sex. But the prof was in management mode. Besides, the sun was rising, the heat building outside, and no doubt tourists would soon be crowding the beach. "Yeah, let's run. Got something you can wear?"

"I can go barefoot if we run on damp, packed sand. I'll wear the top I bought yesterday over the bikini bottom."

He groaned. "You don't have a big sweatshirt or something? You're gonna be way too distracting in an outfit like that."

She beamed. "Sorry, that's it. You're just going to have to suffer."

"You have a mean streak in you, Theresa Fallon." He swung out of bed and got a small measure of revenge when she gaped hungrily at his hard-on. "Give me a couple minutes to get ready." Then he headed for the loo.

When he came out, she was dressed in the outfit she'd described. The shirttails brushed the tops of her thighs, showcasing her long shapely legs and revealing an intriguing flash of green bikini bottom with each step she took. He whipped on a pair of running shorts, then pulled her against him for a quick but intense good morning kiss. The sight and feel of her had his cock growing again, so he said, "If we're going, we better do it now."

Both barefoot, they headed down in the elevator. Outside, they stretched in the shade, then set out at a jog, side by side, on the nearly empty morning beach. When they did pass walkers or other runners, everyone called a cheery "good morning." A few colorful beach towels decorated the sand, and an occasional beach umbrella unfurled like a giant flower.

He let Theresa set the pace, and it was a respectable one. Not as fast as he'd have gone on his own, but enough to give him decent exercise. Though the sun was still low in the sky, heat and exertion were raising a sweat and he saw her face was damp, too. This was a fine start to the day, though he'd rather have woken with her in his arms. "What time did you get up, anyhow?"

"Not long before you. I checked e-mail. We've got a few details sorted out for the wedding. My sister Kat came up with a great idea for e-vites."

"She's the one in Montreal?"

"Yes. I told you she's in PR, didn't I? She's great at her job. Creative as well as businesslike. If only she had better sense when it comes to her love life." She speeded up a little.

He smothered a chuckle. A compliment and an insult, all in one breath.

After a few minutes, the sweat was dripping off him. "Man, I could use a swim."

She glanced his way. "That would feel good. But it's not 'swimsuits optional' this time. And no fooling around."

"Aw, come on, there aren't *that* many people on the beach," he teased.

"Damien!"

He relented. "Nah, we don't want to get arrested. Suits on, and just a swim. I promise." He held up his hands. "Look, ma, no hands."

Next thing he knew, she'd stopped jogging and was unbuttoning her shirt, pulling it off to reveal the sexy bikini she'd worn yesterday. She tossed her shirt to the sand, then stepped into the ocean, and he hurried to join her.

Together they splashed noisily into the water, which felt good on his overheated skin. He dove through a small wave and came up on the other side to find Theresa had disappeared. No, there she was, swimming in an awkward crawl parallel to the beach. He swam too, outdistancing her quickly, then coming back to meet up.

Breathless, she put her feet down and stood. "I told you I'm not very good."

"Doesn't matter. It feels nice, doesn't it?"

"Very. I usually run on a track on campus, so this is a treat."

He glanced at his waterproof watch. "Hate to say it, but we should head back. We'll want to eat breakfast before we go to the airport." He winked. "And, since you don't want to fool around on the beach, we gotta allow some time for that, too."

"I'm very good at time management." Today her eyes reflected the blue of ocean and sky, and sparkled like sunshine glinting off the water.

When they emerged onto the beach, she shook water out of her hair and wiped her face on her shirt. When she slipped into the shirt, it clung in all the right places. A fact he had ample opportunity to notice as they jogged back. By the time they arrived, she'd got him way hotter than the sun ever could.

Inside their room, both of them damp-skinned and breathing hard from the run, he pulled off her shirt, then untied the double-knotted strings of her bathing suit and stripped her naked. His erection was back and he shoved off his shorts as she sat cross-legged on the bed, watching.

He sat in the same position, facing her, then leaned forward to bury his nose in her shoulder. "Mmm, you smell like a jock."

"Takes one to know one." The words sounded automatic,

but then she cocked her head as if reflecting. Expression bemused, she said, "This is so not like me."

"Physical, intellectual, sexy. They're all you."

"I suppose they are," she said thoughtfully, as if the idea hadn't occurred to her before. Gently she touched his face. "Thank you, Damien."

"Nah. Thank *you*." Man, he was glad she'd agreed that they'd keep seeing each other back home in Sydney. Though he'd known her such a short time, no relationship had ever mattered so much before. He reached out to touch her, too. Petal-soft cheek, firm jaw, delicate neck, strong shoulder. Her nipples had beaded and he toyed with one, squeezing it gently.

"I like the way you touch me," she murmured. "*All* the ways you touch me. Sometimes hard and fast, sometimes teasing, sometimes gentle."

"I like touching you. You're so beautiful and you feel so good."

She dipped her head in acknowledgment. "When you touch me, it's like you're . . . appreciating me." Gently she skimmed her hand down his arm, barely touching it. "The feeling's mutual."

"Come sit on my lap," he urged.

"The way we did on the plane? No, I want to see you."

"That's what I mean. Sit across my lap, facing me. No, wait a minute." He reached for a condom, sheathed himself, then said, "Now."

She straddled his thighs, half sitting, half kneeling, arms around his shoulders. Their bodies were still slick with sweat.

Between them, his cock rose. She slid forward to press her pussy against its base and he felt her steamy heat. He wanted to feel that fire from the inside, so he put his hands under her arse and lifted her until the tip of his cock probed her moist folds and began to slide in.

"Mmm, yes," she said, wriggling to urge him on.

When he was fully embedded in her, she stopped squirming and they both sat still, gazing into each other's eyes. Her sheath surrounded his hardness with melting heat, her breasts moved gently with each breath, her multicolored eyes were bright with passion. The longer he looked, the more he saw. Beyond the passion, there was something deeper. More significant. Affection?

He sure as hell hoped so, because he was falling for this woman.

She gazed back at him steadily, eyes searching his.

No wonder he'd never had a serious relationship. He'd been dating the wrong type of woman.

No, that wasn't it. Theresa wasn't a *type*, she was unique.

Her eyes sparkled, crinkled at the corners. "Damien? What are you thinking?"

He pumped his hips gently, caressing her from the inside out. "How special you are. How lucky I am."

"Really?" A shadow crossed her face.

Didn't she feel the same? Or was it that strange vulnerability again? He remembered her ex, and what she'd said about believing he'd been using her from the beginning and had never truly cared for her. "Really." Couldn't she read the truth in his eyes?

"This is all so new to me. I don't have much experience with men."

"I have a fair bit of experience with women, but this is new to me, too. We'll have to figure it out as we go along."

He knew he'd taken things another step. All he'd done before was sound her out about getting together in Sydney, and now he was letting her know she was special to him.

He didn't regret it, though, because her eyes widened with pleased surprise. "I like that. I feel so naïve compared to you. It helps, knowing this is different for you. Knowing you're not so confident, either." Her internal muscles pulsed against him, tightening and releasing in small motions that felt like she was hugging his cock.

"Oh, I'm confident." And suddenly he was. Theirs might be an attraction of opposites, but it was a powerful—and mutual—one. He gave her a big grin. "At least about some things. Like, that you and I are damned fine at making love together." His choice of phrase was deliberate. No way was he going to label their joining as having sex.

Her internal muscles did that hugging thing. "We are." Then she leaned forward and their mouths met in a tender kiss.

While their lips and tongues explored in soft, slow caresses, he held her loosely around her waist, her arms circled his back, and their lower bodies joined in a dance of subtle motions. Tiny movements—shifts, squeezes, the gentlest of thrusts—each barely more than a whisper, a breath, a contraction of muscle. Yet, with each one, his body grew more sensitized. So little stimulation, yet so focused and intense that Damien was painfully hard. He wanted to drive himself into her, to take them both to orgasm, yet he didn't want this to end.

Theresa eased away from the kiss, breathing hard. Her eyes were half closed, her face and chest pink and glossed with sweat, her body taut with tension. She was on the edge, and he wanted her to climax. He reached down between their bodies and strummed her clit.

"Oh!" She let out a gasp of surprise and pleasure, then "oh!" even louder, and her sheath convulsed around him, sucking on him the way the waves ebbed and flowed on the beach.

It took all his self control to hold back from joining her in climax.

A few seconds later, her eyes opened, looking glazed. "Wow, that snuck up on me." Her lips curved. "You give me the best orgasms, Damien."

His body jerked in response. Oh hell, she'd just demolished

all his willpower with a few simple words. Now his hips thrust harder, creating more friction as he slid in and out of her channel, feeling the way she gripped his shaft, then released, her movements matching his.

It felt like she was milking him. Drawing his passion, his energy, pulling it up from deep inside him, pulling it through him as he plunged into her.

She was whimpering, muttering, "Oh yes, just like that," grinding herself against him, her motions as frenzied as his.

The explosion inside him was gathering, ready to release. He caressed her hot button again until she cried out. He gave an immense groan of pure satisfied joy and let go inside her.

For minutes afterward, they clung together, bodies still rocking, muscles still rippling with aftershocks. His emotions rippled with aftershocks, too. She got to him the way no one else ever had. He rested his sweaty forehead against hers. "Oh man, Tezzie."

Half an hour later, he sat across from her at a table in the hotel restaurant. Theresa wore the same navy cotton pants as yesterday and a pale blue sleeveless blouse she'd bought on their shopping trip. She looked fresh and pretty, but he missed the bikini top and sarong, the black dress with all the buttons.

He remembered unbuttoning those buttons, tasting her, seeing her in the moonlight . . .

"Damien?"

Her voice called him back from the memory. He realized a waitress was waiting for his order. "What are you having, Theresa?"

"Fresh fruit and yogurt."

To the waitress, he said, "The same, please. Plus bacon, sausages, scrambled eggs, and pancakes."

When their meals came, he insisted she share his. "It's brunch. We're not going to get decent food on the plane."

As they both tucked in, he said, "Want to start me on that crash course? Comparing the situation with Canadian and American indigenous peoples to that in Australia?"

"Do you have a pen and paper?"

He tapped his head. "Nope. Good memory."

"If you're sure." She began to talk, interspersing words and bites of food.

He listened, asked questions, made mental notes of points he considered particularly relevant. The conversation was so engrossing that, when the waitress came to clear their plates and he glanced at his watch, he exclaimed, "Damn, we've got to get going."

Thank heavens he'd already checked out and checked their bags. He flipped American dollars onto the table, and five minutes later they were climbing into a cab and buckling up.

"This was nice," she said, almost wistfully, as the taxi pulled away.

She was gazing out the window, and he studied her profile. "Very nice," he agreed. He sensed she had the same growing realization that he did. The two of them made a damned fine team. What had started out being a sexual attraction had become much more. And every hour they were together, it got better, deeper, stronger, more complex.

It was too soon to be thinking this way. Once they were back in Sydney, they'd have lots of time to see where their relationship might go. As lovers, and maybe more. Maybe even—strange as it might seem—as colleagues. She'd offered to help with his books. If she meant it . . .

An idea had been niggling away in the back of his mind, growing in scope and taking on a life of its own in the same way as happened with his best story ideas. He leaned back, closed his eyes, and let it form.

What if they collaborated on a book? Not a novel, but a "pop" sociology book about Indigenous Australians? They could draw on her research but put it in layman's terms, and make it come alive with real-life stories. The book wouldn't have as wide a readership as his Kalti series, but they could include it in the Kalti promo, have two-book deals. Do signings of both books, talk on TV and radio shows. They could do this together. Him and Theresa. Pool their talents to create something that might make a real difference.

Would she consider it? Coauthoring a book as well as being lovers? It was risky. If their personal relationship blew up, what would it do to their professional one?

Gut instinct told him they wouldn't be splitting up. Even if he was wrong, they were reasonable adults. They could work things out. Besides, his whole writing career was about risk.

But that was him. Theresa wasn't a risk-taker, and was wary of trusting men. Besides, academic that she was, she might consider a project like this to be beneath her. The whole notion was probably a crazy one. Should he forget it? Hell no; the idea had a grip on him. Talk to her about it? Maybe better to run it by his agent first. If Alex didn't think it was doable, there'd be no reason to mention it to Theresa.

"Damien?"

He became aware she was tugging on his arm. "Sorry. What?"

"Airport?" Her expression was one of amused tolerance. "I didn't want to interrupt when you were deep in thought. I figured you were working on a story idea. But we're almost at the airport."

Glancing out the cab window, he saw she was right. "Sorry to be such bad company."

"No problem. I know what it's like." She closed a small notebook and tossed it in her bag. "I spent the time making more notes for the wedding."

The driver pulled up at the curb and he and Theresa climbed out.

Inside, check-in went smoothly and they headed for the departure gate. "I need to make a call," he said, eager to talk to his agent, and to do it out of the prof's earshot. "Mind picking me up a bottle of water and a snack bar for the flight?"

"Sure. I'll get something for myself, too."

"Leave your carry-on and shopping bag here, and I'll watch them."

The moment she'd turned away, he was dialing. Voice mail, damn it.

He'd called on Alex's direct line, so now tried her assistant. "Hey, Bev, it's Damien. I'm in Honolulu airport, about to catch a flight, and need to talk to Alex. Is she around?"

"I'll hunt her up. Hang on a mo."

He leaned against the wall, impatient, watching as the departure lounge filled. Lots of sunburns and gaudy Hawaiian clothes, tourists heading home from their holiday. Finally he heard Alex's voice. "How was the Honolulu signing?"

"Really good. The woman at the store did a great job."

"How many people? How many books did you sell?"

"I'll e-mail you later. Right now, there's an idea I want to run by you."

"For *Scorched Earth*?"

"No. A different kind of book. I met this woman on the plane from Sydney and—"

"You want to write a sex manual?" she joked. "That'd sell like hotcakes, coming from one of the ten sexiest bachelors in Oz."

He chuckled. Yeah, he and Tezzie could definitely write a sex manual.

15

I found a shop around the corner from the departure gate, where I bought water for Damien and me, snack bars, and a couple of Ghirardelli chocolate bars with raspberry filling.

Leaving the store, I ripped open the wrapper on one of the chocolate bars, broke off a square, and popped it into my mouth. When I bit down, I almost moaned at the combination of rich chocolate and luscious semitart raspberry. Maybe if Damien was especially nice to me, I could be persuaded to share. But then, when had the man ever been anything but especially nice?

I recognized his voice before I turned the corner, and the familiar timbre sent a warm thrill through me. Then, there he was, leaning against a wall with his back to me, casual and masculine in jeans and a white T-shirt that showed off his great musculature. He held his cell phone to his ear.

Not wanting to interrupt his call, I stood there admiring his rear view. Then, with a start, I realized he was talking about me.

"Yeah, she's a sociology prof at the uni in Sydney. Indigenous people are her specialty."

Well, how about that? It seemed he was boasting about me to someone.

"She's researched the issues we'd want to put in the book," he went on.

The book? Was he talking about his next Kalti Brown book and my offer to help?

"Credibility," he said. "I have the rep as a writer and she has credibility as a sociologist. An expert." He listened a moment then said, "I know, but we could cross-promote it with the Kalti books."

So it wasn't one of his Kalti series. A trace of worry shivered through me.

"Yeah, it would sure help if it was put out by the same publisher." His voice took on a teasing tone. "And that's your job, Alex. You can persuade them. After all, I'm their author. They wouldn't want me taking the book somewhere else, would they?"

So, he was speaking to his agent and had an idea for another book. Last night he'd talked about market trends and the need for an author to remain flexible, so maybe he'd come up with a concept for a new series. One he hadn't mentioned to me. And yet now he was talking about me.

I frowned, trying to remember his exact words. He'd said I had researched the issues he'd use in the book, and mentioned my credibility.

"Yeah, I see it as commercial," he said. "Not dull academic stuff. Definitely with a solid foundation, and that would come from Theresa's research, but it would only be the skeleton. It's the flesh that goes on it that makes it exciting. And saleable."

Oh my God. The chocolate bar dropped from my hand. He wanted to use my research as the basis for a book that he'd write, he'd sell, he'd take credit for. I'd offered to help him brainstorm ideas, but I certainly hadn't had anything like this in mind. How dare he?

It was Jeffrey all over again. It was all the boys in school who'd wanted my notes, my tutoring. My brain. To help *them* get ahead. I was numb with shock.

There Damien was, all hyped up about the next big thing, a way to make more money, build an even bigger name for himself. Using my research to do it. Exploiting me, and no doubt also exploiting the Indigenous Australians.

I bent down, picked up the chocolate bar, and heaved the thing in the nearest trash container, wishing I could dispose of Damien so easily.

How could I ever have believed I cared for this man? I remembered staring into his eyes a few hours ago when we'd made love. I'd thought I'd read respect, passion, affection in his gray eyes. I was a naïve idiot. We hadn't been making love, he'd been screwing me—in more than one way. My head pounded with anger and hurt so I couldn't hear what he was saying.

I forced myself to take a few deep breaths before I exploded. And I thought about the things we'd done together, the things he'd said, the way he'd looked at me. The way I'd shifted from labeling him as an airplane gigolo to believing we shared something special. Could I have misjudged him so completely?

Or was I overreacting now? Jumping to the wrong conclusion? I took another breath and focused again on his words.

"Oh sure, the Aboriginal thing will help. I'm a successful Aboriginal Australian, and that'll make people pay attention." He listened. "Why do I need the prof's research? To give the book weight. Credibility, like I said before."

He was going on, but I'd heard enough. I turned on heel.

Oh yes, I'd been right. He intended to exploit me for my research, to make *his* book more saleable. And in the process, he might do serious damage to my professional reputation. I wanted to yank his cell phone out of his hand and whack him in the head with it, but instead I steamed toward the closest ladies' room.

So much for the notion that a man might actually care for me as a whole person. What had he called *Tezzie*? Beautiful, sexy, fun. And I'd actually believed him.

I wanted to slam both fists into the wall of the impersonal gray-walled ladies' room. I wanted to lock myself in a cubicle and cry until long after the flight had left, taking Damien Black out of my life forever. But those reactions would be childish. I was a mature woman, a professional. I would retain my dignity, damn it.

I ran cold water and splashed my face and hands over and over again, but it did nothing to cool my temper. I should have known the whole thing was ridiculous. The idea of me being some kind of sex goddess, with a man like him. And I'd fallen for his manipulative come-on. He'd got his rocks off with an easy lay. He'd fed me a line, softened me up, so that when he asked for my help I'd give it willingly. How he must have chuckled to himself when, under the influence of champagne and moonlight and *him*, damn him, I'd offered to help with his books.

Oooh, I'd been so pitifully needy. I hated myself for having been so damned easy. Just the same as with Jeffrey. So much for learning from my mistakes.

Well, Damien Black had a surprise in store for him. At some point he'd be bound to bring up the subject of this new book of his, hoping I'd gush all over him and offer to help out in any way I could. And he'd soon discover he was no longer dealing with *Tezzie*, but with Dr. Fallon, and she wasn't going to give him the time of day.

My head was pounding, but my cheeks weren't quite so flushed now and tears no longer threatened to spill. Spine rigid with cold determination, I strode back to the departure gate. To my relief, passengers were boarding. Damien was still on his phone so I grabbed my carry-on and string-handled Honolulu shopping bag from beside him, and rushed to join the lineup.

Hurriedly, he said a few words into his cell, then closed it and came to join me. "Hey, sorry, I was talking to my agent."

"Were you?" I kept my voice even, though it took some effort. Then I removed his bottle of water and a couple of snack bars from the bag and shoved them at him, so he was kept busy juggling all his possessions and finding his boarding pass.

When we were shuffling along the ramp toward the plane, he reached for my hand, but I avoided his touch, opening my purse and scrabbling through the contents.

"Lose something?" he asked.

I ignored the question, and continued to rearrange things in my purse until we stepped on the plane, where I wished desperately that I hadn't let him switch his business class seat for economy. It had seemed so sweet at the time—I'd had no clue of his ulterior motive—and now the last thing I wanted was to be crammed side by side for more than five hours.

Hoping I could change seats, my heart sank farther as we inched down the aisle. The plane was packed. Our seats were almost all the way to the back, in the middle section. We had an aisle and a center seat, and as we approached our row I saw the other aisle seat was already occupied. To overflowing. By a bald man reading a huge paperback.

I did *not* want to be trapped between him and Damien.

And I wouldn't be. Damien could damn well sit in the middle. Yes, he'd sacrificed a seat in business class, but only so he could continue to finesse me. Why the hell shouldn't he end up with his big body and long legs jammed into that tiny space?

Giving him a saccharine smile, I said, "Did I mention that I'm claustrophobic? If I sit in the middle, I might have a panic attack." It was a total lie.

He grimaced, then, looking noble—the bastard—said, "No worries. You can have the aisle. I'd better put my bag in the overhead. You want me to put both of yours up?"

"Just this one." I handed him the shopping bag that contained new clothes I'd never wear again and several Damien Black books that would go directly into the garbage. Then I waited, deliberately not watching his muscles stretch as he stowed his bag and clambered into the seat beside the chubby man.

I took the aisle seat and pulled out the wedding bible before I crammed my bag into the small space under the seat in front. Planning a happy-ever-after ceremony. Just what I did *not* feel in the mood for.

Before I could open the book, Damien turned to me, his back to the man who was reading. "I want to tell you about my new book idea. That's what I was doing on the phone, discussing it with my agent." His bare forearm brushed mine on the armrest.

I jerked my arm away and clasped my hands on my lap, atop my book. He was wasting no time. "Oh, really?" *Yes, do please tell me, so I can say no and we can get this over with.*

"Alex isn't sure about marketability. She asked me to tweak it, discuss it with you, write her up a short proposal. But I really think we can make it work." He sounded as excited as a grad student who thought he had a brilliantly original idea for a dissertation.

"Do tell," I said through gritted teeth, staring at my hands rather than at him, amazed he hadn't picked up on my animosity. The man was so full of himself.

"Most of the problems faced by Indigenous Australians stem from either misinformation or prejudice. Right?"

"Yes. Or lack of information." Wasn't that what I'd been saying, or at least implying, yesterday? To reinforce the point, I went on, aware of how stiff, almost priggish, I sounded. "Most Australians don't understand the structural disadvantages, nor the fact that government programs—no matter how well-intentioned—haven't provided effective assistance."

"Prof, are you okay? You seem kind of odd." Well, he'd finally noticed. And damn him, he actually sounded genuinely concerned. "Feeling claustrophobic?" he asked.

More like sick to my stomach. Or to my heart. I resisted

rubbing my pounding temples in case he tried that massage trick again. "I'm fine. Do go on. About your wonderful idea."

He didn't catch my sarcasm and rushed on enthusiastically. "A book that's nonfiction, but presented in an entertaining, easy-to-read style. It'll be based on your research and have facts, some statistics, but they'll come to life through true stories. I want to humanize, personalize, the experiences of the Indigenous Australians. So other Australians can relate. And include some parallels to what's been happening in other countries, like we were talking about earlier. With Hawaii, the continental United States, Canada. So that Aussies will see this is a major social issue, not some odd little Australian idiosyncrasy."

Wow. "And perhaps also include examples of initiatives that have been successful in other countries," I said, before I snapped my mouth shut. He'd drawn me in despite my being pissed off.

"Brilliant," he said enthusiastically.

Damn the man, the book he was proposing could actually be good. And useful. Done well, it would have more impact than all my dry university lectures. The thought infuriated me, even as I felt a grudging respect.

A flight attendant was making takeoff announcements, so I used that excuse to fiddle with my seat belt, while I said neutrally, "It's an interesting idea." Curiosity made me ask, "You think people would actually buy a book like that?" Surely he'd make more money off writing another Kalti book, and it would probably be less work. Could he actually be trying to do a good thing? Aside, that was, from those insignificant issues such as exploiting my research, harming my professional reputation, and crushing my feelings.

He nodded vigorously. "If it's packaged right. It'll appeal to Australians who care about what's going on in their country, and hopefully also to many of my readers. A book like this could really open some eyes to what's going on."

Hmm. Maybe I really had awakened his social conscience. More likely, he was just saying these things as a way of manipulating me to cooperate.

"So, what do you think?" he asked. "You're the one with all the knowledge and statistics." He grabbed my hand, squeezed it, and didn't seem to notice that I didn't return the pressure, or that I'd been avoiding looking at him.

I was tempted to tell him I didn't give a damn, but, being the typical nonconfrontational female, I didn't have it in me. Instead I gave an honest answer. "Do I think it's feasible? Yes. Though it's not likely to hit the bestseller charts as your Kalti books have done."

"And you'll work on it with me, Tezzie?"

There it was. The question. The one he'd been working up to for God knows how long. He'd executed a complex and effective sales campaign that even included a midnight swim, and now he wanted to close the deal.

Finally, I turned my gaze to his face. He looked as excited, as expectant, as a child on Christmas morning. Confident that the packages under the tree held lovely gifts for him. Confident that *Tezzie* would sign on the dotted line.

Well, at least he was laying it out for me and asking, which was more than Jeffrey had.

The truth was, he could write the book without me. Most of my research was in the public domain. As for the rest—comparisons to other countries—he could find that information with a little effort. Damien wasn't stupid. He'd know he didn't need me, but he'd also know I could save him a lot of time. Help him focus on the issues that mattered most. And my willing participation would lend his book that credibility he'd mentioned to his agent.

Credibility with the public for him. Loss of credibility in the academic world for me. A number of my professional colleagues would look down on me for using my research this way, for simplifying it into lay terms and disseminating it in a commercial context. Helping Damien could jeopardize a reputation I'd worked very hard for.

And yet . . . I could make my expertise count, do something constructive to help the people I'd been studying. Whatever I might think of Damien, the man had made me realize there wasn't much point to research unless it was used to better the world.

But, even for an excellent cause, could I work with a man who was using me to build his career? A man I'd been falling for, who'd misled me into believing he might care for me, too? I pulled my hand free of his. "I have to think about it."

His handsome face fell. "I know, you have your own work, your teaching. I guess this is the kind of book an academic like you might think of as superficial."

Many would. Probably before I'd met him I'd have been one of them. Now, I thought it could be valuable if it was done right. Could I trust him, without my help, to do it right? "Look, I said I'll think about it. Besides, you don't even know your agent will go for it. Write up your proposal and if she thinks the book would sell, drop me an e-mail and I'll consider it."

His eyes narrowed and he clipped out a "Fine."

If I did opt in, we could work by e-mail and hopefully I'd never have to see him. Now I knew he hadn't meant those things he'd said about getting together in Sydney. Or, if he had, it was because he thought he could ensure my continued cooperation with great sex.

Great sex. Yes, he'd given me that. As well as a sense that he found me special, that the two of us together had a certain magic. Damn. I had to face it. This whole interlude with Damien proved what I already knew. My instincts about men were appallingly bad.

"I know you have other priorities," he said, voice cool and

distant now. "Just thought you might want your ideas to get some broader exposure. You might want to do some real good, as you said last night at dinner."

Great, he was playing the guilt card. Maybe I should come right out and tell him I didn't appreciate being used.

"Look," he went on, sounding as stiff as I had, "I should tell you my other idea, in case it factors into your decision. I thought I might find some really worthwhile project that benefits Indigenous Australians, like in health, education, or mentoring, and donate my royalties to it. What do you think?"

Oh, great. A double guilt card. Reluctantly, I admitted, "I think it's a great idea." And generous of him. It sounded as if he really did want to do some good.

"I'm not saying you'd have to do it, too," he added quickly. "I mean, if you did agree to work on the book with me."

"Uh . . . I don't follow. Do what, too?"

"Sorry, I mean, it could be just my royalties."

My head was really pounding now. Perhaps that was why I couldn't follow what he was saying. "What are you talking about?"

He took a breath. "Look, I don't mean to offend you, Theresa, but I know the uni doesn't pay huge salaries. What I'm saying is, just because I'd donate my royalties, it doesn't mean you'd have to donate yours."

"My . . . royalties?" Royalties went only to authors. A spark of hope made my pulse speed. I swallowed and tried to collect my thoughts—a hopeless endeavor at this point, what with my confusion and the pounding in my head. "Damien, what exactly are you proposing?"

He looked baffled, exasperated. "What I just said. That we collaborate on a pop sociology book about Indigenous Australians."

"Collaborate?" The word could have a dozen meanings.

"You have the knowledge. I'm a good storyteller. Together, we can write a book that will really have an impact."

Hope beat in my throat, making it hard to speak. "Do you mean, as coauthors?"

"Well, yeah, that was the idea. But you're obviously not so keen." His voice was empty of all his earlier enthusiasm.

"Coauthors. Damien Black and Theresa Fallon."

"Or the other way around if you want. Though we'd have more market recognition if we put my name first."

Recognition. The word resonated through me, carrying a glow of happiness. Damien intended to give me full recognition for my work. Oh no, he wasn't another Jeffrey. What an idiot I'd been to let my own insecurity get in the way, and make me misjudge him so badly.

He was going on. "We make a great team. Hasn't it been fun—and challenging—discussing the issues? Sharing ideas?"

"It has," I said softly, feeling the tension begin to drain from my temples. "Yes, it's been stimulating. And fun."

He nodded, a light sparking in his eyes again. "Imagine it, Tezzie." He took both my hands and this time I returned his warm pressure and let myself enjoy the sense of energy and sexual awareness that flowed between us. "Brainstorming together," he went on. "Arguing over the best way to phrase things." One corner of his mouth tilted up. "Taking sex breaks. Traveling to do research, interviewing people and recording their stories."

As he spoke, I did let myself imagine it. All of it. Damien and me together. Working together. Swimming on Bondi Beach. Being lovers.

Wait. Lovers and business partners? The thought was amazingly appealing but also scary. "Damien, that's . . . big. A book is a long-term project." Had he thought through the implications? "What if we stop getting along?" When I broke up with

Jeffrey, I'd not only left the university he worked at, I'd dropped the field of study I'd specialized in and moved away from Canada. Mixing a personal relationship with a work one could have drastic consequences.

"Does it feel to you like that's going to happen?"

"N-no. But it's so early."

"I know. But we're solid, you and me. Solid enough that, even if the, uh, you know . . . romantic relationship doesn't work out, we'll still be friends. Still be able to work together." He narrowed his eyes, studying me closely. "Don't you think?"

"I'd hope so. But there's no guarantee."

"Life doesn't come with guarantees."

What I had now, with my teaching position and reputation in the academic community, was as close to being safe as anything could be. My career path almost *was* guaranteed.

If I opted into Damien's project and things went well, I'd lose some academic credibility, influence thousands of lives, and have a romantic relationship with a fascinating, gorgeous, sexy man. If things went badly, I could lose everything.

"Damien, right now it seems as if we could work together." I spoke slowly, thinking it out as I went. "I like you and care about you. I want to be with you, figuring it out as we go like we said earlier. But I'm scared. If something goes wrong for us personally, the book project could fall apart." Softly, I added, "When I broke up with Jeffrey, I had to make a whole new start in a different country. I don't want to do that again."

"I'm not Jeffrey. Damn it, Theresa, when are you going to realize that?" He sounded hurt, and genuinely troubled. "Are you going to doubt everything I do, everything I say? I can't live like that. If you don't trust me, then we have nothing."

Trust him. Could I?

"The only lie I've ever told," he went on, "was about us being engaged. And that was stupid. I did it on the spur of the moment, to get rid of Carmen without hurting her feelings."

"You didn't tell me who you were," I said slowly. Then, "But I understand why."

"Theresa, I promise I'll never deceive you again." His expression was fierce, apparently sincere. "Can't you leave Jeffrey behind, and just be with me?"

It was an excellent question. If I hadn't had the bad experience with Jeffrey, I wouldn't be lugging around such a huge weight of insecurity. But Jeffrey was ten years ago. I'd matured a lot since then, and especially in the short time I'd known Damien.

"You're right," I said softly. "I'm finished with Jeffrey. I'm a different woman now. I'm . . ." I smiled at him, knowing I could say the words and believe them. "I'm beautiful and sexy and fun. And smart, confident, and successful." Attractive to men. It wouldn't be hard to find a relationship if I wanted one. But the only man I wanted to be with was the one beside me.

"I trust you, Damien, and I trust me to have good judgment and good common sense." No longer would I let insecurity and fear cripple my life. "Yes, let's do the book if your agent can sell it. And let's swim on Bondi Beach and do everything else we want to. And trust ourselves to work out any problems that come along."

His eyes had brightened as I spoke. He squeezed my hands so hard it hurt. "God, Tezzie, I'm nuts about you."

I gazed into his eyes and saw all those things again. Respect, passion, affection. And I knew his eyes were telling the truth.

Joy bloomed inside me and my own eyes teared up. "I'm nuts about you, too."

Our lips met in a soft kiss, one that hinted of many, many more kisses to come.

"Watch your knees and elbows." A female voice accompanied by a clanking sound jolted me out of my reverie.

Glancing around, I saw that not only was the plane in the air, the flight attendants were wheeling drink trolleys up the aisle. Damien unclipped his seat belt and I noticed how uncomfortable he looked, crammed into that middle seat. "Let's change seats," I suggested.

"What about your claustrophobia?"

"I'm not claustrophobic. I did have a tension headache, but it's gone. It was the Jeffrey thing."

"The . . ." A horrified expression crossed his face. "Oh my God, you thought I wanted to use your work without giving you credit."

"I'm sorry. I overheard you on the phone in the airport and it sounded like . . . Yes, I leaped to a conclusion. The wrong one. Not because of anything you did, but because of my own insecurity. Please forgive me. Honestly, it won't happen again."

He was scowling. "I'd really like to punch that guy out."

"You know," I said slowly, realizing something, "I'm not blameless in that situation. I leaped to a conclusion then, too. And when he tried to explain, I refused to listen. Yes, I still think what he did was shabby, but maybe his intentions weren't as bad as I thought. Or maybe they were, but the point is, I didn't find out. I judged, and I left."

Damien nodded. "I hear you. And?"

"And I won't do it again." I smiled as I thought of something. "If there's a problem, I'll remember what that older woman, Delia, said. Talk things out, make up, and move on."

"Good plan."

"You forgive me?"

He gave me a warm, easy smile, and I knew he was putting the whole thing behind us. "I will if you give me your seat, Prof."

I unfastened my seat belt and stepped into the aisle. "It's all yours."

A couple of minutes later, we had resettled. With our seats reclined a little and the armrest between them pulled up, I turned toward Damien, deliberately putting my back to the bald man, who still seemed intent on his novel. Or was he pretending, out of politeness? How much of our conversation had he heard? It had to have been at least as entertaining as whatever he was reading.

Embarrassed, I said in a businesslike tone, "What's the next step with the book, Damien?"

"We'll come up with a proposal that's so strong, they can't say no." He clasped my hand, as if touching me was the most natural thing in the world. I wasn't even sure he was aware of doing it, which somehow made it even more special. "It would be great to work on it during this flight. Much easier doing it in person than through e-mail."

Oh no, he had no intention of shutting me out. This was *our* project from the start.

"Sounds good." A thought occurred to me. "I know you're part Aboriginal, but only a quarter, and I'm a total outsider. We want to make sure we represent Indigenous Australians accurately and respectfully, not offend the very people we want to help. I think we need to involve some Aborigines and Torres Strait Islanders. Maybe have an advisory board?"

"Fine idea. We could ask some community leaders."

"Perhaps also some people who have no public profile at all. Just normal indigenous people, urban and rural."

"I like that. It would be a good mix."

Tentatively, I said, "Do you think any of your Aboriginal relatives would be interested?"

"Oh, man. Er, let me think."

"You said they thought your Kalti books exploited what they'd taught you. Well, this should be a project they'd approve of." Maybe he could rebuild his relationship with them.

"It should. My granny would like it that I was respecting them and coming to them for guidance. Yeah, that's a cool idea."

"What about your parents? They probably won't like this

project." I'd got the impression he avoided his folks, which seemed sad. I hated to think our book would make things worse.

"I'm a big boy. I don't need approval. Understanding would be good, but that's not likely to happen." His jaw firmed. "You know, it's past time I had a serious talk with them."

"Good for you." I squeezed his hand. "I hope you can help them understand."

"We'll see. How about your parents? Will they think it's a waste of your talent?"

"Uh . . ." I blew out a puff of air as I reflected. "They'll worry about my professional reputation, but when I tell them our goal, how many people we hope to reach, I think they might even be impressed."

He'd started to frown again while I spoke. "Damn, Theresa. Is this going to hurt your reputation? I don't want that."

"I know. And it might, but that's my choice. My decision." I smiled. "And it's made."

"If I'd realized I was asking you to—"

"Decision *made*," I cut him off.

When a flight attendant offered drinks, Damien chose a beer and I went with white wine. We raised our glasses. "Here's to the two of us shaking things up for the better," he said.

I knew he was referring to the impact we hoped our book would have, but when I echoed his words, I was thinking of a broader meaning. Of the effect he'd had on me and my life. He'd shaken me out of my rut, as both a woman and a sociologist. And I'd had an impact on him, too.

"When do you head home to Sydney?" he asked.

"A few days after the wedding. So I'll be there when you get back."

"It's gonna be a long month," he said. "I'll miss you."

"Me too. There's always e-mail and phone."

His eyes gleamed and he leaned close to whisper in my ear,

"We can try our talents at phone sex. That'll make those lonely hotel rooms a lot cheerier." He nibbled my earlobe gently.

The erotic touch, the sexy suggestion, got me so hot and bothered I almost missed it when he said, "Maybe you could join me for the last part of the tour."

"Wow, I . . . Let me think. I have grad students to supervise. But I could do that by e-mail and an occasional phone call."

"I'll give you my schedule. We'll talk about it. My admin assistant Bobby could make the arrangements." He winked. "Might be able to find a beach or two along the route."

The memory of moonlit Waikiki Beach made me squirm. Mindful of the stranger behind me, I said, "Let's get to work on that book proposal."

I was about to reach down for the bag containing my computer when Damien thrust his beer at me and folded his tray table. "Hold this while I get my computer out of the overhead."

When he'd set up and opened a blank document, he turned to me. "Need to think about a title. It's got to be catchy. Let's brainstorm about what we want to say."

For a few minutes, we bounced ideas around, then I said, "How about something around apologies? Perhaps *When Apologies Aren't Enough*?"

"Hey, I like that." He typed it, then mused. "Or maybe *When Sorry Doesn't Cut It*."

"That's good, too."

He typed it as well, fingers as deft on the keyboard as they were on my body. "We'll give Alex half a dozen suggestions and she'll probably have some ideas, too."

After we'd come up with a few more, he said, "Now, what do we say about the book?"

My fingers itched for the keyboard. "I'm used to working alone," I confessed.

"Me, too."

"And I'm a bit of a control freak."

His mouth twitched. "Oh, really? Well, I'm an easygoing bastard. So, Prof, you hinting you want to type?"

"Maybe we could pass the computer back and forth?"

"Here ya go." He shuffled it over to my tray table, taking care not to knock my glass.

I typed for a few minutes, then, feeling self-conscious, showed him the screen.

He read, nodded, frowned, reached for the computer, then revised what I'd written and added a couple of sentences before and after.

When he'd finished, I leaned closer, reading. He'd taken my passive tense, made it active, punchier. Replaced some of the jargon with layperson's wording. I realized I'd been writing as if this were a grant application.

I pointed to the screen and made a couple of suggestions, which we discussed. Then he said, "You want to draft the part about the advisory board? And we'll need a bio for you."

I took the computer back and worked for awhile. Then we discussed, revised, kept adding and honing. And it was stimulating, fun, just as Damien had said it would be. The fact of arms and thighs brushing, the occasional quick kiss, was a bonus. Maybe I didn't do so well with teamwork, but partnership with Damien was working out just fine. I was relieved, almost giddy with pleasure by the time we'd arrived at a draft we felt happy about.

When he'd put his computer away and folded up his tray table, he reached over to hook his arm around my shoulders and pull me against him. I wrapped an arm around his waist, feeling his rangy strength, the heat of his skin beneath the white T-shirt. My lover. My coauthor.

We'd just spent the last hour on the coauthor part and it would have been nice if we could now concentrate on being lovers. I pressed a kiss against his neck, noticing he was getting a five o'clock shadow.

"Not much privacy on this flight," he murmured.

"That's for sure." When I glanced up, I saw the young mother across the aisle watching us, an expression of envy on her face and a baby on her lap. A boy of perhaps six occupied the seat between her and her husband.

The sight reminded me I had a wedding to plan. Reluctantly I eased from Damien's embrace. "I want to have a comprehensive wedding checklist by the time I get home."

"And I've been neglecting those galleys."

My eyes were tired from lack of sleep, so I pulled out my reading glasses and got to work. For the next couple of hours we worked peacefully, arms brushing often. Looking up to buy chicken wraps, drink water, share the remaining Ghirardelli chocolate bar. Exchanging an occasional comment, a caress, a kiss, but mostly concentrating on our tasks. I did my very best to try not to mumble out loud—less because of Damien than out of courtesy for the man on my other side.

Every time I glanced his way, he was deep in his book. In fact, when the male flight attendant came by to ask if he'd like a cup of coffee, he didn't hear. I nudged him. "Sir? The flight attendant wants to know if you'd like coffee."

"Oh, sorry." He turned toward the other man. "Yes, please and thanks. Cream and sugar."

When the coffee was on his tray table, he turned to me. "Thanks."

"No problem. Good book?"

"Yeah, it's a page-turner." He held it up so I could see the cover, which had a "dark and stormy night" image of a man running.

"You like suspense?"

"Suspense and thrillers, the occasional mystery."

I extracted my purse from under the seat in front and found one of Damien's bookmarks. "Here's an author you might enjoy. The books are set in Australia and it's a series with a cop protagonist. There's a touch of the supernatural as well."

He glanced at both sides of the bookmark, then nodded. "Thanks for the tip. I'll look these up." Then he stuck the bookmark into his book and carried on reading.

When I turned away from him, Damien was watching me, a grin on his face. "Good work. Thanks." He stretched, caressed my arm lightly. "How's the wedding coming?"

"It's intimidating and overwhelming, I don't know how we'll ever pull it off. But my plan is almost done. I'll sit down with Merilee and get her input."

We both turned back to our tasks. I'd almost finished skimming through the wedding bible and making notes. Even though there were a million things to do, I was comfortable with the process of project planning. It suited me to think ahead and try to anticipate every eventuality. I wasn't a spontaneous person.

And yet, here I was with Damien. It didn't make sense.

Being with Jeffrey had made sense, at least at the time, given what I thought I'd known about him. We were in the same field, both academics; we were a logical match. Damien and I, though . . . In some ways we were similar, in others we were opposites. It made things exciting.

I thought about my parents. They definitely had things in common, like their strong drive to help people and their desire that their children be happy, healthy, and successful. Yet Dad was most comfortable in a research lab and Mom loved being out in the world, meeting people face-to-face and working to solve their legal problems. Maybe it was partly their differences—the old "opposites attract" thing—that had kept their marriage strong for so many years.

They'd made it clear they wanted happy relationships for their daughters, but so far the oldest three of us had let them down. What was I going to tell them about Damien?

Or was I, yet?

16

Damien finished another chapter of proofreading and stretched, rotating his head. Theresa was staring at him, those professorial reading glasses shoved up on top of her head, messing up her hair. "Hey, Prof, how ya going?"

"Where are you staying in Vancouver?"

Not exactly a response to his question, but he answered her anyhow. "Think it's called the Rosedale. It's close to the radio station where I'll be taping a morning interview, and to the main branch of the library, where I'm scheduled to chat with a buyer later in the morning. And only a few blocks from the store where I'll be signing."

"Hmm. That *is* convenient." Her furrowed brow sent a different message than her words.

"Not a good hotel?"

"Oh, I'm sure it's great. I was just thinking . . ." She trailed off and didn't finish.

He waited. Then prompted, "You were thinking?"

"D'you want to stay at my place?" The words came out in a

quick stream, so fast he barely made sense of them. Then she added, "I mean, my parents' house?"

He'd figured the "meet the parents" thing would happen, and was a bit wary. What would a geneticist and a top-flight lawyer think of their brilliant daughter hooking up with a novelist, albeit a semisuccessful one?

"It's all right if you don't," Theresa said quickly, expression shuttered. "I mean, the hotel would be far more convenient, and I know you have a busy schedule, and—"

"Whoa." He grabbed her hand. "It's just, I've never done this before."

"Done what?"

"Met the parents."

"Oh, come on. With all the women you've dated?"

"Sure, I've occasionally met someone's parents, but never when," he shrugged, "you know, never when it mattered."

"Mattered?"

"Crap, I'm gonna really suck at writing this emotional stuff when I can't even put it in words to you. This is new territory for me. Feeling, you know, like the two of us really have something. Something, uh . . ."

A spark of humor lit her eyes. "Nice to meet a man who can be clear about his intentions."

He gave her a rueful grin. "Something special. Right?"

"Right."

"So of course I'll come meet your parents, Tezzie."

"Thank you." She leaned toward him for a kiss.

It was driving him crazy, being in a full economy class. He wanted to make out with his girl, damn it. But he behaved himself, keeping the kiss soft and chaste. It was no less meaningful for that. A kiss full of promise.

A kiss full of promise. The writer in him recognized it as a damned good line. Maybe Kalti and his new partner could have one of those kisses.

When he and Theresa broke apart, he asked, "What do you think your parents will say?"

She nibbled her bottom lip, which wasn't exactly reassuring. Nor were her words. "They were kind of hard on Jeffrey."

"They didn't approve of a uni prof?"

"They were right, weren't they?"

He held her gaze. "I'm not him."

"No. But they've seen me hurt. And they're protective of all of us girls."

"Course they are. So, any advice?"

That lip got another chew. "Be yourself. You're smart, articulate, successful, and have an interesting career." But she sounded doubtful.

"Thanks for that vote of confidence."

Her face softened. "You've even been known to be charming, and you're not half bad on the eyes. Besides, in the end, it's only my opinion that counts."

True. But if her parents disapproved, it would add tension to his relationship with Theresa. Getting off on the right foot would be important, so he said, "I'd like to stay at your place, but I don't want to inconvenience anyone. Tomorrow I have to be up early and off to the TV station. I can call a cab, right?"

"Maybe I could borrow a car and drive you. Though everyone may be asleep when we get in . . ."

He gazed into her anxious face, guessing what was darting through her perfectionist brain. Late arrival, would anyone be waiting up, where would he sleep, when would they leave in the morning, whose car, when would they get back? And of course, her being in charge and all, she wanted it to go brilliantly.

"You know what?" He felt a combination of relief—hell, he could defer being impressive until tomorrow—and regret, because he didn't want to be apart from her, not with so few hours before he left Vancouver. "I don't think tonight's going to work."

Her nod came quickly. "I agree. But tomorrow, call me when you're finished in town, and I'll either pick you up or you can get a cab. You can hang out at the house, do some work or have a nap, we'll have an early barbecue for dinner, then I'll come to the signing with you and you can come back to the house after."

He chuckled. Trust the prof to come up with an efficient plan on the spur of the moment. "Sounds good. Minimum disruption for you and your family."

"Maybe some of them will come to the store, too."

"Great, then I'd have at least two or three in the audience," he said wryly.

She grinned. "I'll explain that signings are a hit-or-miss proposition, and that you're just starting to get exposure for your books here."

Amazing, how well they'd come to know each other in such a short time. He reached out to pull her into a hug. "I've converted you from a nasty critic to my number-one supporter."

"Great sex will do that," she whispered, breath tickling his ear.

Her words and her soft warm breath made him start to harden.

"You're so shallow," he teased back, voice low. "Give you a couple of orgasms and you lose all your principles."

"More than a couple. And they have to be fabulous ones."

She snuggled against him and he wondered how many people had ever seen this cuddly, teasing, soft side of Professor Fallon. Oh yeah, he was one hell of a lucky man.

She let out a giggle.

"What?"

The face she turned up to him bore an impish grin. "My family isn't going to believe this. Me, the 'I've sworn off men forever' sister, coming home with a sexy guy."

"Happy to oblige."

The flight attendant paused in the aisle. "Sorry to interrupt, but I don't think you heard the announcement. I need you to straighten your seat backs, do up your seat belts, and stow your personal items."

They complied with the attendant's instructions and Theresa put away her reading glasses. Then she said, sounding nervous, "My father's a night owl. If he's not working, he may come to the airport."

"Okay. Guess it doesn't matter whether I meet him tonight or tomorrow."

"No. I'll have to think what to tell him about you."

"There's some reason you can't just say, 'yesterday I climbed on a flight, met a guy, had sex pretty much for twenty-four hours straight, and now we're in a relationship'?" he teased.

She snorted. "Imagine if you had a daughter, Damien. Would that line work for you?"

A daughter. Man. With a woman like Theresa in his life, that possibility didn't seem so distant. "I'd probably want to shoot the guy."

"There you go."

"Oh thanks, that's comforting." He grinned at her. "So, does the senior Dr. Fallon tote a firearm?"

She gave a hoot of laughter. "Not only is he totally nonviolent, he's the most mechanically inept person you can imagine. If he had a gun, he'd shoot himself in the foot. No, his weapon of choice would be some deadly microbe that the coroner would never, in a million years, identify. It'd be ruled death by natural causes and he'd get away scot-free." She leaned close so the soft fullness of her breast brushed his arm, making his pulse race. "So you'd better treat me nice, mister."

"That was my plan. With or without the microbe threat." When she sat back in her seat, he took her hand.

"Let's avoid the subject of how long we've known each other," she said.

"It's your call."

"They'll ask how we met, though. Everyone always asks that."

"Met in a bookstore. You insulted my books. It has the virtue of being the truth."

She slanted him a grin. "I like it."

"And despite your disdain for my writing, my charm won you over."

"And again," she teased, "it's the truth."

The plane jolted slightly and he glanced over to the window. "We're on the ground."

"Welcome to Vancouver."

"My first time here, but I've heard lots of good things."

"It's a lovely city. Mountains, ocean, gardens, shopping, culture, and it's truly cosmopolitan."

"A nice place to grow up?"

"Yes, thanks in large part to my grandmother. My parents were wrapped up in their careers and they were so keen on me doing well in school, I could have spent all my time buried in my studies. At least, when I wasn't trying to organize my sisters. But Gran took us girls out every Sunday. We saw Science Centre, art exhibits, the zoo and aquarium, parks and gardens, Chinatown, Commercial Drive."

"She sounds like a special woman."

A shadow crossed Theresa's face. "She was. She was diagnosed with Alzheimer's three years ago and that person has been disappearing. Last time I was here, I visited her four times and she only recognized me twice."

"Maybe we could go see her together," he found himself saying.

"You want to meet my grandmother?"

"She's important to you." Grandmothers were special, he figured. "And she's disappearing, like you said. Maybe this time she'll recognize you, and you can introduce me." Jeez, he was wading in deeper and deeper with Tezzie, but so far the water felt just fine.

She squeezed his hand. "Thank you. That would mean a lot to me."

The bell pinged to announce that the plane had reached the arrival gate, and they both gathered their things. Damien turned on his mobile and saw there were messages, but they could wait until he was in the taxi on the way to his hotel.

As he and Theresa shuffled down the aisle, he bent close to her ear. "A different kind of flight than the one from Sydney."

Color tinged her cheeks. "This one was good, too. In its own way."

"That it was." Even if he was hungry for her, and wished he could carry her off to his hotel room.

Once they were off the plane and striding side by side up the ramp, he said, voice low, "When am I going to get you alone again? Will your parents let us share a room?"

"You think I'll give them a choice?" She gave him a quick smile. "Actually, they're pretty liberal. Matt's been staying over with Merilee for years."

"You'll have to curb your impulse to scream at the top of your lungs when you come."

Her cheeks were rosy. "I do not."

"Don't have to curb it?" he teased, "or don't do it?"

Her cheeks went brighter.

They were now in the terminal itself and walked hand in hand as they followed the signs to Customs.

"Hey, this is quite something," he said. The building was huge and airy, almost deserted at this hour. Nature sounds met his ears and they walked into a diorama that portrayed a natural setting—forest and beach—and featured some striking art, including a canoe and a giant bird carving. "First Nations art?"

He could see similarities to Indigenous Australian art in the dramatic colors and stylized representations of animals and birds.

"Yes. Lovely, isn't it?"

The diorama was peaceful, intriguing, an odd thing to find in the middle of an international airport. The kind of place that would have made him want to linger, had it not been the middle of the night with Customs to clear, baggage to claim, and transportation to organize.

"It's a pity you can't stay in Vancouver longer," she said. "There are wonderful First Nations galleries and arts and craft stores, as well as all the other things I told you about."

"We'll plan another trip," he said. "When I can arrange for more time and you won't have a wedding to organize. You can show me the city. Like your Gran showed it to you."

"I'd like that." She gazed at him with a touch of wonder in her expression.

He grinned, thinking the future had never looked so bright.

When his first Kalti Brown book had hit the shelves, when his publisher had contracted for books three and four in the series, when he'd first hit a bestseller list, he'd thought life couldn't get any better. Now he knew it could. And it would. Because he'd met Theresa Fallon.

Escalators led down to the Customs floor where he saw a zigzag queue leading to perhaps eight booths with Customs officers. He and the prof were both fast walkers and had passed a number of passengers, but being seated at the back of the plane had put them at a disadvantage. The line was moving quickly, though, and it wasn't long before they reached the front and were cleared to move into the baggage claim area.

Theresa pointed to a luggage inquiry desk. "Hopefully my bag's over there. I'll check while you find yours."

He headed over to the only carousel that had bags circling

on the conveyor belt, and a few minutes later was towing his wheeled bag toward where Theresa was claiming her own.

"Love it when the luggage arrives," she said with a smile. "It makes life so much easier."

They both pulled their bags toward the exit of the baggage area, showed their Customs forms to the officials, and headed for the doors that led out into Arrivals.

"I wonder if Dad will be here?" She sounded excited, a little nervous, as she went ahead of him out the door.

He followed, to hear a young female voice squeal, "Theresa!"

A pretty girl with shoulder-length honey-blond hair was leaping up and down, waving. Then she ran toward Theresa, towing a young man.

"M&M!" Theresa cried, raising her hand to wave back.

Following the pair were a tall, slim, middle-aged man with silvery hair and glasses, and a striking woman who looked like an older version of Theresa.

Ready or not, he was going to meet the whole family tonight.

The girl, Merilee, flung her arms around Theresa and the two hugged tight, bouncing up and down. Then Theresa went to her mother, then father, for hugs that were brief but warm. Finally she stretched up to kiss the young man on the cheek. "Hi there, soon-to-be brother."

"Hey, Theresa. Welcome home."

Now she turned to Damien and held out her hand.

He stepped to her side and caught that hand, gripping it firmly and not letting go.

"Everyone," she said, "I want you to meet Damien Black." She didn't attach a label, not friend or boyfriend or lover. The clasped hands would convey their own message.

The expressions on the four faces were priceless. Bewilderment, disbelief, shock.

"You said you weren't bringing a date to our wedding." Merilee sounded put out.

"I'm not," Theresa said. "Damien's only in town for a couple days, on business."

"Hey, folks!" a male voice shouted.

Glancing around to see what was happening, Damien was momentarily blinded as a flash flared in his face. A camera?

"Damien," a skinny young guy said, lowering the camera and stepping closer, "how'd Prof. Fallon manage what no other girl's been able to do?"

"Huh?"

The guy turned to Theresa. "Wanna flash the ring, Professor?"

"Ring?" she echoed.

The man glanced down. "Damn, he didn't give you one? What's up with that?"

She thrust her shoulders back and gave him a professorial glare. "What are you talking about?"

"That's what I want to know," Damien said.

"This is you two, right? You can't deny it." He thrust a piece of paper toward them—a color image of a newspaper page—and Damien read the headline: *Uni Prof Snags One of Oz's 10 Sexiest!* One of Damien's PR photos of him in an open-necked black shirt sat side by side with a starchy, unflattering image of Theresa. What the hell?

Damien recognized the paper. This was the front page of Australia's most popular tabloid. Oh, shit. He glanced at the beginning of the article. *Single girls, Damien Black's officially out of circulation. A confidential source confirmed his engagement—*

Crap. Carmen. Quickly he turned to Theresa and saw her staring at the page with the same kind of stunned fascination he felt. Being in the tabloids was nothing new for him, but his beautiful Tezzie sure as hell didn't belong there.

Merilee wailed, "You're engaged? What are you trying to do, upstage me?"

Despite his shock, he almost chuckled. Oh yeah, there was some sisterly rivalry.

Theresa turned huge, dazed eyes first on her sister, then, questioningly, on him.

Another flash exploded in their faces, and finally he came to his senses. He put a protective arm around Theresa and she huddled against him. "Damn that Carmen," he muttered in her ear. To the reporter, he said, "We have no comment."

"Oh, come on, man, it wasn't easy figuring out what flight you'd be on, and I came all the way out to the airport after midnight."

Pissing off a reporter was never wise. "Sorry you took the trouble, mate." Damien flashed him a grin. "Give me your card and when we have a statement, we'll call you first."

He snatched the proffered card and urged Theresa toward the door, tugging his bag behind him. Her family trailed them, her father pulling her bag, and the reporter hurried alongside.

As he and Theresa went out the main airport doors, she whispered, "What's going on? What should we do?"

"Don't antagonize this bloke, but don't give him anything. Go on home and I'll call my people, see what the hell's going on, and phone you on your mobile."

"All right." She sounded shaky.

"Damn, Tezzie, I'm sorry about this."

17

Sorry. Damien had said he felt sorry.

Sorry for the embarrassment? Or sorry the media thought we were engaged?

He gave me a quick hug and strode toward the taxi stand.

I stared after him, remembering the confused mix of emotions that had hit when I first saw the tabloid article. Shock and humiliation, yes, but also a strange, proud pleasure. As if I'd have enjoyed being engaged to Damien, and having the world know about it.

"Theresa?" It was the reporter, invading my personal space. "How long—"

"Sorry, no comment." I gave him a pale imitation of Damien's grin.

Dad had stepped up beside me and I gripped his arm. "Let's get of here," he said.

"Theresa, you could have at least told us—" Merilee started.

"Later," I said.

"She's right." Dad stepped between me and the reporter. "Please leave my family alone. We have nothing to say to you."

He loomed over the much younger man, looking distinguished and almost fierce.

"Alls I want is—" the reporter started.

"You won't get it from us." Dad stood firm as I grabbed Mom's and Merilee's hands and we hurried toward the parking garage. Matt, attached to Merilee, came, too.

Hurriedly, Mom crammed the parking stub and her charge card into the payment machine, and by the time it had spat out the receipt my father had joined us. Alone.

"Pretty impressive, Dad," I said, feeling grateful and a little shaky.

He scowled at me. "This family does *not* need to be in some gossip column."

"It's not my fault," I protested. "It's all a mistake."

"I knew it must be," Merilee chimed in.

"Girls!" His voice rose. "Get in the car. Now." He pointed into the parking lot.

It was all rather awe-inspiring, until Mom said, "Actually, Ed, the car's over there." She pointed in the opposite direction. Merilee and I shared a smirk. This was classic for our family. Dad's lab at the university was superorganized, and we always said he had no organizational skills left to deal with real life.

Mom led us unerringly to the old Beemer and we piled in, me in the backseat with Merilee in the middle and Matt on her other side. Dad took the passenger seat, as usual. Once the car was in motion, he turned halfway so he could see me. "What's this all about? What was the piece of paper that reporter was waving?"

"It looked like the front page of an Australian tabloid." Oh God, all of Australia, including my professional colleagues, thought Damien and I were engaged. This was sort of horrible, but sort of funny as well, not to mention flattering in an odd kind of way. "We're not engaged," I said emphatically. "Somehow a flight attendant got that idea, and I guess she told the tabloids and . . ." I pulled my cell phone out of my purse and turned it on so Damien could reach me.

"Why would the tabloids care if you were engaged?" My father raised his eyebrows.

"Of course you're not engaged," Merilee said from within the curve of Matt's arm. "After Jeffrey, you said you'd never get serious about another man. And if you ever did, I know it wouldn't be a guy like that one."

I frowned at her. "What's wrong with Damien?"

"You go for the stuffy intellectual type. That man was seriously hot."

Matt, who was pretty cute himself, shot her an annoyed glance.

"To get back to my question?" Dad said.

"Damien's a bit of a celebrity in Australia. He's a bestselling novelist and, uh . . ." I didn't know whether to be apologetic or proud about this next part. "He's been voted one of the country's ten sexiest bachelors."

Merilee hooted. "You're *so* not engaged to him."

I was about to explain that I *was* dating him, when everyone else started to talk at once.

My cell rang and caller ID told me it was Damien. "What's going on?" I asked him, putting a hand over my free ear to shut out my family's babble.

He groaned. "Panic in the ranks at my end."

I had to grin. "Pretty much the same here."

"Sorry. This is all my fault for telling that stupid lie."

True. "I didn't have to go along with it."

"My agent and the publicist at the publishing house are in a flap. That sexiest bachelor thing has been part of the PR campaign. They're talking about damage control, and trying to figure out how best to spin this."

"Spin it? Don't we just deny it?"

"I'd have thought so. But apparently it's not that simple. Especially when I told them you and I really are involved."

"But we're not engaged." I couldn't see what was so complicated about this.

"I told Carmen we were, so either I have to admit I was lying—and what the hell's a good justification for that? Or I say we got engaged, broke it off, but are still seeing each other. Which doesn't make a hell of a lot of sense."

"None of this makes a hell of a lot of sense. If only you hadn't flirted with that stupid flight attendant, then—"

"He what?" It was Mom. Too late, I realized my family was hanging on my every word.

Oblivious, Damien was going on. "Believe me, I'm never flirting with another flight attendant in my entire life. But as for now, my people are going to come up with a game plan. So we're supposed to keep quiet and not talk to the press."

"I never had any intention of talking to the press," I said a little snippily.

He sighed. "I'm sorry. This isn't how I wanted things to go."

"I know." He sounded so dispirited that I couldn't be angry. "It'll get sorted out."

"Thanks. We'll talk tomorrow. Night, Tezzie. I miss you."

"Me too. Good night, Damien."

After I hung up, my mother the lawyer said, "Can we get the facts straight? Are you or are you not engaged to that man?"

"Not."

"Are you dating him?"

"Yes."

"That doesn't make any—" Merilee started.

Mom cut her off. "And he was flirting with a flight attendant?" Now the lawyer was cross-examining a hostile witness.

I hedged. "She was coming on to him."

"Why would she be doing that if the two of you were all, like, lovey-dovey?" Merilee managed to get a full sentence out.

"We weren't acting *lovey-dovey*."

"But if the two of you were obviously traveling together," Mom took up the charge again, "and holding hands the way you were in the airport, why would this woman come on to him? And you did say he was flirting, Theresa."

"Oh, for God's sake, give me a break, we'd barely met!" The words burst out, fueled by who knows what. Exhaustion, the excitement of the last two days, shock over the tabloid, frustration . . . Who knows, maybe even a subconscious desire to shock the pants off my family.

"You stayed in Hawaii with a man you'd barely met?" Mom's tone mixed disbelief and censure.

Dad and Matt seemed content—or wise enough—to keep quiet while Mom grilled me.

I took a deep breath and this time thought before I spoke. Keeping my voice calm, I said, "Yes, Damien is the reason I changed my plans and stayed over in Hawaii. We wanted some time to get to know each other better."

Finally, everyone was silent. It was a tense silence.

Mom broke it. "You're acting like Jenna."

Jenna, the free spirit, who was always hooking up with a new guy. Never staying with one for more than a few months. My mother's comment took me aback. Was I? But after a moment's reflection, I shook my head firmly. "No. This might have been sudden, and it may seem impulsive to you, but it's not the same thing. In my life, there have only been two men I've been strongly attracted to."

"And look how things worked out with Jeffrey," Merilee said. "What makes you think Damien's any better?"

"He respects me." I was going to mention the book idea, but Mom didn't give me a chance.

"Respects you?" she repeated grimly. "He flirts with a flight attendant and gets your picture plastered on the front page of a tabloid? Theresa, this kind of notoriety could damage your professional reputation."

She was right. Some of my colleagues would brush it off with a laugh. Others, especially the older and more influential ones, would think it unseemly. But then, the same thing would happen if Damien and I went ahead with our book, and I'd already come to terms with that.

Merilee's voice broke my train of thought. "Where did this whole *engagement* thing come from?"

I rubbed my temple, where another headache was starting. I'd never had so many headaches in such a short period of time. "Damien told the flight attendant. As a way of rejecting her without hurting her feelings."

"He flirted with her, then wanted to reject her?" Mom asked.

"By then I'd boarded, and he liked me better."

Matt gave a low whistle and spoke for the first time. "Theresa, you femme fatale."

Merilee elbowed him in the ribs. "She so is *not*."

I glared at her. "Damien chose *me*, and let me tell you Carmen was plenty hot."

"Girls," Mom chastised in the same tone she'd used many times before, "act your age. Now, Theresa, what were you saying on the phone about spinning the situation and not denying the engagement?"

I forgot they'd heard that part, too. "Damien's agent and publicist want to work out the best way to handle things."

"What's wrong with a straightforward denial?" Mom asked.

"They have a whole PR campaign around his book tour and I guess they need to decide if they're adjusting it." I shrugged. "Honestly, I don't understand myself."

"Theresa," Dad finally weighed in, "you can't let others decide how to handle it. This is about your reputation, your career."

"It's about his, too."

"Yours is more important," my father said firmly. "What did you say he is? A novelist? And you're an eminent sociologist of international renown."

No, this didn't seem like the right time to tell my family about the book.

"He's in entertainment," Mom said, "so his career thrives on tabloid exposure. Your career is . . ." She came out with "dignified" just as Merilee said "stodgy."

"Merilee," Mom said warningly. Then, to me, "Your father's right. This could damage your reputation, and it's all that man's fault."

"Okay, it's his fault," I said. "He did something stupid, on the spur of the moment. Haven't you ever done anything stupid?"

There was a pause, then, on a gently teasing note, Dad said, "Who, your mother? No, she's perfect."

"Ed, that's not helping."

"It seems to me," Dad said evenly, "the 'stupid' horse has left the barn. The question now is how to deal with the result. Theresa, don't let that man decide it for you."

Damn, he was right. I'd been so upset when Jeffrey made decisions behind my back that affected me, and now I was handing over responsibility not just to Damien but to his advisers. Advisers who would consider only his interests.

No, all they could do was advise. What he did with their advice was up to him. And I trusted him. After leaping to the wrong conclusion once, I'd promised him I wouldn't do it again, and I was sticking to that promise.

I glanced out the window to see the familiar streets of the neighborhood where I'd grown up. We were silent as Mom pulled into the driveway and buzzed the garage door open.

After we'd all piled out of the car, Dad said, "What do you propose doing about this situation, Theresa?"

"I'll talk to Damien tomorrow, see what his people suggest, and we'll—"

"Oh God, the man has *people*?" Merilee said. "He really is in entertainment. What on earth do the two of you see in each other?"

"Some time, once you've stopped being so judgmental, maybe I'll tell you."

"Girls!" Mom sounded exasperated. "Enough. It's well past midnight and everyone's tired. We'll talk about this tomorrow."

"I'm going to head home now," Matt said.

"Sweetie, why don't you stay over?" Merilee cooed, all sweetness and light now.

He pushed a curl of blond hair behind her ear. "You have to get up early and study, sweetie. You need a good night's sleep."

She smiled up at him. "I guess you're right."

"Thanks for coming to greet me, Matt," I said. "Sorry it turned into such a mess."

He gave me an easy smile. "Hope you get everything sorted out."

We left Merilee and Matt to say their good nights. Inside, after giving each of my parents a quick hug, I headed up to the bedroom that had always been mine. The three-story house was huge, with six bedrooms and two offices in addition to all the normal rooms.

The second floor felt strange now. The bedrooms that had once housed me and my three sisters, that had buzzed with music, arguments, and phone calls, were silent. My room was functional, with the double bed, dresser, and big desk and bookcases, but personal, too, with everything from the ragged stuffed animals I'd loved as a kid to the scholastic awards I'd won over the years. What a different person I'd been than the Theresa of tonight, who'd just spent a wild couple of days with Damien and found her name plastered on the front page of a tabloid.

Merilee popped her head in the door. "Hey, sis, sorry if I was a total beeatch."

Had Matt given her a talking-to? I gave her back the standard sisterly reply. "That's okay, you can't help it."

We shared a half-grin. My sisters and I loved each other to pieces, but so often we managed to bring out the worst in each other. Then we felt guilty—or at least a little guilty, because after all, the other sister was usually equally or more at fault.

"And I'm sorry," I said, "that tonight was about me and Damien. You and Matt came all the way to the airport to greet me, and we should have been talking about the wedding."

"Yeah." She shrugged. "Anyhow, it really is good to have you here."

"It's good to be here. How are you doing, Merilee? You've lost weight and look tired."

"I'm okay. Pretty healthy, just worn down from surgery, then having to make up the semester. Seems like all I do is write papers, study, write exams."

Thinking of all those school prizes I'd won, I said, "If you need any help studying, let me know."

Her face tightened and she gripped the doorframe. "I may not be a 4.0 student, but I'm not actually stupid, you know."

I was tempted to snipe back that there was nothing *actually* wrong with getting a perfect average, but I repressed the urge and tried to see things from her perspective. "I didn't mean it that way. Just, you were sick, you had a surgical procedure, and now you're doing all this makeup work when you'd rather be trying on wedding dresses. It's got to be tough. And let's face it," I gave her a rueful grin, "if there's one thing I know how to do, it's study."

She chuckled. "Yeah, you were always pretty obsessive." Then she sobered. "And I am now too, what with papers, exams, and the wedding. It's a little scary."

I touched her shoulder. "I'm really good at organizing time. And I'm here to help, Merilee. In whatever way I can."

After a moment's careful scrutiny of my face, she relaxed and gave me a hug. "Thanks, Theresa. I can use the help."

I hugged her back. "How about we sit down tomorrow morning and make up a plan?"

"A plan." She paused, and I sensed a taunt coming. But all she said was, "Sounds good."

She turned to leave, then swung back. "I have to ask. Is Damien as hot as he looks?"

"Hotter."

I expected a teasing retort, an unfavorable comparison to Matt, but all she said was, "Wow."

After she'd gone to her room, I hurried through my bathroom routine, set my alarm, and tumbled into my old bed. I was wondering how Damien and I were going to deal with our faux engagement when sleep dragged me under.

Showered and dressed, I checked voice mail and e-mail before heading downstairs, but found no message from Damien. There was no point calling him as he'd be heading off to the radio station. I wondered if the interviewer would ask him about the engagement story.

Downstairs, the scent of coffee greeted me and I found Mom and Dad, dressed for work, and Merilee in a bathrobe sitting at the kitchen table. The usual hodgepodge of cereal, toast, bagels, fruit, and juice was scattered across the table and countertops. My family had never been into cooking real breakfasts.

I poured myself a mug of coffee as we exchanged good mornings, then took a grapefruit from the fruit bowl, sliced it in half, and found a grapefruit spoon.

"Theresa, I have to get to the office soon," Mom said. "But I'll be home for dinner. We've planned a welcome-home barbecue." She exchanged glances with Dad, communicating in their unspoken language. "We want you to invite Damien." It was a pronouncement more than a friendly invitation.

"Uh, good, I'd hoped to ask him over."

"We want to hear what he plans to do about—" Before she could finish her thought, the phone on the counter rang.

Merilee jumped up to answer. "Hey, Kat. Hang on, let me put you on speaker."

When I'd left for university, my parents had bought a fancy conference-type phone so the family at home could gather and talk to the members who were out of town. Now Merilee stretched out the cord, plunked the phone in the middle of the kitchen table, and pushed a button. "Can you hear me?"

"Sure can." Kat's voice came out of the speaker. "Is everyone there?"

Mom and Dad said hello, then I said, "Hi, Kat. I made it home late last night. Are you—" I was going to ask if she was on the train, but before I could finish, she said, "You're engaged? Why didn't you tell me?"

"I'm not. Where did you hear that?" Surely it wasn't in the Canadian papers.

"A friend e-mailed me from Australia. She saw it in some tabloid."

"This is exactly the kind of thing we're concerned about," Mom said.

"It's all a big mistake," I told Kat.

"I thought it must be."

"You'd have known for sure if you'd seen the guy," Merilee said. "He's seriously hot."

"Seen him? You've met him?"

Merilee ignored my frown and said, "Yeah, they were on the same flight. They had some little fling or whatever." She snorted.

"Can you imagine Theresa being engaged to one of the ten sexiest bachelors in Australia?"

"You guys, I'm here!" I said loudly. "And thanks for that vote of confidence."

"What?" Kat's question came out of the phone and Merilee shot me a puzzled look. Across the table my mom was shaking her head and my dad looked like he'd be much happier at the university, safe within the sane world of his lab.

I gave a huff. "You think there's no way I could possibly attract a seriously hot man." Being with my family was reawakening all my self-doubts, and it was hard to cling to the newfound confidence Damien had instilled in me.

After a couple of long, unflattering moments of silence, Kat said, "It's just that you go for the professorial type. Like Jeffrey."

"Except," Merilee put in, "that since Jeffrey, you don't go for any guys at all."

"I *go* for Damien. And he goes for me." I reminded myself of the things we'd said, the way he touched me, the expression in his eyes, and said with certainty, "It's more than a fling. It's a relationship."

There was a long silence, then the voice from the speakerphone said, "Oh my gosh, Theresa has a boyfriend!" Kat sounded like a teenager.

"I do." Her acceptance made me laugh with giddy pleasure. "I really do. And he's not only handsome, sexy, and successful, he's smart and very nice, too." I was aware of my mother crossing her arms across her chest and frowning at me, but ignored her.

"Sounds like the perfect man," Kat said. "Even better than Matt."

"No one's better than Matt," Merilee said huffily.

"How did you meet?" Kat asked.

The question I'd been expecting. "At a bookstore. He's a

novelist. And then on the plane." Before she could probe further, I turned the tables and said to Kat, "And how about you and this man, Nav? Is it serious?" Let her take the heat for a while.

"Nav? Oh, he's great."

"The relationship must be pretty serious if he's willing to come all the way across the country to go to a wedding with you."

"And meet the parents." Mom finally put a word in.

"Right. Well, let's see. He's actually pretty much what Theresa said about her novelist. Except, Nav's a photographer. But he's, you know, all those good things."

It wasn't like Kat to be so reticent about a man. Usually she fell hard and couldn't stop gushing.

"We can't wait to meet him, honey," Mom said. "Right, Ed?"

"Right," Dad said. "Though it's disconcerting to suddenly have men, left, right, and center, trying to take my girls away from me."

"Nav and I aren't about to get married," Kat said quickly.

"Nor are Damien and I."

"Unless his *people* tell him to *spin* it that way," Mom said, sotto voce.

I shot her a nasty look, yet felt uneasy. Surely Damien wouldn't follow his agent's and publicist's advice without involving me in the decision. My heart told me he wasn't another Jeffrey, but my brain reminded me I barely knew him.

"You'll always have Jenna, Dad," Merilee said. "She thinks monogamy sucks."

"I don't want you girls following her example," he said quickly. "It's downright dangerous, as well as foolish, to take up with one man after another."

Merilee and I glanced at each other but buttoned our lips. We knew perfectly well that Jenna didn't believe in serial monogamy. It wasn't always one man *after* another; sometimes she had two or more on the string—and in her bed—at the same time. A small fact our parents had no need to know about. They worried enough about our flaky sister already.

"No news from Jenna about her travel plans?" Kat asked.

"Not a peep," Merilee said. "Unless she got in touch with you, Theresa?"

"No."

There was another long silence, punctuated by Mom drumming her short-nailed fingers on the table. Jenna frustrated her more than the other three of us put together.

I worried about my sister, too. Naïve, optimistic, unrealistic, self-centered—she was all of those things, and you'd have thought she'd have gotten herself into trouble more than once. The weird thing was, somehow she had always come through safely in the end. So far.

"Kat," I said, "Merilee and I are going to discuss wedding plans, then I'll call or drop an e-mail and let you know where things stand."

"And I have the e-vite. I'll send it next time I get Internet access."

"Weren't you in Toronto last night? Couldn't you have sent it from there?"

"I, uh . . . didn't have it ready then."

She'd had hours on the train from Montreal to Toronto, then the evening in a hotel room. Surely she'd have had time. But of course, she might have taken along some work projects she needed to finish first. Or, even more likely, partied with people she'd met on the train.

We said our good-byes, and I was relieved that Kat hadn't asked how we were going to handle the media, and my parents hadn't expressed their annoyance with Damien.

Mom and Dad stood, saying they needed to go to work.

"But make sure Damien's here for dinner," Dad said. "We want to hear what he has to say for himself."

I stood too. Time to act like a grown-up. "I'll invite him. I also want to ask him to spend the night. With me."

Merilee blew out air in a low whistle, then there was a long moment of silence as my parents did another of their wordless communication things. "Invite him," Mom said. "We'll talk to him and see how things stand after that."

I bit my tongue. It was their house, after all. If they decided they didn't want Damien in it, then I wasn't staying, either. "He has a book signing tonight, so can we have an early dinner?"

Mom gave a long-suffering sigh, but everyone agreed, and Merilee said she'd tell Matt.

After they'd gone, Merilee said snippily, "This house hasn't seen so much drama in a long time."

It was interesting being the exciting sister for a change, but I didn't mean to overshadow her. "What are you talking about? Your wedding is our big drama."

She brightened. "You said we could sit down and do some planning?"

"Absolutely. I've drafted a wedding project plan on my computer."

She rolled her eyes. "Of course you have." Then she reached over and grabbed my hand. "Seriously, Theresa, I really appreciate this."

When she went upstairs to shower and dress, I toasted a whole-wheat bagel and smeared cream cheese on it, refilled my coffee mug, and listened to Damien's radio interview. When the interviewer asked him about the tabloid story, he said, in an engagingly offhand manner, "Hope you don't mind, mate, but I'm here to talk about my books, not my personal life." The host respected his wishes, and the interview went off well, with

Damien sounding relaxed, confident, and charming. No surprise there.

I missed him, but shoved that thought away when Merilee came back downstairs carrying my computer. We worked at the kitchen table and within a couple of hours had a schedule roughed out that combined her school responsibilities and the wedding preparations. We barely argued over anything, and by the time we were done we were both exhilarated.

In some ways, it was like I'd never been away. My sisters and I had always been very different, and those differences had led to many squabbles, but there had also been times when we let loose and had fun. Collaborated on a gift for our parents, read stories aloud, danced to the latest hit tune, did each other's hair or toenails.

That was what it was like now when I told Merilee I was going to meet Damien. She offered the loan of her car, then asked what I planned to wear. I showed her the wardrobe I'd packed back in Sydney, which even to my eyes seemed hopelessly boring. She dragged me into her room and tossed clothes at me. Then she perched cross-legged on her bed while I modeled.

We agreed on a camisole-style T-shirt in a gingery shade and a brief denim skirt with a front zipper. She jumped off the bed and found dangly copper wire earrings. "You look really pretty," she said on a note of surprise. "Damien's been good for you."

"You have, too. Thanks for the wardrobe assistance." When things were like this between us, it was definitely wonderful to have a sister.

Amicably we sat down together and I helped her study for an exam.

That's what we were doing when Damien phoned. I congratulated him on the radio show and he brushed it off, saying the interviewer had made it easy.

Nervously I asked, "What's the news from your, uh, people?"

Merilee gave an exaggerated eye roll.

"Tell you when I see you. Did you manage to borrow a car?"

"Merilee's loaning me hers."

"Great. I've arranged a late checkout, so when you get here, park the car and come on in. I figured we could use some private time."

"Oh, yes." To talk, and hopefully hold each other and make love. Not to fight about what he was going to tell the media.

As I drove downtown in my sister's beat-up old Honda, I started to get anxious again. Even if I did trust Damien, my brain could generate half a dozen unpleasant scenarios.

18

When I knocked on Damien's door, he swept me inside, shoved the door closed behind me, then held me at arm's length and examined me. "Wow, Prof, you look like a student, not a teacher."

"Is that a compliment?" I searched his face for signs that he had bad news to deliver, or felt anything other than thrilled to bits to see me, but didn't find them.

"You look great. Very sexy outfit on a very sexy lady." Now he pulled me tight. "I've missed you, Tezzie." His lips met mine hungrily.

It felt so good to be in his arms again, bodies fitting together just right, his hardness and my softness a perfect match. For long minutes we clung together, kissing as if we couldn't get enough of each other's mouths. I could feel the firm press of his erection against my stomach and my legs were weak, my pussy throbbing with need.

I wanted him inside me now, but I also wanted to keep on kissing because his mouth was so delicious, sweet and firm and tempting like a perfect dessert that you never wanted to finish.

Yet, in the back of my mind was anxiety over what his agent and publicist had advised. I broke away. "Damien, I need to know. What about the engagement thing?"

He groaned and tried to pull me back. "Let's talk about that later."

I shook my head. "What did your people recommend?"

A shadow crossed his face.

"I'm not going to like this, am I?"

He shrugged. "Hope not. I didn't. They want me to deny the whole thing. The engagement and our relationship. To say I was joking around with a flight attendant and she took me seriously."

My frown deepened. "They want us to stop seeing each other?"

"They say it's okay to be colleagues—especially if my agent sells our proposal—but they don't want us having a romantic relationship." His mouth twisted. "They even said you might prefer it that way, since the tabloid thing could hurt your professional reputation."

"My parents might prefer it. Damien, what did you tell them?"

"Said I wasn't happy, but I'd talk to you and we'd let them know what we decide."

No, this man definitely wasn't Jeffrey. I wrapped my arms loosely around his waist and gazed up at him. "What do you want to do?"

"Go on like we planned," he said promptly. "Let this relationship develop and see where it takes us."

"In secret? What would you tell the media?"

"Damn, no, not in secret. I don't want to be sneaking around like we're doing something wrong. I guess I'd tell the media we're, what do they call it? An item?"

"An item?" My parents would have a cow, but I kind of liked the idea of being an item with Damien Black. A grin curved the corners of my lips. "What about your sexy bachelor reputation and the PR campaign?"

He shrugged. "Guess they'll have to tone it down. I never wanted my personal life to be such a big part of my image anyhow." Then he narrowed his eyes. "Wait a minute, you haven't said what you want. Do you agree with your folks? Would this hurt that whole distinguished professor thing you've got going?"

"If I get invited to a few less international symposiums, I can live with it. It'll probably up my cred with my students. Besides, if we go ahead with our book, that's going to offend some of the academic purists, too."

"Shit, I'm really wrecking things for you."

"Damien, it's worth it. The book will influence more people than I ever could in my ivory tower. And you—" I grinned at him. "Being an item with you is definitely worth it. I've been happier in the last couple of days than I can remember ever being."

Perhaps I shouldn't have said that, have shown my vulnerability and let him know how important he was to me, but I didn't want to hold back with Damien.

He captured my head between his hands and stared at me. "Hey, you with the billabong eyes, that's how I feel, too." He kissed me, gently and lingeringly, then led me toward the bed.

He sat on the end, positioning me between his legs. Then he undid the button at my waist, slid down the zipper, and watched as the skirt dropped to the floor. His hands caught the hem of the cami tee and slowly he peeled it up, revealing my torso inch by inch until finally he pulled the shirt over my head.

I stood in front of him in only the white lacy bra and bikini panties I'd bought at the lingerie shop in Honolulu.

Damien rested his head against my stomach and sighed, a long, soft whoosh of air against my naked flesh. "Tezzie, it doesn't get any better than this."

I threaded my fingers through his thick, glossy hair, hair twice as long as my own. "No, it doesn't."

We held each other for a long moment, then I said, "Well, it might get better if you took your clothes off."

He chuckled, then stood and efficiently peeled himself out of his shirt, pants, and underwear. "Better?"

"Oh yes." Studying his naked perfection, I marveled at the fact that he was mine to touch, mine to make love with. Slowly I ran my hands down his chest, gently pinched his nipples, watched his flesh quiver. Heard his soft moan. Saw his cock swell, the glistening tip telling me he was as aroused as I.

My panties were damp, my nipples hard against the lace of my bra, my whole being was charged, both erotically and emotionally. "I want you, Damien."

He teased the straps of my bra down my shoulders and reached for the back fastening. "Then take me. Now. However you want."

After the bra fell away, he hooked his fingers in the sides of my panties and tugged them down.

"Me on bottom," I told him. "You on top, as deep inside me as you can reach."

Next thing I knew, I was sprawled across the bed and he was lowering himself, sheathing himself, caressing me between the legs until I squirmed. "Come into me. Now."

With one quick thrust, he obeyed, plunging fast and deep.

Locked together, we gazed into each other's eyes.

Then, slowly, he rose to his knees and as he did, I hooked my legs around his hips to keep him inside me.

"As deep as I can reach?" he asked in a throaty murmur. "Then how about this?"

He lifted my bent legs, one at a time, until my legs were straight out, resting on his shoulders, my body opened to him in a wide V. Oh yes, now he was seated inside me even more deeply.

But he wasn't finished. He leaned forward, bending me

slowly at the waist. I had a vague recollection of some PE gymnastics class where we'd lain on our backs and brought our legs up and over our heads, as far as we could reach. Never had I realized gymnastics could have such a sexy application.

"Is this okay?" he asked.

"Oh, yes." It felt amazing as we adjusted position and he stroked me deep inside. I put my hands at my waist, bracing my body, which let me bend even farther. Breathlessly, I whispered, "That's as far as I can go."

He thrust slowly and gently between my spread legs. The view was an incredible turn-on and I watched, fascinated, as his rigid cock moved in and out, slick with moisture.

My muscles rippled around him, hugging him tight, then releasing, in time with his own motions. The pressure inside me was exquisite as arousal built, an erotic tension that pulsed outward from my center to every cell in my body.

His face was flushed, his breathing ragged. "God, Tezzie. Beautiful Tezzie."

"You make me feel so good." My own words came out between pants. "Making love with you is—" My breath caught as he shifted angle and his penis stroked that gloriously sensitive spot inside me. He hit it again, and again, and . . .

"Damien!" I exploded in orgasm.

He kept pumping, hitting that same angle with each stroke, and before I'd finished climaxing the first time, it was happening again, and this time he came with me, letting out a deep groan of satisfaction.

When we both finally managed to catch our breath, we untangled our bodies and collapsed down on the bed, side by side, holding hands.

Sex had never been like this before. I'd never imagined it could be. Yes, I'd discovered my sex drive, but it wasn't just a physical thing, it was everything I felt for this man. "We're good together."

He rolled on his side, propping himself on an elbow. "Gee, you think?" Then he frowned a little. "Seriously, are you saying it's *only* good? Like, you've had better?"

"No. I've never had anything close to this."

A smug grin curved his lips. "Okay, then."

I raised my eyebrows. "That's all you have to say? Just, 'okay, then'?"

"What I mean is, it's the same with me. This is the best ever. We're so in tune, it's ..." He shook his head. "And again, I can't find the words."

"That's all right. I get the picture." A couple of days ago, I'd have thought he was feeding me a line. Now, I knew Damien. He'd never do that. I also knew that sex between us wasn't only about technique, it was about the way our two personalities—perhaps two souls—meshed.

Damien and I truly did have something special.

After cuddling for a while, we finally, reluctantly, pulled ourselves out of bed.

"It's okay with your folks that I stay at your house?" he asked as I headed for the bathroom.

I turned back. "We'll see. They're not thrilled about the tabloid thing." I hoped Damien's genuineness and charm would win them over. "If not, then we'll get a hotel room."

"Theresa." He came to me and caught my hand. "I don't want to get between you and your parents."

I shook my head. "We'll work things out." I'd make them understand.

Fortunately, he took me at my word and we both got ready to leave.

"What about your grandmother?" he asked as we left the room. "Want to go visit?"

I'd talked to Merilee about Gran. "Apparently she's sharper in the mornings. How about we go tomorrow, on the way to the airport?"

"Sure."

He'd already checked out of the hotel, so we took his luggage down to Merilee's car. As I drove to my parents' house, he used his cell to call his agent, tell her what we'd decided, and ask her to discuss it with his publicist. I listened to his side, as the agent seemed to raise objection after objection and Damien stood firm.

When we pulled into the driveway, he admired the house and yard. Inside, I gave him a quick tour of the main floor, then led him upstairs. "The second floor is me and my sisters, and Mom and Dad's bedroom and offices are on the third floor." Merilee's bedroom door was closed. If she was following the schedule we'd worked out, she'd be inside writing a paper.

I led him into my room to dump his luggage and he gazed around curiously. "Stuffed animals, huh? Cute." Then he grinned and picked one up. "Hey, you even have a koala."

We both gathered our work and headed out to the patio. He called last night's reporter and gave him a quick phone interview, then settled in a lounge chair proofreading his next book. He looked comfortable and at home in khaki shorts and a golf shirt. Having neglected the student exams for too long, I piled the stack of booklets on the metal patio table and began marking.

After perhaps an hour, Damien rose, stretched, and came over to stand behind me and plant a kiss on the top of my head. "I've finished the galleys."

"Congratulations." I tipped my head back and this time the kiss landed on my lips. Soft, lingering.

"Enough of that," he said with a grin, "or I'll want to drag you up to your room."

The sound of throat-clearing made us both jerk upright. "Mom!" I leaped to my feet. "This is Damien. And Damien, this is my mother, Rebecca Fallon."

"Ms. Fallon." Damien stepped forward to offer his hand. "Thanks so much for inviting me over."

She shook firmly but didn't smile. "Believe me, we want to get to know you. And find out what's going on with this crazy engagement business."

"We've sorted it out," I hurried to assure her.

"Good." Still no smile. "When your father gets home, you can tell us all about it." She glanced at her watch. "I must run up and get changed. Theresa, there are steaks and veggies in the kitchen. Can you get things going for dinner?" A frown creased her forehead. "Your dad was supposed to get the steaks marinating. Do you know what he puts in that secret marinade you love so much?"

I shook my head.

"I'm a fair hand with the barbie," Damien said. "If you trust an Aussie to put something together?"

Mom kinked up an eyebrow and studied him. "Trust needs to be earned. Let's see how you do."

When she'd gone upstairs, Damien said, "So, the barbie's the first test. If I pass, then she might trust me with you?"

"It doesn't matter whether she does. I'm an adult."

"Loosen up, Prof, I'm kidding."

"You may be. My mother isn't."

He raised his eyebrows. "Then lead me to the kitchen and let's get going."

I took him there, showed him the basic layout, and helped locate ingredients for his marinade.

"Want to barbecue potatoes and onions, too?" he asked.

"You mean potatoes wrapped in foil?"

"No. You cut them in thick slices, boil them a few minutes, then toss them and some thickly sliced onions into the same marinade as for the steak. Then grill them."

"Sounds good. I'll make a salad and lay out cheese and crackers for appetizers."

We were working companionably when Matt came through the open kitchen door. "Hey, Theresa. Uh, Damien."

I'd never actually introduced them, but Damien was already saying, "G'day, Matt."

I gave Matt a quick hug. "Merilee's in her room, working."

He'd just gone to join her when Dad came in, looking frazzled. "Damn, I was supposed to get the steaks marinating."

"It's under control," Damien said, pointing to the deep bowl that housed the steaks and whatever special mixture he'd concocted. " 'Fraid you're in for an Aussie barbie tonight, Dr. Fallon. Hope I'm not stepping on any toes."

Dad narrowed his eyes. "I'm not territorial about the barbecue. But I warn you, I'm protective of my daughters."

"I appreciate that," Damien said, voice firm, gaze level. "And I'll tell you, I have no intention of doing anything to hurt Theresa."

"She's told you about Jeffrey?"

"Yes. Nothing like that's going to happen this time."

"See that it doesn't."

The two men's eyes locked for a long moment, then Dad's shoulders relaxed a fraction. "Have you worked out what to do about the tabloids?"

"We discussed it and agreed," I told him. "Mom wants to hear about it when we're all together."

"Where is she?" Dad glanced around.

"She went upstairs to change, but that was over half an hour ago, so she probably got onto e-mail or made a phone call. Matt just got here and he's up with Merilee."

"I'll go round them up."

When he'd gone, I said, "Sorry," to Damien.

"Nothing to apologize for. They don't want to see you get hurt. Nor do I."

A few minutes later, we were all assembled in the kitchen.

"Theresa, there's e-mail from Jenna," Merilee said. "She sold her surf board and she's taking a couple jobs with good tips, putting together gas money so she can drive home."

"In that rattletrap MGB?" Dad frowned.

"It got her to California," Mom said. "One hopes it will get her home. In the meantime," she turned and fixed her steady gaze on me, "let's talk about this tabloid issue."

"Damien's agent and publicist wanted to handle it one way," I said, "but he and I talked and we decided we don't care about spin, and even if it might do both of our careers a tiny bit of harm, we want to tell the truth."

Mom and Dad did their silent communication thing, then Dad said, a touch grudgingly, "It's hard to argue with the truth."

"And what, exactly, is the truth?" Mom asked.

When I opened my mouth to answer, she said, "No. I want to hear this from Damien."

He put his arm around my shoulder and I wrapped mine around his waist. "That Tezzie and I care about each other and we're in a committed relationship."

"Committed?" The word burst out of me. Neither of us had used it before.

His body tensed then he dropped his arm and stood in front of me. Gently he cupped my face in both hands. "Isn't that what we've been talking about?"

"Y-yes." Joy flooded through me. Not that I hadn't believed he was serious before, but . . . "Isn't commitment a word men shy away from?"

He gave a soft laugh. "Too right. But then I met you."

"How can you be committed to someone you've just met?" Merilee asked. She probably meant to sound cynical, but instead the question came out almost plaintive.

Happiness bubbling in my veins, I turned to her. "I can't believe you're asking that. Isn't that exactly what happened with you and Matt?"

"Oh!" Her lips rounded around the word and her face brightened. "Of course it is." She gave him a big hug.

"It's just that you met as kids, and we met as adults."

"I see what you mean." A smile flashed. "Okay, I get it. And I'm happy for you, Theresa, I really am." She gave an exaggerated pout. "Even if you *are* stealing my thunder."

Selfishly, I wanted my moment in the sun, with my newfound confidence and sexy lover, but in the interest of family harmony, I said, "I saw champagne chilling in the fridge. Let's open it and toast the bride and groom."

Dad did the honors with the champagne bottle, and when we all held a chilled flute, I made the toast. "Here's to M&M. We've always known they belonged together, and now it's about to be official."

"Best wishes," Damien added. "Here's to a wonderful life together."

"It will be," Merilee said, clicking her glass to Matt's.

Then we settled in, over a couple of platters of cheese, crackers, and olives, to a Fallon-style conversation that ranged here, there, everywhere, and back again. At some point, Damien quietly took charge of the barbecue, and before long we were all sampling the delicious result.

Although my parents hadn't fully accepted him, he was winning them over. Unlike Jeffrey and many of my male colleagues, he was a good listener. He actually paid attention to what others were saying—whether it was Mom discussing a legal technicality, Dad expounding on his latest research, Merilee musing about whether she wanted a short or long train on her wedding gown, or Matt laying out the details of the Mexican Riviera cruise. Damien asked intelligent questions, too. And I knew he wasn't simply being polite, he really was interested.

All too soon, he said, "I'd better run upstairs and change into something more respectable for the signing." He flashed a quick grin. "Good excuse for getting out of doing dishes, isn't it?"

"The cook never has to do the dishes," Mom said.

As soon as he'd gone, she turned to me. "I have to say, Theresa, he's growing on me," and Dad chimed in with, "I agree."

I beamed at them. "Damien has that effect. Now, I'd better get changed, too."

He'd left my door ajar and when I went in, I found him bare-chested, wearing the same pants he'd worn in Honolulu, shaking out a short-sleeved cotton shirt. "Hey, Tezzie. What's the verdict? Did I pass?"

"You're growing on them."

"Like fungus? Or like a guy who deserves to be with their daughter?" He put down the shirt and came over to tug me into a loose embrace. "Hopefully the latter, because I like them. Your parents are caring people and passionate about what they do, and Merilee and Matt are cute. Hope I get a chance to meet your other two sisters one day."

I gazed up at him, thinking how utterly different he was than I'd first assumed. "Damien?"

"Yeah?"

"Where will you be a week from this coming Saturday?"

"Don't remember offhand, but there's bound to be a signing. Why?" Then he snapped his fingers. "Is that the wedding?"

I nodded. "I suppose there's no way it would fit your schedule, but I'd love to have you there as my date."

It took him no more than a second to think about it. "I'll do my damnedest."

"But didn't you say your book tour is hectic?"

"Bobby's an expert at scheduling. Maybe we can juggle things."

"I don't want to completely disrupt your plans or make a lot of extra work for your assistant."

I must have been frowning, because he smoothed my forehead with his thumb. "Theresa, do you want me to be there?"

I would only, always, be honest with him. "Yes, I do."

"Then I want to be there, too."

"That's wonderful." For a long moment, we gazed into each other's eyes. "You know I'm crazy about you?" I said softly.

"Good. Because I've fallen for you, head over heels."

"Really?" I still had trouble believing it.

Tenderly he cupped my face in both hands, staring into my eyes, caressing my skin, pressing a little to feel the bone structure beneath. Like he was testing my feelings, or his own. The expression on his face was so caring, so naked, it brought tears to my eyes.

"It's been one wild ride, hasn't it, Tezzie?" he said softly. "And along the way, you got to me in a way no one else ever has. You challenge me, you turn me on. Sexually, intellectually, emotionally. You make me want . . ."

"What do you want?" My voice came out choky with emotion.

"You." Gently he stroked his thumbs across my temples into my hair, staring tenderly into my face as if he cherished me. "I want you."

"I want you, too." A tear overflowed and tracked its way toward my curved, trembling lips.

"Then that's what we'll have."

As he bent his head to kiss me, I knew I'd never felt so happy and so optimistic about the future.